Praise for The Unmooring of Mrs. Mango

"This was such a fantastic read, rich with interesting, well-developed characters and relationships. The author does an amazing job putting her characters into surprising situations and mixing humor with moments of real emotion. Best of all is the moving perspective on love, commitment and what it means to be a family."

"I fell in love with Mrs. Mango In the 1st paragraph of this book. And laughed and cried and was amazed all the way through."

"The author expertly wove a charming story describing how assumptions, passions and fears, if not expressed as a way to protect our hearts, can tie us down and prevent us from seeing and living the life that we deserve. The characters are so endearing, and it is a gift to join them on their journey as they seek to become 'unmoored.'"

Also by Lynn Rankin-Esquer

My Paperback Cape: The Unlikely Odyssey of a
Bookworm

Murder, Mess, and the Tangerine Dress:
An Order Out of Chaos Mystery (Book 1)

The Unmooring of Mrs. Mango

By Lynn Rankin-Esquer

XandL Press
California

For Elle and Xavier and the dreams that live in each of you.

Unmoor (moor') vt. 1 to free (a ship, etc.) from moorings 2 to heave up all anchors of (a ship) but one -vi. To become unmoored.

-WEBSTER'S NEW WORLD COLLEGE DICTIONARY

CHAPTER 1
Missed Signs

When she locked the letter in the box, her time with Raul was over until next Sunday. She wouldn't think of him. She wouldn't compare him with Joe. She wouldn't imagine what life might have been like if Raul had returned from Vietnam. She wouldn't think about what their children might have looked like, or their grandchildren. Next Sunday morning, at 6:00 a.m., for a precious thirty minutes locked in this old bathroom, she could return to that world, but for now, it was back to the life that came after Raul.

Mrs. Mango leaned back on the closed toilet, folded the letter in thirds, slowly running her fingers along the crease to get it just right. She held the letter against her heart, closed her eyes, and murmured 'God bless' before adding it to the stack of letters in the old steel cashbox. Almost time to move the small stack to the big box in the darkest corner of the garage, the one marked 'knitting extras,' not that anyone would ever notice it in a garage so packed with stuff no car had seen the inside of it for years. She slid the box of letters under the bathroom sink, pushing until it hit against the damp warping wood at the back, replaced the stack of towels on top of it and tucked the key into her bra. She didn't notice the faint mildew smell of the bathroom or the worn-out cabinets or the peeling paint up in the corner or the rust stain rimming the tub drain; it was just a bathroom, serving all the normal bathroom functions plus one more. She firmly shut the chipped vanity doors, locking Raul away until next Sunday in an act as effective as placing him behind a three foot thick steel vault door. Mrs. Mango did not notice that a hinge on the right door had tired of its job, had relaxed enough to let the door swing just a couple of millimeters back open. Had she believed in signs, this might have been the first of several, but Mrs. Mango was too pragmatic for signs. Mrs. Mango didn't over-interpret things and only paid attention to what she thought was necessary, which left a lot out. The unnecessary got explained away in a process most people would recognize as rationalizing, but that Mrs. Mango called common sense. *My daughter just hasn't found the right man yet. I can be in love with Raul and married to Joe. People my age don't care about sex anymore.*

Sunday ritual complete, only pleasant thoughts allowed to drift around her mind, Mrs. Mango slipped out of the house to get the newspaper, feeling her way cautiously down the uneven walkway. The northern California dawn was dark and foggy, like a gray felt bathrobe had been draped over the sky, producing just enough light to see the outlines of the rows of single story ranch houses huddled together in her neighborhood. One moment she was stepping carefully over the cracked edge of where tree roots had pushed up the walkway, and the next she was engulfed in a sudden blizzard of feathers and jabbing beaks, a pack of turkeys charging her with wings spread, necks extended, ambushing her like she held a nest full of their babies in her arms.

Mrs. Mango screamed and waved her hands as she took off running towards the street. The birds were not to be outrun and in fact intensified their attack as she veered to the right, into her yard, and then circled back around to the walk, the turkeys unrelenting in their barrage of beats and pecks. Still screeching, Mrs. Mango swung her hands up, knocking against the gobbler of a furious turkey. Simultaneously she kicked, connecting squarely with the chest of another bird, but in the process losing her balance and slipping in the cold water left from the sprinklers' middle of the night spritzing.

"Stop!" wailed Mrs. Mango, now on her back, her arms tightly shielding her face while a mound of flailing wings and jabbing beaks kept up their angry assault.

"Oh my God," came a tremulous voice from out of the dark. "Is that Elsie?!"

"Holy cow, you alright?" chimed in another voice, sounding closer.

"Get out of here," thundered one of the two child-sized figures as they both waded into the pack of turkeys and started swinging at the birds, the beams of light from their headlamps bouncing wildly around the bizarre scene like a strobe light.

"Shoo! Shoo!" yelled the second person, kicking and shoving at birds.

"You gotta punch 'em," yelled figure number one. "Rooooaaar!" she added even louder as she swung her fist at a turkey, connecting with its back. The turkey took off across the lawn, the rest following after another peck or two.

Figure number two chased them as far as the street. "Get your turkey asses out of here!" she yelled.

"Elsie, you okay?" one of the figures asked, as they both converged back to Mrs. Mango and leaned in over her.

"Oh my God," whimpered Mrs. Mango, moving her hands away from her face and squinting into the glare of the two headlamps. "What the. . . ?" She was at a loss for words.

They snapped off their lights, and Mrs. Mango's eyes adjusted to see the faces of two of her octogenarian neighbors. On her left was Flora Gonzalez, an eighty-five-year-old widow who was two inches under five feet and almost weighed her age. Flora was dressed in the newest Nike running shoes, tights, and a red sweatshirt that said 'Do it till you die.' She had a neoprene belt strapped to her waist with a water bottle and iPhone in it. Her waist was so small that the extra neoprene left over from tightening the straps wrapped around her waist a second time.

Peering down on the opposite side from Flora was fellow widow Velma Costa. Velma didn't let her eighty-three years of age keep her from wearing neon green Lycra leggings, a mini-iPod strapped to her arm, and a tight training jacket that undulated across her bulges, a few of which were in the general location of her chest. Velma was a couple of inches taller than Flora (although a few inches shorter than she used to be, what with her spine compressing and all) and more than a few pounds heavier. The bright pink lipstick she wore to match her headband had bled into the creases around her mouth.

"Damn turkeys," said Flora, leaning down to wipe something gooey off of Mrs. Mango's face. "They've come at us before out on the trail. Never seen them this far into the neighborhood. I literally kicked one in the ass." Flora laughed, pleased with herself.

Mrs. Mango felt around the back of her head, locating a painful bump, not to mention more goo. "Oh my," she said faintly. She tried to pull up to her elbows, but after sixty-something years of use, her arms weren't up to the job. As she squirmed around feeling for injuries, she tugged the hem of her housedress down around her thighs. Only a complete knockout would make Mrs. Mango forget propriety. She looked at her hand. "You don't think . . . "

"Nope," said Flora, making eye contact with Velma, both of them knowing Mrs. Mango was splattered with turkey poop. "Just a little bit of dirt."

Velma crouched down. "Are you hurt?"

"I must have hit my head when I went down." Mrs. Mango shuddered, still unable to understand how she could be so viciously attacked in her own front yard.

"Why are you two out so early?" asked Mrs. Mango, straining again to pull herself up.

"We're going long today, and the pace we move, we don't start early we'll still be running when the sun drops again," said Flora, reaching for Mrs. Mango's arm and holding her steady as she sat up.

Mrs. Mango patted her head to see how badly her hair was messed up. Her helmet of wavy brown hair wasn't cut much for style, but she didn't like it sticking out in funny ways. "Ouch," she said, coming across another bruise and then, as she felt down her neck, collected more goo on her fingers. "Oh my."

"Do you want us to help you stand up?" asked Velma, rubbing her forearm against her forehead to stop the flow of sweat that, despite the cold morning air, was streaming through her wrinkles like they were straws.

"In a moment," said Mrs. Mango. Just sitting up had made her a little dizzy.

"I can't believe they actually knocked you down. Looks like what got you was the sprinkler water," said Flora, gesturing to the wet sidewalk. "Now, that was Velma on her back, I'd assume there was a man around somewhere," Flora laughed.

Velma pretended to be outraged but laughed too. Mrs. Mango grimaced. Bad enough she was wet and bruised, she didn't want to have to hear about Velma's private life.

"Should we get Joe? Or Christine?" Velma asked. Joe was Mrs. Mango's husband and Christine her twenty-eight-year-old daughter who still lived at home. Christine was the youngest and only unmarried one of the four Mango kids, and her mother was both dreading the day she left and longing for it, because it would mean Mrs. Mango could plan a wedding. The three older Mangos were boys, and their mothers-in-law had all gotten that privilege.

"Joe's still asleep, and Christine's not here, stayed at a friend's house last night," said Mrs. Mango. "Went to some late concert I think." Mrs. Mango rolled to her knees, steadied herself with one arm and reached out. "I'm fine, just give me a hand."

Velma grabbed Mrs. Mango's hand, leaned back, and levered Mrs. Mango's pleasantly pillowed frame up as Flora grabbed her under her arm to steady her.

"You sure you're okay?" demanded Flora.

"Yes, I'm fine," said Mrs. Mango, not sure at all but feeling more herself standing up.

"Do you want us to help you into the house?" asked Flora.

"No, no, I'm fine," said Mrs. Mango. "How far you

girls running?"

"Doing a good seven miler," said Velma. "That'll put some steps on the old activity band," she added, shaking her wrist in the air.

Mrs. Mango shook her head, unable to comprehend running, especially at their age.

Flora nodded. "I need my shot of endolphins, you know?"

"Don't go near Gilly Street," Mrs. Mango said. The working class neighborhood they were standing in was only a couple of blocks from the low-income/no-income section of town, and Flora and Velma wouldn't return with anything of value if they ran that direction.

Velma laughed. "Not much they could take from us." She looked down at her wrist. "I'd hate to lose this watch, though. Cost me half a check."

"Don't worry, not headed towards Gilly until my time's up," said Flora. "It's my end-of-life plan but I'm not ready yet."

"Huh?" Mrs. Mango was confused. Was it the bump on her head?

"Didn't plan on living this long so not sure my money'll hold out," explained Flora. "I figure once it runs out, I head to Gilly and let nature take its course. Wouldn't mind going out in a hail of bullets."

Mrs. Mango had no answer for that. "Well, have a good run," she said. "Thanks for your help. See you later." With a weak wave, Mrs. Mango hobbled up the wet walk.

As Mrs. Mango opened her front door, a rectangle of warm light shone into the uninviting chill, backlighting her rumpled dress and hair. Velma and Flora looked at each other, shrugged, and took off running, which in their case was mostly a matter of shuffling feet forward.

CHAPTER 2
A Waste of Mini-pumpkins

Three days later Mrs. Mango stood with her hands on her hips, staring at the dining room table so intently that she was surprised when it didn't magically expand to fit all of the guests she had invited to Thanksgiving.

"Hi Mom," Christine said from the doorway. "I put the pies in the kitchen. Costco was *insane*. Took me twenty minutes just to find a parking space! They were out of carts. *Out of carts!* Do you know how many carts they have there? I had to follow an old man and unload his stuff into his car just to get one. And then a woman tried to steal it from me while I was trying to fit his pallet of peanuts into the back of a Prius."

Christine shook her head. "I thought she was going to pull a gun on me. Honestly. Reminder to self: never go to Costco the day before Thanksgiving."

Mrs. Mango turned her laser eye from the table to her daughter, running her eyes over Christine's loose gray shirt hanging out over ripped up jeans. She noticed that, once again, Christine was not wearing make-up. "Maybe you should wear that cute pink blouse tomorrow. And a little lipstick never hurt anyone."

Christine narrowed her eyes at her mother. "What have you done? Who have you invited?"

Mrs. Mango kept her face blank. "Just the family. And anyone who doesn't have a place to go." Mrs. Mango's years of wedding dreams depended on Christine, who was taking her own sweet time to even date anyone. Christine was very social, almost never home in the evenings, but no boyfriend ever appeared at their house or in the phone conversations Mrs. Mango eavesdropped on.

In the life lived outside of her Sunday 6:00 am half-hour, Mrs. Mango had found a reasonable complacency.

Her husband Joe had stopped bothering her for sex, she was finally retired from the podiatrist's office front desk, she was finding a sense of purpose in a variety of volunteer jobs, and her four kids were raised. If she could plan a wedding for Christine and if any of her kids could, for the love of God, give her grandchildren, she might even call herself happy.

All morning as she prepped for the Thanksgiving meal Mrs. Mango had fantasized about a wedding for Paul and Christine. Finally she could use the contents of the pretty white wicker hope chest she had been stuffing, for years, with ideas for flowers and dresses and chocolate fountains.

Christine's hands went to her hips in an unconscious replica of her mother's. "What's his name?"

"I'm just helping out a friend," defended Mrs. Mango, eyes widening in attempted innocence. "Remember the Greens? Probably not, they moved away when you were little. Their son Paul is back in the area, a *journalist,* and doesn't know many people yet."

"You *need* to stop trying to fix me up," said Christine, nodding hard for emphasis, her long hair bouncing forward, the sunglasses on top of her head flying off. Mrs. Mango got lost for a moment in the beauty of Christine's hair, it was the one part of her appearance she spent time on. Brazilian blowouts and lots of product tamed the frizzy brown hair she inherited from her mother and a couple of well-placed gold highlights drew the eye to the gentle waves. Now if she would just put on some make-up, lose fifteen pounds and stop wearing such loose clothes she'd be a knockout.

"Is that it? Or have you arranged speed dating for me? Exactly how many people are coming?" asked Christine as she scooped her sunglasses from the floor.

"I've counted ten," Mrs. Mango answered. "It's going to be a tight fit. And what is your friend's name?"

"Sarah, with an 'h,'" Christine said. "You've met her, like, four times."

"Hmm, yes," said Mrs. Mango, clearly not

remembering Sarah. "Could you do me a favor and wear some make up tomorrow? You have such a pretty face, I don't know why you don't show it off more. Just some mascara? And lipstick? Maybe a little eyeliner. You're never going to get a boyfriend if you don't show yourself off."

"You're a real confidence booster," Christine said. "If I have such a pretty face, why would I need make-up," she added, thinking *you can stop worrying about the boyfriend thing. Permanently.* That thought gave her a flash of panic. What if she couldn't go through with it? Time to change the subject. "What else do you need help with?"

"Could you take me to the store?" Mrs. Mango didn't like to drive unless it was absolutely necessary. Plus, a little time in the car might give her a chance to casually mention Paul again and how great he was. "I want to get some mini-pumpkins. I saw a thing on TV about using them to make little individual flower arrangements. You know, so they don't stick up too high in middle of the table."
******

"What else can I do?" asked Rita, third son Danny's wife. It was Thanksgiving day and the turkey was due out of the oven in minutes, which meant a rush of activity to get everything to the table. Rita was tall and slim, and even on a holiday looked like the attorney she was. With her well-fitting pencil skirt, red silk blouse, and flinty expression she could have arrived straight from the courtroom. Rita laid down the oven mitts she had been wearing, having just transferred the sweet potato casserole from the oven to a trivet on the side table in the dining room.

Mrs. Mango was faced towards the sink, away from Rita, so Rita didn't see Mrs. Mango roll her eyes or hear her mutter under her breath, "not much."

Mrs. Mango looked around the kitchen to find a job for Rita that didn't involve cooking. Privately Mrs. Mango didn't believe that what Rita did could be called cooking

and she wasn't going to let her ruin any of her tasty dishes.
She grabbed a ceramic pitcher. "If you could fill this with
water and add it to the glasses on the table, that would be
great."

Rita took the pitcher, filled it with water and strode
purposefully through the swinging door.

Bang! The door hit into Mimi who was coming
from the dining room and bounced back into Rita,
knocking the pitcher into her chest. Mr. Mango's sister
Mimi, her husband Leo, and their grown son Timmy had
made their yearly pilgrimage from the Central Valley.
While Mimi helped in the kitchen, Leo and Timmy were
sitting on the couch nibbling on the tray of vegetables Mrs.
Mango had stuck no so subtly in front of her husband. So
he could stand to lose a few pounds, who couldn't at their
age?

"Oh!" exclaimed Rita. "Sorry," she added, looking
down at the water spreading down her silk shirt, face
tightened in way that suggested she was sorry for the dry
cleaning to come, not for hitting Mimi.

"Wow," said Mimi, carefully entering the kitchen,
holding her elbow that had taken most of the blow. "You
move kind of fast there."

Rita shrugged, stepped around Mimi, and took the
half full pitcher into the dining room.

Mimi and Mrs. Mango shook their heads at each
other. Rita's shortcomings (wound *way* too tight, poor
cook, a bit of a control freak) had been the topic of many
discussions.

"I'll bet she's hell on wheels in court," said Mimi,
looking back at the door. Although Mimi was Mr. Mango's
sister, she looked more like Mrs. Mango's sister—both
with the same comfortable shape, sometimes wavy, mostly
frizzy hair, and resting irritated faces. Not that menopause
had anything to do with it, they would both be quick to say.
The irritation, that is.

"She's hell on wheels other places too," answered
Mrs. Mango, adding cream to the mixer where the mashed

potatoes were spinning. She shot a quick look at the door
to make sure Rita hadn't come through and added a stick of
butter. Rita would never eat the potatoes if she saw how
much butter and cream went in. As far as Mrs. Mango
could see, the reason Rita's food didn't taste so great was
that she didn't put anything tasty in it. No butter, or salt or
anything with sugar. There is healthy and then there is
rabbit food and Mrs. Mango was no fan of rabbit food.
Probably also the reason Rita hadn't gotten pregnant yet
too. A woman needs a little fat on her to get that job done
and Rita was as thin as a shish kebab skewer. And as stiff.

Mimi grabbed the asparagus casserole and bumped
the swinging door open with her ample hip, waited to make
sure Rita wasn't on the other side of it and then slid
through. Her hair was freshly permed and had just been set
yesterday, but the steam in the kitchen had loosened up the
waves. After setting the dish on the side table, Mimi wiped
at her hair with the back of her wrist, trying to tame the
wildness she could feel rising out of her head. She lifted
her arms and fanned at herself. "Darned if I'm not still
having hot flashes. That should have been over a long time
ago."

Rita looked up from pouring water into the glasses.
Was everything in a woman's life driven by hormones?
Those ridiculously uncontrollable things that were making
her life miserable too. Two years of negative pregnancy
tests made it clear that hormones were one thing Rita
couldn't control. Even a break from her job at the law firm
hadn't helped and now she was hustling around the clock to
catch up on the partner track.

Rita nodded in appreciation. Her dark hair, in a
sleek shoulder cut, bounced with the nod and caught in her
red lipstick. "Men have no idea."

Mimi was already headed back towards the kitchen
but snorted over her shoulder, "You got that right."
Complaining about men united women throughout the
world and the Mango house was no exception.

Mrs. Mango sent Rita to gather everyone to the

table. She found Paul, Sarah and Christine (banned from the kitchen to 'entertain' Paul) huddled around the crab dip in the living room. Christine had convinced her parents to let her switch out the old plaid couch for a sleeker new off-white one. It didn't quite fit with the old armchair or faded striped wall paper but then again no one in the living room seemed to be looking at the furnishings. Rita looked at Paul and Christine huddled on either side of Sarah and smiled to herself, it didn't take someone with her IQ to notice both Paul and Christine staring longingly at Sarah. Rita told them dinner was ready and headed towards the family room, shaking her head in wonderment at how clueless everyone in the house seemed to be. If the living room was a cauldron of desire, the family room was like a museum display of male behavior: Mr. Mango was cranked back in his Barclounger, beer in hand, eyes fixed zombie-like on the TV, ignoring cousin Timmy's running commentary on the football game, not that Timmy seemed to notice. Leo sat in peaceful silence, although that could have been sleep, she couldn't tell. And Rita's husband Danny slumped on the computer table chair, turned to face the TV, but with his head down as he scrolled and scrolled on his phone.

"Dinner's ready," Rita said to the tableaux.

"Damn, what happened to your shirt?" asked Timmy as he leapt up, never one to linger when there was food around.

Rita looked down at the water stains on her silk blouse. "Accident."

Timmy chortled. "I hope it wasn't for a wet t-shirt contest, not for nothing, but I think you'd lose."

Rita had endured Timmy before but it never got easier. She cringed looking at his button-down that gapped and strained from his big soft belly to his neck, leaving a scalloped line of hairy flesh. His thinning brown hair, freed from its customary baseball hat, was stuck against his head in the shape of the hat. At thirty-two, Timmy had no strong career ambitions and sold refurbished cell phones out of his 'home office.' There wasn't much going on in his head, but all of it came out of his mouth.

"As would you," Rita whispered under her breath. She truly loved her husband but his family was another matter. She wasn't sure how he had come from them.

Mr. Mango struggled out of his chair and poked at Leo. "Wake up, dinner," he said and then, "come on Danny." Danny hadn't moved yet. "Nose in the phone, all the time," Mr. Mango said in Danny's direction. "Your generation is the start of the end, you know that, right?"

Danny shrugged. His dad always had something to criticize about the world and arguing back did nothing to stop him. "Returning some patient emails," he said without looking up.

"It's Thanksgiving!" said Mr. Mango. "And you're a dermatologist, what kind of emergency could be happening? Someone's Botox wore off in the middle of dinner?" Mr. Mango laughed at his joke, then shook his head. "Kids are practically autistic these days, don't know how to actually look someone in the eye. Just staring at the devices." He pointed the remote at the TV, muted it, gave one last longing look at the silent football game, and headed towards the dining room.

Even with both leaves in the table, the small dining room was crowded, and the guests sat shoulder wedged against shoulder, mini-pumpkins fighting for space with glasses and plates and platters of food. Mrs. Mango told everyone to hold hands as she motioned for Mr. Mango to start the blessing and she looked over to where Christine and Paul sat, thrilled that they would actually be touching. She choked, right in the middle of Joe's 'Father in heaven,' because Christine was holding hands on one side with her uncle Leo and on the other with Sarah, not Paul. Mr. Mango shot her a look from his bowed head and kept on praying. "—thank you for bringing our family and friends together today, bless this food we are about to receive. . ."

Mrs. Mango couldn't even listen. What happened? Somebody must have switched the place cards. Of course it was Christine, always rebellious, probably trying to show her mother who's boss. *Huh*, thought Mrs. Mango. *You think I'm some kind of amateur?*

Before she made Paul look like the greatest catch on earth it was time to make Sarah look like the worst. Mrs. Mango had seen the way Paul was looking at Sarah and she didn't like it. Time to take her down a notch.

Sarah turned out to be a worthy foe. "The asparagus casserole is delicious, Mrs. Mango," she said with a friendly smile before Mrs. Mango could start grilling her. "If you give out recipes, I'd love to have it."

"Of course, dear," said Mrs. Mango pleasantly, thinking *what a suck-up*. "Now, tell me about yourself. Are you from this area? And what do you do?"

"I'm from Sacramento originally," said Sarah. "I teach fourth grade, and I just *love* it."

Timmy and Paul were both staring at Sarah in appreciation. With her smooth long brown hair, big brown eyes and thin yet curvy body she could have been Italian or Spanish or South American. Something exotic in the engaging tilt of her eyes. She had that multicultural appeal that Ralph Lauren seemed to feature every couple of years.

Mrs. Mango was frustrated. Sarah had just the right amount of make-up on and had dressed in a lovely pink sweater and slim off white capris that hugged her curves just right. What was Christine thinking, with a beauty like Sarah around no man would look at Christine. And now here Sarah was being all nice and teaching fourth grade for Pete's sake. Mrs. Mango figured she was probably a big fake and mean at the core.

Christine took a deep breath. Once her mother turned her attention on a person there was not much she would miss. Even though Christine was ready, her heart started beating triple time. This was it, she started to raise from her seat—and then Timmy spoke up before either Christine or Mrs. Mango could say anything.

"Hey, Uncle Joe, you put any bets on the games today?" Without waiting for an answer Timmy launched into a detailed description of his Thanksgiving Day fantasy picks. "I'm going to clean up. Put down a C note!"

Mr. Mango stopped eating long enough to give Timmy a hard look. The kid had no sense, talking about gambling when he owed Mr. Mango almost a thousand dollars.

Mimi and Leo shook their heads, aware of Mr. Mango's stare and in complete agreement with him. Timmy was their kid but they had no illusions about him.

When Timmy paused long enough to shovel asparagus into his mouth, Christine took a breath. This was it.

Christine's mouth was open but before a sound came out Mrs. Mango said, "Mimi, we haven't even heard about the store yet. What is new there?" Mimi and Joe had grown up working in the family grocery store and Mimi continued to run it.

While Mimi answered Christine chugged a couple of swallows of wine to get her heart to slow down. She could literally feel it beating in her ears. Sarah gave a quick squeeze on her leg.

Finally, Christine stood up abruptly and tapped her wine glass to get everyone's attention. She cleared her throat and with half a smile looked nervously around the group.

"I have, uh, something to tell you all," she started. She looked at Sarah who nodded her encouragement.

Maybe she got a promotion, thought Mrs. Mango. Immediately her mind spun off with possibilities. *Maybe she'll be included in new meetings now, meetings where she'll meet men who were higher up the corporate ladder, men with good incomes and even better future earning potential.* Mrs. Mango thought that as a personal banker at a local bank, maybe Christine wasn't meeting the kinds of men she would want to marry. She thought sadly of Paul, *but he'll find someone,* she reassured herself. *Maybe he can have Sarah after all.*

Christine continued. "I just want you all to know, I

am so happy, and I don't like having to hide my happiness from you. I know you might not completely understand what I am going to tell you, but please just remember that this is who I am, and it makes me happy, okay?" She looked around at puzzled but nodding faces.

My goodness, thought Mrs. Mango, *what in the world is she going to tell us? Maybe she got a job in another city.* Mrs. Mango felt a pang of sadness and started imagining daily life without Christine. *Imagine, just me and the old coot from now on; well, that should be interesting. Thank goodness I've been doing all this volunteering. But maybe just to be safe, I'll take up a new hobby. Maybe I'll try that tae bo thing.*

As if she needed a focal point, Christine fixed her gaze on Rita, across the table from her, and said, "I'm gay, and Sarah is my girlfriend."

Nobody moved, then Mrs. Mango said, "My God, speak up Christine, I can't hear you, I could swear you just said you're gay!"

Christine faced her mother. "That's exactly what I said. I'm gay. I'm a lesbian."

Mrs. Mango gave a high-pitched laugh. "Well, don't be silly, of course you're not." Mrs. Mango smiled and looked around the table to let people know that Christine was joking. *That Christine,* she thought, *doesn't know how to be funny, poor girl. I'll have to take her aside later and let her know it's not nice to make fun of people who are Different.*

Rita looked at Danny and said, "I told you so."

"Not now," Danny hissed.

Timmy got a big smile on his face and looked back and forth between Christine and Sarah. "Do you ever let anyone watch?" he asked.

Aunt Mimi glared at Timmy, "Be quiet, you ignoramus." She rolled her eyes and said to the ceiling, "How could I have raised such a monster?" She looked around the table at no one in particular, "You know they say you should bite off the head of your first born and start again, you never get it right the first time. I don't know why I didn't do that." She narrowed her eyes at Timmy. "Maybe it's not too late."

Mrs. Mango jumped up and said, "I'll get the dessert," even though plates were still full of food. She ran into the kitchen, leaving the door banging back and forth behind her.

There was silence as everyone but Timmy tried to find somewhere to look besides Christine and Sarah. It didn't seem right to keep eating, but what were they supposed to do?

"Well?" Christine said. Still silence. "Isn't anybody going to say anything?"

"What the hell do you want us to say?" said Danny. "Congratulations? Like you just won the lottery or something?"

"Sure, that would work," said Christine. "Or how about, we're happy for you?"

"Well, of course we're happy for you," Danny said. "But honestly, give us some time; it takes some getting used to."

"What takes getting used to? When you met Rita, I didn't have to 'get used to it,'" said Christine, making air quotes around 'get used to it.'

"True," said Danny, tilting his head to the side. "Okay, I am happy for you. Glad you found each other." Danny nodded at Sarah and then Christine.

"*I'm* very happy for you too," said Rita. "Congratulations. You are a lovely couple." Rita smiled triumphantly at Danny. She loved being right.

"Hey," Timmy said, "you guys Lipstick Lesbians?" He elbowed Danny, "Some of them are pretty hot, you know what I mean."

Danny turned to Timmy. "Shut *up*."

Mr. Mango kept eating his turkey. No reason he should let his food get cold just because his daughter was, as they said down at the dock, playing for the other team.

Uncle Leo turned and looked at his niece,

"Christine, not for nothin', but are you sure? Cause I'm
pretty sure you go to hell for that."

"Yes, honey," chimed in Mimi, "how are you going
to go to church now? St. Andrews won't let you take
communion or anything, I'm almost positive."

"If that's true, screw God," Christine said.

Mimi gasped and crossed herself. "Take that back!
What are you doing, asking for trouble like that!" She
looked up at the cross with Jesus on it hanging on the wall.
"Jesus, please forgive her, she doesn't know what she is
saying!" Mimi jumped up and ran into the kitchen.

"Dad, you got anything to add to that?" Christine
asked her father, anger on the edge of her voice.

Mr. Mango looked up from his food, "Nope." He
reached for the sweet potatoes in front of him, scooped out
a big pile of it on top of his turkey, there being no more
room on his plate, and went back to eating. Mr. Mango was
secretly a little bit relieved because he wasn't sure where
he was going to get the money to pay for the wedding of
his wife's dreams. He'd overheard enough over the years to
know her plans were not on the economic side. This was
the one occasion that would not be sourced from Costco.
He'd never lived down the fact that their own wedding was
in front of a justice of the peace with a $6 wedding band
and no flowers. Elsie had *said* she didn't want a big "to do"
but somehow had held the small "to do" against him since
the beginning. Then it occurred to him that maybe his
daughter would still want a wedding and he'd have to pay
for two dresses and two bouquets, and that thought made
him weak so he shoved it out of his mind and hunkered
down over his food.

The kitchen door burst open as Mrs. Mango ran in,
slammed down a pumpkin pie and an apple pie and ran
back out. She returned in a huff, threw a bottle of whipped
cream at the table where it landed in the asparagus
casserole and ran back out again. She passed Mimi in the
kitchen, kneeling down in prayer, grabbed her purse and
the car keys, and went out the back door, muttering.

"Lesbian? Lesbian? What does she mean, lesbian? I should've never let her play soccer. My goodness, what will the neighbors think?"

Mimi had the right idea back there, praying, but this occasion called for an actual church. Mrs. Mango stomped around the side of the house, climbed in the Buick, adjusted the seat up close to the steering wheel and threw the car into reverse. Now was not the time to think about how much she hated driving. She didn't even bother to maneuver into the driveway, just backed straight across the lawn. On the way she took out one of her Princess Diana rose bushes but didn't pause to assess the damage. With roses hanging off the back bumper, Mrs. Mango shot into the street. Luckily, everyone else was in the middle of their dinners so she didn't hit anyone, but she did scare the Melucci's cat Binky into leaping onto Danny's brand new dark blue BMW SUV. Mrs. Mango put the car in drive and hit the gas, headed towards St. Andrews.

Meanwhile, back at the table, Paul was sitting there thinking he had nothing but bad luck. Sarah was the first woman he had been excited about in a long time and she turned out to be gay. What was he thinking, moving back here? Everyone acted like it was a big deal he was a journalist and wrote for a newspaper, but in reality, he was writing filler for an online local newsletter. At his age, he should be writing about something more than the U12 soccer team winning the weekend tournament in Manteca. Maybe the only way to salvage this day was to get shit-faced. Maybe he'd get Timmy to go to a bar with him. Friends with Timmy—yeah, he was definitely moving up in the world.

Sarah hadn't spoken since Christine made her announcement, but she gave Christine little squeezes under the table cloth to let her know she was there for her. On the whole, Sarah thought this was going better than when she came out to her family. Her parents had immediately thrown her out of the house, at the tender age of fifteen. They didn't speak to her for a year, and it took a number of years to get a relationship back with her mother. Her father still didn't accept it, and his only communication was to periodically send her fundamentalist Christian literature. Sarah thought Mr. Mango showed some encouraging signs of apathy. At least he wasn't angry. He didn't seem to care one way or the other, which she thought was vastly better. Her thought was confirmed when he turned to her and in a normal voice and making eye contact, asked her to pass the wine.

Mr. Mango got the wine bottle in hand and stood up. "Okay, now, listen up," he started, not sure of what he was going to say, but feeling a growing sense of importance with them all looking expectantly at him. He finally had recognized that this was the rare occasion in which Mrs. Mango was not going to take charge; in fact, she seemed to have disappeared. "I'm going to pour us all some more wine, and we, uh . . ." he fumbled furiously for something to say, and then, perhaps inspired by the wedding thoughts he had just been having, continued, "we are going to toast my daughter and her friend Sarah, her *girlfriend* Sarah, and wish them every happiness."

Mr. Mango walked around the table sloshing wine into glasses, whether they were full or not. He ran out before getting to Christine but she grabbed another bottle and handed it to him. He made a big flourish filling her glass and then Sarah's. He got back to his own seat, picked up his glass, and held it up, feeling the effects of taking charge, not to mention the four pre-dinner beers. "To Christine and Sarah!"

The rest of the table obediently held up their glasses and drank. The toast worked; everyone relaxed and started laughing and eating again. Paul was happy for the opportunity to start getting shit-faced, and Timmy was already well on his way there. Christine and Sarah were surprised and delighted at this turn of events, and kept holding their glasses up and toasting Mr. Mango, "To Dad!" Danny couldn't believe his dad had actually taken charge of the family, and he sat back in his seat happily feeling like a kid again. Rita sat beside him, glowing with the knowledge that she was right; she had told Danny ages ago that she thought Christine was gay. She was also relieved that Christine knew she was gay; she'd been worried that Christine was an 'embryo,' which she explained to Danny was someone who was gay but didn't know it yet.

Mimi was still in the kitchen, praying, when she heard the laughter float in from the dining room. She couldn't think how they could all just act like nothing was wrong. She was certainly not going to join that bunch of savages; they were all headed for hell! Mimi had left a full plate of food in the dining room and was regretting it, so she got a fork and picked at the mash potatoes stuck to the side of the mixing bowl and then at the extra tray of asparagus casserole. She made some coffee and sat in the kitchen, getting more and more irritated, wishing she could go in and get some pie but not sure how to do so without God confusing her for one of the heathens. She wished Father Steven was here to tell her what to do. Finally, she could take it no longer and decided that someone needed to go in and save them from themselves. It was a bigger job than she should have to take on, but apparently no one else was going to do it.

"Mimi," said Mr. Mango expansively, enjoying his new potency, "Come and eat with us! Rita here was just telling us the funniest dumb criminal story."

"Yes," said Rita, "this guy butt dialed 911 in the middle of breaking in to someone's house!" and everyone at the table started laughing again.

Lord have mercy, Mimi thought, *they're drunk! This is going to be harder than I thought.*

Leo patted her empty chair, "com'ere, babe, sit down." Leo hadn't called her babe in years, and Mimi was so surprised she obeyed him, walking over and sitting down without a word. He put his arm along the back of her chair and let his hand dangle on her shoulder. Mimi sat back so that her back touched his arm too and thought it wouldn't hurt to wait a bit on her 'duty' and just enjoy this moment. She couldn't remember the last time Leo had touched her.

It wasn't long before the wine was gone and Mr. Mango broke out the Schnapps. He handed out Dixie cups since he couldn't find shot glasses, and with their brightly colored little wax cups, they continued to toast. "To turkey!" "To love!" "To winning the lottery!"

Mimi decided she better have at least one shot so that the heathens would respect her as one of them; then she could help them see the error of their ways. Join them, then save them, she thought. She threw it back and shuddered at the raw alcohol taste. Mmm, that flavor wasn't so bad.

At St. Andrews, Mrs. Mango was busily lighting Novenas for her daughter's soul. She emptied the entire box sitting beside the wrought iron candle holder, and the whole back of the church was glowing with all the flames. Even as she cried, she couldn't help but notice how pretty all the light was in the darkened church. She decided to put a note in the hope chest about dark churches with lots of candles and then remembered she was never going to plan a wedding and started crying even harder. She went into the back pew and settled herself onto the kneeler. With her head lying on her folded hands on the back of the pew in front of her, she cried and asked God for guidance. Never in her life had He been so silent. 'What am I to do?' she asked over and over and still no answer.

On a normal day, Mrs. Mango tended towards wearing either cotton house dresses or basic pants (blue or khaki) with a nice blouse. Always clean and ironed but nothing wildly fashionable, she found that Kohls or Penny's seemed to have everything she might need. She didn't like to have to put a lot of effort into her clothes on a daily basis, but on holidays she enjoyed going a little fancier. Today, Mrs. Mango had on a black silk dress with a pattern of red and pink roses. With her head down she noticed she hadn't even taken off the pretty pink apron.

Who could get worked up over wearing an apron out in pubic when the devil had possessed her daughter? And forget planning a wedding, her daughter's soul was at risk. Then it hit her: she needed a sacrifice; maybe that would exorcise the devil. What would she sacrifice? Very quickly her brain came up with the exact right thing. She begged God to help her think of something else, but nothing would come, so she stood up, picked up her purse, and headed back to the parking lot.

As she walked through the vestibule, she saw a poster that said 'LGBT meeting Thursday at 6:00' and shuddered. Maybe the *church* wasn't even going to help her.

As Mrs. Mango approached the Buick, she noticed the Princess Diana rose bush hanging off the back bumper, and tears welled up again; it looked just like a car ready for a bride and groom to jump in and head off for their honeymoon! She didn't have the energy to take the flowers off, so she got back in and drove home dragging the roses along the road behind her.

When Mrs. Mango got home, she heard the hysteria in the dining room but ignored it and went to get her sacrifice. She took it to the family room, wedged it in the fireplace, and set a match to it. The match burned out without lighting the sacrifice, so she stuck some newspaper around it and lit it again. The newspaper caught on fire but quickly burned out. In frustration, Mrs. Mango looked around and saw the bar cart Christine had given her parents for their anniversary. She grabbed a bottle of Jim Beam off the cart and liberally doused the sacrifice. She put more newspaper around it and threw in a match. Whoom! The fire lit up the room and the sacrifice started burning. Lighting fires was Mr. Mango's job, so Mrs. Mango didn't realize that she was supposed to open the flue before burning something. Fire shot out the front of the fireplace, licking the edges of the mantel above it and burning the carpet around the hearth. The room quickly filled with smoke, bringing the drunken group running into the room.

"What's going on? What's on fire?" yelled Mr. Mango, the first one in.

The rest piled after him, running into each other with their impaired motor skills. Christine and Sarah made it into the family room after Mr. Mango, but Leo was moving side to side and too slow for those behind him. Like Keystone cops, Danny accordioned into Leo, Rita into Danny, Mimi into Rita. In trying to back up, Rita knocked Mimi down, and Timmy and Paul, with too much forward motion to stop, stepped on top of her. Timmy and Paul managed to push forward and land in the family room with Danny and Leo, while Rita and Mimi tried to untangle themselves in the hallway.

Timmy heard his uncle yelling fire and took up the call. "Fire! Fire!" he yelled, darting around the living room looking for a phone to call the fire department.

Christine was close to the fireplace by now and saw what was burning. "Mom! Why are you burning the hope chest?" she yelled, while she stamped on the burning rug.

Mrs. Mango bravely looked at the Satan she knew her daughter to be. "There's no need for it anymore, now is there?"

Unfortunately, Mrs. Mango, in addition to not knowing about opening the flue, also didn't realize that video tapes don't burn well, nor do plastic favors. Dark, smelly smoke billowed into the room as Mr. Mango and Leo tried to get the flue open.

"Open the doors!" screamed Mimi, as she finally stumbled into the room, heading for the windows to open them.

Timmy, in an uncharacteristic act of altruism, opened Poker the dog's cage to let him out before escaping the house himself, sure it was burning to the ground. The cat knew trouble when he saw it and left the vegetable dip he was working on to run out the door with Timmy. Poker, excited by the frenzy in the family room, started running around, jumping on people and barking like he knew he should rescue the family but didn't exactly know how. He knocked Mimi down right as she got to the window and she laid on the floor screaming for Leo to come save her, sure she was about to die of smoke inhalation. Poker sprung off Mimi and careened into Mrs. Mango, throwing her into Mr. Mango, and the two of them went down on top of the remnants of the vegetables and dip, shattering the coffee table with their fall.

Christine stood calmly beside Sarah, explaining the significance of the hope chest burning in front of them. "I don't think she realizes I could still have a wedding," Christine said, deciding that humor was the only way to go.

Sarah giggled and they looked away from each other, talk of weddings was way too early in their relationship but there was such a zing of attraction that, well, who knew?

"Not that I'd have used anything in that chest," Christine added. "I'm more rustic barn and jam jar cocktails and she's more rose petal cannon."

"Huh? What's that?" asked Sarah looking back at Christine.

"Yep, someone had one at their wedding. Which I know because she ripped the page out of the magazine and showed me before she stuck it in there," Christine gestured at the smoking hope chest. "And other insane stuff, like engraved martini glass favors and a Do It Yourself boutonniere station. Like we could afford any of that."

By this time, Leo had the flue open and Paul had the sliding doors to the patio open, and new smoke headed mostly up the chimney. Rita ran in from the dining room with the water pitcher and threw it at the fireplace. Unfortunately it was still hard to see the fireplace and her aim was not good to begin with, so she ended up dousing Paul instead.

Leo went over to try to raise Mimi, but all at once the Schnapps hit him and he started seeing double. He lunged for where he thought her right arm was but got a handful of her breast instead. "What are you *doing*," she said, her face getting hot. "There are *people* around." He grabbed again, missed her body completely, and fell onto the floor himself. The world seemed to calm down once he was on the floor, so he decided to rest there for a while. He could tell the smoke was clearing and could feel the air coming in the door so knew he wasn't about to burn up. Plus, he knew how much Mimi prayed and went to church and knew that God wasn't going to take her this way, and as long as he was alongside her, he'd be fine. Face down on the carpet with his butt still up in the air, he closed his eyes and went to sleep.

Outside, Timmy shakily dialed 911 on the cell phone he retrieved from the dining room table and screamed at the operator to send a truck quick, there was a house burning down. He gave the address, ended the call, and then stood looking around the yard. It occurred to him that the cars might explode when the fire got to them, and, feeling very smart for realizing how volatile the gas tanks were, decided to move them away from the house. In the absence of keys (there was no way he was going back in to get the keys), he decided he could just put them in neutral and drift them down the slightly sloped driveway. One by one he coasted them into the street, and since the street was flat, couldn't move them beyond the front of the Mango house. By the time the fire truck came screaming around the corner, he had effectively blockaded the street with the Mango collection of cars. With screeching brakes, the fire truck fishtailed, sideswiped Danny's BMW, and slid into the rebuilt convertible, pushing it into the Buick and obliterating the remnants of the Princess Diana roses.

Across the street, nosy neighbor Mrs. Melucci, hearing the sound of metal on metal in the street, ran out of her house without completely finishing her business in the bathroom. She managed to get her stretch pants pulled up but failed to notice the toilet paper trailing out the back of them. Mr. Melucci, on the hunt for Thanksgiving leftovers, called her name throughout the house. He found it easier than usual to find her because, in her haste to get out of the bathroom, she left the toilet paper attached to the roll, thus he was able to follow the long strip from the bathroom to his front yard where he found Mrs. Melucci pacing back and forth, like a helium balloon on a string.

The firemen sprang into action and within seconds had the hoses unfurled and in place. Just as they were about to let loose a stream of water towards the smoking side window, Mr. Mango ran out of the house and yelled, "No! No! The fire is under control! It's in the fireplace!" Several of the firemen looked disappointed and insisted on going in the house with Mr. Mango to make sure.

Mrs. Melucci couldn't take the suspense anymore and started to weave her way through the haphazard arrangement of Mango cars in the street. Her husband debated whether to rip the toilet paper off her behind or see just how far one roll stretched. To his misfortune, he chose the second option. For the record, the roll lasted well up into the Mango's front yard.

Christine and Sarah sat down on the couch and stared at the burning hope chest through the lifting smoke. Christine turned to Sarah and said, "That went well, didn't it?" and started giggling uncontrollably. Sarah joined in, and when the firemen and Mr. Mango came in, they were hanging on each other in hysterics. The firemen looked at the floor scattered with remains of vegetables and dip, a broken table, Mimi and Leo. They saw the burning hope chest, smelled the acrid scent of burnt plastic, and heard the manic laughter of Sarah and Christine. Paul stood in the corner, dripping and staring into space. They looked at each other and shook their heads. Just another family Thanksgiving.

Mrs. Mango limped out of the house in a daze, staring dully at the truck and the cars scattered around, barely feeling the pain down her entire right side from falling on the vegetable dip. Mrs. Melucci ran up to her. "Elsie! What happened? Are you alright? What's that down the side of your dress?"

Mrs. Mango looked blankly at her dress. "I guess

that would be ranch dip.”

“What happened?” Mrs. Melucci asked again. “Was there a fire?”

“Hmm, yes, a little bit,” Mrs. Mango said absently, still staring at her dress.

Mrs. Melucci decided Mrs. Mango was in shock. “Maybe you should sit down.”

Mrs. Mango looked directly at Mrs. Melucci for the first time and said, “Mary, whatever do you have on your pants?”

Mrs. Melucci looked down. “Nothing. What do you mean?”

“Turn around, let me see. Why . . . it’s toilet paper,” said Mrs. Mango, grabbing at the paper and ripping it off at the top of her pants.

Mrs. Melucci looked at the paper in Mrs. Mango’s hand and then looked back towards her house, seeing the winding trail of white through the cars and leading into her front door. She also saw her husband running for the garage. Her face turned red, and she stammered, “Well, I, uh, don’t know, uh, oh goodness,” and she grabbed the paper out of Mrs. Mango’s hand and ran back to her house.

It took the rest of the afternoon to remove the cars, clean up the dishes, sober up the guests and make a start on fixing the living room. Mrs. Mango usually would have been the leader in any cleaning operation, barking out orders for the troops. This time, however, she said she had a headache and went to the bedroom to lie down. She locked the door and ignored the periodic knocks that Christine and Mr. Mango made.

“She’ll come around, don’t worry,” Mr. Mango said to Christine, not so sure himself but seeing how unhappy his daughter was and wanting to make her feel better.

Mr. Mango picked up the pieces of the destroyed coffee table and threw them in the garbage can he had dragged into the room. “I never liked that table,” he said. Christine followed him with a garbage bag full of crab dip, crackers, stomped on vegetables, empty wine bottles, and all the rest of the detritus of a Thanksgiving gone south.

Christine and Sarah cleaned the carpet the best they could, leaving the charred portions alone. Mr. Mango said he had some carpet scraps that he might be able to use to replace the burnt parts and that he'd get right on that tomorrow. Leaving the door and windows open had cleared out the smoke, but the burnt smell hung heavily in the air. The cars involved in the fender benders all had dents but were drivable.

"I'm going to drive Sarah home," said Christine, looking around at the straightened up family room.

Mr. Mango nodded and then hugged his daughter. Stepping back from the hug he motioned to Sarah who was standing behind Christine. "Bring it in," he said and hugged her too.

Christine patted her dad's shoulder. "Thanks," she said, her face crinkling up as if she was going to cry at the same time she was smiling.

Before Christine could say anything too emotional Mr. Mango said, "Ah, get on out of here," grabbing the remote and turning towards the TV.

Sarah slipped her hand into Christine's and squeezed as they walked out.

Left alone in the smelly family room Mr. Mango settled himself in his easy chair, and flipped through the channels. *What the hell*, he thought. A lesbian for a daughter. He tried to get himself worked up about it but found it really didn't bother him so much. Not that he'd ever given it much thought but as he cast back over Christine's life he found he wasn't so surprised after all. He knew Mrs. Mango was not going to get over this quickly, if at all, so he decided he better save his energy for dealing with her. With that, he cranked the chair back as far as it would go and fell asleep.

CHAPTER 3
After the Fall

Dear Raul,

My heart is breaking. It's just too awful to even write down. I have had very bad news about my daughter. She is not who I thought she was. She is a stranger to me. It is like the daughter I knew has died, and I can't stop crying about it. And no one else seems to understand. They are all fine with it. I don't know how they got their brains to do that. My baby girl. My sweet, sweet girl. Gone, for all intents and purposes. And now this imposter, this stranger, is living in my house. I don't know how to talk to her. I can't even look her in the eye.

Thanksgiving was the worst day I have had in many years. The entire thing was ruined. And now I don't know how to speak to my daughter.

Oh Raul, this would never have happened if you were still in my life. I just know it. When our time is up today, I will somehow keep moving forward, but there is now another hole in my heart. You were the first, and that hole never healed. And now Christine is gone too. Eventually, there will be nothing but holes, no heart at all, and I'll just die. And in a way, that is a comfort, knowing I will see you again.

I know, I know, I can hear you saying that I should not rush to join you. I know that is what you would say. But death has no real sting for me, unless it would mean not seeing grandchildren, but no one seems to be doing anything about giving me those.

Sometimes I wonder what this whole life thing is about anyway. A lot of suffering. I'm not sure how much more suffering I can take. Why would she do this to me?

You know, I'm going to forget Christine for the next few minutes. I'm going back to the time we spent the whole day at the Santa Cruz boardwalk. I'm going to relive every moment, every ride, the stuffed gorilla you won me. How the sun sparkled on the water, and the warm sand squished up around our toes. The way our hands fit so perfectly together. The way the sides of your eyes crinkled when you smiled at me.

Ahh, thank you. I'm back. That was pure joy, those minutes. Maybe I can last a little longer.

God bless you and hold you for me,
Yours,
Elsie

"Mom, can I talk to you?" Christine said to her mother's back. Mrs. Mango was standing facing the old coffee maker that soldiered on day after day doing its duty to bring three poor sleepers awake every morning. She didn't move, or speak, or given any indication she heard Christine.

"Mom, I'm the same person," Christine said, walking to the refrigerator and pulling out the half and half.

No answer. Christine set the half and half next to her mother. Mrs. Mango picked it up without turning her head, poured some in her mug, set it down, and still didn't turn around.

"Mom!" said Christine. "This is ridiculous. You can't act like I'm not even standing here. It's been three days and you are acting like I'm dead or something."

Mrs. Mango stared rigidly ahead at the cabinet a foot from her face, moving only to lift her coffee cup to her lips. Her glazed eyes didn't see the cluttered counters in front of her, or the faded yellow of her kitchen walls, or the worn wood grain of the cabinets. They didn't see the muddle of well-loved mugs or prescription bottles alongside unopened Omega Three Fatty Acid bottles.

Christine sighed and walked to the family room where she plopped down on the couch next to her dad, who looked ready to spend the day on the couch. He was in sweats from top to bottom and surrounded by food and newspapers. The TV flashed with football, set on a low volume. Mr. Mango shifted a stiff throw pillow from behind him and tossed it onto the floor. Christine periodically tried to get her parents to update the furnishings in the house but was fighting a losing battle. Her addition of colorful 'accent' pillows and a throw blanket were just so much lipstick on a pig, in her dad's opinion. Mr. Mango didn't understand why people were always trying to remodel their houses or their lives. It all worked and was comfortable and that was enough for him.

The cat jumped into Christine's lap and rubbed his butt along her stomach.

"She'll come around," said Mr. Mango, folding his spread newspaper in half lengthwise to make room for Christine. His feet were propped on the coffee table they had moved from the living room to replace the one smashed at Thanksgiving. Christine had said it ruined the 'aesthetic' of the room, but Mr. Mango was enjoying its larger size. More room for snacks and feet. So what that it was dark wood when the rest of the wood in the room was light?

"How do you know?" asked Christine.

"I just know. She loves you more than she hates the idea of you with a girl," he said. "Your mother is just, hmm . . . " Mr. Mango searched for a way to reassure his daughter without actually saying that her mother was close to phobic about anything sexual, even the 'normal' stuff. "She's, uh, conservative. Careful. Ladylike."

Christine glanced at her dad and laughed. "Are you trying to tell me mom is uptight? 'Cause I know that!"

Mr. Mango grimaced. "Well, you know, she's from a different era."

"She was a teen in the sixties!" Christine exclaimed. "Wasn't that all the free love stuff?"

"Not for everyone. Your mom is more fifties. Or Victorian." The cat moved onto Mr. Mango's lap, rustling against the newspaper, and he gently swatted it off him.

"What about you?"

"What about me?" Mr. Mango gave up on the newspaper, picked up the remote and switched the TV from football to golf, increasing the volume.

"Are you more sixties or, I don't know, something else?"

"If you are asking do I care that you're gay, no, I don't. I can't really get worked up about it. Which, to be honest with you, kind of takes me by surprise. Not that I ever really thought about it." Mr. Mango waved the remote at the TV. "Jesus Christ, this kid's about to give away his first major. Would you look at that, he was six strokes in the lead and now he's two back. Christ." Mr. Mango shook his head in disgust. "Complete meltdown."

"What should I do about Mom? She is literally acting like I don't exist," said Christine.

"Give her time. And just act normal. One of these days she'll join back in," said Mr. Mango. Without taking his eyes off the TV, he slid his arm around Christine's shoulders and gave her a hug. "We both want you to be happy. I just got less idea about what that is than your mom."

The sound of the front door closing drifted back to the family room. Mr. Mango looked at his watch. "Huh, your mother must be going to church by herself." He smiled. "Maybe the silver lining of all this, huh? That I don't need to go with her every time." Historically, Mrs. Mango refused to go to church without Mr. Mango, unwilling to drive herself. It was a weekly battle, football or mass, and today was one of the battles Mr. Mango had won. Mr. Mango didn't think God would begrudge him the pleasure of a Sunday morning football game, otherwise why schedule them at 10:00 a.m.? For that matter, why put so many exciting sports events on Sundays at all, if they weren't there for a man to relax and enjoy? Unless it was a stinker, Mr. Mango resented missing the early game on Sunday mornings. Mrs. Mango's intensified motivation to get to church seemed to have solved the problem, at least for Mr. Mango.

Christine gave her dad back a weak smile. "Must be going to pray for my soul," Christine said. "I guess I can't go anymore either. According to Mom and Aunt Mimi anyway."

Mr. Mango shook his head. "Don't listen to all that. You go to church if you want. Go to a different one if the Catholics are going to be buttheads about it. Besides, I don't think they are against it anymore."

"Dad!" Christine exclaimed in shock. "Calling your religion buttheads? That's sacrilegious."

Mr. Mango chuckled. "Don't much care for religious hypocrites. Either we love everyone or we don't. The older I get, the less I believe in all the horseshit *humans* have added to religion. There's God and He loves us all, and the rest of it is made up, you ask me. So, don't be feeling like God doesn't love you. He loves you just as much as anyone else. Maybe more because you've been brave."

Christine welled up with tears as her dad squeezed her shoulders again in another hug.

"Ahh, would you look at that?" Mr. Mango rolled his head in frustration. "Kid just bogeyed the fourth. He's got no frickin' chance." Mr. Mango smacked the remote against his leg. "I hate it when I let myself care. Shouldn't have gotten so involved in watching this guy. Christ, golf'll break your balls, it will."

At church, Mrs. Mango slid into her normal pew, third from the back, and nodded to her regular pew neighbors. She slid onto her knees on the kneeler and

looked around the sanctuary with satisfaction. The altar
flowers were just lovely, huge sprays of green and white on
either side of the altar, towering above rows of poinsettias
lining the steps. Mrs. Mango loved this church, loved the
vaguely Mediterranean look with white walls and dark
beams, loved the stained glass windows. She looked for her
favorite window, St. Anthony of Padua, the miracle
worker. Mrs. Mango lowered her head and silently asked
St. Anthony to work some of his magic on Christine. She
begged God for forgiveness for Christine and asked for
guidance. Crossing herself, she opened her eyes and eased
herself up onto the pew.

"Where's Joe?" whispered Pearl Bussman, an 80-
something-year-old deacon wearing her brown wig too far
forward on her head. She raised her heavily drawn-in
eyebrows, and they hit the wig. "He's not sick, is he?"

"Do we need to add him to the prayers?" asked
Winky Bussman-Wessman from the other side of Pearl.
Winky was Pearl's 60-something-year-old daughter and
had returned to live with her mother now that they were
both widows. Church attendance was like their weekly soap
opera viewing where they scoped out every detail on every
parishioner, giving them enough to talk about the rest of the
week.

"He's fine, just, ah, overslept, and I came by
myself."

Pearl and Winky exchanged glances. They had
never seen Elsie at church alone. Either she and Joe came
together, or they didn't come. Pearl privately decided to
pray for their marriage because clearly something was
going on. Both of them mentally tucked the information
onto the front of the discussion list for the week. And Elsie
was being uncharacteristically quiet. Normally, she would
have fired questions about their week at the mother-
daughter duo. She hadn't even asked about Winky's
haircut—that was a detail Elsie would never have missed.

Mrs. Mango had a hard time following the sermon.
She stared blankly into the back of the head of the woman

in the pew in front of her, not even noticing the flattened sleep spot in her hairdo. She kneeled and stood and sang automatically, but nothing really entered her head, filled as it was with the constant prayer to save Christine's soul.

As soon as the service ended, Mrs. Mango hurried to the restroom and stayed in a stall until the church could be safely assumed to have cleared out. She didn't want to have to talk to anyone. Those nosy ladies, wondering why Joe wasn't with her! She was afraid someone would figure out what a sham their family was if she had to have any conversation at all. Shoot! Mrs. Mango remembered she had agreed to stay after the service and help manage the Angel Tree. Well, someone else was going to have to hang more children's names. Once all noise had died down, she came out, slipped over to the Angel Tree to grab a name, and then made her way slowly to her car. As she approached it, she saw the dent left over from the fire truck pushing the convertible into her Buick and wondered if she should go back in the church and say another rosary. The alternative was driving home, and all of a sudden Mrs. Mango couldn't stand the idea of spending the day at home ignoring Christine. She wondered if Christine had maybe gone somewhere. She wondered if she herself should go somewhere. Maybe back in the church? No, she couldn't face anyone.

Mrs. Mango climbed in the car and sat there without putting the keys in the ignition. Where could she go?

Was her life really that small? That she could think of nowhere to go?

Finally, Mrs. Mango stuck the keys in the ignition, started up the car, and headed to the bakery. Maybe a good eclair or three would soothe her pain.

CHAPTER 4
Bill Becomes Tripod

"Jeez, not allowed to forget a thing," Mr. Mango grumbled to himself as he stomped out of the house towards his still-warm pickup truck. Mrs. Mango had asked him to pick up green Jello mix on his way home from his last delivery, and between saying yes and heading home, he had hauled four huge boxes out of his truck and up a skinny switchback set of steps in the Berkeley hills. The only thing in his mind when he climbed back in his truck and maneuvered down the crooked street cluttered with cars on both sides was that he was getting too old for this, even as a part-time gig. He wasn't sure who designed the streets that were basically terraced into the side of the hill, but he thought it might have been Hobbits, given the narrowness of the streets and the hairpin angles of the turns. Definitely not designed for big delivery trucks or anything larger than a golf cart. The fog that had just rolled in didn't help any either. After leaving the delivery truck in the lock-up yard, his drive home in his pickup was completed listening to Tupac and thinking about a cold beer. Listening to Tupac is no memory device for remembering Jello, so Mr. Mango sat in the westbound traffic with the hundred thousand other people headed east from the SF bay until he was off the freeway and into his driveway. Christine wasn't supposed to be home until after 8:00, and Mrs. Mango didn't like driving at night if she didn't have to. Or on the freeway. Or to anywhere except her well-traveled little circles in their corner of suburbia. Over forty years of marriage had taught Mr. Mango it was just all-around easier to do what his wife wanted. He wondered what Tupac would have done if his wife demanded he go buy Jello. The world would never know. Tupac exited before dealing with such mundane minutiae.

Sighing with the inevitability of heading out to the store when he was ready for his easy chair, Mr. Mango climbed back in the pickup. He turned the key and heard a thump and a screech that made him sure Satan had finally come for him (Mr. Mango had some guilty secrets of the online variety), and luckily his hand was still on the key and his reflex made him turn the ignition back off. He got out of the truck and fearfully reached for the hood. He had been working on cars his whole life and should know what to do, but on the other hand he was also a Catholic and hadn't made confession in a year, and in all his years working on cars he had never heard *that* sound. He put his hands under the hood, said a quick prayer begging for forgiveness, and lifted the hood.

Right as he lifted the hood, something dropped on his foot, screeched again, and scrambled past his leg in a blur of blood and fur. Blood was not Mr. Mango's friend. He screamed, dropped the hood on his hands, and fainted. Because his hands were stuck under the hood he didn't actually fall clear to the ground but toppled forward onto the hood, thus further pinning his hands with his own body weight

Mrs. Mango, coming out to see if she could catch Mr. Mango before he left and add a can of mandarin oranges to the list, found him slumped over the hood of the car with a grisly trail of blood leading away from him. Having raised four kids, she was less worried about the blood than the lack of movement from Mr. Mango, so she poked at him and yelled his name. "Joe! Joe! What the hell are you doing?" as if he had picked the hood for a place to take a nap instead of getting on about the business of picking up her Jello.

She shook him, and that moved his hands a bit under the hood, and he woke up howling with pain. He tried to tell her to pick up the hood, but all she could make out was something that sounded like "Pood! Pood!"

He leaned back, and she finally saw that his hands were pinned and, by now, numb enough he couldn't get them out himself. She grabbed at the hood and said, "My goodness, why are you standing here with your hands stuck in there?"

Once released, Mr. Mango fell to the ground, writhing in pain and mumbling about 'my livelihood.' Reassured that he was alive, Mrs. Mango decided to investigate the blood trail and followed it around the side of the house. She found Bill the cat tearing around the back yard in circles, darting and falling, darting and falling, screeching and flinging blood like a salad spinner. Mrs. Mango was no dummy and realized that although many mysterious things happen in the world, it was likely that the scene out front had something to do with the scene in the back.

Mrs. Mango shook her head while she contemplated how to catch the cat. "Darn, I'm never going to get that Jello set," she muttered. She tried cornering the cat, she tried luring it into its cage, and finally had to get an old sheet and throw it over the cat, grabbing at the corners to tie it up like a load of laundry. She knotted the top and dragged it around to the front of the house, kicking and howling like an alien trying to get out of Sigourney Weaver's stomach, blood stains causing abstract designs on the sheet. She found Mr. Mango sitting up where she'd left him, looking pale but at least conscious, staring at his hands.

"Goddamn," he said. "What the hell *was* that? Do you realize my hands may never work again?"

"Don't get any funny ideas about retiring," she said. "It was the cat and somehow he lost a leg, do you have any idea how that happened?"

"It was the *cat*?" he said and then felt overwhelmed by a feeling of relief. *Thank you God,* he silently mouthed, *Thank You.* And then realized he had promised God not to look at any more porn on the internet if he just protected him from the engine Satan. Would God really hold him to that? Something to think about later; there had to be a loophole because he wasn't giving up porn for a goddamn cat. He made that deal when he thought it was Satan.

Meanwhile, across the street, their neighborhood watch specialist Mrs. Melucci couldn't stand it anymore. She had been pacing the width of her front window, peering out trying to get a good angle on the action. Once Mrs. Mango came around the corner with the bloody kicking sheet, she decided she might need help. Mrs. Melucci flew out of her front door and up the Mangos' driveway in her housecoat and slippers with holes cut out for her bunions. "Are you okay?" she said to Mr. Mango.

"Jesus," he said, cradling his hands, "I don't know. I creamed my hands in that hood. Goddamn cat." And with that, he looked over at the screeching, rolling, bloody sheet and passed out again.

Mrs. Mango shook her head. "He never could stand the sight of blood. The doctor said it's one of those phobia things. He'll wake up in a minute or two. Can you believe it, the cat ripped its back leg off."

Mrs. Melucci gasped. "My lord! How?"

"I think it got caught in the engine; it likes to climb up there and get warm. But I don't know, ask Sleepy here."

Then Mrs. Mango was struck by the thought that maybe there was a bad energy attached to their house now that Christine was . . . she couldn't bring herself to actually think the word. Maybe God was punishing the family, and it was the poor cat that caught His wrath. She realized Mrs. Melucci was talking and forced herself to focus on Mrs. Melucci's words, not her own thoughts.

"You know, these days they can reattach limbs and such." Mrs. Melucci shook her head in wonder. "I don't know if they've done it with animals, but I read the other day in Parade magazine in the Sundee paper about a guy had his arm chopped off by a thresher and they sewed it right back on. Be important to get it on in the right direction, wouldn't it?"

Mrs. Melucci and Mrs. Mango looked at each other and then at Mr. Mango, still unconscious. "Well, it's not going to be him that goes looking for it," Mrs. Mango said.

"How much do you like that cat?" said Mrs. Melucci.

Mrs. Mango thought about it. "Enough to look under the truck but not in it," she said. She got down on her hands and knees and peered under the truck. "I can't see anything," she said, getting up. She looked in the bed of the pickup and found a flashlight and went back around to the front. Both Mrs. Melucci and Mrs. Mango got down on their knees and peered warily under the truck.

Mr. Smolensky was walking his dog Buster and noticed Mrs. Melucci's feet sticking out from the front of the truck and thought Mrs. Mango might have had a heart attack, or worse yet, been run over by Mr. Mango. Who really knew what went on in peoples' houses? He thought they got along, but you never know; just a month ago, a guy three streets over ran over his wife and then backed up and ran over her again. When the police came, he said it was because she bought the wrong brand of hot dogs, but Mr. Smolensky suspected it was more than that; I mean, really, whoever killed over a Ballpark Frank? Ever the good neighbor, he walked closer and yelled out "Hello? Mrs. Mango?"

Mrs. Mango jumped and bumped her head on, ironically, the bumper and swore. Mrs. Melucci sat up, looked around the bumper, and said, "Hello, Bobby, we're looking for the cat's leg."

As Mr. Smolensky came closer, Buster smelled the intoxicating combination of cat and blood and ripped the leash out of Mr. Smolensky's hand, shooting like a Patriot missile straight under the truck and reemerging a split second later on the other side carrying a bloody stump. Without losing a step, he took off down the street with the leg in his mouth, leash bumping along behind him so fast it gave off sparks. Mr. Smolensky yelled, "I'm sorry!" and took off down the street after the dog, yelling "Buster! *Buster!* Stay! Stay! *Buster!*"

"Well, that's that," said Mrs. Mango, secretly glad she didn't have to pick up the leg. "I better get these two some help." Mrs. Melucci leaned her hefty weight onto Mr. Mango's shoulder, trying to get herself up. "I swear, this arthritis is getting worse by the day." Mr. Mango woke up with the feeling of Mrs. Melucci's knobby hand on his shoulder and her cabbage smell five inches from his face and came close to passing out again. Comatose was so much more peaceful than real life; it was really underrated, he thought, as he half-heartedly fought to stay awake.

Mrs. Mango realized she was yet again in a traumatic situation that called for her to drive, and that made her think of the last traumatic situation that called for her to drive—and that was even more distressing than a ripped-off cat's leg. While she loaded Mr. Mango and the cat into the car and slowly eased the car out of the driveway, she tried to think about the cat and not Thanksgiving. She figured there was no need for her to drive so fast they got in an accident and finished the job Mr. Mango had so ably begun, so she took her time.

Partway down the street, she saw Rosa Cabasso out walking the little white ball of frizz she called a dog. Rosa looked at Mrs. Mango in astonishment, having never seen Mr. Mango as a passenger in her car. Either Mrs. Mango drove alone, or she rode with Mr. Mango. Rosa gave a big wave.

Mrs. Mango slowed the car, pulling over towards the sidewalk beside Rosa, and hit the button to put down the passenger-side window. "Hi Rosa! How's your mother doing? It's been, what, a month since her hip surgery?"

"She's doing well, thanks," said Rosa. "Constipated from the pain killers, but otherwise doing good. Driving me crazy ringing that bell for help, though. Why're you driving? Joe, you okay?" Rosa leaned into the passenger window and peered in at Mr. Mango.

"Gotta get this guy to the doctor," Mrs. Mango said, gesturing at Mr. Mango who was leaned back, eyes closed, in the passenger seat, thinking he had fallen into some sort of hell.

Mr. Mango didn't open his eyes. He was done with

these ladies and their lack of urgency. His fingers would probably drop off before he got to the hospital. He tried not to think about how he would drive and unload his delivery truck without the use of his hands.

"Joe!" Rosa said again and, getting no response, looked at Mrs. Mango. "What is it? Heart attack? Stroke?"

"No, crushed his fingers in the hood of the truck."

There was a yowl from the back seat.

"And the cat ripped its leg off; got to get him to the vet."

"Hmm, don't that beat all. Think he'd know better," said Rosa, removing her head and shushing the yapping dog at her feet. "Joe, I mean. Not the cat. Well, better get Punkin on her way here."

Mrs. Mango gave a wave and hit the button to raise the window before putting the car back in gear. She got to the end of the road leading out of their neighborhood and considered whether she should take the cat or her husband for help first. She decided the cat was in a more dire position, and, plus, it was bleeding all over her car despite her best efforts to pad the back seat with towels, so she headed for the vet first.

Mr. Mango, feeling the direction of the car, opened his eyes and yelled, "Where the hell are you going? The hospital's the other way."

"I'm dropping the cat off first; she lost a leg, you just bumped your hands."

Mr. Mango looked at his swollen and purpled hands, realized for the millionth time in his marriage that he had no control over Mrs. Mango, and sat back and closed his eyes again. Maybe he'd never open them.

What with all the vet and hospital visits and cleaning the blood out of the back seat, Mrs. Mango never did get that Jello made and had to go to bridge club the next day with a dessert bought at the Safeway. The ladies were privately delighted to get an almond ring instead of Jello, even though it was because the cat lost a leg. They didn't know the cat and, besides, it wasn't going to give the cat its leg back if they didn't eat the almond ring. After that, everybody took to calling the cat Tripod, after Mr. Mango noticed how much his legs looked like the doohickey his camera stood on to get group shots.

CHAPTER 5
Mr. Mango Gets Frisky

"Goddamn it," Mr. Mango mumbled under his breath as he turned over yet again in the bed, unable to sleep. He fumbled with the rolled-up towel under his head, trying to get it into a position that might feel comfortable. A week earlier, Mrs. Mango had seen a story on TV about dust mites in beds and pillows and realized their pillows were thirty years old. She immediately threw out all the pillows in the house and bought new ones at Costco. Mr. Mango hadn't slept through the night since. If he had known how badly he would sleep on the new pillow, he would have followed the garbage truck to the dump and retrieved his old one, but unfortunately it was collected before he made that discovery. The new pillow was too high, and he got a neck ache from it. He bought another new pillow at Target, but that didn't work either. After that, he tried sleeping without a pillow, and that left him with a backache in addition to the neck ache. Now, he was working on using a rolled-up towel to try to get the right height, but he could already tell it wasn't going to work.

Meanwhile, Mrs. Mango had been solidly asleep for several hours. He could tell by the level of snoring and the way she hadn't moved from the same spot since climbing into bed. He flipped over again and 'accidentally' bumped her back, and she still didn't wake up. After lying there with growing resentment and watching the clock flip every minute from 12:07 to 12:51, he finally got out of bed.

In the family room, Mr. Mango looked at the TV and then he looked at the computer and decided he would go online. He knew what that meant, but he just couldn't stop himself. Here he was, with Mrs. Mango fast asleep, while he was wide awake, and it was her fault! Christine was off on some sort of retreat for three days, so it was just the two of them. There couldn't be a better time, and in his anger, he assured himself he deserved some kind of pleasure. Mr. Mango had only started using a computer consistently a year ago when he switched to part-time work and just recently had discovered the unlimited amounts of pornography available on the internet. Before the internet, he would have said he was about as interested in naked women as the next guy, which to him meant looking at a buddy's Playboy if it were around but not going out of his way to get a subscription. This online business changed all that. Now it was easy and private, and there was such a wealth of pictures! He grabbed a couple of beers from the refrigerator, hoping they might help him get sleepy, and sat down at the computer. An hour later, he hit the button to disconnect and wandered back into the bedroom.

"What the hell," he thought, feeling horny and a little buzzed from the beer, so he climbed into bed and started spooning up against Mrs. Mango.

There was no response, so he threw his arm around her and started hugging. There was still no response, so he started nuzzling the back of her neck. He ran into bristling curlers, but he was so aroused by the internet pictures he kept on going. He could feel her starting to wake up, so he increased the nuzzling and hugging, sliding his arm around her and putting his hand on her breast.

"What are you *doing*?!" Mrs. Mango said loudly, flipping over to face him and pushing him away at the same time.

They hadn't had sex in years, so Mr. Mango felt a little bit silly, but he felt a lot horny so he didn't give up. "I just thought, you know," he said, "we might have, ah, a little action."

Mrs. Mango propped herself up with her elbows, "What?! Are you kidding?! It is the middle of the night, for Pete's sake! Are you *drunk*?"

"Hey, it's *your* fault I can't sleep," Mr. Mango said, "why'd you have to go and change the pillows?"

"And *that* means you can get all, all . . . ." Mrs. Mango sputtered, unable to name what he was doing.

"Forget it," Mr. Mango said, rolling onto his side facing away from Mrs. Mango. "Just forget it."

Now Mrs. Mango was wide awake. "I can't believe you woke me up, you owe me an apology. What is *wrong* with you? All over a couple of *pillows*?"

Mr. Mango turned back towards her. "Do you really want to have this conversation?" He knew she didn't, knew she would do anything to avoid having sex, talking about sex, admitting there even was such a thing as sex.

Mrs. Mango said, "Hmph!" and pulled the covers towards her as she flipped on her side facing away from Mr. Mango.

Mr. Mango stared at the ceiling, steaming. That old woman acted like he was some kind of pervert. For Pete's sake, there was nothing wrong with wanting to have sex with your wife. She made it seem like *he* was the one with the problem, and he had let them both agree with that for too long. Even those old crones Velma and Flora were getting some. Was it too much to ask, after a lifetime of fidelity and mortgage payments with no complaint, that he get a little pleasure? He looked up at the wall facing their bed and saw the cross with Jesus hanging on it that dominated the bedroom. He believed in God, but having the crucifixion in every room was too much for him. You won again, buddy, he silently said to Jesus. After letting out a couple of irritated snorts, he picked up his rolled-up towel-pillow and walked out of the bedroom. He made no effort to be quiet and in fact intentionally opened and closed the door slowly so it would extend that creaking noise no amount of WD40 could remove.

Out in the living room, Mr. Mango defiantly sat down at the computer again, and this time, he didn't just look at the pictures. Afterwards, he settled himself on the couch, feeling at once physically relieved and mentally agitated. Pulling the throw blanket around him, he did the sign of the cross on himself, whispered a prayer asking for forgiveness, and fell into the best sleep he'd had since Mrs. Mango threw out his pillow.

When Mr. Mango left the room, Mrs. Mango tried to slide back into sleep, but she was too angry. She felt guilty, and as usual when she felt guilty, she turned it quickly into irritation at Mr. Mango. What had gotten into the old goat? Why did he have to go and upset the fine balance they had achieved (she didn't complain about the thousand things wrong with him, and he didn't try to have sex with her)? She sent a silent prayer up to Jesus on the wall, asking him to set her husband straight. And thinking the word 'straight' sent her right back to obsessing about Christine, which brought her brain even more awake. With each toss and turn, Mrs. Mango cursed Mr. Mango, her anger at him mounting with each tick of the clock. How could he have woken her up for *that*?

Mrs. Mango finally fell into a restless sleep, and by the time she woke at 7:30, her brain had efficiently stuffed any remnants of sexual issues back into their boxes, allowing her to hang on to the irritation without actually thinking about what had caused it.

Anyone looking in the window in the morning would have seen the normal routine of Mrs. Mango making coffee and pouring two cups, and Mr. Mango handing Mrs. Mango the Life section of the newspaper. There would be nothing to show the slow drifting apart, like two sticks caught in different currents.

Dear Raul,

Oh, how complicated life is. Joe approached me the other night. You know, for relations. And I just couldn't bring myself to. It has been the dilemma of my life, feeling unfaithful to you and unfaithful to him all at the same time. Maybe I should have never married, but then again, I wouldn't have Joe Jr. and Danny and Michael and Christine. Ouch. Hard to even write her name. I know I am breaking her heart, but it is hard for me to even look at her these days. I just can't bring myself to accept it. Accept her.

Maybe the whole world would be better without sex. Just find a way to procreate in the test tube and never have to deal with all this messiness. When we were young, seemed like such a natural concept. I don't know how it all got so complicated. Not that you'd want that from me now anyway. I'm old and look it.

Enough whining. I'm going to remember the time we were Christmas shopping in San Francisco.

Ahh, that was lovely. Back again. I remember walking next to you, our sides touching the whole time. I was wearing your pea coat, and I just felt so surrounded by your love. The lights were beautiful, and the sounds of the cars and street cars and people were like music. It felt like we were in a movie, and I felt so content, like I would never want anything else again. You kept pointing out things you could buy me, and I couldn't work up any interest in them. I already had all I needed walking right beside me. Thank you for those moments.

Yours,
Elsie

CHAPTER 6
The Triathletes

Christine came limping up the sidewalk from her attempted run. She suspected that you had to run more than you walk to actually call it a run. She was breathless and hunched over trying to both breathe and not throw up and to ignore the fact she hadn't even made a mile. She had jogged down a series of streets similar to her own, little single-story houses shoulder to shoulder, with small front yards and driveways wide enough for one large car or two small ones. Every so often, someone had added a second story to their house, dwarfing the houses around it like a teenager stuck in a class with seven year olds. Traffic and cars moving in and out of driveways meant she had to stop and/or walk plenty, but she still found herself out of breath by the time she reached the opening to the community trail. The plan had been to run for a while on the trail, a paved pathway that snaked alongside an eleven-mile meandering creek bed; however, Christine was tired enough that she glanced across the trail at the almost dry creek bed and turned around to head home. She'd join the crowd of people running and walking and skating along the trail next time.

"Hiya Christine." Christine looked up to see Flora and Velma walking towards her, each pushing a 21-speed bike. "You okay?" Velma added, peering at Christine as they stopped in front of her.

"Not dead yet," gasped Christine.

"Good for you honey, out running," said Flora, stretching stringy legs that looked like one long Achilles tendon from foot to butt. "How far did you go?"

"Maybe a mile," said Christine.

"Well now, that's a good start, you just keep at it," said Flora.

Christine pulled herself to standing and noticed the

bikes. "You guys are biking now?"

"We're training for a triathlon, and today was a riding day but dang if my chain didn't come off five minutes into it and I can't get it back on," said Velma.

Christine noticed they had on biking shorts with the padded behinds giving them both an attractive roundness they hadn't had in at least twenty years. The biker shorts were topped with tight brightly colored shirts, adorned with pockets for water bottles and other biking paraphernalia. Christine pulled her shirt from around her neck and stretched it up to wipe her forehead. "Let me take a look at it."

The 'girls' pushed their bikes up the driveway, and sure enough, Christine could see Velma's chain dangling off. Christine got down on her knees and fumbled with it for a while, getting greasy hands but making no progress at getting the chain back on.

"Let me get my dad; he could do this in a second, I'm sure," Christine said.

Christine found her father asleep on the couch in the family room and gently nudged him. "Are you okay, dad? You seem to be sleeping a lot these days."

"Hmm? Huh!" he said coming awake. "What?"

"You're sleeping a lot," Christine repeated. "Are you feeling okay?"

"For crissakes, I can't sleep at all at *night*," he grumbled. "I'm getting maybe three hours total, now that your mother went and threw out my pillow. Now, you won't even let me sleep in the day."

"I'm sorry," Christine said. "Go back to sleep. It's not a big deal. It just that Velma and Flora are outside. Velma's chain came off her bike, and I thought you might put it back on."

"What's she doing riding a bike," her father muttered under his breath, but he got up and headed to the driveway.

It was the rainy season, but there was no rain yet; instead, the December Saturday had warmed from 39 degrees at sunrise to a balmy 63 by afternoon. Sometimes you got several seasons in a day in the Bay Area. Mr. Mango squinted as his eyes adjusted from the dim family room to the bright afternoon, and he was hit by a stab of the guilt that can come from doing nothing on such a beautiful day. A quick glance around his street added to the feeling, neighbors on every side were out mowing or decorating for Christmas or exercising. Mr. Mango gave a quick shake of his head to come further awake and greeted Velma and Flora.

Velma and Flora were almost twenty years older than he and Mrs. Mango, and he couldn't help but have some respect for their health obsession. They seemed to have more energy than he and Mrs. Mango combined. As he dug around his toolbox to come up with something to fix the chain, he thought about how those two old ladies were having the time of their life and his wife acted like sex with your spouse was illegal. He wondered if there was any way to ask them how they got themselves going on this whole new program.

Mr. Mango easily slipped the chain back on and stood up. "Hey, Velma, Flora, how'd you two get on this health kick, anyhow?"

"It was a combination of things that happened all at the same time," said Flora. "First, Sam died, bless his soul." She crossed herself and looked up into the sky for a second. "And I was kind of bored, and then on account of the osteroferosis, I went to one of them water aerobics classes at the Y, and Velma was there. Hadn't seen her in a year of yesterdays."

Velma took up the story. "We did one of the classes, and we weren't sure it was helping much, but we had paid for it so we kept going, and then one of the seniors had an 'accident'"—she widened her eyes and lifted her eyebrows—"in the pool, and they had to cancel class for a while to drain the pool and clean it up."

"Someone crapped in the pool?" Mr. Mango said, trying not to laugh.

"Yeah, *diarrhea*. That was me, it would be time for Dr. Kevorkian," said Velma. "Actually, I don't need him, I got all my pills saved up for when it's my time."

Flora nodded. "I've got my Gilly Street plan, but I'm still paying on my Nautilus Society arrangements; got to at least get that taken care of before I kick. No way I want my family to have to pay for that."

"What's the Nautilus Society?" asked Christine.

"Pre-arrangement Cremation Services," said Flora. "Anyway, with the class cancelled, we decided to try something else, and I was watching Jack Lalane one night and I thought if that old fart could look that good, so could we," said Velma. "I mean, it was a rerun—that guy kicked the bucket already—but you know, he looked younger than his age right up until he died."

Flora nodded again. "So we got on the internets and got some workout programs for ourselves. A little weightlifting, some running, some biking. You know you got to have your cardio and your resistance work too."

"And then we added in the diet part, the wheat grass and omega threes and such," said Velma. "I figure if the government is going to stop paying for my prescriptions, I better get myself in shape to not need them anymore. So, we do all that, and presto!"

"You got that right about the prescriptions," said Mr. Mango, snapping his toolbox shut.

Christine sighed, her dad was about to go off on one of his favorite rants.

"Obamacare has ruined this nation, you know that," Mr. Mango continued.

Before he could say any more, Christine tried to get back to what Flora and Velma were talking about. "I think it's great, this health stuff you are doing," she said. "Is that all of it?"

"Well, there was one more part," added Flora, tilting her head at Velma. Velma smiled but didn't say anything.

Mr. Mango forgot about his Obama obsession; this

might be the part he wanted to hear but didn't know how to get her to say it. "What was the other thing?"

Flora and Velma looked at each other again and said nothing.

Mr. Mango tried one more time. "I, uh, noticed the two of you ladies have, uh, been dating a lot."

Velma snorted. "Huh! Not much to pick from in our age group; they're all dead. But yeah, we've found some younger men to, uh, spend time with. There are still a few 70-year-olds with some life in them, if you know what I mean."

"Most men don't age as well as you have," said Flora giving Mr. Mango a flirty smile.

Christine winced. She agreed, had always thought her dad was handsome, but it felt creepy to have an old lady flirting with him.

"Uh huh, uh huh," Mr. Mango said, ignoring the comment and hoping to get one of them to expand on the topic of their dating. Neither said anything, so he said, "So with your husbands, uh, passed on, I guess there were some things you, uh, missed."

"Is he talking about sex?" Flora asked Velma. "I could swear he is asking us about our sex lives!"

"Well, I never," said Velma, pretending to be offended.

Flora started laughing, "That's not what you told me about last weekend!" They both started giggling.

Mr. Mango was desperate now. "What? What?! Was it the omega three whatevers? The wheatgrass? What else are you girls *on*?"

"Oh, he means the *cream,*" Velma said. "Okay, here's the deal; there's a cream for women to use on their, uh, special parts. That cream is like Viagra in a tube. I call it 'resurrection cream,' because it brought my dead parts right back to life.

Flora twisted her head to the side and raised her eyebrows. "I call it Ball Park Franks because it plumps, you know?" Then she giggled again. "I can't believe we are talking about this.”

"Well, why not? Maybe the man knows someone who could benefit from the cream.” Velma looked meaningfully at Flora. “He should tell this person to go to her lady doctor; that's what he should do.”

After her father headed back into the house, Christine watched the 'girls' ride away and stood shaking her head. “And *I'm* the one with the abnormal sex life?” she muttered to herself.

CHAPTER 7
Unexpected Entanglements

Mrs. Mango heaved a dusty box of books onto a long table in front of the library. It was one of ten long tables, all rapidly filling up with the boxes of used books library patrons dropped off when cleaning out or downsizing or just generally tired of storing The Da Vinci Code and its brethren. It was book sale day, and the volunteers were behind in getting the books arranged on the tables. She rotated the box so that its sign "Young Adult" faced the front and looked right and left to make sure it was with the other Young Adult used books.

Marion Kniess, an actual employee of the library, moved quickly from table to table, issuing instructions, brushing dust off of stacks of books, straightening boxes into neat rows. Marion, somewhere over fifty with a blond-going-gray bob cut, was five feet of discipline, attention to detail, and organizational efficiency. Mrs. Mango had often thought that Marine sergeants could learn from Marion, a woman Mrs. Mango liked but was scared of, too.

"No Early Birds!" Marion barked at an elderly man who was poking through the "History" box. He jumped and mumbled something and wandered back towards the parking lot where other Early Birds were gathered, waiting for the sign from Marion that they could descend on the tables and walk away with months' worth of reading for under $10.

Marion finally gave the okay, and packs of people surged towards the tables. Mrs. Mango stepped back out of the way and enjoyed watching all the different types of people poking around in the books. There were old couples and young kids and singles and packs of moms and toddlers, just about every stage of life represented.

"Hi Mrs. Mango," said a thirty something year old woman with two braids sticking out of a baseball cap.

"Oh, hello Tina," said Mrs. Mango smiling. "And Monica! How are you?" she added to the ponytailed woman beside Tina.

"You girls don't miss a sale, do you?" asked Mrs. Mango. She knew the regulars at the book sale and had always enjoyed the cheerful banter of Tina and Monica.

"Nope, gotta get our supply," said Monica, arms already full of books. Tina gave Monica a pat on the shoulders. "Here, I have the bag, you can stick those in," she said, opening a reusable Trader Joe's bag for Monica.

Something in the pat and the smile between the women hit Mrs. Mango like a stone. It had never occurred to her that they might be . . . *a couple*. No. No way.

"You're so thoughtful," Monica said.

"I'm full of something, that's for sure," laughed Tina.

"See you two later," Mrs. Mango said quickly. She walked to the Romance table and straightened up the already straight boxes, letting her attention focus on a little blond woman cruising around with a little white terrier, no more than fifteen pounds, if that, twisting its leash in and around her feet. Mrs. Mango was struck, not for the first time, by how much dogs and owners can look alike. Dog and woman both had cute little faces on cute little bodies but it was the length and curl to the hair that put the twinning over the top.

As Mrs. Mango watched, the terrier darted away from the owner, yanking at the leash and pulling one foot out from under her.

The owner screeched and grabbed the table for balance, spinning around to unwind the rest of the twists of the leash. "Bella!" she yelled, yanking back on the leash as the dog tried to pull her towards another dog headed their way.

The other dog looked like some kind of black lab-pit bull mix and definitely had at least 30 pounds on Bella. At the end of the lab-pit bull's leash was a man who looked like he'd been assembled from the bread-proofing oven at

Subway: smooth round doughy rolls stuck together in the shape of a man. He saw Bella straining to get at his dog and smiled. "Is your dog friendly?" he asked Bella's owner.

Having gotten herself straightened out, she smiled back. "Yes," and then to Bella, "Hey, Bella, say hello to this nice dog." Her voice went up an octave, like she was talking to a little baby.

"This is Ranger," said the doughy man, as the dogs came at each other's noses. Bella easily fit under Ranger's body and squirmed from his head to his tail where she came out and started sniffing.

Bella's owner dropped the leash that had gotten tangled with Ranger's leash. Before she could pick it up, the dogs started jumping around each other in play, and then Ranger mounted Bella.

"No!" screamed Bella's owner. "My baby! He'll kill her!"

Ranger's owner yanked on his leash and yelled "Stop!" but Ranger was a dog on a mission and nothing was stopping him now.

Bella's owner scrambled on the ground to grab her leash but couldn't get to it. "Bella, baby! I'll save you," she screamed, as she started hitting Ranger to try to dislodge him.

The crowd around the closest table all turned to see what was going on, and two teenage boys were laughing so hard they were on the ground, which didn't prevent them from holding their phones towards the dogs to record the action.

"Dude! The little dog is just *takin' it,*" the taller of the boys yelled.

"Dude, they can't get them apart," laughed his buddy. "It's doggie porno!"

"Get him OFF!" yelled Bella's owner, pushing at Ranger.

Ranger's owner yelled and pushed too, but nothing was stopping it. He stood staring at his dog, helpless, and secretly a little bit proud.

"Oh my God, I think he's actually stuck," cried the taller of the boys, and from his ground level view, he had the most accurate assessment of the situation.

"Nooooo!" wailed Bella's owner.

Bella stared straight ahead, a deadness to her eyes. Hard to tell if it was shock or tolerance or even enjoyment.

"Do something," wailed Bella's owner. She grabbed Ranger's leash from his owner and started pulling on it, which just wheeled Ranger around, still stuck on Bella.

A man who had been looking through the Suspense and Thriller section stepped closer. "You need to leave them be."

"What???" said both dog owners.

"Yes, the male's penis becomes swollen, and the female's vagina clamps down on it. It is perfectly normal. It can last up to thirty minutes, and you shouldn't try to separate them." His voice was professorial and sounded sure enough that people became silent as his words settled in.

"Oh my God!" sobbed Bella's owner. "I just wanted to look at some books," she cried.

The crowd stared at the dogs. Ranger had stopped moving but remained on top of Bella. Bella's owner closed her eyes and seemed to be praying.

The teenage boys were laughing so hard they couldn't breathe, and both had dropped their phones. They rolled around on the ground gasping for breath and wiping at their eyes. Every once in a while, one would gasp out "Dude!" and they'd both laugh even harder.

Suddenly a heavy stream of water hit the dogs and Bella's owner, ricocheting onto the teenagers. She spluttered and jumped back, as the stream continued to pound into the dogs and the boys just kept laughing.

Marion had pulled a hose from somewhere and expertly trained it on the dogs, most particularly Ranger. Within a couple of seconds, Ranger jumped off of Bella and started shaking himself off, spraying the crowd around him with water.

Bella's owner scooped her up and started crying. "Oh my poor baby, my poor baby, mommy is so sorry." She looked daggers at Ranger's owner. "I'm going to SUE YOU."

Mrs. Mango had not moved from her spot near the dogs, stunned by the speed with which the whole thing unfolded. A man next to her jabbed her in the side with his elbow. "The call of the wild, eh?"

Mrs. Mango looked at him with bewilderment. Only at a book sale.

An hour later, dogs and owners untangled and gone, teenagers off to show their friends their excellent video, Mrs. Mango was rearranging the books in one of the Kids board book boxes, propping them back up in a neat line after several waves of toddlers and their mothers had rummaged through the box and left them in a haphazard state. As she finished, a girl of about eight tapped her arm and held up a book. "This book is inappropriate."

Mrs. Mango stared in horror at the page the girl had opened the book to and was holding up to Mrs. Mango. It was a cartoon drawing of a naked woman on top of a naked man, and at the top of the page it said "Making Love, Sexual Intercourse."

"Let me see!" said a boy coming around the back of Mrs. Mango. He was about the same age as the girl. He grabbed the book out of the girl's hands. "Hah!" he yelled. "Look at this! They are naked!" Two other boys crowded around him as he flipped the pages of "It's Perfectly Normal."

"Holy cow, there's a boy's dingie!" said one of the other boys pointing at the page. "Eww, it's got hair on it."

Mrs. Mango was paralyzed, knowing she should do something but not sure what. The dog experience had deadened her to processing any more sexual content. "Hey, um, why don't you give me that book? There are some good chapter books right over there," she said faintly, pointing.

The boys didn't seem to hear and kept flipping pages.

Mrs. Mango made another try. "Here, now, give me the book," she said, reaching towards the book. The boy holding it darted away, and his two friends followed him.

Marion appeared by Mrs. Mango. "What is going on here?" she said, seeing the boys run.

"Uh, well, uh," said Mrs. Mango. "They somehow found a, a, well, an inappropriate book."

"What? About what?" demanded Marion.

"Uh, I think it was a kind of book for parents to teach their kids the, uh, birds and the bees. But it had pictures. Not of birds or bees," fumbled Mrs. Mango.

"Oh, for Pete's sake, we need to go get that book," said Marion, stomping off in the direction the boys had taken. Mrs. Mango trailed unhappily behind her.

They found the boys around the corner of the library, giggling and punching each other in discomfort while two women in front of them, presumably their mothers, yelled at them.

"Where did you get this?" said one mother, a tall woman dressed in workout clothes with her brown hair pulled into a pony tail. She flung the book back and forth at the boys.

The original boy pointed at Mrs. Mango.

"What? I didn't give them that book!" exclaimed Mrs. Mango.

The other mother, dressed in jeans and a sweatshirt, her short dark hair held back from her face by a pair of large sunglasses, jumped in. "This is unacceptable! That 8-year-old boys are given an S-E-X book to look at!"

"Mom, we can spell; we know it is sex," said the smaller of the boys, a blond wearing Nike gear from top to toes.

Marion shook her head in agreement with the moms. In a calm voice intended to soothe, she said, "You are right. This book shouldn't even be in the boxes. I am so sorry." She looked at Mrs. Mango. "You should have known better."

This accusation freed up Mrs. Mango's tongue. "I didn't put that out! A girl brought it to me telling me it was inappropriate and before she could give it to me, the boys grabbed it. I was just about to get it back from them."

"What kind of show are you running around here?" asked pony-tailed mom.

"Again, our apologies," said Marion. "We get so many donations, and the volunteers go through all the boxes, sorting them, and this must have slipped through."

Sunglasses woman chimed in. "It is a VERY private matter when we talk to our children about sex! I don't need him finding it out here!"

Marion nodded. "Of course, and again, it was a mistake, and we are sorry." She reached out and took the book out of pony-tailed mom's hands. "I'll put this away inside."

Mrs. Mango stood there, face in flames, wondering how things could go wrong so fast. She wanted to tell the moms that the boys were out of control, grabbing the book from the girl and ignoring her request to give it back. She wanted to question their parenting and put the blame somewhere back in their direction, but she had a feeling Marion wouldn't like that at all. And she was more scared of Marion than these two stressed and stretched moms.

"Come on, Elsie," commanded Marion and swept her inside the library, away from the moms.

As they made their way to a back storeroom, Marion said, "Wow, talk about an overreaction."

Mrs. Mango was confused. "Me?" she asked.

"No, those two twits," said Marion. "That was a book written for kids, helping them to understand their bodies and how babies are made. Do those two think they are going to escape *that* discussion?" She shook her head as she tossed the book onto a shelf in the storage room. "It's normal, their interest. Of course, probably not best to have that out at a book sale, but, oh well, mistakes happen."

Mrs. Mango felt a rush of relief. She wasn't in trouble!

"I wonder if there is something in the air, maybe a full moon tonight? Somehow today has been all about sex!"

Mrs. Mango shrugged, uncomfortable. Starting to wonder if it was her, if somehow her own discomfort with all things sexual was making all things sexual follow her around.

"I wish I could be around to see them give their kids the talk," said Marion, giggling.

Mrs. Mango had never seen this side of Marion, didn't know she had a sense of humor at all. "Me too," Mrs. Mango said, smiling in faint support even though that was one of the last things she'd want to see.

Come to think of it, Mrs. Mango wasn't sure she had ever given her own children 'the talk.'

CHAPTER 8
Broken Fences

Dear Raul,

You know I always drove myself to work and on a few errands, but when I retired and started volunteering, I realized I had gotten so limited in the places I felt comfortable driving. And so I've made it to more places on my own these days, but not on a highway yet. It's probably been twenty years since I did that! But I keep thinking about the ocean and thinking that maybe one of these days I'll just get in the car and drive the whole way there. I can't wait for Joe to take me; he has no feeling for the ocean. Not like I do. Not like you did. And I've been driving to the church and praying for C. Can't say I see that the prayers have made any difference, but it can't hurt. I just don't know why God would give me this burden. There is only so much pain a person can take. What kind of life is she going to have? People are going to judge, and she won't get to be married and have babies. Oh, I know, those kind DO, but it can't be the same. I keep thinking that maybe it is just a matter of finding the right man. Like you were for me. Like the world finally makes sense. Like there really is a God, and he loved me so much he set the perfect man in front of me. And then he took you away.

The more I think about it, the more I am angry with God. There. I said it. I'm angry with God. If a lightning bolt is coming for me, I don't care. Maybe I'll stop going to church. Maybe it has always been a waste of time anyway. First he took you, and now he took Christine. It's too much.

Sorry. I'm back. I had a little cry just there. How has the sting never gone away? It's been so many years, I don't even want to count.

And why is that girl insisting on hurting me so much? Why now? Why did she have to go and ruin our lives?

And you know what I don't get? Joe seems just fine with it. That man has a strong opinion about everything, and this *he doesn't seem to care about. I thought I knew him so well, but this is a surprise. Although I guess he might say he knows me well too, but we both know he really doesn't know me at all. Maybe that is the lie couples believe, that they really know each other, when in fact there might be huge chunks of a person that remain unknown. Maybe nobody really knows anyone else.*

I never thought about Joe that way. I wonder what I don't know about him.

That evening from her spot on the couch, Mrs. Mango stared at Mr. Mango, kicked back in his easy chair, eyes locked on the TV in front of him, remote resting on his round belly. Her letter to Raul floated into her head, and she batted it away. Her regular life was allowed into the Raul life, but not the opposite. Like a pesky fly, the thought returned. What might there be about Joe that she didn't know? What secret dreams did he have? What ruined hopes? Maybe there was more to him than she saw.

"Want some watermelon?" Mrs. Mango asked Mr. Mango. "It's cold."

The two of them had agreed to try to limit carbs and to start exercising. Not much had happened on the exercise front, but they had managed to decrease their bread intake.

"Hmph," snorted Mr. Mango. "I guess so. I guess ice cream is out of the question."

"Well, if you want to go off the diet, go right ahead," said Mrs. Mango, but her tone was friendly. She stood up. "I'll get us some watermelon."

She returned a few minutes later with two bowls and handed one to Mr. Mango.

He sat forward and looked into the bowl. "I'll be damned! You made 'em in balls. Haven't had it this way in years."

Mrs. Mango smiled at her husband, her face relaxed and friendly. Mr. Mango stared; it seemed like years since that face had been directed at him.

"I don't know why I got out of the habit," said Mrs. Mango. "Lazy, I guess. Took me a while to find the melon baller, that's for sure." Mrs. Mango sat back on the couch with her own bowl of balls and put her eyes on the TV.

"Want to watch a movie?" Mr. Mango asked, picking up the remote and also looking towards the TV.

The moment had taken them both by surprise.

Mrs. Mango gave a little smile that no one else could have noticed. He never asked her what she wanted to watch. "No sports on?" she said.

He shrugged. "There's always sports. But I could take a movie."

Two hours later, Mr. Mango clicked the TV off. "Goddamn, but they don't make movies like that anymore!"

Mrs. Mango nodded. "It was very good." She pushed herself up from the couch. "Not even easy to stand up anymore," she grumbled, but there was a lightness to the grumble. She picked up their bowls and moved creakily towards the kitchen.

Mr. Mango stared at her as she walked away and then clicked the TV back on. "Maybe I'll just watch a while longer. Get a quick SportsCenter update," he said to her back.

"Hmm hmm," said Mrs. Mango as she eased into the kitchen.

In separate rooms, they each allowed themselves the smallest of smiles, now that no one was looking.

That night, Mrs. Mango dreamed about Raul. He looked nothing like himself, was old and out of shape, but she knew it was him. He was standing across a gray street, in a fog, like he was in England or somewhere similarly gray. He was waving at her and shouting something, but she couldn't hear the sounds coming out of his mouth. In the morning, she woke in an odd combination of disturbed and happy.

Mr. Mango was already up and off to an early delivery job, so Mrs. Mango allowed herself to linger in bed, wanting to hold on to the remnants of the dream, the wispy bits of love still floating in her half-asleep state. As her brain came more awake, she glanced up at the cross with Jesus hanging across from her bed and felt a stab of guilt. What was she doing? For these many years, even her dream world had kept the no-Raul rule, and she didn't like to think what might happen if the boundary started to fray—but on the other hand, it had felt so delicious to be close to him again. No, no, no, she told herself. Do not go there. Do. Not. Go. There.

Why was this happening? What fence had broken, letting Raul into her dreams? She wondered if her anger at God had anything to do with it, so she hastily crossed herself and said a prayer of apology.

CHAPTER 9
Mrs. Mango Goes for a Walk

"Hey mom, I'm going to go for a walk. You want to come along?" Christine said to her mother, aware that her mother and father had been inspired by Flora and Velma and had made a vow to go for a walk three times a week. She hadn't seen any walking yet, but maybe this was her chance to reconnect.

Mrs. Mango was sitting at the kitchen table, drinking coffee, reading the newspaper, and nibbling on the rice cakes with peanut butter she had been trying, without much success, to like. It had been nine days since the big reveal, and Mrs. Mango had not yet spoken to Christine, but Christine kept acting like she had.

Mrs. Mango looked up. "Are you saying I'm fat?"

"No, just wondered if you wanted to walk a bit," said Christine carefully, trying to mask her surprise that her mother had finally answered her, not to mention actually looked at her. "In case you forgot, I sit at a desk most of the day," added Christine, referring to her job as a personal banker in the Willow Grove branch of Wells Fargo. "So I need to move around some on my days off."

Mrs. Mango sighed. "Well, it wouldn't hurt to get out there, I guess. Let me go put on my tennis shoes."

They stepped outside into a gray chill that made them both rethink the plan. It was clearly a day to stay inside and drink a hot beverage, not try to overcome decades of inertia. The gray overwhelmed everything; even the Christmas decorations around the neighborhood seemed depressed, like a failed attempt at cheer.

Christine was afraid if they headed back inside, her mother would revert to ignoring her, so she strode down the front walk and turned left onto the sidewalk. Her mother had no choice but to follow.

Catching up to Christine Mrs. Mango fiddled

around with how to hold her water bottle. She kept shifting hands and trying different positions, first swinging it with arm down, then holding it up near her waist, but nothing felt right. She was committed to the diet, though, and was sure that drinking a lot of water was a good and healthy part of their plan.

"So how did Jenny lose the weight again?" Christine asked mother. She knew the answer but wanted to ask a safe question. She couldn't believe her mother was actually talking, like nothing had happened. As usual, her dad had been right. Just keep acting normal, and eventually her mother would come around.

"Atkins. She lost sixty-eight pounds!" said Mrs. Mango. "I should be able to lose ten to fifteen, if *she* could do that." Somewhere in the back of her mind, Mrs. Mango knew that thirty to forty would be more in the ballpark of what she should lose but figured she should set her goal as something that actually sounded achievable.

"So that's why we've been eating cauliflower instead of rice?" said Christine.

"Well, that was one of the recipes Jenny talked the most about, but I don't think it tastes that great all ground up, so I'm just serving cauliflower with cheese sauce instead."

Christine was afraid to ask if her mother had lost any weight yet; to the eye, it didn't look like it.

The two were walking towards Daisy Street because that was where the nicer neighborhood started and Mrs. Mango liked looking at the houses and perfectly manicured lawns. Their own home was in the buffer zone between the middle-class neighborhoods where houses were spotlessly maintained and the hopeless neighborhoods where houses looked like they were one good storm away from falling down and where the apartment buildings looked like abandoned prison blocks. The Mangos' neighborhood was one where people were just hanging on, but most of them were doing it with pride. Unless they were retired, families in their neighborhood were two-income by necessity. This left little time for home maintenance, but most of the residents had not given up. Residents might live with peeling trim a little longer than in the nicer neighborhood, but they were aware of it and worried about it until it was repainted. Garage doors eventually got replaced, and most yards had some attempt at landscaping. In the hopeless neighborhoods, people seemed to have given up on the possibility of any aesthetic appeal to their homes. They were more focused on survival; edging your lawn tends to take a back seat to finding food and not getting shot.

They rounded the corner of Sunset Drive and Daisy Drive, and Mrs. Mango looked up at the large, faintly Victorian house that faced Daisy Drive. She loved looking at that house and often said hello to the fifty-something man who lived there alone.

"Look at those roses!" Mrs. Mango said, gesturing towards a line of pale peach roses that spilled gracefully over the perfectly white, perfectly proportional picket fence in the front of the yard. As they admired the roses, the owner came running out of the house and down the walkway toward them. "Hey!" he yelled as he came closer. "Hello there! I don't know what to do!"

He opened the gate and grabbed Mrs. Mango and Christine by their hands. "Come with me; he's not awake, he's not awake!"

Mrs. Mango and Christine looked at each other and allowed themselves to be dragged back up the walkway. "I don't know what to do; he passed out and the ambulance is taking forever!" the man said as he hustled them up his front steps.

Mrs. Mango could see real fear in his face. He was a tall man, in good shape. He had a full head of dark hair just starting to go gray. His skin was quite tan, probably from all the time he spent in his garden (she had seen him there often), but today his skin matched the gray of the day.

They came into the front room of his house, and the first thing Mrs. Mango noticed was that the house was beautifully furnished, with expensive-looking dark wood pieces arranged artfully on a beautiful Persian rug. Then she noticed there was a man lying on the rug, and he indeed looked like he had passed out, or even died. He also looked to be in his fifties, but he was pudgy and almost bald and had a sheen of sweat over his entire face and head. He was wearing a tan button-down shirt and gray pants that had been unzipped and had something bulky sitting right over the zipper part. Peering closer, Mrs. Mango saw that it was a ziplock baggy with ice in it.

Mrs. Mango and Christine looked back at the owner of the house, unable to come up with anything to say.

"It's my neighbor Bob," the owner said. "He, uh, stopped by to, uh, borrow a weed wacker, and we were talking about gardening and then before I could get him the wacker, he just, uh, just, passed out."

Mrs. Mango looked at him, waiting for the ice-in-the-pants part. He didn't say anything else, but he ran over to the window to peek out, presumably still looking for the ambulance.

Christine crouched down near the man's head. "He is breathing, at least," she said.

"Oh, thank God," the house owner said as he ran to the front door. "Here are the paramedics."

A tall man and a short woman came in the door carrying all sorts of equipment. Christine and Mrs. Mango moved against the wall to get out of their way. They got right to business working on the passed-out man. They seemed to be testing things like his heart and breathing, and pretty soon he was mumbling something. They asked the house owner what had happened, and he said the same thing as he had told Mrs. Mango.

The ambulance crew was less discreet. "Why does he have ice down his pants?" asked the male paramedic.

The owner looked around the room, "Uh, well, he was sweating pretty badly, and he, uh, grabbed his, uh, crotch area, so when he passed out, I got ice for his head and then thought maybe something, uh, down there was wrong."

The tall guy had muscles bulging out of his tight navy t-shirt and seemed to be in charge. He had a young face but eyes that looked like they had seen plenty. "Did he take anything?" he asked.

"No, not that I know of," the owner said.

"You know, like Viagra or a stimulant or something?" the ambulance guy pressed on.

"Not that I know of," the owner said, looking more anxious if that was possible.

"Look, sir," the ambulance guy said. "I don't care what you guys were doing, but I need to know why you put ice on his genitals."

The owner sat down in the chair behind him, clutching his chest, "I don't know what you mean," he said. "He's my neighbor, that's all."

Mrs. Mango edged toward the door, tugging on Christine's sleeve. "We better go," she murmured.

The short woman stopped them. "Hold on, you have to help us understand what is going on."

"We don't know anything," Mrs. Mango said, unable to take her eyes off the guy on the floor because at this point, the ambulance guy had removed the bag of ice to reveal the hugest erection she had ever seen. She was horrified and couldn't take her eyes off it.

"Yeah, he just grabbed us from outside; we didn't see anything before this," said Christine, her eyes equally glued to the erection.

At that moment, the front door opened and Velma and Flora stuck their heads in. "We thought maybe you might need some help in here," Velma said, eyes scanning the room hopefully.

"Yeah," said Flora. "I just took one of them CPR courses so if anyone needs to be revived, here I am."

As the crew turned to look at the new arrivals, there was a thud, and when they all turned towards the thud, they saw the owner of the house on the floor, apparently passed out himself.

"What are these hose doing here?" said Velma,

picking up a pair of panty hose from the floor. She handed them to Flora who examined them closely.

"These are the good kind, the ones that come in the silver egg," Flora said, stretching them and holding them up in the air. "And they don't even have a run in them; these are brand new!"

The short woman was working on the owner of the house, and having passed what looked like smelling salts under his nose, he was now conscious again.

"I'll bet them two were doing that automobile-erotic thing!" said Velma.

"Yes!" said Flora, nodding in agreement. "That's what you use the hose for, to strangle yourself into some kind of state. Me and Henry Bidenon thought about trying it but I was afraid he might choke to death, you know he has emphysema. Probably not a good idea to choke someone who's only got 20% of a lung left. He barely made it through the deed as it was. Plus we could never figure out how to work the automobile part in."

Everyone turned to look at the old women. The owner of the house looked like he was about to pass out again.

"Is that what was going on here?" asked the ambulance guy. He bent down and started examining the bald guy's neck.

"Oh God," said the owner with his hand over his face. "Oh God. I just want to know, is he all right?"

The man on the floor had his eyes open, but it didn't look like much was registering in them. His erection was still strong.

"Holy cow," said Velma, "look at that ding dong! I never seen anything that big."

Flora elbowed Velma, "And you've seen a *lot* of 'em." They both giggled.

Mrs. Mango thought she might be the next person to pass out. She moved again towards the door, not even bothering to get Christine. This time, she didn't say anything as she slipped past the old women and ran down the front steps.

In front of the house, there was a crowd gathered on the sidewalk by the ambulance. People looked expectantly at Mrs. Mango, and a few asked her what was happening, but she pushed through them without answering and powerwalked towards home.

Christine caught up with her a block away. "Mom! Wait up," she said, jogging alongside Mrs. Mango's fast walk.

Mrs. Mango was shaking her head and refused to speak. A person could take just so much perversion in the world.

"Mom!" Christine tried again.

"Just leave me alone for now," Mrs. Mango said through tight lips, elbows pumping as she scooted along. "I'm getting my exercise."

Christine slowed to a walk and let her mother race on home alone. *So much for pretending everything was back to normal*, she thought, as she watched her mother stalk away.

Upon getting home, Mrs. Mango grabbed her purse and car keys and got in the car. She drove straight to St. Andrews to make a confession.

"Father, I don't know how to say this, so I'll just say it straight out. I just looked at a man's penis, and it wasn't my husband's." She burst into tears.

The priest eventually was able to determine that it wasn't her fault that she saw the penis and that she had done nothing wrong.

"I know you say that, Father, and you are a man of God and all, but I just know it was wrong! It was wrong!" With that, she left the confessional and walked slowly to her car, wondering if the world had gone crazy. Was everyone gay? She had never in her life known one person who was gay, and now all of a sudden it was all around her. Christine claiming she was a lesbian and those two men who were up to *something,* she couldn't imagine what, but it was something sexual together. Was she that blind? Had it always been all around her and she just hadn't noticed?

Mrs. Mango longed for a return to the 'don't ask, don't tell' era.

CHAPTER 10
The Joy of Rudeness

Monday morning, Mrs. Mango sat in the kitchen, staring at the small counter TV wedged between the baking canisters and the paper towel stand, mindlessly taking in the morning shows as she tried to wake up with her second cup of coffee. The dingy morning light barely showing through the window didn't help. She'd lived in the house long enough to know that even though it looked like it was about to rain, the gloom was just the outer reaches of the marine layer that seeped over the Oakland and Berkeley hills, and that by afternoon, it would be gone. There were days when Mrs. Mango appreciated a cool gray morning, but when her mood was already dampened, she didn't enjoy it at all. She could have never lived in Berkeley; some days that gray never burned off. Mr. Mango still slept soundly on the couch, where he apparently had landed in the middle of the night. Mrs. Mango had slept badly for two nights now, images of the bald man's penis haunting her sleep. The harder she tried to put it out of her mind, the more it seemed to be front and center. *What was wrong with people?* she wondered. *Were Velma and Flora right, were those two men really gay?* She couldn't figure out any other explanation. *But then, what were they doing that would make the bald man pass out and need ice? Why would the house owner have put a bag of ice on the bald man's penis?* She just couldn't get over it, that nice man who was always out gardening—gay!

Mrs. Mango turned to look at the TV. *My, that Kelly Ripa was showing a lot of leg these days,* she thought. She gasped, *Oh my God, does noticing Kelly's legs make me a lesbian?*

There was a knock on the door, and when Mrs. Mango opened it, Mary Melucci was standing there with a covered plate.

"Hello, Elsie, I've got some pound cake here and thought you might like some," Mrs. Melucci said, peeking past Mrs. Mango to see if there was anyone else there. Mrs. Melucci refused to give up on her mission to find out what was going on with Mrs. Mango.

"Oh, hi, Mary," Mrs. Mango said, still distracted by the penis images. What would Mary think if she knew what was in her mind, Mrs. Mango wondered. Mrs. Melucci told her own daughter she was going to hell for wearing a push-up bra, and she had put a block on their TV to keep her husband from watching R-rated movies. Mrs. Melucci prayed three times a day and believed a clean mind was the way to get close to God. Mrs. Mango shuddered to think about what Mrs. Melucci would say about a woman obsessed with a penis.

Mrs. Mango was exhausted by the effort it took to hide their increasing store of family secrets. Christine wasn't who she seemed to be, Mrs. Mango wasn't either anymore, and what about that old sex-crazed goat of a husband coming after her in the middle of the night last week? Mrs. Mango decided she had to get Mary out of the house before she sniffed out all their sordid secrets.

"That is so thoughtful to bring us some cake, but Joe and I are trying to cut down on carbs right now," Mrs. Mango said. "Maybe you should keep it all for yourself."

Mrs. Melucci looked at Mrs. Mango with surprise because she had *never* heard Elsie turn down cake. First of all, she loved to eat it, and second of all, she knew what a slight that would be, turning down an offering of food! And third, Mrs. Mango never turned down an offer to chat. Now she knew something was really wrong. "Well! Okay, then. But are you sure you don't want to keep it around for guests or something?"

Mrs. Mango was so busy keeping penis images under control (or, more accurately, agonizing about them being out of control) that she had no energy left for her normal politeness. "No, if it is here, we will eat it and then I'll never lose the weight," she said. "You take it back."

Mrs. Mango moved to close the door.

Mrs. Melucci felt offended not just by the rejection of her pound cake, but also by the failure of Mrs. Mango to invite her in. The Elsie she knew would have at least invited her in to have a piece of the cake she brought. "Okay . . . well, goodbye, then," Mrs. Melucci said, turning around to leave.

Just as Mrs. Mango had the door almost shut, Mrs. Melucci whirled around to face her again and stuck her foot in the door. "Elsie, is something going on? Are you all right? You are just not acting yourself."

Mrs. Mango pulled the door back open. "I'm just fine, Mary, really. I'm just tired, that's all. Joe tossed and turned all night complaining about me throwing out his pillow, and I barely slept." She started pushing the door again.

Mrs. Melucci stepped back. "Okay, then, but you let me know if you need anything, all right?"

"Sure, sure," said Mrs. Mango, willing to say anything to get that nebby Mary out of her doorway. How had she never noticed how annoying Mary was? For years, the two had been friends, chatting about everything from grandbabies to the sale over at Joanne's Fabric.

Mary tried one last time. "Hey, did you hear an ambulance was over at that big Victorian house on Daisy Saturday? I wonder what happened."

"That's none of our business!" Mrs. Mango barked, slamming the door shut abruptly on Mary and feeling a surprising pleasure at the sight of Mary's stunned face staring back through the window panes. Mrs. Mango rarely passed up a chance to chat. She was built to connect, to turn the kindly laser of interest on the person in front of her without any conscious thought, so Mrs. Melucci couldn't be faulted for being so surprised. *Maybe I'll be rude more often,* Mrs. Mango thought. *That was fun.*

Mrs. Mango walked into the living room and saw Mr. Mango still snoring on the couch, the dog asleep across his feet. Flush with her door slamming success, she went to the closet, pulled out the vacuum cleaner, plugged it in, and positioned it beside Mr. Mango's head. She paused before turning it on, savoring the moment. She hit the switch, and both Mr. Mango and the dog jumped, and in a tangle of man and dog fell to the floor, banging into the coffee table on the way down. Poker scrambled away by planting his paws hard into Mr. Mango's crotch and chest, leaving Mr. Mango to writhe on the floor, stunned by the speed with which he was awakened, knocked off the couch, and kicked in the nuts. Mr. Mango looked like he might have said "What the hell are you doing?!" but Mrs. Mango wasn't sure because she couldn't hear over the roar of the old Hoover upright. She feigned innocence and kept vacuuming, moving neatly around the furniture and making careful strips up and down the middle while she laughed herself silly inside.

After Mrs. Mango finally turned off the vacuum, carefully coiled the cord around the handle and returned it to the closet, she turned to face Mr. Mango sitting on the couch, arms folded tightly into his chest, staring at her like she was a python who escaped from the zoo. He spoke quietly, a pause between each word. "What . . . was . . . that?"

"What?" Mrs. Mango said, with a blank face. "I was just vacuuming." She couldn't contain herself, though, and broke into laughter. "Oh my goodness, you should have seen your face!"

She sat down in a chair and fanned her face, laughing harder. "And the dog!" She kept laughing until she could barely breathe, tears running down her face, grasping at her stomach.

Mr. Mango stared at his wife, sure she was having a nervous breakdown. He knew she was upset about Christine, and he knew she had seen something upsetting Saturday at that big house over on Daisy, and he knew she was still menopausal even though she refused to admit it. He figured the combination of these things had finally sent her over the edge, and he wasn't sure what to do. Was there someone you can call? A nice van or something that shows up and takes away a crazy spouse? He doubted it because he'd never seen one on TV. He supposed he could call Christine, but how would she know what to do? Maybe one of their sons? The priest?

Twenty minutes later, she was still laughing and the living room was full of neighbors staring at her, waiting for her to wind down. Mr. Mango had called Mary Melucci, and she had swept up two other women from the neighborhood to come with her to see what was going on with Elsie.

Mrs. Mango wiped at her eyes and finally gasped out some words. "Oh my, I don't care if I go to Hell; that was the funniest thing I've ever seen."

She broke into another fit of laughing, eventually slowing down enough to talk again. "Did he tell you what I did?" She giggled some more. "He was sleeping," she laughed and then continued, "and I turned on the vacuum cleaner . . ." She couldn't continue because she was off on another laughing fit, doubled over in her chair, pounding on her knees.

Mr. Mango shook his head and finished the story. "I'm sleeping, *finally* sleeping, and this . . ." he gestured at Mrs. Mango, "*this crazy woman* turns the vacuum cleaner on right in my ear. The dog took out my nads getting away, I end up on the floor, and she just sits there laughing."

Mary Melucci looked outraged on Mr. Mango's behalf, but Ginger Simon had to hide her mouth with her hand to keep from laughing. Sue Hatanaka didn't even try to hide her mouth; she burst out laughing too.

Mr. Mango looked at Marion. "What is wrong with you women? All a man wants is a little sleep, and you think it's funny when he doesn't get it?"

With that, Ginger started laughing too.

Mary Melucci was torn. She wanted to support Mr. Mango, and she desperately wanted to feel morally superior to Mrs. Mango, but she also wanted to feel like she belonged with the women. She really didn't see why it was so funny, but she smiled too.

Mr. Mango got up and left the room in disgust. *Holy Sam*, he muttered to himself as he stomped to the kitchen, *what is up with these women? I will go to my grave without cracking the mystery of women.* He grabbed a banana and left the house.

Mr. Mango walked down his driveway, shaking his head at the craziness of the women in his house. He looked at the banana and frowned and tossed it in the bushes. A banana! That's not what a man needs to start his day. Screw the diet; he decided to walk over to the Jack in the Box and get a couple of breakfast sandwiches. Let the women take care of Elsie if she was breaking down. He was done with it. A man can be pushed only so far! She wouldn't touch him, she threw out his pillow, and now she blasts him out of sleep with the vacuum cleaner. Not to mention the years of telling him what to do. Although their kids had always teased their mother for her chattiness with anyone around her, stranger or friend, he knew that people enjoyed her intense curiosity. It just had been so many years since he was the recipient of that. It seemed she saved all the irritated demands for him. Not to mention . . . He didn't even let himself think of the not to mention.

As Mr. Mango turned out of his driveway towards the Jack in the Box, he saw Manny Melucci across the street in his driveway. Manny gave a wave, and Mr. Mango waved back.

Manny started walking towards Mr. Mango and said, "Hey Joe, what's going on?"

Mr. Mango shook his head and waited for Manny to get closer so he wasn't yelling across the street. "Bunch of crazy women in there, that's what. Christ, I was just sleeping on the couch, minding my own business, when Elsie cranked the vacuum cleaner up right by my head! On purpose!"

Manny was a tall thin man with lots of veins in his nose and an overall redness to his face. He shook his head in sympathy, "Sheesh, these women, huh?" he said.

Mr. Mango didn't make it a practice to discuss his business outside of the family, but he was so irritated that he couldn't stop himself. "I don't know what's got into Elsie, honestly. Maybe it is the change, maybe it is frustration with Christine, maybe the old bird just needs to, you know, get some." Mr. Mango couldn't believe he said that last part, but that's what she had driven him to, talking to other men about their private life.

Manny nodded sympathetically. "Man, that's tough."

"I mean, you put yourself out, day in and day out, for *years* bringing home the mortgage money, and this is the thanks I get?"

"Tell me about it," Manny got into the spirit. "All these years, I work my fingers to the bone, two sometimes *three* jobs, so she could have nice furniture and send the kids to college, and I'm not even allowed to eat an effing sandwich in my own living room! Everything in that room is covered in plastic; Christ, you slide right off. Even so, I've got to watch TV in the garage if I want to eat at the same time."

It was common knowledge that Manny watched TV in the garage so he could drink too, but no one ever talked about that.

"You know, nothin's been the same since Thanksgiving," Manny said, thinking about how he let Mary walk across the street with toilet paper coming out the back of her pants.

"Ain't that the truth," said Mr. Mango, thinking about how Christine came out and Elsie started going to church every day. She thought he didn't know, but he did—had seen her car there a number of times. He knew a lot more about his wife than she realized. Even though she never talked about it, he was sure that her sexual hang-ups were because of being so religious. He figured she thought it was wrong to enjoy sexual intercourse, wrong to even have sexual intercourse without the intent of procreation.

He thought she had almost enjoyed sex a couple of times, when they were much younger and she'd had a drink or two. He guessed that she felt guilty that she might have enjoyed it, even a bit, and felt like that made her a 'loose woman,' and that upset her so much she never had a drink again. On the rare occasions they had sex, he felt like she was merely tolerating him. For a number of years, he lived with that, and finally it got to him and he stopped initiating. He had hoped he'd be able to show her how fun sex could be, and he finally realized he wasn't going to change her. Jesus was too strong of an opponent.

It felt great to complain to another man, so Mr. Mango asked Manny if he wanted to walk up to the Jack in the Box with him.

Manny agreed and they took off. "I'll tell you what I'd do, woman woke me up like that. I'd cut up all her credit cards, that's what I'd do. Hit 'em where it hurts is what I say."

Mr. Mango shook his head. "That wouldn't stop her. I think she's lost her mind."

"And good Christ," Manny continued, "if the woman ain't giving you the business, you gotta take care of *that*. Can't miss out on your sumpin sumpin, why that'll drive a man over the edge. That's what happened to John Hinkley, you know. He tried to shoot Reagan 'cause he was what you called sexually backed up. It can make you murder; I've heard research on that. I'm not taking chances, if you know what I mean. I got a Plan B. And I got a Plan C too, although she isn't one you'd want to look at too closely in the light." He elbowed Mr. Mango in the arm for the fifth time and laughed.

They weren't even a block from their houses, and Mr. Mango already regretted inviting Manny along. Just not his kind of guy. Sure, Mr. Mango was frustrated with his marriage, but it didn't turn him into a woman-hater.

CHAPTER 11
Beginnings

Dear Raul,

Mrs. Mango looked up from the note pad on her lap and stared unseeing at the shower wall in front of her. Her mind flitted between memories; which one did she want to relive today? She thought back to meeting Raul; that was a good one. Maybe she'd start all over from the beginning. Yes, that was it.

Almost before her eyes closed, she could smell and feel the dry dust of the nearby fields on her skin, could see the last streaks of pink and purple and gray-blue across the sky left by the sun that had dropped out of sight over the distant hills, the ones that looked like an unending rampart between the ocean and the fields in this long center of California. Mrs. Mango remembered how big the sky looked in Mivida, her small central California town—not like where she lived now. Surrounded by fields and more fields, the sky and the land stretched as far as one could look to the east; in the day, a brightness that lit up everything; at night, a sky so full of stars you'd think you were looking out from the surface of the moon. Even when the fog came, there was always a solid sense of the space above and beyond the fog. Everything felt wide open then, everything. She could hear the muffled music coming out of the old warehouse that was serving as a dance hall, as she and her best friend Sandy made their way from the parking lot. They were seventeen and sneaking into a dance when they were supposed to be at the movies. Sandy, in all her curvy flirtatiousness, sailed towards the back of the warehouse with full confidence, while Elsie, nervous but excited, trailed behind her.

Mrs. Mango remembered the crunch of their feet on

the gravel and the excited fear in her throat as they slipped
in a back door held open by the boy Sandy had promised to
meet there, the one old enough to go in the front door. It
was dark and loud, and Sandy held her arm, dragging her
past people as they both followed the boy.

What was his name? Mrs. Mango couldn't
remember, which she found interesting since it was
Sandy's determination to meet him that led to Mrs. Mango
meeting Raul.

Sandy had promised, over and over, not to abandon
Elsie once she met up with him, and for a good half hour,
she was true to her word. Finally, Sandy's boy enticed her
onto the dance floor, and Elsie sat at the little table,
clutching both their purses. It was the table furthest to the
back so she had the wall behind her, and, in time, she
relaxed as she realized no one was paying attention to her.
She even found herself tapping her foot to the music and
enjoying watching the dance, both literal and metaphorical,
in front of her. Eventually, Elsie had to go the bathroom, so
she draped her sweater around her chair to save it, got up,
and wandered towards a door that looked promising.
Having found it, and on her way back to their table, a
couple came stumbling off the dance floor and banged into
her from behind. Elsie was propelled forward and was
caught from falling by a pair of strong arms.

"Oh, sorry!" Elsie gasped. The couple that hit her
were on the ground laughing and oblivious to having
knocked into her. Elsie looked up to see who caught her,
and felt a rush of energy.

She was looking into a pair of brown eyes, in a
brown face, lit up by a bright and easy smile. "Hey, there,"
he said. "You okay?" His arms were firmly holding her
under her elbows.

Mrs. Mango sighed and went over every detail of
that face again. Beautiful tanned skin with a flush that
spoke of a lot of time in the sun. Smiling eyes. Carefully
cut brown hair brushed to the side with an adorable little
cowlick on the left. Starched white shirt matching the teeth

showing in the smile. Fresh, clean, kind. Handsome.

Mexican.

Although that didn't matter, not then.

Mrs. Mango let the full memory unfold: how he walked her back to her table, talking easily. Laughing at the couple who'd knocked into her, making sure she was okay. Then it seemed perfectly natural that he would sit down. They exchanged their stories: she, a dutiful Catholic schoolgirl; he, finished with high school, working the fields. In the moment, she was just enjoying herself and the attention of such a handsome boy. An *older* boy, by two years, which is a lot when you are a teenager. Enjoying his ease with her and, seemingly, with the whole world. Aware that he was someone she would not normally run into, and thrilling at her daring at even being at this forbidden dance. No thought at all to what her parents might say or even that there would be something to say anything about.

Mrs. Mango lingered over the details of that night, intentionally staying away from the events that followed, eventually, inevitably. Focused instead on how it felt when Raul finally convinced her to dance, the feeling of their bodies grazing against each other in the dark music. The rightness of it. Like all this time, her life had been a movie with the soundtrack always a bit off, and now everything matched up.

Ahh, that was lovely. I miss you, Raul. I miss your handsome smile. I miss your confidence and comfort in the world. When I was with you, I felt it too. Felt like everything would always be okay. Would be great, in fact. Till next week,

Yours,
Elsie

Later that morning, Mrs. Mango looked around her helplessly. The family room was littered with boxes of

Christmas decorations, and she didn't know what to work on first.

Christine walked in, perfectly timing her arrival home so as to miss going to church with her mother, and exclaimed in delight. "Oh! Yes! Let's decorate today. I'll help."

Mrs. Mango sighed. "Let me change out of my church clothes, and we'll get to it."

Christine's shoulders dropped a couple of inches in relief. She was waiting for her mother to ask where she had been all night. Up until the big reveal, her mother had no reaction to the times she stayed overnight with a friend, accepting that they were late at a concert or were closer to a party. Now that she had announced a girlfriend, she walked through the door feeling like she was wearing a big scarlet L on her chest.

Christine rummaged through a box near her. "Look at this! I made this candy cane in—what—must have been third grade." She sank down beside the box and started pulling out tree ornaments, enthusing over each one, sounding as innocent and happy as she had been as a child.

For a second, Mrs. Mango was back in time, remembering Christine's bubbly joy at everything Christmas. Even more than the yells and excitement of the boys' getting presents, Christine had been crazy for the holiday. And, as she was the youngest, they all got to live in her joy even when the Santa thrill had paled for the older ones. What a darling girl she had been.

And then she was back in the present, and the disappointment felt even more intense. That darling girl was a lie. Her lips pressed into a thin line, Mrs. Mango marched past Christine to change her clothes.

In her bedroom, Mrs. Mango's brain took off with her, spiraling through the disappointment in Christine, running its judgmental laps until the Christmas mood was ruined. Tugging at her waistband to try to button her old jeans, something from church that morning slipped in among the judgments. There had been a line in the lighting of the advent calendar that pierced through her Christine ruminations. She didn't remember the beginning, but one phrase stuck with her: "May we bring light and love to all we meet, that the darkness of sin and fear may be overcome." Mrs. Mango's brain seized on that phrase and repeated it, "May we bring light and love to all we meet." She stood still thinking about it and realized the important word was 'all.' Which included Christine. Just for today, maybe she'd try to bring light and love to Christine. Maybe that was the way to handle this whole thing. Bring her back to the light with love, and then maybe she'd see the error of her ways.

Determined to keep the feeling of Christmas, and to bring light and love, Mrs. Mango returned to the family room. She and Christine worked peacefully for a while, and then Mrs. Mango moved on to unload a few things in the kitchen. She stood back to admire the row of Santa mugs on the counter and smiled.

There were a few boxes left in the garage that were too heavy for Mrs. Mango, so she went to find Mr. Mango for help. Discovering him on the living room couch asleep, she was about to poke him awake but the Christmassy feeling inside her stopped her hand. Maybe it wouldn't hurt to wait till he woke up. Maybe that was the way to share a little light with him too.

An hour later, as Mrs. Mango was hanging the garland around the front door frame, Mr. Mango appeared.

"Looks good; I've always liked how you do the door," he said, reaching up to help her get the garland over the nail left in place for that purpose.

Mrs. Mango smiled. "Me too. Everyone else, they have maybe one strand of light around the door. I added five strands. It lights up so nice."

Mrs. Mango took a few steps down her walkway, adjusting the line of light-up candy canes that marked the edges of the walkway and looked across the street at the Meluccis'. The one strand of lights that hung from their gutters glimmered weakly in the daylight. Not hard to do since it stayed up all year and just got plugged in at Christmas time. She turned around and stared at her own doorway with satisfaction. It shone bright, all those strands of light woven through the realistically green garland, looped in a gentle dip from either side of the door and trailing down the sides. The wreath she had helped make at church, with its big red bow and gold sprayed pine cones, looked perfect. Mrs. Mango took another look at the Meluccis' and felt sad for their house. One strand of lights was worse than nothing. All that said was, *hey, look how feeble my owners are.*

Mrs. Mango looked at the house to the left of the Meluccis' and noticed that Dan Carpenter was out putting up Christmas decorations as well. A partially unfolded wire reindeer sat beside a completely folded metal reindeer. *Oh good,* thought Mrs. Mango, *I love those reindeer.* For as long as she could remember, the Carpenters had put a pair of graceful reindeer in their front yard, bright with hundreds of little white twinkle lights. Mrs. Mango looked more closely and noticed Dan yanking on the partially unfolded reindeer and shaking his head. There were miles of twinkle lights jumbled around him on the ground, some lit, some dark. She smiled; it was part of the seasonal ritual to watch Dan fight to get the deer set up and lit. Every year, he was sure they were done for, he gave up, then bought more lights for the burnt-out strands, and went back to trying to get them to work, managing to resurrect them every time. It was their own neighborhood Christmas miracle. She saw him stand up and give the reindeer a hard kick and then walk back towards his garage. Of course, it lit up as he walked away, giving Mrs. Mango a good giggle.

"Hey Dan," she called. "Turn around!"

Dan turned around, shaking his head, curse words evident even from the distance. Then he noticed the reindeer and started laughing. "Holy Jesus, I'm tired of these things!" he yelled back.

Mrs. Mango gave him an encouraging wave. "It

wouldn't be Christmas without the reindeer challenge," she answered in a cheery yell and then turned around to face her own door. "You should go help him," she said to Mr. Mango, who was fiddling with the garland around the door to make the trailing sides even.

"Not a chance," said Mr. Mango. "I got no patience for those lights anymore. No quality. All made in China and don't even last a season! I don't know how anyone even stays in business anymore, just churning out cheap stuff, knowing us idiots will keep replacing the shit that broke."

"Merry Christmas to you too," said Mrs. Mango. It was hard to stay in the Christmas spirit when someone could get that grouchy that fast.

Christine popped her head out the front door. "Dad, come help me with the tree," she said.

"Just a minute," said Mr. Mango. He gave one last teeny adjustment to the garland and went to help Christine.

Well, if her husband wasn't going to offer, she would. Mrs. Mango slid a pair of fake poinsettias on either side of the door and then walked over to the Carpenters'.

Dan was back to kneeling in front of the first reindeer as Mrs. Mango approached.

"Hey there, need any help?" asked Mrs. Mango, coming around the other side of the reindeer so she was facing Dan.

"I don't know, probably only God is going to make these things work again," said Dan, plugging and unplugging a whole train of twinkle light plugs together, then trying them in the power strip at his side. The front half of the reindeer was lit but the back strings of lights stayed stubbornly dark.

"How's Nancy?" asked Mrs. Mango. "How's her foot healing?" Nancy was several weeks into recovery from foot surgery. Mrs. Mango knew the details of the lives of everyone up and down their street, and several streets beyond.

"Healing well," said Dan, plugging in a new strand

of lights and exclaiming in joy. "Holy cow! A string that works!" He started weaving it through the dark strands of lights. "Doctor says she can get out of the boot next week."

Mrs. Mango nodded in approval. "She gets around well in that thing, but I'm sure she's ready to be done with it."

"Hey, and thanks again for the dinners you brought." Dan looked over his shoulder to see if his wife was around and then, seeing that she wasn't, leaned towards Mrs. Mango. "I got to tell you, we ate way better after her surgery than we did before!" he leaned back and laughed. "Lot of good cooks in this neighborhood!"

Mrs. Mango puffed up with the pride of being one of the good cooks and then thought about Nancy, who she really liked. "Nancy's good at so many things; it wouldn't be fair if she was good at everything." Mrs. Mango was still feeling the effect of the morning sermon and had always felt loyal to Nancy.

"Sonovabitch!" grumped Dan as the entire reindeer went dark. He slumped back on his heels. "This is it. The reindeers are done for. I can't keep doing this. There's some good football on in there, and I'm out here wrestling with these . . . these. . ." He struggled not to swear anymore in front of Mrs. Mango.

Just then, the Carpenters' front door opened, and Nancy clumped onto the porch. "Hi, Elsie!" she called. "Dan, please tell me those reindeer are working."

Dan looked at his wife's face and back at the unlit reindeer. "Shit," he whispered under his breath. "Still working on it," he called back to his wife. He looked up at Mrs. Mango. "I think I gotta work on this myself for a while, but thanks anyway."

Mrs. Mango nodded. The offer had been made; neighborly relations in order, she said her goodbyes to Nancy and Dan and headed back across the street. As she walked, she looked around the neighborhood, her community for these many years. She normally felt connected and protected with all these people around her, comforted by knowing her spot in the social fabric. For some reason, the image of the expansive sky and land of Mivida flitted across her mind, making the neighborhood feel claustrophobic, not friendly. She looked up at the sky and saw the grid of telephone wires and cables and felt even more pinned in. For a second, life felt small and confined, and she wondered how long it had been since she looked up at a wide, unfettered sky.

What's wrong with me? thought Mrs. Mango. *It's Christmas. I love Christmas.*

Determined to get back in the holiday mood, she started humming 'Deck the Halls.'

CHAPTER 12
A Tree-climbing Dog

The Mango family had bad luck with cars. Tripod was not the first casualty and surely wouldn't be the last. For years, Mr. Mango had lusted after a convertible, any make, and then about a year ago, a customer towed one into his buddy Artie's mechanic shop. Artie had indulged Mr. Mango's hobby of fixing up cars for so long sometimes he gave him an occasional paid job. Mr. Mango was tinkering with a transmission when the customer with the convertible said, "I'll give anyone here twenty dollars to take this piece of shit off my hands." Mr. Mango had his wallet out by the word 'shit' and was running across the floor. He should've known right then this was a bad move because on the way over, he hit a grease spot and fell ass over teakettle. He banged his elbow so bad it grew a softball-size welt that he eventually had to have drained three times. Still, he managed to convince the guy the car should be his, and after his shifts driving his delivery truck, he worked on the car's engine. It was a 20-something-year-old Mustang with rusted out side panels and long cracks in the seat leather, but the canvas roof was intact, which was ironic because Mr. Mango never planned to put it up.

Once he got the engine working, he drove the car home, and his wife, hearing the mufflerless car pull into the driveway (well, actually, the yard—the driveway was full of other cast-off cars Mr. Mango was working on), crossed herself and muttered, *Jesus help us.*

"Hey, Elsie, come look!" he called.

She came to the door, looked out over their five cars, two parked along the street in front of the house, two in the driveway and one in the yard to the side of the driveway, and as she'd done countless times before, shook her head at the sight. "You'd think a family of six lived here! It's only us three, and I don't even drive much, and we got five cars. Five cars. And now I'll never get that grass to grow." Mrs. Mango had been trying to get grass to grow in their little front yard for thirty years now. While her kids were growing up, they wouldn't stay off it long enough for seeds to take root, and even when she got little blades of grass to struggle up through the hard dirt, the kids would wear them down with all their games, running back and forth and sliding around. Then, when the kids were grown and gone, she thought for sure, but the sprinklers never managed to really water it right and she suspected Buster from down the street peed on it a little too often and now the old fool had taken to parking cars on it.

"I'm thinking of getting rid of the Dodge," he said, but she knew he wouldn't.

The convertible had been fixed up and looked pretty good, and then a week ago, Artie had asked to borrow it for the weekend. Mr. Mango appreciated all the free garage time, so he said yes and Artie had brought it back with thanks and a thumbs-up on Mr. Mango's work on it. It rained on and off that week, so Mr. Mango left the roof up, and because he worked some extra deliveries, he didn't have time to drive it himself. So no one realized that Artie had left a bunch of half-filled fast food bags in the back seat.

Monday, Mr. Mango came out front for his morning ritual of letting Poker the dog do his business while he surveyed his collection of cars to decide which would be his project for the day. Having gone to part-time as a delivery driver, he needed something to keep Mrs. Mango from hounding him to death. Poker sniffed at the line of plastic candy canes lining the walkway and then wandered around the yard looking for the right spot for his business. As Mr. Mango waited for Poker, he noticed a big slash in the canvas roof of the convertible. "Damn those gang bangers," he said, sure that one of them had done this. Did he not lend money to just about all of them? And did he not ignore it when they didn't pay back? Was this the thanks he got?

He looked at Poker to make sure he wasn't leaving the yard and went over to look at the rip. As he got closer, he saw something moving in the car. Was it possible someone was sleeping in there? Or doing something worse? He moved around to the window and put his face up to it to get a closer look and found himself staring into a pair of dark, beady eyes. He yelled and jumped backwards as a raccoon the size of a forklift leapt out of the car (making yet another rip), landed on his chest, dug its sharp claws in for traction, and then leapt off of Mr. Mango towards Poker.

As soon as his lungs started to work again, Mr. Mango said, "What the . . . ?" and twisted around on the ground to see where the raccoon went. The raccoon had Poker up a tree and was circling around underneath it. Poker's back legs were straddling one branch while his chin hung over another and his two front legs shook violently hanging onto a third. As Mr. Mango watched, a stream of urine dribbled down from the dog but that seemed to have no effect on the raccoon. Mr. Mango remembered that raccoons can have rabies (or maybe all have rabies? His memory was a little vague on that) and thought he better get inside. Although Poker looked to be in a precarious position, at least he was out of harm's way for the moment. Mr. Mango figured if raccoons could climb trees, he'd already be up there. Or maybe he just liked stalking Poker.

Mr. Mango quietly got up and crept back slowly until he was by the corner of the house, at which point he ran around the house and pounded on the back door.

When Mrs. Mango finally came to the door, coffee mug in hand, he pushed past her and slammed the door shut behind them.

"What is wrong with you?" she said. "Where is Poker?"

"Jesus, Mary, Joseph," he said. "There was a raccoon in the car, and he's treed Poker. He landed on my *chest.*"

"You mean Poker treed the raccoon," she said.

"No, I mean *Poker* is in the tree."

"Dogs don't climb trees; this I got to see," she said, slamming down the coffee mug and running to the front window. On her way, the phone rang and she grabbed it mid-stride. It was Mrs. Melucci from across the street. "Elsie, you have a raccoon in your front yard!"

Mrs. Mango was a little irritated that Mrs. Melucci knew her business before she did, but by this point she was at the window, and, sure enough, the raccoon was still circling the tree and Poker was still barely hanging on.

Mrs. Melucci said, "Those raccoons can be so bold! Look at that thing; you'd think in the bright daylight, he'd be scared and run off."

"We've got to get him out of here; that poor dog isn't going to last much longer," Mrs. Mango said to both Mrs. Melucci and Mr. Mango and then noticed Mr. Mango wasn't with her. "What do you think we should do?" she asked Mrs. Melucci, sure she'd have an opinion.

"I was just reading in the Reader's Digest that raccoons can carry all sorts of diseases and the best thing to do is make sure your garbage cans are strapped shut."

"I think it was in the car, not the garbage cans," said Mrs. Mango, offended that Mrs. Melucci would think she had no more sense than to leave her cans unstrapped. My goodness, what kind of fool did she take her for? Did she think they were somehow dirty because a raccoon was in their yard? "I meant, how do we get it away from the dog?"

"I think you should throw something at it," said Mrs. Melucci, and apparently Mr. Mango had the same idea because he came into the front room with a collection of balls and various other things from the garage that seemed useful for throwing. He eased open the front door and tossed a football at the raccoon, which was about fifteen feet away. The football landed right beside the raccoon, and he didn't even flinch.

Next, Mr. Mango tried a couple of baseballs and then pulled out a bag of old tennis balls and starting throwing one right after the other, like some kind of bizarre pitching machine. At first, he opened and closed the door between every throw, making the wreath hanging on it slam back and forth, but then got bold enough to leave it open a crack as he reloaded. About two thirds of the balls actually hit the raccoon, but it didn't waver from its snuffling around the base of the tree and staring at the dog.

Mrs. Mango opened the window a hair and yelled, "Hold on, Poker!" like the dog just needed a little encouragement to stay up there.

Mr. Mango had run out of tennis balls and moved on to gardening tools. He threw a trowel as hard as he could, and it spun end over end like a magician's knife flung at an assistant. Bulls-eye! The sharp end of the trowel landed right smack on the back of the head of the raccoon. "Gottem!" Mrs. Melucci yelled so loudly into her phone that she almost blew out Mrs. Mango's ear drum. "Ow!" yelled Mrs. Mango, and the dog, hearing the 'Ow!' turned instinctively towards the window, having a deep attachment to Mrs. Mango, his source of food. With that turn, Poker's front legs slid and he started to scramble, legs grabbing at air. Meanwhile, the raccoon had turned in the direction of the trowel and was staring viciously at the front door, which Mr. Mango had forgotten to close as he debated between a claw-like implement or a set of shears for his next throw.

The raccoon pawed the ground like a bull and stared into the open door. Mrs. Mango didn't know where to look, at the dog or the raccoon. Mr. Mango looked up to see if the trowel had been enough and found himself, for the second time that morning, staring into the angry eyes of a hulking raccoon. Mrs. Melucci didn't see any of this because she was looking at the trio of Eddie Cabasso, Rosa Cabasso, and Eddie's 90-year-old mother Angelica edging down the sidewalk at the speed of a glacier.

As the raccoon charged at the door, Mr. Mango did

the same, throwing himself at it in hopes of getting it closed in time. Before he could get to the door, a streak of black and white whizzed by him and out the door. With a war-cry screech, Tripod shot at the raccoon, landing in front of it and scratching madly at the raccoon's head like it was hitting the speed bag at the boxing gym.

As Tripod beat up the raccoon, the branch in the tree broke, dropping Poker into the assortment of balls and gardening implements. Barely even touching the ground, Poker streaked out of the yard like a comet, head down and legs pumping, and after ripping through the row of candy canes lights lining the walk, it only took half a second for him to plow right into the middle of the Cabasso trio. As a bowler, Mrs. Melucci had to appreciate the accuracy of Poker's strike, scattering the Cabassos like a collection of balsa wood bowling pins. Poker didn't stop to admire his accuracy but continued putting as much distance between himself and the raccoon as he could manage, the string of candy cane lights flowing behind him like a bizarre Christmas cape. He cut between the finally-up-and-working metal reindeer in the Carpenters' yard, and the cape of candy cane lights caught around the reindeer's legs, ripping them both off the ground. They banged along behind Poker for a couple of yards before catching on some bushes. The candy cane lights, firmly caught on the reindeer, pulled taut around Poker's throat, whiplashing him backwards. The backwards motion loosened the string of lights from Poker's neck, and with a yelp, he took off again, this time free of Christmas impediments.

With a haunting yowl, the raccoon finally freed itself from Tripod and charged blindly straight ahead, running into the front door. It hit the door so hard the wreath fell down, neatly ringing its head, at which point, Tripod leaped on the raccoon again and started pummeling him from behind.

Meanwhile, Mr. Mango had slammed the door and rushed to the front window to see what was going on. Mrs. Mango was jumping up and down and yelling, "Poker! He got away! The cat did it!" and then saying into the phone, "What? Good Lord! Where are they?"

She turned to Mr. Mango. "Poker knocked down the Cabassos!"

"You mean Eddie?" Mr. Mango said.

"Eddie and Rosa and Angelica! She's ninety years old and just had her hip replaced two months ago."

"I don't mind seeing Eddie on the ground, that sonofa. . ."

"Joe! What about the poor women? And what if they sue us?"

She put the forgotten phone back to her ear. "Mary, what's the raccoon doing now?"

Mrs. Melucci tore her eyes away from the Cabassos and looked at the Mangos' front door. "Holy sweet Jesus, it's got your wreath on it, and the cat is attacking it!

"Dang," said Mrs. Mango, craning out her window to see the front door. "I liked that wreath!"

The raccoon and the cat rolled into view, screeching and clawing at each other like a cartoon fight, legs and fur flying in all directions.

" I better hang up and call for help," said Mrs. Melucci. "I think the Cabassos are really hurt. Not even Eddie is up yet—you know he's over sixty himself. I'll call you right back."

If there was one thing besides snooping and cleaning that Mrs. Melucci was good at, it was rousing the troops. Eventually, an ambulance, a fire truck, and animal control all showed up in front of the Mango house. Eddie and Rosa Cabasso were merely stunned and a little bruised. Angelica broke her other hip, for which she later came and thanked the Mangos because she'd been trying to get insurance to pay for a replacement for that side but they wouldn't until Poker broke it.

The raccoon, hampered by the wreath stuck around its neck, and scratched to a bloody mess, was cornered behind the (strapped) garbage cans and was taken away in a cage, wreath and all. Tripod strutted around the front yard, fur mangled and bloody, puffed up with protecting his family.

The reindeer were well and truly done for, and Dan, after secretly doing the sign of the cross in relief, replaced them with a blow-up Santa whose only maintenance involved plugging him in.

Later that day, after the remains of the fast food had been properly disposed of (in strapped trash cans), the balls had been cleaned up, the trucks were all gone, and Poker had been found in the park hiding under a picnic table, Mr. and Mrs. Mango stood looking at the rips in the convertible roof.

"Are you happy now?" Mrs. Mango said. "Nothing but trouble, that's what that car is."

"Hmm," Mr. Mango grunted, not willing to concede anything.

"You best take that thing back to the garage; I think it's cursed," she said, but privately Mrs. Mango was wondering if their house was cursed now that Christine had come out. "No wonder someone paid you to take it off his hands. I'll give someone *$40* to take it off our hands."

"We'll see," he said, knowing full well he planned to keep it but not wanting to argue with Mrs. Mango. Forty years of marriage had taught him he could get what he wanted but not by taking her on directly. The trick was to half agree, but not in a way that she could accuse him later of lying. Then let the matter sit for a while until something else caught her attention, then do what he wanted to. If she got mad at that point, he could plead a poor memory for what they had decided. Master of strategy, that's how Mr. Mango liked to think of himself. Better than thinking of himself as a man whose wife kept his balls strapped as firmly in a jar as the garbage was strapped in its can.

CHAPTER 13
Pork Rinds and Mangos

Christine dropped onto the couch and arranged her laptop on her legs. It was a Sunday afternoon, and her dad was practicing his religion, which was watching football and yelling at the TV.

"Hey, Dad, what was your mother's father's name?" she asked, clicking on some keys and peering at the screen.

"What?" said Mr. Mango from the depths of his easy chair, not able to look away from the TV. "Holy cow, did you see that catch?"

"Your mother's father's name. I'm doing a family tree," said Christine.

"Paddy," answered Mr. Mango, knocking back a handful of peanuts. "Paddy Connolly. Just a little bit Irish," he laughed.

"So you're part Italian, part Irish?" asked Christine, typing in Paddy's name.

"I guess, probably some other stuff in there too. I think there was a German somewhere, a couple of English maybe."

"Hmm." Christine stared at her dad. "I always thought you were mostly Italian."

Mr. Mango shrugged. "You ask my granddad, the Italian is the only part that matters. And if you're Sicilian? Forget about it. One drop of Sicilian blood trumps everything else."

Christine moved her cursor around and found Mr. Mango's dad and his side of the tree. "So your dad was Jack, and then his dad was Michael, right?"

"Right. Big Mike was the one who came from Italy."

"Big Mike? Was there a Little Mike?"

"No, he was just a big guy and people called him that," said Mr. Mango, eyes still glued to the Raiders melting down, once again. "Goddamn, but we haven't had a good team since Gruden was here." He shook his head in disgust.

"Why did he leave Italy? And when—was he a kid? An adult?" asked Christine. "I can't believe I don't know any of this. How come I don't know my family's history?"

Mr. Mango grunted. "Never comes up, I guess. Too busy making a living." He dug around the bag of peanuts and came up empty. Without looking away from the TV, he fumbled around the side of his easy chair and pulled up a barrel of pork rinds the size of a small keg.

"Oh my God, what are you eating?" said Christine, eyes wide at the size of the pork rind container.

"Pork rinds. From Costco. They only come in one size."

Christine closed her eyes briefly. She knew she wasn't the healthiest eater in the world, but at least she gave it some effort, at some meals. "What happened to cutting carbs, eating healthier?"

"That's exactly what I'm doing! These arc not carbs, they're protein! And they are basically air."

Christine knew she had zero chance of influencing her dad's eating behavior, so she returned to the family tree. "So when did Big Mike come from Italy? And why?"

"I'm not sure when he came. Young man, maybe? There was some story that he had to leave the country. Some kind of trouble, I think."

Christine leaned forward, fascinated. "Really? Like the mafia or something?"

"I have no idea. I always kind of thought it had something to do with a girl, but I don't know where I got that idea."

"So the name Mango is Italian?"

Mr. Mango laughed. "No, that part I do know. Our name should be Mazzocchetti. Big Mike changed it when he got here."

"Mazzo- what?" Christine asked. "Spell it."

Mr. Mango spelled it.

Christine looked up and stared into the distance. "Whoa. I could be Christine Mazzocchetti? That feels weird."

Mr. Mango nodded and looked at Christine. There was a commercial on, and he could afford to look away from the train wreck of a football game. "I didn't know until I saw some stuff of my granddad's once. I was snooping through his drawers—boy, I got a smack for that one." He laughed at the memory. "I wanted to try one of his cigars. He caught me, standing there with it in my hand like a fool."

"And?"

"And he made me smoke the whole thing, right there. I got sick as a dog, never wanted to smoke anything again. Puked my guts out."

"Eww, that's gross."

"But effective," chuckled Mr. Mango.

"But how did you find out about the different name?"

"In the drawer, there was this metal-like thing, heavy, like a piece of jewelry almost, had a shield or a coat of arms on it for the 'Mazzocchetti family.' Once I got over throwing up from smoking the cigar, I asked him about it."

"And?" Christine wanted to hear the whole story, but the game had come back on and Mr. Mango's eyes were on the screen. Before he could answer, there was a tinkle of dog tags and Poker launched himself up over the side of the easy chair at the barrel of pork rinds on Mr. Mango's lap.

"What the?!!!" yelled Mr. Mango, as the barrel flew over the side of the chair, followed by Poker, who dug his paws into Mr. Mango's groin and then dove onto the floor where the pork rinds were spilled all over the carpet.

"Poker!" he yelled, jumping up and grabbing his

crotch as he lunged at the pork rind barrel. "Jesus Christ, is this dog ever not hungry?"

Christine set the computer on the coffee table in front of her and came around it to help her dad. "Poker!" she yelled. "Leave it!"

Poker had never responded to commands in his life, and he wasn't about to start now, not with so much crunchy deliciousness right in front of his snout. He snuffled and chomped like a truffle pig on speed, knowing his time was limited. Mr. Mango righted the barrel and held it up in the air, where Christine grabbed it and heaved it onto the back of the nearby desk, theoretically out of Poker's reach.

"How'd he get out of the garage?" grumbled Mr. Mango, sinking back onto his chair, ceding the rest of the pork rinds on the floor to the dog.

Christine came back around the couch and glared down at the dog. "He's supposed to be on a diet."

Mr. Mango snorted. "Aren't we all?"

Poker finished cleaning the floor and looked up at Christine hopefully, searching for more low-hanging snacks. Christine grabbed his collar and dragged him back to the garage.

Returning to the family room, she sat back down on the couch, picked up her computer, and continued. "You were saying about the Mazzo-whatever thing. How Big Mike was not a Mango."

Mr. Mango had gingerly settled back into his chair with a few discreet arrangements of his pants. "Ahh, yeah. Turns out he changed his name when he moved to the United States. Ah jeez, look at that!" He waved a hand at the TV. "He took a dive. Didn't even try to avoid the tackle! Bunch of pussies. Something about making the name shorter. Lotta immigrants did that. And you know, Italians weren't that popular in our area at that time anyway. Big Mike was always proud to be Italian, but he was a smart businessman and knew a store with the name 'Mango' would do better than one with 'Mazzocchetti.'"

"Hmm," said Christine, thinking. "How did he pick

Mango?"

"His family had a small mango farm in Italy. Everyone always called his dad 'Mr. Mango' so I guess he just decided he'd be Mr. Mango too. That's all I know; he never talked about it much."

Christine flopped back against the pillows on the couch. "I can't believe I never heard this story."

Mr. Mango shrugged. "Really? We never talked about it?" Mr. Mango's family had run a small grocery store for decades. His sister Mimi still ran it, although it made less and less money, the closer the big grocery stores got to their small town.

"I mean, I know your family has a store, I knew someone came from Italy; that was about it." Christine laughed. "No wonder I couldn't find any documents for family before Michael Mango. I had the wrong name." She started typing again.

"What's with all the family interest?" asked Mr. Mango.

"I don't know; I saw an ad for this genealogy site, and I got kind of curious."

Mr. Mango nodded knowingly. "Offered it for free, got you hooked, and then started charging you for it, right? It's the selfie generation, always a sucker to know more about themselves. My day, we didn't go in for so much 'me me me' business."

Christine laughed. "Whatever. I don't know, it is really interesting."

"Don't bother your mother with that stuff," said Mr. Mango.

"Why?" asked Christine, even as she realized that had been her instinct too.

"She's not much on digging up the past," said Mr. Mango.

"Or for accepting the present," said Christine.

Mr. Mango found a pork rind on his chair and ate it. "She's a complicated one, you know?"

Christine stopped her typing and looked at her dad

in surprise. She had always thought of her mother as kind
of a simple person, not complicated at all. For the briefest
of seconds, she considered asking her dad what he meant,
but that felt like it might segue into a conversation about
their marriage and she didn't want to go there at all.
Somewhere in her brain, she had a vague awareness that
her parents were no model for ageless romance, but she
didn't want to know any more than that. The thought had
the same cringy feeling as all those stupid Viagra
commercials. Better not to have an image for some things.

"Interception!" Mr. Mango yelled, banging the
remote down hard on the arm of his chair and scaring
Christine with his sudden shout.

Mr. Mango thrust the remote towards the TV and
clicked it off. "I can't watch this bullshit! I can't watch it."
He stood up and lumbered towards the kitchen. "I've gotta
go help Charlie with a repair. Might as well do it now.
Can't see wasting a Sunday afternoon watching lazy
millionaires tackle like girls."

CHAPTER 14
No Bingobucks for You

Mrs. Mango stood in front of the all-purpose, room-turned-bingo-parlor at Aegis. Folks in wheelchairs were rolling in, folks with canes were stabbing their way to seats, and those who could walk were already in place. The room was big enough for five rows of tables, with two long tables in each row, for a total of ten tables, all of which were filled. Pushed against the soft pink walls were an assortment of lightweight foam armchairs covered in a subtle angular mauve-and-gray pattern. When the room wasn't in use for bingo, the chairs were arranged in conversational groups around little tables, and the room served as a gathering spot. In the light of the afternoon sun streaming through the one wall of windows, the color scheme showed its age, but at night, when the room turned into a cocktail lounge, the soft colors were just right. A focus on healthy living was balanced by an enjoyment of life, and no one begrudged the residents their nightly tipple.

Alicia, the volunteer coordinator, was showing Mrs. Mango the bingo set-up. Alicia was close to forty and had been driving an hour each way to get to this job for almost ten years. Nothing fazed her, and she had a genuine love for the residents, no matter how grumpy they got. "So, you pull a ball out of the cage and read it as loud as you can. Then slide the tab over on the board so you know you've called that number. And say 'B' or 'G' clearly too; those two sound a lot alike."

Mrs. Mango nodded. How hard could it be? She had volunteered at Aegis for several months now, but this was her first time calling bingo. The normal Tuesday volunteer was sick, and no backups had been available.

Alicia slid a hand over her light brown bob, smoothing it back. "When someone calls 'Bingo,' you'll need to review their card, make sure they have all the spots for that game. Sometimes people get a bit confused. And when they win, they get a Bingobuck." She showed Mrs. Mango a stack of printed fake bucks. "They can exchange these for treats in the store."

"Where's Bob!" demanded a large woman seated at the left front table. Her walker was parked beside her, decorated in five different kinds of patterned duct tape. After her exclamation, the woman pulled out her dentures and set them neatly on a paper plate beside the three bingo cards she had lined up.

"Hello, Geraldine," Alicia said in a pleasant voice. "Bob's sick. This is Elsie; she's going to call it today."

Geraldine didn't move so well these last few years, and more than one part of her body was deteriorating, but those parts didn't include her brain. She was the unofficial official of Bingo. She shifted the folds of her voluminous dress and found a pocket, pulling a packet of tissues out of it and setting them next to her denture plate.

Geraldine shook her head and grunted. "Wass wrong wif Bob?" Without teeth, her words were harder to decipher, but the meaning was clear.

"Turns out, all the coughing? Pneumonia," said Alicia, smiling brightly to take the sting out of the diagnosis. "He needs some bedrest, but then he'll be back."

Geraldine pointed at Mrs. Mango. "Be loud!" she instructed.

At the right front table, a woman with a lilac silk scarf covering her head, tied in a complicated knot at the back, stared at Mrs. Mango. "We got a new face!" she proclaimed, smiling in delight.

"Hello, Marjorie," Alicia nodded to the woman in the scarf. Marjorie had soft loose skin hanging gently off of prominent cheekbones, balanced by arching eyebrows, and it was easy to see the beauty she'd been all her life. A very straight posture, head held erect in a way that showed inner dignity. If she felt her body was betraying her, she didn't show it. Mrs. Mango looked at Marjorie and thought she must have been a dancer. Such a beauty and presence. And such style, the way that scarf was wrapped just so.

Mrs. Mango glanced around the room that was close to full of the Aegis residents. There were maybe four or five women for every man, and aside from one wildly unnatural red-headed woman, puffs of gray and white hair dotted the room. It looked like a room full of George Washingtons, all of whom were staring at Mrs. Mango, some with welcoming smiles, some scowling at a change in routine.

Mrs. Mango smiled at the group as Alicia introduced her.

"We have Elsie Mango here today, filling in for Bob. I'm sure you will all be happy to help her feel welcome!" said Alicia.

"Mango?!" yelled a small gentleman bent like a comma over the second row of tables. His thin white hair was wild and sprouted in equal portions from his head, his nose, and around the hearing aids in his ears.

"Dom, do you have your hearing aids turned on?" asked Alicia, pointing dramatically at her own ears.

Dom rolled his eyes and reached up to his ears and clicked at something.

Mrs. Mango nodded. "You heard right, like the fruit."

"What kind of name is Mango?" said Dom, in only a slightly lower voice.

"My husband's family is from Italy," Mrs. Mango started to explain.

Dom waved a hand. "Mango is not Italian!"

Mrs. Mango nodded in agreement. "You're right; when they moved here, they changed it from Mazzocchetti."

Dom shook his head in disgust. "Ethnic cleansing, that's what that is."

Marjorie turned around to look at Dom. "That's a little exaggerated, don't you think?" She turned back towards Mrs. Mango. "I think it is a lovely name."

Mrs. Mango was feeling less confident about this

bingo-calling.

"Let's get started, shall we?" said Alicia. She turned to Mrs. Mango. "Rotate the drum, then pull out a number, and call it."

Mrs. Mango rotated the drum, stopped it, opened the little door, and pulled out a number. "B 6" she called.

"Huh? Louder!" yelled a voice from the back of the room. "Was that a 'B' or a 'G'?"

Mrs. Mango raised her voice. "B. B 6" she repeated.

The sound of discs landing on cards broke the silence.

Mrs. Mango spun and picked again. "N 43"

Alicia leaned in and whispered, "Say it twice, and the second time, if the number is double digits, say the digits, so 'N four three.'"

"N four three," called Mrs. Mango.

"Louder!" came the same voice from the back.

"An' fasser," grumped Geraldine, waving her fist in the air in circles in a 'speed it up' move.

Alicia gave Mrs. Mango an encouraging smile and slipped out of the room. Alicia was in charge of too many programs to stick around watching over a bingo sub.

Mrs. Mango got louder and faster, and then a woman beside Dom yelled 'Bingo!' in a wavery voice.

"Norma doesn't have Bingo!" yelled Dom, pointing a gnarled finger at her card. "Look at her card, she doesn't have it!"

Mrs. Mango walked to Norma and looked at her card.

"Yes, I do," said Norma calmly, peering through chunky glasses tucked into a deep ridge on the bridge of her nose that looked like it had worn into her face from a lifetime of wearing glasses. The glasses were so large they were even with the bottom of her nose and ended well above her eyebrows.

Geraldine grunted. "Hah somun reah em bah," she mumbled.

The lone red-headed woman in the room was sitting

on the other side of Norma and said, "Go back to the board; I'll read off her numbers to you."

"*Thank you,* Flo," said someone in the back.

Mrs. Mango went back to the board where she had placed each ball as she read the numbers. Three numbers in, she said in a friendly voice, "Whoops, looks like you got that wrong. There's no O 65."

Norma narrowed her eyes at Mrs. Mango, looking like Mr. Magoo behind her large glasses. "I did NOT!" she said firmly.

Dom shook his head and swore under his breath. "Why is she IN here?" he demanded. "She doesn't know what she's doing. Holds up the whole enchilada."

"Enchilada?" said a voice behind Dom. "I'd love an enchilada!"

The aide, a tall muscular man in khakis and a blue Aegis shirt was almost done passing out smoothies to the group. He leaned in to the enchilada-hungry woman and said "Look, Dorothy, I just gave you this smoothie. And you had lunch right before this."

"I did not!" said Dorothy indignantly. "I'm telling my daughter you people are starving me! This place is a prison!"

Mrs. Mango knew she was losing the room.

"Keep calling!" called another voice from the back. "I'm one square away! I want my Bingobucks!"

Mrs. Mango pulled another ball and called it.

"I already HAVE Bingo!" yelled Norma, standing up so abruptly she knocked the table forward, dislodging all the discs on the three cards each Dom and Flo had spread out.

"Jesus Christ!" bellowed Dom. "She ruined my cards!" He stood up and gave Norma a shove. Arms flailing, Norma hit both her smoothie and Flo's before tumbling onto Flo's lap, knocking the chair with them both over onto the floor, smoothies on their sides on the table cascading on top of them.

The aide came running from the back where he was

getting the last of the smoothies off the cart to distribute to the front tables.

"Dom! You can't be violent," he said evenly but firmly. He put his hand on Dom's arm, as if to calm him, as he passed him to get to the tangle of Norma and Flo on the floor.

"I think I banged my head!" yelled Norma, squirming and pushing on Flo to get up, as smoothie dripped down her back. "I think I broke my back!" Norma added.

"Why is she IN here?" yelled Dom again. "She doesn't know where she is. She doesn't even know *who* she is!"

Alicia appeared in the doorway. "What's going on?" she said, hurrying over to Norma and Flo as the aide helped them sit up.

Mrs. Mango felt awful. How had this happened? And so quickly?

Geraldine was shaking her head. She popped her dentures back in and looked at Mrs. Mango with angry eyes. "Not everyone is good at calling bingo."

"We still have half an hour left!" said a voice from somewhere on the left. "Clean them up and let's keep playing."

Alicia and the aide had Norma up, and the aide walked her out of the room saying, "Let's just get that smoothie out of your hair, okay?"

Flo's chair was righted; she sat back in it and wiped at her shirt with a towel.

Alicia grabbed two Bingobucks from the stack on the table and handed them to Flo. "Your lucky day! You get some Bingobucks for being such a good sport."

"Dom, you're going to have to leave," said Alicia. "You can't push people. You know that."

Dom reached up and turned his hearing aids back off. He gave a disgusted wave at the group. "Ridiculous. Everyone in here knows she shouldn't have been here, but *I'm* the one in trouble."

Alicia stared hard at Dom, walked towards him, and followed him as he stomped off.

Flo smiled and shot a look at Mrs. Mango to let her know there were no hard feelings. "Play on!" she said.

Mrs. Mango called three more numbers and then 'Bingo!' from Marjorie, in the front. She read back her numbers, and Mrs. Mango was thrilled to find they all matched. She gave Marjorie her Bingobuck and started calling the next round.

A chorus of "Clear! Wait, start again" kind of words came at her.

"Right," said Mrs. Mango. "Clear your cards. Okay, here we go."

Two numbers later, there was another ruckus in the back of the room.

"Goddamn it, I deserve to play this!" grumped Dom as he stomped back into the room. "Not my fault I got stuck by cotton-for-brains."

Mrs. Mango was at a loss for what to do with no aide or Alicia in the room.

"You need to leave," said Flo.

"Yes," agreed a man in the third row. "You'll really be in trouble if Alicia finds you here again."

"Pah!" yelled Dom. "Like I care. We're all one foot in the grave! What do I care if little Alicia is mad at me? What threat does she have that the grim reaper doesn't have 100 times more?"

Winces from most of the group. A couple of people hissed boos.

Mrs. Mango grabbed another ball and called, "I 25! I two five!" in a loud voice.

"Give me a card," demanded Dom, making his way to the front.

"Uh, I think you should probably go," said Mrs. Mango, grabbing the stack of extra cards and holding them against her chest.

"Oh you do? Who are you? Crappy substitute for Bob! That's all you are. You stink at this!" At that, Dom grabbed the cage of uncalled numbers and took off. "If I can't play, nobody plays!" he yelled, rounding the front tables and heading for the door in the back of the room.

Someone stuck a cane out and tripped Dom, and he went down with a crash of the cage, spilling all the bingo balls.

A skeletal woman with a sloppy bun of thin white hair stood up near Dom and yelled, "This is my favorite thing in my whole week! And you ruined it, you horse's ass!" She picked up her full smoothie and dumped it on top of him.

Another woman on the same side of the room stood up with her smoothie and dumped it on Dom too. "Me too! We all know Norma doesn't know what she's doing. So what? *You're* the one that ruined it for everybody!"

"Ah, I think everyone needs to just calm down," said Mrs. Mango, but no one seemed to hear her. They were too busy yelling at Dom and dumping smoothies on him.

Marjorie was the only one sitting calmly. She looked at Mrs. Mango. "A lot of anger around here."

Mrs. Mango was still clutching the bingo cards to her chest, paralyzed. She gave a little nod to acknowledge Marjorie's words. She had nothing to add.

"He went too far, with the grim reaper thing?" Marjorie shook her head, then smoothed the scarf that had shifted with the shake. "We all *know* but don't need to have it shoved in our face during bingo. He went over a line."

Mrs. Mango had a feeling this was her last bingo-calling assignment. It would be back to cleaning up the library, she was sure. And maybe it was for the best.

CHAPTER 15
No Massage Oil for You

Mrs. Mango and Christine were at the mall working on the last of their Christmas shopping along with several thousand other people who seemed to have the same idea. They walked slowly, unable to move any faster than the thick stream of people coursing along each side of the mall. Huge swathes of green garland looped across the long hall every twenty feet or so, sprayed with silver and dripping with silver and gold oversized ornaments. Christmas music played maniacally, and the scents fought with each other: cinnamon and frosting from Cinnabon clashing with Abercrombie and Fitch cologne, fake fir mixing in with the buttery, salty smell of the pretzel shop. Mrs. Mango silently cursed herself for leaving it this long, hating the overstimulation of every one of her senses.

It had been three and a half weeks since Thanksgiving, and although Mrs. Mango and Christine had come to an uneasy avoidance of the gay issue, Mrs. Mango was finding it harder to avoid the issue in her own head. Normally, Mrs. Mango's river of Denial ran strong and fast, sweeping problems into a vast sea from which they never returned. This Christine issue, though, was leaping and fighting its way up the river like salmon fiercely intent on procreating. Walking around the mall, Mrs. Mango couldn't help but notice all the families and couples. She felt a deep stab of pain to think Christine wouldn't be part of that kind of world and wondered yet again why she was insisting on being attracted to women. She pushed the thought from her mind and said, "Oh look, Crabtree and Evelyn has the loveliest gift basket in the window; let's go in."

They wandered around Crabtree and Evelyn, trying out the lotions and smelling the soaps. Mrs. Mango looked across the store to see Christine holding a bottle of massage lotion and felt a wave of disgust. She marched over, grabbed it out of her hand, and put it down firmly on the shelf.

"That stuff is no good," she said as she steered Christine towards the aloe soap. "Here, now this is a great smell," she said as she handed Christine a bar of soap.

"It's okay, Mom," Christine said. "I wasn't going to buy the oil for myself. I was getting it for Susan, a friend of mine at work. She's taking a massage class and has been practicing a lot on her *husband*."

"Oh. Well, anyway," said Mrs. Mango, flustered. "I still don't think that oil is a good present. Awfully personal."

They left the store after Christine insisted on getting the oil and after she had also whispered to the clerk to save the basket in the window for her. She knew her mother would love the basket but would never buy it for herself since the price was $75.

They headed for the food court where Christine got in line at Great Khan Mongolian Xpress and Mrs. Mango got in line at the Steak Your Escape. They met back in the middle, hovered over people who looked almost done eating until they finished in a huff, and brushed at the sticky table to get a clean spot to put their food.

Christine stared at her food. "I don't know why I always get this Mongolian beef; it never tastes as good as it looks.

Mrs. Mango looked at Christine's plate and wrinkled her nose. "I don't know why anyone would want to eat something cooked on top of the leftovers of so many other people's food."

"They clean the grill off, Mom," Christine said. "It's just that there is never as much flavor as I think there will be." Christine ripped open packets of soy sauce and stirred them around in the noodles.

"So, I still need something for Danny," said Christine. "He's so hard to buy for—doesn't seem to want a lot and when he does, he buys it himself."

Mrs. Mango nodded. "Something for his exercise obsession?"

Christine pondered that. Danny had always worked out in some way, starting with lifting weights in high school to try to bulk himself up. He took up running during medical school and had recently added biking and swimming to that, in preparation for a triathlon. Christine had zero interest in exercise. The only reason she exercised even infrequently was to continue to fit in her clothes. "Maybe? But I don't know what sorts of things he needs. Maybe a gift certificate to Athletes' Basement?"

They chatted for a few minutes about what to buy for the rest of the people left on the list, and then Christine pushed her food away and looked at her mother.

"Look, Mom," she started, "we can't keep pretending nothing happened at Thanksgiving. I'm not going to keep pretending Sarah doesn't exist."

"Oh, please, let's not go into that right now," Mrs. Mango said. "We are having such a nice day."

"No, I really think we need to talk about it," said Christine.

"Okay, Christine," Mrs. Mango cut her daughter off. "Of course, men are kind of disgusting, and they don't get any better as they age; they get worse. Do you think I'm attracted to a man with hair growing out his ears and his belly hanging over his belt? It's nature, though; that's how families work. I don't know any woman my age who is still attracted to her husband, well, almost none."

Mrs. Mango took a bite of her steak sandwich, pieces of pepper and onion sliding out the sides. She tilted her head to the side as she chewed. "Well, Nelly Frinoni won't shut up about, you know, *it*, but I think that's from the hormones she's on, 'cause have you ever seen Benny? I mean, frankly, I did my part and got you four, and I'd be just as happy to leave it at that. And I think your father would agree. You get to a certain point, sex is just not such an interest anymore. I'll let you in on a little secret: I don't think it is ever that big a deal to women. But the point is,

Christine, just because you don't find men attractive doesn't mean you have to go looking at women. Once the sexual desire dies away, it would just be easier all around if you were with a man."

Christine didn't think her dad would agree. Having unfortunately stumbled upon the search history on his computer, she knew his interest in sex was thriving. "I have to say, you're not making much of a case for men or marriage. And what about Velma and Flora? Those two are in their eighties and all they talk about is sex."

Mrs. Mango waved her Diet Coke at Christine. "Velma and Flora are all talk. Easy to do when your husband is dead. Men and women, that's just how it works."

"No, that's not how it *always* works," said Christine. "Why do I need a man?"

"You just do, that's all," said Mrs. Mango. "Maybe you just haven't met the *right* man?"

"It isn't about finding the right man; there is no right man." Christine tried to stay patient. "I've never been attracted to a man. Never."

Mrs. Mango was silent for a moment, then said, "Is it your dad? Is this his fault? He DOES have a lot of disgusting habits, but I'm sure not all men are like that." Mrs. Mango wasn't sure of that at all, but she wasn't going to tell Christine that.

Christine laughed. "No, it is not his fault. I was born this way."

"Not all men cut their toenails in the living room over a paper and then accidentally scatter them when they pick up the paper. And not all men look like they are pregnant with that big potbelly." Mrs. Mango got lost for a moment contemplating Mr. Mango's belly. Not for the first time, she had the thought that they should make maternity-style clothes for men, because there sure were a lot of them with those big stomachs. They could have shirts that widen towards the bottom, like maternity shirts. They could make the pop-out portion to pants so that she wouldn't have to look at those stupid jeans slung low around his huge belly.

"Don't you want me to be happy?" Christine asked, spearing a slice of mushroom and swirling her fork to pick up noodles.

"Don't be silly. Of course I want you to be happy!" harrumphed Mrs. Mango.

"But you want to tell me how to be happy," said Christine. "You want me to be *your* version of happy."

"That is not exactly true!" said Mrs. Mango. "Every parent wants their children to be happy. And parents have more experience with life. We can see what might be coming to make you unhappy, and we just want you to learn from our mistakes."

"The way you complain about Dad makes me think you feel like he was a mistake." Christine smiled, pleased at turning her mom's words against her. "Maybe you should have married a woman."

"Christine!" Mrs. Mango gasped so loud people stopped mid-transfatty-bites to look at them.

Christine laughed, feeling mean but pleased to have shocked her mother. Maybe the only way to handle this situation was to get some humor out of it. Might as well amuse herself. "You know, Mom, some people think older women are more likely to turn gay after menopause. You know, all the nurturing hormones go away, and the balance with testosterone makes them more, you know, like men."

Mrs. Mango gasped again. "That is ridiculous! How are you talking like this?"

Christine shrugged. "I don't know, you seemed to be looking pretty close at that magazine with Kathy Lee Gifford on it. Maybe you have a girl crush."

Mrs. Mango stood up abruptly. "That's enough. I'm going to the As-Seen-On-TV store. If you get some kind of respect back, you can come join me."

Mrs. Mango stomped off, leaving Christine giggling into her Mongolian beef. It was better than crying.

Mrs. Mango paused by the Just Nuts kiosk in the

middle of the mall. The nuts smelled good and had some cute packaging, maybe she could get a tin for Mimi for Christmas.

An emaciated gangly teen with big holes in the lobes of his ears leaned off his stool by the kiosk. "Can I help you?" he asked.

"No," said Mrs. Mango, still staring at the array of loose and boxed up nuts. "I'm just looking at your nuts."

An elderly man standing next to Mrs. Mango snorted with laughter. The gangly teen broke into what might have been his first smile since he was nine.

"What?" said Mrs. Mango. She didn't wait for an answer but wandered off. What was wrong with people?

Wandering through the As-Seen-On-TV store, Mrs. Mango saw a personal groomer and wondered if it was up to the job of deforesting Mr. Mango. She took one off the shelf, and, then, thinking about the hair that grew so copiously in his ears and nose and even down the back of his neck, took a second one. That hair looked like the fur on an ungroomed dog, all matted and unruly. It shot out in every direction, sticking out over the collar of his shirts, and, when left unshaved for too long, almost meeting up with the ear hair. How in the world could he think she would be interested in having sex with him, looking like that? She didn't enjoy sex when they were young and good-looking; why would she want to rub her sagging body up against his fat hairy one?

Mrs. Mango looked around the store but still no Christine. She was probably sitting there, still laughing at the thought of her mother with a woman. Mrs. Mango shook the thought out of her head and went back to ruminating about Mr. Mango.

The old fool was losing his hearing and wouldn't admit it. For a long time, she thought he was just intentionally ignoring her, but she finally had to conclude he wasn't hearing well because she heard his friend Roger tell him a dirty joke and he didn't even laugh. He said 'eh?' a lot, and he didn't respond until you repeated what you said in a louder voice. About a year ago, Mrs. Mango saw an ad in the classifieds for hearing aids, and she bought them for him. She couldn't understand why he wouldn't wear them; the man who used them before his family sold them said they worked just fine. She didn't see anything wrong with wearing a dead man's hearing aids; at least you knew they worked!

"Let's stop at Starbucks," said Christine, breaking into her mother's ruminations. "I need to get some gift cards there. And maybe a coffee."

"Oh, there you are," Mrs. Mango said. Christine waited with her mom while she paid for the personal groomers and a back support pillow, and then they headed back into the scrum of shoppers.

As they fought their way towards Starbucks, Mrs. Mango said, "I don't get this fancy coffee stuff. What's a latte-dah or whatever they're called? Just get me a plain old cup of coffee."

While Christine waited in line for their coffee, Mrs. Mango wandered into the Williams-Sonoma next door. It reminded her that at some point, Christine would need to stock her own apartment. Mrs. Mango had always assumed she could register for all that stuff when she got married, but, well, that plan was a bust. Did every thought have to lead back to that?

Mrs. Mango decided that while she couldn't support Christine having a girlfriend, she could show some goodwill by buying her household goods. It was a vague gesture at faith that she might actually get married to a man some day. She wandered towards a display of pots and pans. Stunning. The shine and beautiful stacking arrangement on the All-Clad eleven-piece set was irresistible. She glanced down at the price tag and almost had a stroke. $1,599 *marked down* from $2,310! She decided to go to HomeGoods instead and carefully backed away, afraid if she bumped the set and it toppled, she'd owe all that money.

That's what was wrong with this world, she

decided, as she safely made it out of the store. People paying over fifteen hundred dollars for a set of pans! That was a house payment for crying out loud. There was no common sense anymore. None. Her daughter was confused, her husband was really getting on her last nerve, and no one was producing grandchildren for her. All of a sudden, the crowds felt suffocating. The holiday seemed ridiculous and commercialized. Mrs. Mango just wanted to be home surrounded by grandchildren.

That was the only thing she wanted anymore in life. Grandchildren.

CHAPTER 16
Shamans and Brussels Sprouts

Mrs. Mango did not see herself as a truck person and so did not care for riding in her husband's truck, but they had so much to take to Danny and Rita's for Christmas that she had no alternative. Even though she had also loaded up Christine's car before she took off to pick up Sarah, there was still too much to fit in the Buick. Christine had casually let it drop that Sarah was coming, and Mrs. Mango had pressed her lips together and pushed the information out of her head.

Presents cluttered the truck bed, and food covered the entire backseat. Rita said she would cook the dinner, but in Mrs. Mango's experience, Rita's meals were on the sparse side. Although it might be healthy, three spears of asparagus and a piece of poached chicken did not make a meal. Danny said they were making a prime rib, but Mrs. Mango didn't believe he'd actually get Rita to agree to such a carnivorously delicious meat. So she had prepared her homemade macaroni and cheese, her boys' favorite potatoes au gratin, a green bean casserole, and a bag of dinner rolls. She added the Honeybaked ham she had picked up earlier just in case Rita was short on meat.

Mrs. Mango tapped her heels on the rubber mat in the front seat, annoyed at her husband. She tugged at the hem of her red silk dress, unaccustomed to such a bright color. The dress, brought out once a year, still fit over all her curves and rolls but was just this side of too short, especially when she was sitting down. She felt for the neck; yes, still buttoned correctly. And the dainty gold chain with its cross hung just right. She rearranged the black sweater around her shoulders, staring out the window at the weak sunlight. Of course California always needed rain, but she was glad that today was clear; it was no fun loading and unloading all the presents and food in the rain. Where was that old fool? She had cooked, shopped, wrapped, and packed the entire truck and was ready to go. All he had to do was get himself dressed, and where was he? She leaned over and honked the horn, knowing full well it would make him go slower but unable to control her irritation. When he didn't appear, she climbed out of the truck and stomped into the house.

"Joe? Where are you? We need to *go!*" Mrs. Mango spied the bunch of ripe bananas in the fruit bowl. Thinking you could never bring enough food to Rita and Danny's, she grabbed them and tucked them under her arm.

Mr. Mango ambled into the kitchen, zipping his jacket up over a white collared shirt under a navy V-necked sweater and neatly creased khakis. Around the house, Mr. Mango dressed like a homeless man, but to the world outside he always presented the neat, clean, pressed version of himself. He had a lot of ideas about how a man should act in the world, and being presentable was one of them. "Ready?" he said, as if it had just occurred to him they should leave, as if he hadn't heard her yelling and honking.

"Hmph," said Mrs. Mango, rolling her eyes. "I've been ready an hour!"

Mr. Mango glanced at the clock on the microwave. "We've got plenty of time."

"Not if there's traffic. Or an accident. You just never know around here. Let's go," she answered, turning around and heading out the door.

"Where's Meredith?" Mrs. Mango asked, giving second son Michael a hug. They hadn't yet made it into Danny's house but were standing in the driveway, unpacking the truck. "Her family got you guys at Thanksgiving; so glad we get you for Christmas!" As she said the word 'Thanksgiving,' Mrs. Mango cringed, wondering if she would ever enjoy that holiday again.

"She's, uh, not going to make it today," said Michael, his brown eyes darting to the side, not able to look his mother in the eye. A girlfriend had once told Michael that he was good- looking in a 'third look' kind of way, and he couldn't really argue with that. He had a nice-enough face, brown eyes, thick brows, strong nose, but it took some time for women to put that all together in a pleasing way. Most didn't bother after one look, but Meredith had. Until she hadn't.

"Oh, poor thing, she's sick? Are *you* sick?" Mrs. Mango said, leaning back and feeling Michael's head for a fever.

Before Michael could actually answer, Danny came up behind his mother and hugged her. "Hey, Mom, Merry Christmas; is there more in the car to bring in?"

Michael and Danny gave each other a meaningful look as Danny led Mrs. Mango away. Michael slid his hand around to his lower back and grimaced when his mother wasn't looking. Now was no time to tell her about his marriage. Or his back pain. He didn't need her advice or worrying. Because when his mother started worrying, it took over everything.

"Pops, you remember my brother?" Rita said, giving Mr. Mango a hug and gesturing to a tall, bearded man beside her. They were standing in the high-ceilinged kitchen that Rita and Danny had just finished remodeling. It was full of light and seemingly acres of white cabinets, with a view of a deep backyard rimmed by beautiful old live oaks.

Mr. Mango squinted, not recognizing him. Rita and Danny's wedding had taken place five years earlier, and although he had a vague recollection of a brother, he didn't remember anyone looking like this guy. This guy had a rumpled gray linen shirt hanging untucked over flowy white linen pants. Several strands of beads and charms circled his neck, and a leather woven bracelet hung from his wrist. His brown wavy hair was cut closer on the sides of his head than the top and his beard was carefully trimmed to about an inch below his chin.

"I'm Don Paz," Rita's brother said, stepping
forward and grabbing Mr. Mango's hand in both of his
hands. "Blessed to see you."

"Uh, yeah, uh, nice to see you too, Don," said Mr.
Mango.

"It's Don *Paz*," said Don Paz. "'Paz' as in 'peace.'"

Mr. Mango couldn't stop himself from rolling his
eyes. Don Paz just gave him an understanding smile that
irritated Mr. Mango even more than the silly name.

Rita gave a high-pitched laugh. "Don Paz is his
chosen name, Pops. When you met him at the wedding, it
was just Bill." Rita gave her brother a squeeze to soften her
words. "Who isn't for more peace in this world, huh?"

Don Paz gave a slow nod with the same goofy
smile, and Mr. Mango wondered if he was high on
something. Good Christ, this was going to be a long day.

"Come on, let's get you something to drink," Rita
said, linking her arm in Mr. Mango's and pulling him away
from Don Paz.

Mr. Mango found Danny in the backyard, heating
up the grill. Danny was dressed in gray jeans that were
snug clear to his ankles and a maroon, thinly knit sweater
that strained a bit across his shoulders. Danny was a good
advertisement for his medical profession, slim and toned,
with a healthy glow to his face even when he wasn't
sweating over a grill. Mr. Mango couldn't argue with the
results but was bewildered by how many hours Danny put
in on his treadmill and fancy stationary bike. How could a
person give so much of their life working so hard to going
exactly nowhere? Mr. Mango waved his beer bottle at
Danny, "Here you are. Couldn't find you."

"Yeah," Danny grunted, scraping old black shreds
of unrecognizable meat off the grill.

"Hiding, maybe?" Mr. Mango said.

Danny didn't answer.

Mr. Mango looked around the back yard. "Well,
you are in the middle of it now, huh? Looks like it's going

to be nice." The back yard was torn up, with pallets of stone stacked to one side and all manner of PVC tubing and sprinkler heads scattered around.

Danny nodded. "Yeah, am happy with the flagstone we picked out, and the landscaping is going to be killer." He sprayed some water on the grill and scraped a few more times, then closed the lid. "Shouldn't take too long to heat up."

"You're doing a prime rib on the grill?" Mr. Mango asked.

"Huh!" Danny barked, raking his fingers through his short, light brown hair. "Rita, uh, miscalculated on the prime rib. It came out of the oven an hour ago. Pretty much ruined."

Mr. Mango took a breath and reminded himself not to criticize his children's choices of mates. But, goddamn, he had been looking forward to that prime rib.

"I knew I should've cooked it," grumbled Danny. His dad's self-control in not criticizing Rita opened up the possibility for him to. "A hundred and twenty bucks worth of meat turned into a pile of charcoal. Apparently, she forgot to turn the heat down after the first 15 minutes. So we'll be having steaks. And burgers. Not that the Dalai Lama in there eats meat. I guess he can have some alfalfa."

Mr. Mango stared at Danny in surprise because Danny never broke the boundaries of his marriage. This was the first time he had ever complained, even though Mr. Mango knew Rita could be a bit of a ball breaker.

"Yeah, what's up with him?" Mr. Mango said, finishing the last of his beer and looking around for an outside cooler.

Danny walked over to a partially completed outdoor kitchen and opened a door to reveal an under-counter refrigerator. He pulled out a beer and handed it to his dad, then pulled out another one for himself. "He's a 'shaman,' if you can believe it. Dropped out of Stanford Business School to be a freaking shaman."

"What the heck is a shaman?" asked Mr. Mango.

Danny shook his head. "Something about the spirit world. Like, that he is some sort of messenger between the spirits and the rest of the world. And something about healing."

"Doesn't seem like there'd be a lot of money in that," said Mr. Mango.

Danny shrugged. "Hopefully, not my problem. I don't get it, but he seems pretty harmless."

"Harmless? Not earning your way in the world is not 'harmless.' Who do you think is paying for all the services that guy uses? Us! The taxpayers of the world. The people who do honest work for honest pay. We don't float around all airy-fairy 'healing' people. We get out and get our hands dirty."

Danny took four quick slugs of his beer. "I get it, Dad; I probably even agree with you. But it is Christmas Day, and Rita's already stressed about the stupid meat and probably deep down worried about her brother, and I'm sure Mom is in there making her even more stressed, so for today, just for today, could you not make a big deal out of it?

"Fine. But one more word of advice: don't give that guy any money. I know how that works. Do you know how many people 'live the dream' on someone else's dime?"

Danny had a feeling his dad's words were hitting close to home. His oldest brother, Joe Jr., was forty years old and still chasing the dream of being an actor. Everyone in the family had secretly sent him some money, but the big break still hadn't come. Maybe every family had that member.

Christine was giving Sarah a tour of Danny and Rita's house, and Sarah was so entranced there was a chance they would not finish by dinner.

"Look at these hardwood floors; they are beautiful!" Sarah enthused, slipping her loafer off and running her bare foot along the living room floor. "And I love the colors, so soothing," she added, looking around the room full of white and light wood.

"They pretty much gutted this place and updated everything," said Christine, finding herself proud of her brother as she saw his house through Sarah's eyes.

Sarah nodded, still scanning the room. "Love the built-ins along that wall," she said, gesturing towards the end wall filled with books and artistically placed objets d'art. "And that piece—just gorgeous," she added, walking towards an antique-looking armoire. "What is this?" she asked, peering more closely at it.

"I think it is some sort of Indian thing," said Christine, wishing she had listened more when her brother and Rita enthused about their various finds.

"It's a carved Indian cabinet," said Rita, who had appeared in the doorway without them hearing her. "Isn't it just so cool? I wanted one really unique item in here, and when I saw that, I knew it was the piece." Rita was talking fast—friendly but with an undercurrent of holiday chef stress just beneath the surface.

"Oh my God, I just love your house," said Sarah. "I love everything you've done with it. The colors are gorgeous, and everything just flows so well! Where did you find the chandelier in the entry? I've never seen anything like it."

"There are so many antique shops and unique little design places in this area," said Rita. "I found that way up above St. Helena."

"And the floors, are they reclaimed wood?" said Sarah.

Christine felt a happy glow. Rita was friendly and as animated as she'd ever seen her, and Sarah seemed more at ease than either of them had thought was possible. Who knew that interior design would be the entry for Sarah into the family? She watched Sarah and Rita chatter away at each other and trailed behind as Rita took Sarah to see the chandelier in the dining room.

"Let me show you this real quick, and then I'll do a proper tour after dinner," said Rita as they trooped out.

"Oh, and you don't even have a glass of wine yet; let's grab one from the kitchen."

Christine had never liked Rita as much as she did in that moment.

"Does anyone want more ham?" Mrs. Mango held up the platter, triumphant in her decision to bring it. She had just known that prime rib was not going to materialize. They were gathered around the long distressed-pine dining room table, digging into the meal. The dining room was one of the biggest rooms in the house, stretching along a good section of the back of the house, the entire wall covered in a series of French doors opening out onto the gray flagstone patio. Opposite the doors, Rita had positioned a triptych of mirrors, and the light of the funky elegant chandelier bounced off the mirrors and around the room in a pleasing way. Comfortable parsons chairs covered in thick linen with a faint mattress ticking stripe lined each side of the table, and it all sat on a soft grayish-blue rug. Mrs. Mango had once told Rita it looked like a room straight out of a catalog and didn't understand why Rita was offended by the comment. It was top praise for her.

No one said yes, but Rita's shoulders slid towards her ears. "I'm fine, Mom," said Danny. "The steak is enough for me."

"Potatoes? Green bean casserole?" said Mrs. Mango.

Danny sent her a dagger look. Could she not see how stressed Rita was? And here she was offering up only the food she had brought. "Hey, I'll take some more of the kale-brussels sprout thing," said Danny, gesturing towards the end of the table with his fork.

"Me too," said Christine, understanding what Danny was up to. She grabbed the kale-brussels sprout mix, heaped a pile on her plate, and passed it along. "Rita, I'm going to have to have this recipe," Christine said.

Sarah had one goal in mind, which was pleasing

Mrs. Mango, so she passed the bowl along without taking any. She and Christine had agreed it would be progress if Mrs. Mango just tolerated Sarah being at Christmas dinner. Actual conversation could be a goal for the future. For her part, Mrs. Mango pretended Sarah wasn't there and never even looked towards her.

Mrs. Mango turned to Michael. "Tell me again why Meredith isn't here. Is she that sick? What's she got? Is it contagious? If so, maybe you shouldn't be here."

Mrs. Mango peered more closely at her son. "You don't look good; are you okay?"

"She's fine. Well, not fine. Just, uh, not up to being here today," fumbled Michael.

Mrs. Mango's mother instinct spun into top speed. "What does that mean? What are you hiding?"

"Meredith and I are, uh, taking a bit of a break," sighed Michael. Hoping to change the subject, he turned to his dad and said, "Gas is $2.45 a gallon! Can you believe it? Filled up my Yukon on the way here for barely forty bucks."

Mr. Mango shook his head. "Just goes to show you what I've been saying all along. You think all of a sudden there's more oil? Those oil companies have had us by the balls since the engine was invented. They set the price as high as they can 'cause they know we'll pay it. And then, boom, all of a sudden people are buying less gas, and what happens? The price magically goes down."

"What do you mean, you and Meredith are 'taking a break'?" Mrs. Mango's eyes drilled into Michael's.

"Dad, there *is* more oil available now; well, I mean we have more available in our country," said Michael, ignoring his mother.

"Exactly! But it won't last forever. And I didn't believe in it at first, but now that there's all those alternative energies and people don't need the oil as much, isn't it amazing how the thing that cost over four dollars now costs almost half that?"

Mrs. Mango had not broken her stare at Michael. "Mikey? What's going on with Meredith?"

Mr. Mango turned to Mrs. Mango. "Crissakes, Elsie, can't you tell he doesn't want to talk about it?"

"Talk about what?" Danny asked, returning to the room having just hopped up to get another bottle of wine and the salt and pepper shakers.

"The price of gas," Michael said.

"You don't want to talk about the price of gas?" Danny said, shaking salt on his kale-brussels sprout salad.

"It needed salt?" Rita said in a shrill voice.

"He and Meredith are having problems," said Mrs. Mango. "And he has to tell us now, at Christmas? Just ruin the day?"

"Mom!" said Michael. "I didn't bring it up! You are the one who kept pushing to know why Meredith wasn't here. You just couldn't let it be."

"I don't know how I'm the problem here all of a sudden," huffed Mrs. Mango. "Excuse me for caring."

"What does this all have to do with the price of gas?" asked Danny, still trying to catch up.

"I was saying that I've been right all along," said Mr. Mango. "The oil companies have lied to us for years, acting like oil is worth more than gold, then all of a sudden, the demand goes down, and what do they do? Sell it for less. The price of gas has always been some magical moneymaker for them, and we all just handed over our wallets and let them take what they wanted."

"And don't forget all the suffering that's been caused in the world getting that oil," chimed in Don Paz.

Mr. Mango turned towards Don Paz, surprised to have an ally. "True. We wouldn't have soldiers in the Middle East it wasn't for all the oil they're sitting on. Hah! We always act like we are there to spread democracy or something when it's really about the oil."

Don Paz nodded. "A lot of pain."

Mr. Mango couldn't believe he agreed with Don Paz, but you never know where allies are going to come from.

"Pain and suffering. I'll tell you about suffering," said Mrs. Mango, a tear running down her face. "I'm never going to get grandchildren." She looked around the table, eyes full of judgment and disappointment. "That's all I want. Grandchildren!" She banged her water glass down so hard the water slopped out onto the table.

Rita leapt out of her seat so fast she knocked her chair over but didn't stop to right it, just ran out of the room. The sound of her sobs carried back as she flew out the door.

Silence took over the room, everyone looking around at each other, and then all ending up staring at Mrs. Mango.

"What?" asked Mrs. Mango. "What was that?"

Danny let out a big sigh as his head fell into his hands. Taking another big breath, he stood up and followed Rita out of the room.

"What?" said Mrs. Mango again, looking around. Her eyes fell on Christine. "Well, I'm not getting grandchildren from *you*," she said. "And Joe and Jenny are too poor; thank God they are smart enough to know that. And now it looks like they won't come from Meredith, at least not any time soon. So . . ."

Christine shook her head. "Mom, you know that Rita and Danny want kids . . ."

"Yes! And they should get to it!"

"They've been *trying*. And trying. And it hasn't worked out. So, Rita is a little sensitive about that right now," said Christine.

"Well, how was I to know?" demanded Mrs. Mango. "Nobody tells me anything."

"It's not necessarily the kind of thing you give your mom details about," said Michael. He mimicked holding a phone to his ear, "Hey Mom! How are you? Want to hear about all the baby sex we've been having and how it isn't working?"

"Oh for goodness sake, Michael," Mrs. Mango put

her hands over her ears. "Stop that!"

"Besides, Mom, maybe *I* will have a baby sometime. I've got a working uterus. Maybe I'm your best shot at grandchildren," said Christine with a sly smile. "In fact, we've got two!" she gestured at Sarah.

"Oh my God, just everybody stop!" said Mrs. Mango.

Michael snorted with laughter at Christine. What with his separation and almost unbearable back issues, he didn't get much of a chance to laugh. Christine started giggling back. Mr. Mango fought back a smile, and Mrs. Mango noticed. "Now *you're* laughing? This is not funny!"

With each of Mrs. Mango's protests, the family started laughing harder. Her outrage was bringing the whole family together.

Mrs. Mango had worked herself into a toxic mix of fury and disappointment. Her oldest broke and chasing an impossible dream, her second separated, and her youngest with this gay foolishness. Rita and Danny had been her only hope, and now even they had failed her. And nobody was eating the ham.

Don Paz beamed at them, "Yes, laughter is such a great way to restore harmony!"

CHAPTER 17
No Danger in Sight

Dear Raul,

Wherever you are, I hope you had a blessed Christmas, because I didn't. The day was such a disappointment. I get so excited for holidays, and then someone in my family always ruins them. How was I to know that Rita hasn't been able to get pregnant? No one tells me anything. Or, they tell me too much. But never what I want to hear. I'm just so tired of it all.

Mrs. Mango looked up from her writing and sorted through her memories to see which one would do the trick today. She remembered that recently she had gone back to the beginning, the night she first met Raul. She decided to pick it up there. She closed her eyes and let her mind travel back to the end of the evening she met Raul. By the sixth deep breath, she could hear the background music, see the dim lights, feel the excitement of sitting in the almost dark with her head tilted in towards Raul's. How natural it seemed that he ask her to meet him the following weekend for a date. A quick squeeze of her hand when they said goodbye, and the way she self-consciously walked to the car with Sandy, knowing he was watching her. Like walking a tightrope, she held herself together, like it was any other old walk to a car, until she and Sandy were in the car, the windows up, before she let out a giggly scream.

Mrs. Mango gave herself over to the memories of that week, how she and Sandy discussed the details of that night endlessly, how they plotted out her date for Friday in a way that would leave her parents clueless. Because there was something about Raul Elsie just knew her parents would not approve of.

Too many times she had listened to their dreams for her life: a proper upbringing, a good college, a reasonable job for a woman, marriage to an educated man. Neither of her parents had gone to college, but both believed it was the only road to Oz. Her mother's fondest dream for Elsie was that she would become a nurse, marry a doctor, and live happily ever after. Elsie knew that her parents would not be pleased at the idea of her dating a farm worker who had no college plans. And although they were not vocally racist, she also had the uncomfortable feeling that her parents lived in a narrow definition of what the 'right' kind of person was, and it didn't involve any of the darker shades of skin.

The plan Raul had offered was to meet at Rocky's Burgers—which worked perfectly for Elsie. It was one town over and not a place she was likely to be seen by her parents or friends. Elsie and Sandy obsessed all week. Would Raul show? Did Elsie even remember the time right? What were his words again? What was her answer? It was a delicious and anxious week. When Elsie got too scared, sure that she couldn't do it herself, Sandy took charge and set up her own date at the same place. The girls would drive there together in Sandy's car and then split up and sit at different tables with their dates.

Elsie's eyes were shut and her head tilted back as she remembered that night. Walking in the diner door, her heart pounding, her cheeks flushed with the fear that she had it all wrong, that he wouldn't be there, and then again, fear that he would. In a second, she saw him standing up from a back corner table, smiling and walking towards her.

He was even more handsome than she remembered, and her heart beat faster, all these years later, as the image played in her mind. He took her hand and led her back to the table, where they talked for three straight hours, barely even touching the food in front of them. Those friendly brown eyes, on her with an intense focus. The way he seemed to find everything she said fascinating. The way it felt to be adored, because that is how it felt, right from those early moments. The strength of her attraction to him deep and fast, like going over rapids, a thrilling experience with danger bubbling all around. What was the danger? Mrs. Mango drifted back towards the present as she wondered that. The danger of falling that hard? The danger of knowing her parents would never approve? The danger of looking that deeply into another person and letting him look that deeply into you? As she had done back then, she let herself fall into the danger. Let herself feel the delicious, potent joy of feeling so *known*.

Ten minutes later, Mrs. Mango opened her eyes and glanced at the clock.

Oh, Raul, I miss you so much. I have just never stopped loving you or remembering your love for me. I'm so sorry for all my parents did. I hated them for so long. It has been so many years that I find it hard to summon up the hate anymore, but I never forgave them. I just know you wouldn't have enlisted if you weren't trying to prove something to them. I know in my heart they caused your death.

All my love,
Elsie

With a deep breath, Mrs. Mango started the ritual of stuffing the memories back in their vault, like putting a genie back in the bottle, seemingly impossible but somehow managed, every week.

With the turn of the key in the lock, letter safely stowed, the ritual was complete. No danger in sight.

****

Mrs. Mango was by the end of her driveway, trying to stabilize their dangling mailbox. It had been installed over thirty years ago, and the rainy winters and scorching summers had finally weakened the thin wrought-iron post holding up the aluminum box. The screws had come loose because the holes around them had rusted out enough to be too wide to hold the screw, even with washers added. Mr. Mango kept almost everything in the house in good order, but every time Mrs. Mango asked him to fix the mailbox, he claimed they needed to buy a new one, that this one was beyond fixing. And then somehow they never got around to buying a new one. When Mrs. Mango came out today to get the mail and it swung loose and off to the side yet again, she decided on the spot that she would fix it. She went into the house and dug around until she found a roll of duct tape, and she brought it outside with some old scissors and went to work, glancing periodically at the dark clouds that were multiplying. She'd need to get this finished before the rain started. As she was wrapping the duct tape around the box for the fifth time, Velma and Flora came walking by, elbows flying into the air as they scuffed their feet quickly along the ground.

Flora's thin and bony body was decked out in purple spandex with a rainbow headband holding her sparse gray hair out of her face. Velma, looking like Marilyn Monroe might have looked had she made it to her eighties, was dressed in head-to-toe yellow spandex that was straining to hold everything in place. Her bust was mostly above her waist and her behind was mostly below it, and that was enough for her.

"Hey, Elsie, how ya doing?" Velma called out as they got closer.

"Fine, how are you girls doing? *What* are you girls doing?" said Mrs. Mango.

"Speed walking," said Flora as they neared Mrs. Mango.

"Let's take a break," said Velma, and Flora nodded.

"Okey dokey," said Flora. She looked up at the sky. "Not sure how much longer we have anyway before the heavens let loose."

The women stopped and peered at Mrs. Mango's work as they unstrapped water bottles from their waists and took drinks.

"That's a fine bit of duck taping there," said Flora, wiping her mouth with the back of her hand, water dripping down her chin.

"Thank you," said Mrs. Mango. "I just got tired of waiting for Joe to fix this, so I thought I'd do it myself. The darn mailbox keeps tipping off of its pole."

"Where is Joe? I thought he went to part-time, but I never see him around," said Velma.

"He's been driving extra shifts for Norm, a guy at work," said Mrs. Mango, stepping back to survey her work. "His wife has The Cancer, and he took off so much time he doesn't have any left. Joe's been driving his shifts so he doesn't lose his job."

"Well, if that don't beat all. Nice guy, that Joe," said Flora.

"Hmph, I think he just wanted an excuse to get out of the house," said Mrs. Mango, adding another strip of duct tape to the mailbox.

Flora and Velma shot each other looks. Mrs. Mango would never give her husband credit for anything. Seemed like everyone except his wife knew what a good guy Joe Mango was.

"Come to think of it, I haven't seen Christine around for ages either. She still live here?" asked Velma.

"Of course, just busy," said Mrs. Mango. It was true Christine had not been around much, but Mrs. Mango preferred not to think about where she was.

"She got a honey?" asked Flora.

"No, uh, I don't know," said Mrs. Mango, flustered. She pulled a strip of duct tape and cut it, even though she had been done with the mailbox. She needed to do something to cover her discomfort with that question.

Velma raised her eyebrows at Flora. They both had an idea of what was going on.

Velma leaned in close to Flora's face. "Flora, you've got to get out your tweezers; your chin hair is growing back."

"Huh, thank you very much, that is a rogue eyebrow hair," said Flora, rubbing at her chin.

"Who are you kidding, old woman, we got more hair on our chins than Abe Lincoln. No shame in that, just got to keep it trimmed, you know?" said Velma.

Flora started laughing. "I know, but I heard that line somewhere and thought it was funny. I guess I forgot to pluck this week."

"Every night, I put my teeth right next to my personal groomer so I don't forget to check in the morning," said Velma. "I learned about these memory tricks from that TV doctor. When you get old, you need to put things right where you'll see them and remember. Like, I also keep my reading glasses with The Rabbit."

Flora looked at Velma and raised her eyebrows in a what-does-that-mean face.

Mrs. Mango wrinkled her brow. "You have a rabbit?"

Velma laughed. "The Rabbit is the finest vibrator around. I keep it by my glasses so I can read my 'romance' novel at the same time. Or, if I have company, so I can see what is, uh, coming my way."

They both turned to Mrs. Mango. "You have to trim your chin yet, Elsie?" asked Velma.

Mrs. Mango wanted no part of this conversation. Rabbits and 'company'! "My goodness, look at the time, I need to get inside!" she said. She grabbed the duct tape and scissors and walked quickly towards the house.

What is wrong with those women, she thought as she walked. Can't anything stay private anymore? The fact was, Mrs. Mango hated all the things that were growing on her body as it aged. It seemed like every week, there were new moles and new wrinkles and expanding rolls of fat despite her walking regime. There were yellowing toenails and hair on her chin and her hair *down there* was all gray. She tried her best not to even look at her body when she got out of the shower. She dried off and dressed with her back to the mirror and only checked herself once she was fully clothed. Even then, it was just a quick glance to make sure things were zippered and buttoned correctly.

"Let's see if we can't get in another mile before the rain starts," said Velma.

Flora agreed, and they took off, elbows pumping. With one last look back at the Mangos' house, Flora said, "That woman has to loosen up; she is going to rupture something one of these days."

"Huh, a little rupturing might be just the thing for her," said Velma. "I ruptured myself last night and I still feel *good.*"

CHAPTER 18
Not Your Normal Thursday

To her great discomfort, Mrs. Mango was sitting in the dentist chair, mouth numbed up and tooth filed down to a nub, while she waited for the dentist to finish working on the temporary crown in the lab. An easy-listen radio station played music that was annoying in its blandness, and she shivered, wishing she hadn't left her sweater in the car. Why did they always keep it so cold in professional offices?

In addition to the irritation with the temperature and the music, Mrs. Mango couldn't distract her brain from her family. She had always thought once the kids were grown, she could relax and stop worrying, but the problems were even bigger in adulthood than they had been in the teenage years. Her thoughts zigged and zagged from one of her children to the next like a ball in a pinball machine. Christine, no, don't think about her. Michael, what in the world was going on with him and Meredith? Joe Jr., no, he was almost out of money, again. Danny and Rita? Didn't want to think about them either; the scene of everyone staring at her in anger at Christmas was painful, their laughing at her even worse.

Trying to push her family from her mind, Mrs. Mango scanned the ceiling wondering why dentists never seemed to look up at their own ceilings and put something more interesting up there, like a picture or something. Or at least fix the stains in the acoustic ceiling, like the one above her right now. She looked at the crisscrosses of aluminum strips that held the panels in place and contemplated the position of the three panels that were fluorescent lights instead of acoustic tile. All of a sudden, she heard a pitter-patter sound in the ceiling and thought, *that sounds just like when we had rats in the attic*. She realized the office was on the second floor of a two-story building, and if there was an attic, it was right above her. She heard the sound again, scrabbling closer and closer, and then saw a form go right across the translucent plastic over the light. An assistant walked past the door and Mrs. Mango tried to get her attention with a "Hey!" but the assistant just chirped "he'll be right back" and kept walking.

The dentist, a small man as pale as the fluorescent lighting, came back in with the crown and saw Mrs. Mango squirming and pointing at the ceiling as the scrabbling sound continued.

The dentist looked up. "Oh, our furry friend is back," he said and looked back down at Mrs. Mango. "Don't worry; we think it is a squirrel or something—it always goes away."

The dentist got back to work in her mouth, trying out the crown before pulling it out to shave it down. Right as he started the drill, the sounds in the ceiling got louder and more frantic. As Mrs. Mango stared up, there was a loud crack, and she saw the panel above her head slip out of its aluminum frame, tilt down towards the floor, and release a rat. The rat fell screeching onto the dentist's head, dug its claws into his thick hair, and then scrambled down his neck. The dentist screamed, and in standing up, stepped down fully on the floor drill control pedal. The drill wound up to warp speed as he flung it away, grabbing for his neck.

"Naw!!!" yelled Mrs. Mango as she tried to roll out of the chair, away from the rat on the dentist's head. She was prevented from getting away because the drill landed in her hair and wound itself up to her scalp. She screamed in pain as her hair was pulled into a tight spiral around the drill. Luckily, in jumping around, the dentist stepped off of the drill pedal. Mrs. Mango pulled on the drill, ripping out a good chunk of hair. She rolled her body off of the chair, scrambled on her hands and knees to the door, and ran out of the office, sobbing.

The rat, scared by the fall and the screams, was frantically looking for a place to hide. After crawling down the dentist's neck, he found an open collar and slid inside where it was at least a little darker. The dental assistants came running into the room and stopped short at the sight of their boss, a quiet, almost passive man, screaming and writhing around, banging into walls and tearing at his clothes.

Mr. Magill was finally going for a checkup after twenty years of no dentists. His back molar was hurting so badly the entire left side of his face was in pain, and his wife had badgered him into getting it taken care of. Just as he got to the door, it whipped open and a woman came bolting out screaming, her eyes and mouth wide open, fear in her eyes and a little stump of a tooth in her mouth. She was bleeding from one side of her head while the hygienic drape streamed out behind her, bouncing on its little chain. Behind her, office staff and other patients were knocking each other down to get to the door, and behind them, he thought he saw the dentist staggering around in circles, screaming and grabbing at his clothes.

Mr. Magill turned around, went home and pulled the molar himself, swearing never to return to a dentist again. He told his wife he'd pull out all his teeth and puree his food before he'd go through whatever that poor woman had gone through.

Mrs. Mango had a hard time eating dinner that night because shreds of flank steak and broccoli kept sticking in the tooth stump left without its crown.

"I can't believe I'm going to have to go back there and get that crown," she said to Mr. Mango, wondering if the dentist could even find the crown or would have to make a new one. "I can't live like this."

Mr. Mango grunted in response, then wiped his mouth with his napkin, and got up from the table. Without saying anything else, he walked into the family room, sat down, and turned the TV on. He didn't even notice the smoke smell anymore. Mrs. Mango followed him and said,

"Are you finished with dinner?"

Mr. Mango mumbled a yes.

"Well, you could at least say thank you for dinner or maybe even think about putting your plate in the sink," she said.

"I don't feel so good," he said, eyes on the TV.

In truth, he did look a little green, but Mrs. Mango ignored that in her anger over his abrupt ending to dinner.

"Oh sure, how convenient, right at the time for dishes," she said, but there wasn't much venom in her tone because, in fact, Mr. Mango never helped with the dishes. He didn't believe men did dishes, and Mrs. Mango had never seen other men doing the dishes except on TV, so she didn't really believe men did dishes either.

"And I suppose you aren't going to finish fixing that door either," Mrs. Mango said, motioning to the wall unit door that Mr. Mango had off its hinges. One of the hinges had pulled out of the side of the unit leaving the door dangling. Mr. Mango had taken off the door and hinge and was in the middle of repairing the screw holes inside the unit so that he could reattach it. He gave his wife a dark look; she was the one that made him stop in the middle of the project for dinner.

Mrs. Mango went back to the kitchen and sat down at the table. In fact, she had been finished as well, but to make a point she ate some more off of her plate and then finished off Mr. Mango's plate as well. Then she clanged the dishes around as she cleaned up the kitchen, hoping the banging noise would remind her husband that he was sitting there doing nothing while she was working.

After Mrs. Mango threw in a load of laundry, sorted the mail, replaced a light bulb, and set up the coffee maker for the morning, she walked back into the family room intending to sit down with the latest Ladies' Home Journal. There were some interesting-looking recipes in there, and Kathy Lee Gifford was on the front, and she always liked to see what Kathie Lee was up to.

Mrs. Mango sat down on the couch and looked at

Mr. Mango in his easy chair. He was pale and sweaty and breathing hard. "What is going on?" she asked. "You don't look so good."

"I don't feel good at all," he said in between labored breaths. "I think I'm going to throw up."

"Don't even think it was my flank steak; I know you don't like it so much but there was nothing wrong with it," she said. "Maybe you got an air bubble in your stomach."

"No, no, not that," he wheezed. "My chest hurts too; it's like an elephant is sitting on it."

Mrs. Mango frowned, thinking that it was just another one of Mr. Mango's exaggerations, but in fact he looked like this was for real. "Maybe I should call Danny," she said.

"Yeah, go ahead," he said. "And while you're at it, call Christine and see if she's going to be home soon."

When the paramedics arrived, Mrs. Mango noticed that one of them was the tall young guy who had been on the scene at the big house on Daisy Street. He was a reminder of something too weird for her to even think about, so she directed her comments towards the other paramedic, a mid-thirties man with a Fu Manchu mustache and beard and several sets of beads around his neck.

"My son said we should call you right away," she said. "He said to tell you that Joe is probably having a heart attack and we should get him to the hospital immediately."

The Daisy Street paramedic was already taking vital signs and asking Mr. Mango about his symptoms.

"My son is a doctor, so he knows what he is talking about," she continued. "His wife is an attorney—don't you think that is a great combination? So if anyone even thinks about suing him, there she is to defend him for free!"

"Ma'am, we need to take your husband to the hospital right away. We are going to St. Barnaby's and you can meet us there."

They whisked Mr. Mango out on the stretcher, and

Mrs. Mango was left to follow. Unable to reach Christine, she realized she'd have to drive herself so she grabbed her purse and went outside to get into the car. A crowd had gathered on the sidewalk near the ambulance, and Mrs. Mango saw several neighbors craning their necks to catch a glimpse of Joe on the stretcher, now inside the ambulance.

"Hi, Ethel," she called out. "Can't talk right now, I'm following the ambulance to the hospital. It looks like Joe is having a heart attack."

As Mrs. Mango backed her car into the street, the crowd parted to let her drive away, and she looked in her rearview mirror to see them. She felt like someone famous, all those people watching her!

Mrs. Mango circled the hospital parking garage, looking for a double spot. For most of her adult life her driving consisted of local errands and going to work (now to volunteer jobs) and none of those trips involved freeways or tight parking garages. She passed spot after spot, all of them looking too narrow to fit her Buick into. How in the world anyone made the turn and slid into slots the width of a slice of bread was beyond her. Finally, on Level Eight, she found a double spot and eased the car into it, taking up exactly half of both spots. She would return to find an angry note and a couple new dents.

After waiting in two wrong lines in the emergency room, she was finally directed to Mr. Mango. She found him in a curtained-off section of a big room, attached to enough cords and wires to connect him to Mars. She reached for the sheet to cover his chest; it was really too much to look at, all that gray and black hair, not to mention the moles that seem to arrive with the AARP card.

The nurse grabbed at her arm. "Don't touch that! We don't want to disturb the electrodes."

Mrs. Mango rolled her eyes. "Sorry. Just trying to keep him, uh, warm."

Mr. Mango looked to the side and shook his head slightly. He was staring death in the face, and she was worried about covering him up?

"Well?" she said, looking back and forth between Mr. Mango and the nurse.

"I had a heart attack," said Mr. Mango, "and they are checking how bad."

The curtain snapped back, and a young woman bustled in, dressed in scrubs and a white coat with all sorts of stuff hanging out of her pockets.

"Hello, Mrs. Mango?" she said, glancing at Mrs. Mango.

Mrs. Mango nodded.

"I'm Dr. Miller. Your husband is a lucky one tonight. He was smart to get in here right away. We've got some further testing to do before we know what we are looking at, but he definitely had a heart attack."

Dr. Miller started firing more questions at Mr. Mango as Mrs. Mango tried not to look at that mess of chest hair and electrodes. She focused on the doctor. Young. Young was the first thing that sprang to mind. She didn't look much over eighteen, for crying out loud. Had they gotten the Doogie Howser of St. Barnaby's? Probably gave them the brand new doctor 'cause of their low-budget healthcare plan. It was worse than nothing, because you got nothing but paid anyway.

Mrs. Mango's cell phone rang. Must be Danny checking in. She fumbled in her purse to try to find the phone.

Dr. Miller stopped talking and gave her a dirty look. "We don't allow cell phones to be on in here," she said, gesturing at a sign of a cell phone with a red slash over it.

"Sorry, sorry," mumbled Mrs. Mango. She still couldn't find the phone, and the ridiculous Jailhouse Rock ringtone that Michael had put on for a joke was blaring into the emergency room. Finally, she dumped the purse onto the foot of the bed, knocking half the contents to the floor. As a brush, lipstick, Kleenex, mints, and a packet of coupons bounced on the floor, Mrs. Mango spotted the phone under her wallet, grabbed it, and answered it.

Mr. Mango and Dr. Miller stared at her in disbelief.

"Hello? Danny, yes, I'm here," she shouted into the phone. Mrs. Mango never believed that the other person could hear her without shouting.

The nurse sidled up to Mrs. Mango. "You need to shut that off," she said.

Mrs. Mango covered the bottom of the phone, "It's our son Danny. It's okay, he's a doctor."

Mr. Mango snapped, "Shut it off, Elsie!"

Machines started beeping.

"See what she does to me?" Mr. Mango pointed at Mrs. Mango. "*That* is why I had a heart attack. I can't take it anymore."

"Danny, I'll call you back, they are getting angry for some reason. What? He's okay. He had a heart attack. I'll call you back."

She poked at the phone to hit 'end' and looked around the cubicle. "What? I got off the phone. No need to get all huffy."

Just then, Christine appeared around the curtain, eyes frantic. "Dad! Are you okay?" she said, stopping short of the bed.

"Still kickin'," said Mr. Mango, but his voice trembled a little as he said it. Christine's concern scared him in a way that Mrs. Mango's business-as-usual demeanor had not.

****

Dear Raul,

I can't believe it. Joe had a heart attack three days ago. It didn't really hit me until last night that he could have died. I don't know what the delayed reaction is about, but all of a sudden, it became real. And I have been a mess since. And now, I don't know how to sit here in my time with you, knowing he's out there with a bad heart. It feels like my fault, like somehow he knows about these letters, and it has broken his heart.

I'm back. I just had myself a cry right there. In fact, it seems like that's all I do anymore. Like all the tears I never bothered to turn loose over the years are now forcing their way out. I need to go early today; talk to you next week.

Elsie

CHAPTER 19
The Cloud

Mr. Mango stepped down off of the three-rung ladder he had positioned at the end of the family room window and stared up in satisfaction. "There. That's been bugging your mother forever," he said to his son Danny, who had just arrived to check on his dad. Mr. Mango motioned at the corner of the window. "Curtain rod bracket was loose and leaning, whole curtain was crooked because of it. Just needed a couple of mollies."

"Maybe you shouldn't have been up on a ladder, exerting yourself," said Danny.

Mr. Mango gave a wave of disgust, picked up his small toolbox and the ladder and returned them to the garage. When he got back, he sank into his easy chair and turned the TV sound up to better hear the football game. Or to drown out Danny.

"I know you're busy. You didn't need to rush on down here," said Mr. Mango, digging into a bag of corn chips he had grabbed on his way back from the garage.

Danny peered at his dad, looking for signs he was unwell. He looked the same.

"Dad, you had a heart attack. I just want to make sure you are recovering all right," Danny said, sagging back against the couch and staring at the TV while he talked. Danny and his father followed the unwritten rule of male communication, never looking at each other while talking about sensitive issues. "And I doubt those chips are on your recommended eating list."

"I'm fine. I know you're a doctor, but I got a doctor and he's says I'm fine. And not for nuthin' but you're a dermatologist."

Danny sighed. His wife, Rita, had predicted exactly this conversation, but he had to try, right?

"You see Michael lately?" Mr. Mango said, hoping

to take the focus off of himself.

"Last week. They're about to launch a new product so he's working extra hard these days, but I got a quick beer with him."

Mr. Mango snorted. "New product. Not something that actually exists in real life, right?" Mr. Mango had a limited understanding of the tech business and didn't really understand what his second son did for a living. Or how it possibly made him money, which it did. In large amounts.

"A lot of tech stuff is, you know, online or digital," said Danny. "It doesn't have to be something you actually buy in a box."

"Yeah, what's that mean? Probably that it's in the 'cloud,' whatever the hell *that* is," said Mr. Mango.

Danny wasn't sure himself exactly what the cloud was.

"Does anyone actually know what the cloud is or where it is or where all the information goes?" Mr. Mango asked. "Straight into the government's data base, that's where!"

"I don't think that is how it works," said Danny, moving a stack of magazines and a couple of empty soda cans over so he could prop his legs on the coffee table.

"Ha! Prove it isn't. It is all a conspiracy. And guess who is responsible? Al Gore! You got that right, Al Gore. Started the internet with all this in mind. Wanted to know everything about every American, like it was his business."

"Dad, Al Gore's a Democrat; it is the Republicans who are the ones who love the Patriot Act and want data on everyone."

"Kid, I got news for you. There is no such thing as Republican or Democrat. It is all a scheme the politicians dreamed up so we'd all believe we have a two-party system. They are all alike. They just get in these secret rooms and draw straws to see who will play the Republican and who will play the Democrat. And then they bring government to a halt, all while getting paid by *us,* the dummies of the world. We just hand over our money to them for doing shit-all up there in Washington. They eat, drink, and hump on our money and don't do shit for the country except gather more information about how to keep us asleep. Al Gore knows what kind of beer I drink and how much, and he's got me by the balls. It's the old magician's trick. Distract with your left hand, 'Hey, the glaciers are melting!' and do the magic with your right hand, 'Hey, where'd your money go?'

"Al Gore isn't in government anymore, Dad."

"That's what he *wants* you to think. See!? He's brilliant, that scheming son of a bitch. He's just behind the scenes now."

"You really believe that?"

"Goddamn right I do," Mr. Mango was getting worked up now. He took a gulp of his soda. "And while those bastard politicians are living it up on our tax dollars, what do think the terrorists are doing? Fully organized. Fully focused on one thing, which is how much they hate us. They don't have to pass a law or pretend to try to pass a law. If they want to do something, they just do it. If we could just point them at the politicians and not regular citizens, maybe we could clean that shit out and get us a real government back."

"I know there are some politicians who are in it for the wrong reasons, but you really don't think there are some who are in it because they care?" Danny knew he should be trying to calm his dad down, but he couldn't resist one question.

"Good God, no. Any morality they might have had is wiped clean by the oath of office. Christ, do you really think they are focused? Every week a new one is found to be cheating on his wife or putting pictures of his dick on the internet. You don't beat ISIS putting your dick on the internet! Those guys are living in caves and eating dirt and bugs so they can maintain a sharp focus on one thing: killing us."

Danny shook his head, realizing there was no

arguing with the old man.

"Took out a permit to carry concealed. The bastards aren't going to get me. Or your mother."

"Dad, you didn't! Why do you need to carry a gun?"

Mr. Mango shook his head at his son's naïveté. "You don't think they already have terrorist cells all over this country? They do! You know what they're called? 7-Eleven."

"Dad, that's ridiculous. 7-Eleven is a convenience store, not a terrorist organization."

"Yep. Most of those 7-Eleven employees are foreign, haven't you noticed?"

"Doesn't make them terrorists."

"Prove they're not."

Danny looked down and closed his eyes. There was no arguing with his dad.

"Do you keep it loaded?" Danny asked, looking up again.

"Of course I keep it loaded! What's the point of having a gun for protection if it isn't loaded? You think the asswipe that breaks into my house is going to wait while I load the gun? Jesus, sometimes I think you have no brains at all."

Danny decided this conversation could only end with another heart attack and that there was zero chance he'd get his dad to see reason, so he just shook his head and mumbled that he was going to the kitchen for a sandwich.

"Don't bother your mother," Mr. Mango said before Danny was out the door. "She's not really herself these days."

Once Danny was gone, Mr. Mango slid his hand under the easy chair to check for his gun. Yep, still there, ready to go once the attacks started. Kids. Didn't know shit about the world.

In the kitchen, Mrs. Mango remained seated at the table with Christine while Danny made himself a sandwich.

Things were definitely off kilter; Mrs. Mango never let her sons make themselves food, not when they were kids and not when they were grown-ups. Until now. He put the sandwich on a plate, added some chips, and sat down with them.

"Where's mine?" joked Christine, looking up from her computer where she was busily tapping away.

"You want a sandwich?" Mrs. Mango started to get up.

"No, just wanted him to offer," said Christine, pulling her ponytail twistie out, rearranging her hair, and retying the ponytail.

"So, is Dad doing what he's supposed to?" Danny asked, chewing.

"Don't talk with your mouth full," Mrs. Mango said, almost on auto-pilot.

Christine shrugged. "Yes and no. Mostly, I guess." Christine looked at the clock on the microwave; she was due to meet Sarah in an hour and wanted to leave enough time to freshen her makeup. She finally was regularly wearing make-up and it was killing her mother.

Mrs. Mango gulped her tea. "I just can't believe it. A heart attack!" Mrs. Mango's eyes had bags under them, and her hair was not in its normal waves. Instead, it looked like she had forgotten half her curlers, leaving some parts curled, some parts straight, some parts somewhere in between.

"Mom, it's not all bad," said Danny. "He survived it and now can do the things that will help him be even healthier. Think of it like a wake-up call."

"But we had already started! We were walking and cutting down on carbs and everything," Mrs. Mango said. "And now he's going to be an invalid. Forever."

Danny shook his head. "Not at all. He can go back to doing just about everything. He'll just focus more on healthy behaviors, which is good."

Mrs. Mango looked doubtful.

Christine nodded. "I think that is a good approach.

Think of it as a good motivator to be more healthy."

"The thing is, those rants of his," said Danny. "They get him so worked up. Maybe it's time to turn the 24-hour Fox News station off."

They all looked up at the small TV on the counter that was brightly broadcasting its message of fear.

Mrs. Mango got up and turned off the TV. "Fine with me." Now if only she could turn off the message of fear in her head, the one that said she had broken her husband's heart.

Mrs. Mango broke her stare at the dark TV and went to the refrigerator and grabbed a bag of green beans, which she rinsed and then brought with a bowl to the table.

"So, Mom," said Christine as Mrs. Mango sat down and started popping off the ends of the green beans. "Your mom was Jane and her mom was Pearl, but I don't remember her dad's name. What was your granddad's first name?"

"Buzz," said Mrs. Mango. "What are you doing there?"

"It's a way to trace your family tree," said Christine, sneaking a glance at her mother to see if she was upset, remembering her dad's advice not to dig into the past with her mother, but too fascinated by the research to stop.

"Huh," said Mrs. Mango, tossing another bean into the bowl beside her.

"Buzz sounds like a nickname," said Danny. "What was his real name?"

"George," said Mrs. Mango. "George Ingalls."

"How do you get Buzz out of George?" asked Christine.

Mrs. Mango shrugged. "No idea. That was a big family. He had eight brothers and sisters."

Danny stared at his mother; she never had mentioned that. Then again, she never mentioned her family at all. It was one of the unspoken rules absorbed by the Mango children: you just didn't ask or talk about mom's side of the family.

Christine tapped keys for a while and then turned the computer towards her mother. "Look at this, the census from 1930: here's his name, shows him married to Pearl, one daughter Jane."

Mrs. Mango dropped the bean she was holding and pulled the computer towards her. "My goodness, look at that! You've got to be kidding me."

Mrs. Mango peered at the screen and ran her finger along the line of the document showing her grandfather's name. "Yes, he was a laborer. Oh my, I can't believe you can find this stuff on here. And look, it shows where he lived, and that he was married to Pearl."

Mrs. Mango looked up at Christine. "This is amazing. I hadn't thought about Grandpa Ingalls in a long time. He died when I was just a girl, maybe seven years old?" Her eyes softened, as if she was looking beyond the room and into the past. "I used to love visiting them. He would throw me up in the air and laugh and laugh and then we'd walk down the street and he'd buy me penny candy. Probably sounds boring to you but it was such a treat."

Danny looked like he wanted to ask something, but Christine gave him a dagger look, one that said, 'Don't screw this up, I've got her talking.'

"So, looks like your mom was born in 1920," ventured Christine, knowing her mother had been estranged from her own mother for as long as Christine had been alive. She looked down at her computer to hide her guilty eyes, thinking about the secret visit they had made to meet Grandma Walker. She was afraid to look at Danny; maybe he'd give it away. Christine always thought her mother could see right through her to the truth, but she was starting to think maybe that wasn't completely accurate. Her mother had clearly been blindsided by the discovery that she was gay, so maybe she wasn't all-knowing.

"Hmm, that sounds right," said Mrs. Mango, resuming the snap, snap, snapping at the beans.

"And she married your dad in . . . ?"

"Not sure," said Mrs. Mango, standing and scraping the ends of the beans into a grocery bag and picking up the bowl of cleaned beans. She walked to the sink and dumped the grocery bag into the garbage can under the sink and started rinsing the beans.

"And your dad's dad was named?" Christine asked, sensing that the earlier generations of the family held less emotional charge, or at least less negative emotional charge.

"He was William, just like my dad. William, Senior, and his wife was Margaret." Mrs. Mango emptied the beans into a pot, added an inch of water, and set it on the stove.

"And wasn't your dad the first person to own a Model T in your area?" asked Danny.

Mrs. Mango snapped her head towards Danny. "How could you know that?"

Christine wanted to whack Danny over the head with her computer.

"Uh, I don't know, you must have mentioned it," fumbled Danny.

"No, I didn't." Mrs. Mango crossed her arms over her chest and glared at Danny and then at Christine.

Silence.

Mrs. Mango narrowed her eyes at them. "What's going on? What's with the family tree interest?"

Christine shrugged. "I just got interested is all. There are some cool stories. Like our name is supposed to be Mazzocchetti."

"What?" said Danny. "Says who?"

"Dad. He told me about how his grandfather came from Italy and changed the name to Mango."

Mrs. Mango was not to be distracted about Mr. Mango's family. "How did you know about the Model T?" she demanded again, moving closer to Danny and staring down at him with narrowed eyes.

Danny shrugged. "I don't know, someone must have mentioned it."

Christine didn't look up from her computer. Were they busted? Was her mother to find out they went behind her back to meet their grandmother? Because of course that is who told them the story.

Mr. Mango ambled into the kitchen looking for more food.

Mrs. Mango transferred her glare to him. "So. I see you've been talking behind my back."

Mr. Mango stood in the tractor light of her stare. "What?"

Mrs. Mango tapped her foot in a fast staccato. "Telling the kids about my family. Behind my back."

Mr. Mango glanced at Danny and Christine, both looking down, and waved his hand in a casual dismissal. "Ahh, of course I probably did over the years. Nothing big. Couple names, couple good stories, right?" He made his voice easy and jokey, and Christine and Danny looked up at him in relief. Sharing secrets was a dangerous business.

"Hmpf!" said Mrs. Mango. "I'll thank you to leave the family stories to me."

"Okay," said Mr. Mango, moving to the cupboard where they kept the cereal and pulling out a box. "Do I have time for one more snack before dinner?"

"Fine," said Mrs. Mango, looking up at the wall clock. "But don't fill up. I have some nice salmon."

The tension in the room seem to float away as Mr. Mango took the box and left the room.

Under the table, Christine texted Danny. "Dad just saved your ass. How could you be such an idiot?"

CHAPTER 20
The Vegevape 6200 Pro Blender Party

Mrs. Mango fussed with the cocktail napkins she had laid out on her dining room table and looked around the room. It was as neat as she ever got it, meaning that things were mostly put away, and the candlesticks and platters that had been displayed on the sideboard since before the kids were born were dusted. The hutch on the opposite wall was crammed with china and crystal that never got used, but looking at it always gave Mrs. Mango a warm feeling inside, like she was a proper homemaker with a cupboard full of the good stuff. A home design expert would probably have recommended taking out fifty percent of the stuff in the room, but Mrs. Mango liked having her things around her.

Although Mrs. Mango was technically hosting a party, the real hostess was Dawn Starbrite, a blond blur of light flying between the kitchen and the dining room. Dawn had taken control, and Flora and Velma, the ones who had talked her into using her home for a Vegevape 6200 Pro blender party, were not here yet.

The kitchen door flew open, and Dawn charged through it carrying a large platter of cut-up vegetables. She whirled around and made it back through the door before it swung shut then reappeared with containers of fruit. Her hands moving faster than a Vegas dealer, Dawn arranged the table with several industrial-looking blenders, the vegetables, and fruit. Then, she started arranging cups that had odd-looking tops, tops with little screens and inverted cones sticking up.

"You are just going to *love* this stuff, I promise you," chirped Dawn. "I was depressed and fat and barely got off the couch for six years, and then I found veggie vaporizing and look at me now!"

Mrs. Mango dutifully stared as Dawn waved her

hand down her slim body. Dawn wore a silky black shirt, snakeskin pants and high black boots. Her wrists and neck were encircled by stacks of silver, and her platinum blond hair cascaded around her perfectly made-up face. Mrs. Mango had to admit she looked good and she had more energy than a nuclear power plant running at full capacity.

Dawn settled a little ear-to-cheek microphone over her right ear and said, "Check, check, can you hear me clearly?"

Mrs. Mango was less than five feet away and wondered about the need for a microphone in her small dining room but just nodded. The doorbell rang and, relieved to escape, Mrs. Mango pulled off her unnecessary apron and went to let in her guests.

Flora bounded into the house, her arms loaded with bags of fruit, and Velma crowded behind her with a cardboard box marked 'herbs and supplements.' Not for the first time, Mrs. Mango wondered how these two 80-something-year-olds had so much energy. And bounciness.

"Don't you both look nice," said Mrs. Mango, noticing their outfits.

"Chico's had a sale," said Velma, twirling around to flare her black skirt. She had on a knit boat neck shirt with a chunky silver set of necklaces over it. Flora had on taupe linen capri pants with a dark green satin wraparound shirt, also topped off with a chunky set of necklaces, but hers were gold. Both of them had on sneakers. Their commitment to fashion stopped at uncomfortable feet.

"Yes, we ran that salesgirl ragged, didn't we, Vel?" said Flora. Then she held up her bag with a pineapple sticking out. "Where do you want this?"

"Dining room," Mrs. Mango said faintly. What had she gotten herself into?

Mrs. Mango stayed by the door ushering in the rest of the guests while Flora and Velma took their offerings to the blender goddess. The chatter from the room grew intense, and Mrs. Mango felt like she was stuck in the exotic bird wing of the zoo. Cackles and crows and high pitched excitement were no match for the thin walls of her house.

Soon the dining room was filled with neighbors, Christine and Sarah, and a number of Mrs. Mango's friends who had been guilted into coming by the fact the Mrs. Mango had gone to their product parties. More guests spilled into the living room.

Dawn greeted the guests with a big 'Hello!' and was off on her spiel. She talked so fast and with such excitement that Mrs. Mango didn't completely follow it all, but the gist of it, if she got it right, was that the contraption Dawn was selling wasn't even a blender; it was so much more powerful that it wasn't correct to call it that. Its blades were so fast that they *vaporized* the fruits and vegetables, and then all you had to do was *inhale* the vapor. You got all the nutritional value with none of the calories.

The ladies were swooning and screaming at the idea. Mrs. Mango wondered if there was a brain cell in the bunch. There was no way inhaling something gave you nutrition. Maybe Dawn was so thin because she wasn't actually eating.

She ventured a question as to how this could actually happen, and Dawn said, "Great question, Elsie!" Mrs. Mango immediately regretted the question because Dawn started spouting science gibberish. How the essential part of the vegetable is such a small molecule that it can float in the air once liberated from the casing of the actual vegetable. Or some such.

Dawn finished her twenty-minute presentation, seemingly without once taking a breath, and pressed each person to come try the vapor. Mrs. Mango hung back, ending up in the back of the room with Flora and Velma, each of whom already had their own Vegevape and were letting others inhale before they did.

"Elsie, this stuff will energize you like you don't believe," enthused Velma. "I took a couple of puffs before I came over.

"Mm hmm." Mrs. Mango thought it was just so

much snake oil.

"How're you sleeping?" demanded Flora.

"What? Fine. Pretty well," said Mrs. Mango. "Well, actually, not great. Always waking up to check on Joe."

"And how's your energy?" asked Velma.

"Decent, really, actually pretty good," said Mrs. Mango, thinking that her energy was too fueled by anxiety these days.

"And your poops? Are they curved or straight? Do they float?" said Flora, putting her face close to Mrs. Mango's.

"What?!" exclaimed Mrs. Mango, stepping backwards. What was wrong with these ladies? Asking personal questions like that. The next thing you know they'd be asking about her sex life.

"Yeah, and how's the old libido?" chimed in Flora. "You know, some good vapor and a little cream, and we'll get your chi *flowing*." She laughed as she pointed below her belt. "Although Joe probably has to wait a while since the heart attack. Is he ready again yet?"

"If your poop floats, you're eating too much fat," said Velma. "And it needs to be shaped like an 's' too. How's your shape?"

"Uh, I, uh," Mrs. Mango could not believe she was having this conversation.

Christine floated back to her mom. "I might just have to buy one of these!" she enthused.

Mrs. Mango stared at her daughter. Christine hated stuff like this. She had agreed to stick around for it only when Mrs. Mango said she could invite Sarah.

Christine giggled, "Smelled great!"

Sarah joined her, oblivious of the cold stare coming from Mrs. Mango. "Delicious. Without even eating."

Velma grabbed Mrs. Mango's arm. "Come on, your turn to inhale."

"I inhaled, unlike a certain past president," Christine giggled again. Flora, Christine, and Sarah all laughed, like it was the greatest joke ever.

Mrs. Mango found herself at the front of the room, a black plastic cone over her mouth. The cone attached to a cup below that was swirling with a bright green smoke. 'Dear God in heaven, save me,' she thought to herself as the smell drifted up into her nose. She tried to hold her breath and not take any in, but Dawn had the cup over her mouth in a death grip and was pinching off her nose so she finally she had to fully breathe in.

Hmm. Not bad. A pleasant kind of appley, lettucey kind of taste. Or was it a smell? And something else, which she couldn't put a name to. A sort of herb, probably. Maybe thyme? Rosemary? She let herself breathe in again. What could it hurt? At least it wasn't adding calories to ruin her diet.

A half hour later, Mr. Mango came home from his dinner at Fresh Choice. He had gone with his buddy Charlie with the idea of eating healthy but, as usual, he had overdone it on the all-you-can-eat pasta bar and ice cream. He had stayed away until the party was supposed to be over, but instead his house sounded like a thousand seagulls fighting over a cheeseburger. Before he could turn around and leave, Mrs. Mango grabbed his arm.

"Come try this! It is amazing! You're going to love it, which is good because we bought one." Mrs. Mango's face was red and her eyes were happy in a way Mr. Mango hadn't seen for a long time.

Mrs. Mango flung her arm around Sarah and said, "Isn't it amazing?"

Mr. Mango's eyes widened. She was talking to Sarah? The supposed 'devil who has ruined our daughter'?

Sarah nodded and looked straight at Mr. Mango, "Go up there, have a sniff."

"Yeah, Dad, please, please have something healthy for once," begged Christine.

"Nah, I'm good," said Mr. Mango, making his way out of the room. He shut himself in their bedroom and looked for a ballgame on TV.

The frenzied laughter and general maniacal behavior lasted for several more hours.

Most of the partygoers awoke in the morning feeling foggy-headed. Most of them also wondered how they could have been so quickly convinced to buy a $350 blender when they already owned a blender. Velma and Flora already had the secret, which is that in order for the Vegevape to have the 'fun' effect, you had to purchase the supplemental herbs to add to the mix. Velma had enough of a past to guess what was in the supplemental herbs and was happy that it was legal now. The guests would all find out too, since almost every one of them had signed up for the Boost Your Juice club, thus tacking on a monthly fee of $50 for shipments of extra supplements and herbs. Mrs. Mango had paid for the blender, and since they had hosted the party, they got a free half-year of Boost Your Juice club membership.

Christine was packing her lunch in the dim dawn light while Mrs. Mango sipped on her first cup of coffee. One soft light over the sink was lit, but otherwise the kitchen was dark and still half asleep, like its inhabitants.

"I can't believe how fun that party was," enthused Christine, sticking the cold pack in the bottom of her lunch bag and adding a sandwich on top of it.

"Mm hmm," said Mrs. Mango. She was trying to remember everything that had happened. Why did it all seem so hazy? Was the Alzheimer's starting?

"Thanks for being so nice to Sarah," said Christine, turning to face her mother. "That means so much to me, to us."

Mrs. Mango felt a weight settle in her chest. She had a floaty memory of her arm around Sarah's shoulder. How had *that* happened? She felt a hot flash coming on, and the tears that seemed so close to the edge of her eyes these days threatened to start pouring. *Just hang on till Christine leaves* she begged herself. She didn't want Christine to see how close she was to a breakdown. She was sure she was losing her sanity and was fighting to keep that to herself.

"Does that mean . . .?" Christine trailed off.

Mrs. Mango made the mistake of looking into her daughter's eyes, and the hope lighting them up was almost too much to bear. The little girl with the happy brown eyes, the giggly, full-of-life sparkplug that had been the delight of her mother's life was right there, shining out at her. After three boys, it had been so much fun to have a girl, especially one so full of joy. Her girl was still there, and seeing that was not going to help. Mrs. Mango tightened her insides, like pulling the strings on a corset.

"I just can never accept this," Mrs. Mango said, looking straight towards the window. "She seems like a very nice person, but I just can't, well, I just can't."

"Why are you being like this!?" cried Christine, in a rare outburst at her mother.

"Why are *you* being like this?" Mrs. Mango said.

"Why won't you accept me? This is who I am, this is what I want," said Christine, zipping her lunch pack with force and stomping out of the kitchen.

Mrs. Mango felt a strange reverberation in the room, as if time had shifted for the briefest of seconds and it was her voice saying those same words. *This is what I want.*

Were the Mango women doomed to want what they couldn't have? Mrs. Mango tightened her lips and pushed images of a sparkplug little girl and an older, long-ago image of a passionate teenaged girl out of her brain.

CHAPTER 21
Unsettled

Mr. Mango stared at the phone, letting it fall to his lap where it landed on his open wallet. He was sitting at the small computer desk in the corner of the family room, a place of order and accountability. The accordion folder with paid bills neatly arranged sat on his left and a cup full of pens and pencils on his right. Otherwise, the desk held only the laptop computer and a slim scratch pad. Clutter might build up in other areas of the house but not the desk. Mr. Mango was selectively obsessed with neatness in two places: his tool bench and the desk. He had just hung up with a debt collection agency and was thinking that maybe it would have been better if he had died from that heart attack. All the hospital bills and insurance statements and paperwork that blossomed from his 'cardiac event' were threatening to cause another one. And now, this. A collection agency! He had paid his bills on time and in full his whole life. He had an organized filing system and could show you the date and payment of any bill stretching back thirty years. How could this have happened? Actually, he could see how this happened. It seemed like every single person who worked in a hospital sent a separate bill. Not to mention the ambulance. This wasn't a health care system; it was a health dare system. As in, 'dare to let your health depend on it.'

Mrs. Mango walked into the living room and swept up the empty plate and glass Mr. Mango had left on the coffee table.

"Holy crap, Elsie," said Mr. Mango. "We are in debt collection! How did that happen?"

Mrs. Mango stopped and stared back at him. "How could that be? You never miss a bill. We paid everything. And then some."

Mr. Mango shook his head. "You sure you gave me

every bill that came in?"

"Of course I did. I always put them right on the desk."

Mr. Mango held his chest. "I don't feel so good."

"What happened? How do you know? It's too soon; don't they take months to turn bills over?"

Mr. Mango grabbed the pad of paper on the desk. He waved it at Mrs. Mango. "Some kind of lab," he looked at the pad of paper. "TechLab America, it's called, says we missed their bill and now our credit rating's gonna be ruined. All those years of perfect bill-paying screwed up."

"How much?" asked Mrs. Mango.

"Eight hundred fifty dollars! Had to pay it with the credit card. The guy on the phone was an asshole. I mean, no understanding at all. I told him we never got that bill, and he says not his problem but it is our problem because we were about to get arrested. Arrested!"

Mrs. Mango gasped and clattered the plate and glass back down. "No!" She stumbled backwards and felt for the couch and sank onto it.

"Calm down, we won't be. I paid it, but Jesus Christ. Is there no understanding here? We didn't even get a bill, and we're gonna be arrested? Is that how this country works now? Have a heart attack, go straight to jail. For crissakes. Obama has ruined this country. Just ruined it."

Mrs. Mango still kind of liked Obama, but she'd never admit it to Mr. Mango. And now was not the time to get into an argument—but she doubted it was Obama's fault that they didn't get a bill.

Mr. Mango pulled himself up from the chair and lumbered over to the pile of magazines on the side table. "Any chance a bill got stuck somewhere it shouldn't?"

"No chance. I sort the mail the second I take it out of the mailbox," said Mrs. Mango.

Mr. Mango glared at Mrs. Mango, looming over her. "Never saw anything from that lab. Elsie, get your affairs in order. Health care in this country is done for.

Done for. The politicians have screwed us over."

Mrs. Mango sighed. Once he mentioned politicians, she was in for it.

"And you know that there's gonna be nothing left in Social Security soon. Nothin'. So don't count on *that* money. Better make sure, you come down with something, it's something on your skin so Danny can treat, because he's it. A son for a doctor is all we got for health. We can't count on anything from the government or insurance. 'Insurance!' My ass, 'insurance.' Insurance is just another word for government, which is just another word for 'take my money and give me shit back.'"

Mrs. Mango stood up, grabbed the plate and glass, and tried to slip out of the room.

"You know our kids are the first generation that won't live longer than their parents? You know that, right? You know why they're saying that? Because there's no health care to take care of them."

Mrs. Mango was pretty sure it was because so many people were overweight these days, but there was no arguing now. She just had to ride out the rant.

****

"Elsie! Elsie! *El*sie!" Two days later, Mr. Mango stomped through the house looking for his wife, waving the phone. Finally he found her in the garage, where she was half-heartedly putting Christmas decorations away. It was hard to do because all the boxes still seemed full, but she hadn't actually put anything back in them yet. The boxes were all still so full because, although she added to her collection of decorations every year, she never threw out the decorations she didn't use. The boxes held the accumulation of forty-three years of marriage and still contained the kids' Christmas art from elementary school, even though her oldest, Joseph Jr., was forty.

"Jesus Christ, I couldn't find you. Someone stole the credit card!" he said, waving the phone around.

Mrs. Mango jumped up. "Where's my purse?! Did they get my whole wallet?"

"No, no," Mr. Mango said in disgust. "They got the *numbers*, not the actual card. Just bought six iPads and five iPhones at a store in Colorado." He didn't even mention the rest of the charges. There are all sorts of things you can buy in Colorado.

Mrs. Mango grabbed at her chest. "Oh my God, those things are like $800, right?" She sank back onto the floor. "What are we going to do?"

Mr. Mango shook his head at her. The woman understood nothing. "I just got off the phone with Visa. *They* called *us* to see if we were making the purchase. I told them, no, of course not. I still use my first iPhone for crying out loud. But they got to send us a new card."

"Oh my goodness," Mrs. Mango said, still trying to understand.

"They wanted to know, did anyone ask us for the numbers lately?"

She shook her head no.

"Did we order anything online? I mean, you don't normally, and I didn't, but they asked."

"Nooooo," she said, thinking.

"When was the last time you used the credit card?" He was sure this was somehow her fault. Some dumb thing she bought, some scam she fell for.

"Did you buy any magazines lately? Give money to any jackasses at the front door pretending to be school kids raising money for a field trip?" His voice was hoarse in anger.

"No. I haven't used it in a while. Oh wait, what about the collection agency? You used a credit card with them."

Mr. Mango rolled his eyes. "That was *paying a bill*, not buying something." Sometimes he wondered if Mrs. Mango had any sense at all.

"Well, how do you know you were paying a bill? We never got that bill. Maybe *you* got scammed." Mrs.

Mango was tired of her husband always blaming her for stuff. Always acting like she was some kind of idiot. Who was the one who finished a year of college? Not him.

Mr. Mango stared at Mrs. Mango as the wheels in his head started turning. Without a word, he spun around and charged to the computer. Typed in 'collection scam' and found 42,700,000 results (in .31 seconds, Google helpfully told him). He clicked on one with a sick feeling that Mrs. Mango was right. Sure enough, it was like the caller from the so-called collection agency had read his script from this site. Intimidation, threats, a demand to pay immediately, by credit card. It was all there. No number to call them back. He typed the lab name into the Google search window. Goddammit. No TechLab America existed.

Mr. Mango sat back in his chair, his hand going to his chest. That was becoming an automatic reaction to everything, as if he could hold his heart steady from the outside.

Jesus Christ on the Cross. Those motherfuckers. They were not getting away with this. Mr. Mango picked up the phone and called the police.

Dear Raul,

I'm feeling very churned up inside these days. Very unsettled. Like nothing is normal anymore. Joe got scammed (and tried to blame me!). And that Vegevape party messed everything up. Somehow I've given Christine the impression that I'm okay with her, what's the word for it, lifestyle. I think there must have been something in the supplements they put in that thing because my brain got all fuzzy and Sarah seemed nice and not at all a problem. And then in the morning, it all seemed wrong again. Or maybe I'm just losing my mind. There. I said it. I can say it to you. I think I might be going crazy. This is even worse than when the menopausal stuff started, and, believe me, that was bad. One moment I feel okay, the next I'm in tears and unable to stop.

And it is hard to know what is going to happen with Joe. He isn't allowed to drive his delivery truck for six weeks, at least. There is a lot of heavy lifting involved, and I don't know if he'll ever be able to do that again. It is hard to have him around the house all day, and, yet, I know he needs to rest and do the exercises that will get him back in shape. And he's refusing to go to the heart class he's supposed to go to. I don't like having our regular routines so thrown off.

Mrs. Mango sat back on the toilet, closed her eyes, and tried to summon up one of her favorite Raul memories, but the image of Joe in the emergency room bed, looking so vulnerable, kept creeping in. She opened her eyes, shook her head like she was shaking out cobwebs, and closed her eyes again. Trying to summon up the image of Raul the night she met him, she instead saw Joe the night she met *him.* Handsome in a completely different way than Raul, and the first night she had actually had a bit of fun since word of Raul's death reached her. She remembered the thrill of his interest in her, remembered how every girl there wanted him to ask her to dance but it was Elsie who somehow drew his attention. Maybe because she didn't care to chase him like the rest of the girls, didn't seem silly and boy crazy. Mrs. Mango shook her head, banishing the image, and tried again. She could imagine walking with Raul on the beach at night and then, out of nowhere there was the young Joe, smooth smile, laughing eyes, and then all of a sudden there was Joe, sitting in the living room, sweaty and green. She opened her eyes again. Was that a memory or premonition? Should she go to the living room right now and check on him?

Mrs. Mango looked at her watch. Darn it, she was almost out of time. This was the most unsatisfying Sunday morning.

Even though she knew it was irrational, she was

annoyed with Raul for the first time in many, many years. After she had the news of his death, there had been months of tears. And then the anger. First at her parents and then finally at Raul for trying so hard to prove himself to her parents that he got himself killed. And of course at her country for sending all those boys over there to die. And then many more months of tears. And then a snap decision to marry Joe and show her parents they had no control over her. They hadn't approved of Joe either, and it pleased Mrs. Mango to hurt her parents, even though it didn't balance out in any way.

Annoyed, Mrs. Mango just wanted to be out of the room. Before the half hour was even up, she hastily shoved the unsigned letter and box away.

CHAPTER 22
Good Intentions

"Elsie!" Mr. Mango called for his wife, angry and sure she knew the source of it. "Elsie? Where are you?" He stomped through the house, turning on lights. Where was she? Calling bingo? Walking shelter dogs? Clerking at the Hospice Shop? What new hell was she putting him through with all this volunteering? And why were there no dinner smells? He looked at his watch. Yep, six o'clock and no one home. No one around to explain the pile of unmentionables on the front porch.

Mr. Mango opened the refrigerator and stared into it. No covered casserole dish ready for the oven. Nothing that said 'dinner is not far off.' He yanked open the meat drawer and pulled out a half-eaten pack of salami and then found a bag of individually wrapped little cheese rounds and pulled that out too. He dumped five cheese rounds on a plate, added the rest of the salami, tucked an unopened beer under his arm and headed to the family room. Halfway through the six o'clock news, he heard his wife come in.

"Oh, hi, you are already eating," Mrs. Mango said, peeking into the family room.

"What is that crap on the front porch?" Mr. Mango demanded, sticking the last cheese round in his mouth.

"I'm collecting items for the women's shelter," said Mrs. Mango. "They literally have nothing."

"So that's why," Mr. Mango spluttered. "That's why there are big bales of *personal products* on our porch? There's no other place to collect those?"

Mrs. Mango laughed. "Bales, that's a funny word. The bag isn't *that* big. And don't worry, I'll bring them in. No need to get bent out of shape. Of course, they need *everything.* Shampoo, soap, deodorant, clothes. *Personal products.*"

"How did our house get to be the drop-off spot?

You don't care that the neighbors see this?"

"I'm just grateful that so many people are contributing," said Mrs. Mango.

"How long is this collection going on?" asked Mr. Mango.

"As long as we need it to," said Mrs. Mango.

"Good Christ, we're going to have this stuff on our porch all the time?"

"Wow, here I am trying to help someone and you are worried about how our house looks." Mrs. Mango clucked to herself. "If it offends you, I'll put out a big box."

"Please," barked Mr. Mango.

"Are you still hungry or did you eat enough?" Mrs. Mango said, looking at the empty plate in front of Mr. Mango.

"Still hungry. Do you have something for dinner?"

"I ate at my meeting, but I brought you a salad," said Mrs. Mango.

Mr. Mango dropped his head to his chest. "A salad."

"You are supposed to be eating healthy!" said Mrs. Mango. "And it has chicken on it. I'll go get it."

Mr. Mango turned to look at Mrs. Mango as she left the room. Was she trying to turn him into a woman? Sanitary pads and salads? Next thing the rooms would be painted pink.

Christine smiled at Sarah across the tiny table in the bar section of The Cheesecake Factory. "I love this place," she said, leaning in so Sarah could hear her over the clatter of the crowd. "Glad you picked it."

"Me too," said Sarah. "So many choices!" She held up the thick laminated menu book.

Christine sighed, flipping through her own book of a thousand choices. "I know. Too many. I'm just going off the skinny menu tonight. Maybe that'll narrow it down. We should tell my parents to come here; I can't seem to get my dad to eat healthy and there are so many healthy options here."

Sarah nodded. "How's he doing with his diet?"

"Hah! You'd have better luck getting a duck to moo instead of quack. And my mom, bless her, I love her food but she never met a stick of butter she didn't love."

Sarah smiled in support. The first rule of dealing with a person's family vents is to support the complaints but not actually *add* to the complaints. A sort of 'yes, that's hard' combined with a 'but I still love your mom/dad/brother' kind of attitude.

Around them, waiters maneuvered their trays through groups of people who hovered over occupied tables and stared intently at the diners in an attempt to hurry them into finishing and leaving. The dining room was dark and cavernous, subtle light coming from the tops of the columns scattered through the room and the bar with its flickering TV's and backlit rows of liquor bottles.

Having finally narrowed down their choices and ordered, Sarah and Christine tapped their glasses together (red wine for Christine, beer for Sarah). "To the end of a good day," said Sarah.

"To us," said Christine, enjoying the way the light from the bar slanted across Sarah's beautiful cheekbones.

Sarah smiled wide, and then her mouth retracted a bit. "Talking about us . . ."

Christine sighed. "I know, I know. It just never seems like a good time."

Sarah nodded in sympathy. "I get it, but . . ."

It had become an old topic. Christine and Sarah were about to tell Christine's parents that they had decided to move in together when her dad had his heart attack. Christine wanted to wait until things calmed down a bit and she was sure he was doing okay. Sarah had been fully supportive of that, but Christine couldn't seem to come up with a way to know he was okay.

"And . . . now my Mom seems like she's kind of losing it," said Christine. "I swear she's been crying in private. Which freaks me out, to tell you the truth. Because

I didn't think she would get that emotional over Dad. She *never* cries. I mean, she's grumpy with him but so chatty-friendly with everyone else that it's weird to think of her crying."

Sarah dug into the hot bread that had just landed on their table, smearing butter over a ripped-open steaming roll. "Well, of course she would be worried about your dad. He had something serious happen. And maybe she just never expected something like that."

"I just don't want to be the one who puts her over the edge," said Christine, taking the buttered roll that Sarah handed her.

"I know, I get it," said Sarah. "But . . ."

Christine was completely sure Sarah was the one for her. She loved the thought of living together, and when she was with Sarah, it seemed obvious and easy. But when she was at home with her parents, it felt like she belonged there. She wasn't sure why it was so hard to leave them. After all, she had lived away at college, and her return home was always intended to be temporary. Save up some money and move into her own apartment. So why was she left with the feeling that she would be removing one leg of a three-legged stool? Why did she feel like her leaving would topple her parents?

"I know, she's a grown woman. I don't know what's wrong with me," said Christine, finishing off the roll. "That's it. I'm telling them tonight!"

Christine felt a firm sense of conviction even while a filament of doubt floated through her head, whispering that her resolve would fail once she was facing her mother.

She pushed the doubt aside to dig in to the Cajun Jambalaya Pasta that had just arrived in front of her. She'd order skinny next time.

By the time Christine got home, her mother was in bed and her father was asleep in his easy chair. In the back of her mind, she knew she had delayed her return enough that this was the likely scenario. In the front of her mind, she allowed herself to be annoyed at her parents for not being available for her news.

Tomorrow for sure, she told herself and went to bed feeling virtuous and relieved all at once.

In the morning, Christine left the house earlier than her normal time with the intention of treating herself to a latte before work. It was just a coincidence that this meant she was gone before her parents were up.

CHAPTER 23

A Dream Comes True

"What're you doing?" Mr. Mango stood in the doorway of their bedroom staring at the open suitcase on the bed. Mrs. Mango was darting around the room grabbing clothes and throwing them into the suitcase. Had it finally happened? Had she finally had enough of him that she was leaving? Hard to believe she would have the gumption, although if he was honest with himself (and he never really was), he would admit she didn't seem that happy. Come to think of it, he probably wasn't that happy either, but it wasn't anything he felt like he should do something about. Just a fact of life, like needing glasses and taking Metamucil.

Mrs. Mango stopped her whirlwind. She looked up at Mr. Mango, face flushed and glowing with happiness. "You'll never believe it! It's a miracle! Danny and Rita have a baby!"

"What?" Mr. Mango couldn't get his mind around what Mrs. Mango just said. He just saw Danny last week, and he made no mention of it. What about that whole Christmas debacle when Mrs. Mango had Rita in tears? "They're *having* a baby? She's pregnant?"

"They *have* a baby. They've adopted! It happened in an instant! I'm going over to help them just as soon as I get packed and you get the car gassed up to take me." Mrs. Mango almost skipped towards the bathroom to get her toiletries.

Mr. Mango followed her. "What the hell? How? I didn't even know they wanted to adopt!"

Mrs. Mango shoved bottles and tubes into a ziplock bag and talked over her shoulder. "I don't care how it happened!"

Mrs. Mango hustled back to her suitcase, tossed in the ziplock, and scooted over to the closet. "A baby got delivered at Danny's hospital and the mother didn't want to keep it and I guess the doctor who delivered it is a friend of his and called him in and there it was. She turned it over to them!"

Mrs. Mango zipped the suitcase shut. "They have nothing for a baby! They don't know anything about babies!" She was deliriously happy. She was a grandmother! She was needed! It was like God had just stuck paddles on her chest and jolted her back to life after years of lying in a coma.

Mrs. Mango slid the suitcase to the floor and motioned to Mr. Mango to get it. "Let's go! They are bringing the baby home this afternoon! They need *everything*. They don't have a crib or anything." Mrs. Mango gave a big happy sigh. "This is the greatest news!"

"Is it a girl or a boy?" Mr. Mango asked.

"It's a girl!" Mrs. Mango couldn't believe her luck. Now all her plans for Christine could be transferred to the new baby. Maybe there was a girl wedding in her future after all.

Mrs. Mango prodded Mr. Mango. "Let's go!"

"I'm hungry! I haven't had lunch," he protested, picking up the suitcase as he said it. "I was over working on Charlie's truck and he had nothing to eat in that house. Nothing. He was going to eat a can of beans for lunch."

"We'll grab something on the way." Mrs. Mango's whole body was vibrating with the need to get that baby in her arms. She felt like if she didn't get on the road soon, she would wake up and find out it was just a dream. Although she was desperate to get to that baby, she hadn't driven on a freeway in forty years and didn't see why she'd have to start now. Joe would just have to get himself together and drive.

Mr. Mango knew Mrs. Mango well enough to know there'd be no stopping, so he detoured to the kitchen and made himself a quick bologna sandwich.

Mrs. Mango normally would have been angry at Mr. Mango for taking the time to get the sandwich, but she was still flying high. "We're grandparents! Finally! I can't believe it," she laughed as they made their way to the car.

As Mr. Mango loaded the suitcase into the trunk, Mrs. Mango caught site of Mrs. Melucci staring out her front window. Normally, they would both have pretended Mrs. Melucci wasn't spying, but Mrs. Mango gave a big wave and yelled, "I'm a grandma!"

Mrs. Melucci couldn't hear through the glass but made her way out to the front lawn. "What'd you say?"

"I'm a grandma! Headed over to Danny's! They adopted a baby girl."

Mr. Mango was already in the car. Mrs. Mango gave another wave to Mrs. Melucci and climbed in the passenger seat. "Let's go!"

As Mr. Mango backed out of the driveway, he couldn't help but wonder how Elsie could move so fast when it came to a baby but so slow when he was having a heart attack. Guess he knew where he stood on her priority list.

Christine scraped the last bite of leftover jambalaya pasta out of the to-go box and glanced at her watch. Her time in the break room of the bank was just about over, which was fine with her because Lance had taken the same break time. She was tired of him already, and he'd only been in his position at the bank for three weeks. Pushy, ambitious, and cocky enough about his appearance that he thought he could turn her straight. The first day he started at the bank, in the same Personal Banker position as Christine, she remembered thinking he was handsome in a British-guy kind of way: dark hair, pale skin, slim, and seemingly self-deprecating. Within three days, she couldn't see anything attractive about him, and the only thing that seemed British were his crooked teeth.

"You and the babe eat out last night?" Lance said staring at her to-go box.

Christine closed her eyes and sighed. Opening them, she answered, "Wow, nothing gets by you."

"I was over at Metro, happened to run into Wallace at the bar. We had a great time. Practically closed the place down." Lance rubbed his hand across his forehead, like he had a headache but was proud of it.

Wallace was their branch bank manager, and Christine was sure Lance had stalked him to Metro and then feigned surprise at running into him. She had no time for that kind of ambition or the kind of person with that kind of ambition.

"Way to go," Christine said, just to say something.

"Metro is a great bar; you should check it out sometime," Lance said to the young woman sitting next to Christine. "Oh, right, you're not old enough!" he laughed, the only one in the room that found himself amusing.

Christine glanced at the young woman, a college student earning extra money by working as a teller. "He's a charmer, isn't he, Stephanie?" she said.

Stephanie rolled her eyes and looked back down at her phone. Her long, light brown hair was fastened back into a smooth ponytail and her face lightly made up. With her careful hair and her conservative clothes, she managed to look professional despite her youth. Christine had seen her out of work and barely recognized her, dressed as she was in a mini skirt and boots, hair down and flowing. It seemed to Christine that Stephanie was doing a good job of keeping her professional versus college-girl lives straight. Stephanie had figured Lance out even faster than Christine had and normally spent her break eating a salad and scrolling on her phone.

Christine's phone buzzed with a text. She glanced at it and then looked more intently. "Oh my God," she said staring at her phone in shock.

"What's going on?" asked Stephanie, looking up again. News via a phone was interesting.

"My brother just got a baby!" gasped Christine. "What in the world?"

"Just *got* a baby, what's that mean?" asked Stephanie.

"I knew they wanted one but didn't know they were trying to adopt, and, all of a sudden, they have a baby! A little girl!" Christine looked around the break room in wonder. "I'm an aunt!"

Mrs. Mango had overcome her aversion to technology, not to mention Christine, and had texted Christine the good news. "My parents are on their way up to see her. Wow."

Christine's heart sank with the thought that, once again, telling her parents she was moving out was delayed. Then she felt a stab of guilt that she could so quickly take the news in a selfish way. She really was happy for Danny and Rita. Maybe this would gentle Rita a bit.

"You have a brother?" asked Lance, shoveling a burrito into his mouth as he talked.

"I have three," said Christine, still absorbing the news about the baby.

"Three? Who knew? What do they do?" asked Lance, ever searching for networking opportunities.

"Joe is an actor, Michael is a tech guy, and Danny is a doctor," said Christine. She was proud of her brothers and couldn't resist bragging, even to Lance. Or especially to Lance.

"Michael was project manager for the Gallant," Christine said, referring to the latest phone-tablet phenomenon.

"No way! I bought one of those," said Lance. "I'm an early adopter, you know."

"Of course you are," said Christine.

"You must get tons of free swag," said Lance.

"Not really," said Christine, shrugging and standing up with her empty to-go box. "But he can fix anything I don't know how to fix or use."

"He must be loaded," said Lance.

Christine walked towards the garbage can and dropped her box in. "He's done well."

As she pulled open the door to leave, Lance added, "What happened to you?"

Christine walked out and pulled the door shut without answering. What a dick.

An hour and a half later, after driving through rounded hills and past scattered vineyards north of the San Francisco Bay, they pulled into Danny and Rita's driveway. On previous trips to Danny's, Mrs. Mango always took time to appreciate the beauty of the area around his house and the pristine upkeep of his neighborhood. She loved driving past the fancy neighborhood right before his, admiring the planned-to-look-unplanned look of the houses in that development, all different architectural plans but similar in their size and landscaping. And then, on the road to Danny's, the houses became more spread apart, set back further from the road. Some with gates and enough mature landscaping you couldn't even see the house, while others allowed a peek of a Mediterranean villa here, a more French design there. Danny's house didn't look as fancy from the outside, but he and Rita had gutted the rambling ranch house and created a light-filled inviting home. They both said they had fallen for the grounds of the place and knew they could turn the house into something worthy of the spot.

Today, Mrs. Mango didn't even notice the arch of curvy live oaks lining the driveway or even the egret standing curious by the lily pad-filled pond to the left of the driveway. Her hand was on the door handle, ready to spring out before the car was even close to a stop.

Seeing the car door actually opening, Mr. Mango slowed up and Mrs. Mango leaped out, left the door open, and ran to the front door, leaving Mr. Mango to park in the turnaround, shut off the car, pull out her suitcase, and shut the passenger door.

He found Mrs. Mango with Danny and Rita in their kitchen. Rita was cradling a bundle that he assumed must be the baby, although he couldn't see anything beyond a frilly white blanket. Mrs. Mango was hovering by Rita, bent over and cooing at the bundle, her arms twitching at her sides with the effort not to grab the baby.

Danny was leaning on a bar stool, smiling and shaking his head. "Hey, Dad! Can you believe it? We have a baby!"

Mr. Mango dropped the suitcase and went over to his son. Instead of their more usual backslap or handshake, Danny and Mr. Mango hugged.

"Congratulations, son," said Mr. Mango, pulling back. "What a surprise! You almost gave your mother a heart attack."

"No more of those, huh?" said Danny, still full of smiles. "Come here, look at her," he said, walking over to Rita and leaning over the bundle. He pulled the blanket down a bit, and a little circle of baby face peeked out. "This is Emma Rose."

Mr. Mango peered in as Mrs. Mango breathed in and out with big sighs. "Oh my, she's precious," Mrs. Mango said. "Just precious."

Mr. Mango nodded.

Rita gave a big grin, "It's just so hard to believe! Yesterday, we woke up in the morning, life as usual. And then, by noon, we find out about this angel, and today, here she is!" Rita's face was softer than either Mr. or Mrs. Mango had ever seen it. The slightly pinched look that Mrs. Mango had always assumed came from being a trial attorney was gone. She looked ten years younger. "We had done all the preparatory paperwork and were going to go through a regular agency, and then this happened!" Rita added.

Mrs. Mango was itching to get that baby in her arms. It was all she could do not to rip her away from Rita. Luckily, in addition to a strong instinct to hold the baby, another instinct had kicked in, the one that tells you not to offend your daughter-in-law when she is the gatekeeper to your grandchild. Mrs. Mango had been holding her tongue about Rita for a long time. Right now, she was overcome with the urge to please Rita. To help her and support her and make sure access to Emma Rose would never be denied.

"Can I get you anything?" Mrs. Mango asked Rita. "A cup of tea? Something stronger? A sandwich?"

Sure, offer her *a sandwich,* thought Mr. Mango. He had the sinking feeling he had just dropped a rung down on the food chain. Any further, and he'd be scrounging in garbage cans for food.

"No thanks, I'm fine," said Rita. "But I do have to get a bottle ready. Would you like to hold her?"

Mrs. Mango tried to act nonchalant. "Sure, would love to."

Emma Rose settled into Mrs. Mango's soft curves like she had come home. Or at least that was the way it felt to Mrs. Mango. It was like a part of her body had been missing for many aching years, and it had just gotten reattached. Or like the stories about a child losing a beloved stuffed animal only to have it found and returned years later. Everything finally in its rightful place. "Ooh, lovey, hello lovey," she crooned, slipping into the gentle swaying that had put every one of her kids to sleep countless times. She started softly humming, putting herself and the baby into a trance.

Mr. Mango stared at his wife, seeing in her softened face a glimpse of the happy woman he had fallen in love with. Every once in a while, that woman appeared, a lightening up, if only for a moment, a return to joy and warmth. It didn't happen much these days, so Mr. Mango took the time to watch his wife and appreciate seeing that girl again. Maybe she was still in there, beneath that frazzled older woman. For so many years, he had seen her as that happy woman, way past the time she stopped showing that side. He always figured she was in there somewhere but realized, now, seeing her lit-up face, that somewhere along the way he had stopped thinking of her as the happy girl. He wondered when his vision had shifted. A sharp melancholy filled him, and he turned away, surprised by the intensity of emotion. *Damn heart attack,* he mumbled to himself. *Making me weak.*

The doorbell rang. "Oh, that must be Martin, bringing the crib," said Danny, heading out of the room.

It turned out that Danny and Rita's friends, most of whom had kids already, had rallied to bring them the furnishings and equipment modern-day babies seem to require. By the end of the afternoon, there was a crib, changing table, boxes of diapers and wipes and formula, carrying contraptions that strapped on the chest, carrying contraptions that strapped on the back, a bathtub, an educational mobile, and more.

CHAPTER 24
A Keeper

It was five in the evening and Emma Rose was tucked away in her new crib on freshly washed sheets, swaddled in a freshly washed blanket, bolstered on either side by little soft rolls attached to a pad to keep her from rolling over, even though the chance of rolling over was zero at this point in her young life. They all gathered around the video monitor staring at her. Finally, Mrs. Mango stepped back and looked around the kitchen, strewn with baby items and paperwork, and felt happy. She had always liked Danny's house (although thinking it kind of big for just two of them), but now it felt like a *home*, not just a house. It had baby stuff in it. It was not perfectly organized and clean. It was not a showcase; it was a house with a life.

"Let me make you some dinner," Mrs. Mango said, as Danny opened a bottle of champagne that had arrived with a diaper genie. She bustled to the refrigerator to see what she had to work with.

Rita collapsed into a chair. "That would be great. I can't even think about food!"

Mrs. Mango found enough to fix dinner, but while she was looking, she started making out a shopping list. "I'll send Joe to the store," she said. "Do you both like French toast? I can make that for breakfast tomorrow."

Rita and Danny looked at each other. "Are you staying?" Danny asked.

"Of course I'm staying!" Mrs. Mango said, straightening up from looking in the crisper drawer and turning around. "I'm sure you'll get up to speed fast, but for right now you need someone in the house who knows something about babies!"

Danny looked at Rita, eyebrows raised in a

question. Clearly, this was going to be up to her. He looked like he was holding his breath.

Rita's face softened even more, if that was possible. "Really? Could you? Because I'm scared to death! We don't know what we are doing yet."

Danny was about to comment that he was, after all, a doctor and could probably manage to keep a baby alive. Then he looked around at all the unfamiliar gear littering the room and realized maybe he didn't know that much about all the stuff past feeding it and making sure it was breathing.

Mrs. Mango nodded. "No question. I'm here as long as you need me."

It occurred to Mr. Mango that he had not packed anything. The only one prepared to stay here was Mrs. Mango. Well, he could manage one night, at least.

"Joe, put my suitcase in the guest room," Mrs. Mango ordered. "Then I'll have a list ready and you can go get the groceries. Oh, and if you are thinking of staying, you better let Christine know to let Poker out when she gets home."

The doorbell rang again, and Danny went to answer it, coming back with two friends and a jogging stroller.

"Mom, Dad, this is Crawford and Lauren," Danny said. "Hey, guys, can I give you some champagne?"

Crawford and Lauren were only too happy to have champagne and gather around the baby monitor and hear the story of the adoption.

As Mr. Mango picked up Mrs. Mango's suitcase and headed towards the guest room, the doorbell rang again. Things were turning into a party, and he was uninvited. More like the hired help. 'Go to the grocery store and then go home.' This wasn't the time to make a fuss in front of Danny and Rita, but he wouldn't mind if the soft version of his wife was turned towards him once in a while.

Later that night at Sarah's apartment, Christine was

snuggled into the couch with Sarah, watching America Ninja Warrior. Christine loved Sarah's apartment and not just because Sarah was in it. Sarah had a knack for decorating, making her basic apartment in a basic apartment building something special. They were sitting on a comfy gray couch with a fluffy, faintly patterned off-white and slate blue rug under it and a reclaimed wood coffee table in front of it. To either side of the couch were intricately carved wood Tibetan garden stools. Christine always felt more classy sitting in this room, like she was one of the stylish people. She loved the colors and the furniture choices and the art but could never have picked that stuff out herself.

"I'm so sorry; I meant to tell them tonight, and, well, now they are up at Danny's and staying over," said Christine.

"I know; I get it. Well, at least you can stay here tonight."

"Nope, got to go home and let Poker out. And feed the cat."

"Oh shoot, forgot about the animals," said Sarah. She pulled Christine closer and fluffed a nubby white blanket over them both. "Maybe I just won't let you go. Clean up the poop in the morning."

Christine laughed and gave her a quick kiss on the cheek. "Ha ha. Hey, come with me! No one's home."

Sarah sat back away from Christine and looked intently at her. "Really? Are you sure?"

Christine nodded. "Let's do it!"

"Come with you to let the dog out and then come back here, or come with you and stay?"

"Stay!" said Christine, feeling reckless.

"All right," said Sarah, standing up. "Let me get my stuff for tomorrow."

The batteries on the motion sensor light over the Mangos' front door had died, leaving Sarah and Christine to approach the house in complete darkness. As they fumbled towards the front door, Sarah's foot ran into something, and she collided with the huge stack of shelter supplies Mrs. Mango had never put out a box for.

"Oh my God, are you okay?" said Christine.

"Yes, not sure what I ran into, a big pile of something," said Sarah getting to her feet.

Christine got the front door open and turned on the light. Bags of shampoo and clothes and sanitary pads and tampons were piled to the left of the front door. "Oh, this is the shelter stuff my mom is helping to collect. I guess when she took off for Danny's, she forgot about it."

Sarah giggled. "Wow. There is a *lot* of stuff here."

"No kidding," laughed Christine. "I better remind my mom about it. Maybe someone can come pick it up."

Sarah restacked the bags she had knocked over. "I guess if either of us has a need . . . wouldn't have to go far."

Across the street, Mrs. Melucci sat in the dark at her front window, staring at Christine and Sarah and the piles of goods surrounding them at the door. Things were getting strange at that Mango house, and she wasn't going to miss a minute of it.

In the morning, Christine got up early and made Sarah steel-cut oatmeal for breakfast, enjoying the chance to actually do that in her own house. Sarah came into the kitchen freshly showered and wearing Christine's robe.

"Wow, what a nice surprise," Sarah said, sitting down to her oatmeal. "We could do this every day, you know."

Christine smiled. "I know!" Then frowned. "I have to tell them."

"You can do it; I know you can," said Sarah, sprinkling brown sugar on her oatmeal.

"I will. I will," said Christine. "But right now, I need a shower." Christine gave Sarah a peck on the cheek and disappeared.

Two minutes later, Mr. Mango walked in and

stopped in surprise.

Sarah looked up and stared back in just as much surprise.

"Well, hello," said Mr. Mango, his brain processing the scene in front of him and coming up with a 'what the hell' reaction. An 'oh well, what the hell,' not an angry 'what the hell.'

"Hello," said Sarah, surreptitiously pulling the robe more firmly shut.

Ten minutes later, as Christine walked back into the kitchen, she said, "I promise, I'm telling them tonight," and then stopped dead in her tracks at the sight of her dad sitting at the table drinking a cup of coffee with Sarah.

"Hey, Christine," said Mr. Mango.

"Oh, shoot. I mean, oh—" sputtered Christine. "What are you doing home? I thought you were staying at Danny's?" And then, before he could answer, her voice rising in panic, "Where's mom?"

"Still at Danny's," said Mr. Mango. "Your mom forgot her blood pressure medication, and I couldn't sleep, so I figured I'd drive down for it before the rush hour traffic hit. I think she's planning on staying at Danny's for a while."

Christine couldn't move. The awkwardness was beyond measuring. Her dad was no dummy, so he must have easily figured out that Sarah slept over. She was sitting there in Christine's robe! Hair wet! Her brain spun and came up with nothing.

"Good thing your mom isn't along," Mr. Mango said with a mischievous smile. "Especially since she hasn't had her blood pressure medication."

Christine closed her eyes and said a quick thank you to God.

Sarah giggled, and Mr. Mango laughed with her.

"Tell us what?" asked Mr. Mango.

"Huh?" said Christine.

"You said 'I'm telling them tonight,' and I assume 'them' is us."

Christine stared, unable to bring herself to tell him.

"Go ahead," urged Sarah. "Your dad is cool. He'll be okay."

"I don't know," said Christine, sinking into a chair at the table. Her brain was finally working again and processing the information that her mother was staying at Danny's for a while. "Mom is staying? What about you?"

"I'm going to take her medicine up and then come home again. Too much craziness there for me right now. And there's Poker and Tripod to take care of. You're gone a lot, which is fine, but someone needs to take care of the animals."

Christine's heart got heavy. She couldn't leave her dad alone here. Could she? His heart attack was not that long ago. She looked at Sarah and saw the happiness in her eyes. Shoot. She didn't want to let her down either.

"What could there be left to tell us?" Mr. Mango said.

Christine took a deep breath. "Well, we were talking about, I mean, we were thinking, I mean, I was thinking of moving in with Sarah." She let out a deep sigh. There. She'd said it. "But I don't want to leave you alone—I mean, if mom is gone for long."

Mr. Mango waved his hand. "Won't be long. And I'm fine. Jesus Christ, everyone is treating me like a cripple." He took a sip of his coffee and looked at Sarah and then back at Christine. "I guess that makes sense. Moving in together. Good for you."

Christine stared at her dad, trying to figure out if he really meant it. If he really was supporting this.

"Of course your mother won't see it that way," Mr. Mango added.

Christine stared down into her coffee mug, cold now since it was poured before her shower.

"Then again, this might be perfect timing," Mr. Mango said, staring up at the ceiling, deep in thought. "She's so goddamn happy about that baby, nothing could bring her down." He nodded to himself. "Yep. Good timing. While she's still in baby bliss."

Christine looked up. "Really? Do you really think so?"

"Yes."

"Well, then, could you tell her?" Christine laughed.

"I'll have to think on that one," said Mr. Mango. "By the way, want to see a picture of the baby?" He pulled out his phone and poked at it until he pulled up a picture.

"Awww, adorable," said Christine. "I can't believe how fast it happened. But awesome, just awesome for them." She handed Sarah the phone.

"Oh, she's so cute," said Sarah. "So little! And just so so so cute." She passed the phone back to Mr. Mango.

Mr. Mango reached over and patted Sarah's hand while he looked at Christine. "This one's a keeper." He stood up. "Well, I'd better go find that medicine," he said and left the room.

Christine stared at Sarah. "What in the world did you guys talk about? How did you get him to be so friendly?"

Sarah shrugged. "Like the man said, I'm 'a keeper.'"

CHAPTER 25
A Matter of the Heart

Mr. Mango traveled back to Danny's several times over the next week, mostly to bring Mrs. Mango things she had forgotten. Pills and her pillow and her curlers and her fluffing comb. Each time, he felt further shuffled into a corner and each time, he thought maybe Mrs. Mango would be leaving with him, but she stayed on.

Exactly a week after the baby arrived, Mr. Mango arrived at Danny's with Mrs. Mango's knee brace and her hormone replacement pill refill.

He walked into the kitchen to find Rita in tears and Danny comforting her. The fog hadn't cleared yet even though it was midmorning, and with only a single light on in the kitchen, the gloom extended inside. Mr. Mango didn't do well with tears, so he said a quick hello and then exited to find Mrs. Mango. He wandered towards the guest room only to find it empty, not just of Mrs. Mango, but also all of her clothes and toiletries.

Now where the hell did she go? he wondered.

He slowly walked through the family room and edged towards the kitchen, listening to hear if Rita was still crying.

Soft murmurs from Danny that sounded something like, "It will work out, we'll find someone, don't worry. People do it all the time."

Mr. Mango decided to slip out to the back yard and see how the work back there was going. In addition to the new landscaping, Danny and Rita were also fixing up a little house behind the pool as a guest house.

As he picked his way past the stack of stones waiting installation and gave a wave to the four workers digging and shifting dirt, he saw Mrs. Mango making her way up the path leading from the little house.

"There you are! Do you have my brace?"

"Hello to you too. I wouldn't go in there if I were you," he thumbed back towards the house. "Rita's crying about something. Maybe give them some privacy."

"Hmph!" Mrs. Mango said. What did he know about anything? She picked up speed, heading straight for the French doors that opened into the kitchen. "Poor thing, must be feeling stressed. It's hard to get into the rhythm of taking care of a baby."

Mr. Mango stared at the workers without really seeing them, shaking his head. Why did he even bother?

He followed after Mrs. Mango, deciding he better make sure she didn't interfere too much.

By the time he got into the kitchen, Rita's tears were stopped and she and Danny looked calmer. All the lights in the kitchen had been turned on, and Mrs. Mango was standing facing them, her arms crossed, her face beaming.

Mrs. Mango turned to Mr. Mango, "They're so worried about finding help. Rita has to get back to work, and they don't have a nanny yet. So I told them I can stay 'til they find the right person. No problem!"

Rita gave Mrs. Mango a weak smile. "I'm sorry. I just don't know how long these things take. None of my friends knows of someone available this fast. And I can't just leave her with a stranger!" Rita clutched at her heart, like someone was standing over her threatening to rip it out. "I can't believe I have to work already, but the firm was just as surprised about all this as we were. I got to take care of some stuff, and then maybe I can work out a way to have a real maternity leave."

Mrs. Mango nodded. "I know, I know, it is hard to even imagine they can live without you!"

Rita nodded. "I don't know if I can do this. I mean, I love my work. I want to go back, but I can't leave Emma Rose, I just can't. I just got to get things ironed out at work, and then, well, we'll see."

Danny said, "You can, you will. Lauren said she

went through the same thing. Somehow it works out. And maybe I can figure out a way to adjust my hours too.”

“Danny, don’t be silly; you can’t stop working,” said Mrs. Mango, not noticing the little squint that comment caused in Rita. “And no need to worry; of course it will work out!” said Mrs. Mango. “Until you find someone, you’ve got me. And I have to tell you, you did a beautiful job on the guest house! I’ll be completely comfortable there. And out of your hair when you don’t need me.” Mrs. Mango gave a satisfied sigh.

Mr. Mango couldn’t help himself. “What about me? And the house? And all your volunteer jobs? Those bingo numbers don’t call themselves.”

Mrs. Mango snorted. “I’m retired. I can do what I want. It’s not like I have a boss to get mad at me! And besides, I’m sure I’ll never be asked to call bingo again.”

Danny shot his dad a worried look. “Maybe you should stay here too.”

Mrs. Mango’s face clouded over.

Mr. Mango shook his head. “We’ve got Poker and the cat, and I promised Artie I’d help at the garage. He’s short, and I can’t drive my routes yet.”

Danny looked at his Mom. “Maybe Dad does need you there. You know, he’s just getting over the heart attack. And he’s got his follow-up visits with his doctor. I’m not even sure he should be driving back and forth so much.”

Rita’s smile had disappeared. “Oh, how could I be so selfish?” she wailed. “Of course you can’t stay here any longer,” she said to Mrs. Mango.

Mrs. Mango shook her head. “Joe’s fine! He knows what he is supposed to do. And Christine is there. At least, she’s there in the evenings.” Mrs. Mango said it as much to convince herself as the others.

It wasn’t so much that Mr. Mango wanted Mrs. Mango home, but he didn’t like feeling so low on her list. If a heart attack didn’t buy him any attention, he wondered if anything would. The look on Rita’s face made it clear to him, though. She wanted Mrs. Mango’s help, and he couldn't stand the thought of Rita starting to cry again, which she very much looked she was about to do.

"No, no," Mr. Mango said waving his hand. "I'll be fine. I am fine. Of course Elsie will stay and help you out. And Christine is there if I need anything." The lie came out so easily it scared Mr. Mango. But no need to inform his wife yet that her daughter had gone another step down the forbidden road. If Mrs. Mango couldn't be bothered to come home, he couldn't be bothered to tell her about Christine moving out.

Rita's frown smoothed out. "If you are sure . . ." she said, staring at Mr. Mango.

"Yes, of course I am," he said. "It'll give you time to find the help you need."

"She's so tiny," cooed Christine as she rocked Emma Rose gently in her arms. It was later that afternoon, and Christine was sitting on Danny and Rita's sleek living room couch, well supported by pillows around her and under the eagle eye of Rita in case she proved inept at holding babies. In these first few days of Emma Rose's arrival, everyone wanted to see her and everyone wanted to hold her, and Rita lived in fear someone would drop her. Just when all of her prayers had been answered.

Across the room, Mrs. Mango fought her rising emotions. How much she loved that little baby! And the sight of Christine holding the baby was so bittersweet. How much she wished she could see Christine married, to a man, holding a baby. But no, there was Sarah, bold as anything sitting at Christine's side, oohing and ahhing over Emma Rose. They had arrived with a huge shopping bag full of presents and were as besotted with Emma Rose as everyone else. Right after their arrival, Don Paz had shown up too, also with a gift bag.

Mr. Mango sat in one of the armchairs flanking the fireplace, watching the whole scene and plotting how he could escape. Don Paz annoyed him, and he was trying to keep his annoyances to a minimum these days. He couldn't help but notice that Don Paz, with his loose white linen shirt and beige linen pants, fit the elegant aesthetic of the room more than Mr. Mango. Mr. Mango liked comfortable furniture that a person didn't worry about messing up with food and couldn't imagine how Danny and Rita were going to raise a child in a room like this. All the furniture was covered in white, the floors a light wood polished to a beautiful shine, the glass coffee and side tables all hard edges. The only color in the room came from a neatly arranged wall of books. It was an Architectural Digest room, and nothing you could imagine a child playing in. Mr. Mango winced with the thought that Danny and Rita could turn out to be the kind of parents that refused to allow a child to actually live in their house, refuse them the chance to scatter toys and crayons and all the stuff that made a home feel comfortable.

"Hello, little niece," crooned Christine in a sing-song voice. "I'm your Aunt Christine. And this is your Aunt Sarah."

Mrs. Mango felt a wave of nausea and hurried out of the room, muttering about getting the baby a bottle, even though she had just finished one.

'Aunt Sarah.' Please.

In the kitchen, Mrs. Mango leaned against the counter with her head down in prayer.

Don Paz came in and waited patiently for Mrs. Mango's head to rise and for her to see him.

Mrs. Mango crossed herself and looked up, thinking she'd make herself a cup of tea.

"How are you?" Don Paz said, his face full of compassion.

"Fine, why do you ask?" said Mrs. Mango, turning to search the cabinets for her favorite cup. The one that said "Marriage is a relationship in which one is always right and the other is the husband."

"You seem upset," said Don Paz, and he nodded his head towards the living room. "This seems difficult for you."

"It's not difficult, I love being a grandmother," said Mrs. Mango.

"Not that. I mean the situation with your daughter."

"I don't know what you are talking about," said Mrs. Mango, filling the cup with water and opening the tea drawer. Mrs. Mango loved how Danny and Rita had an entire drawer devoted to tea. Neatly arranged boxes with a selection so large she could take ten minutes just to settle on one.

"She's a good soul, Christine," said Don Paz. "A lovely, good soul."

"I know that," huffed Mrs. Mango, grabbing a mint lemongrass bag. "I don't need you to tell me that."

"People are what they are, Elsie," said Don Paz softly. "Who knows why some people have a different path in this life? But she is still a daughter who, I'm sure, wishes for a mother to accept her."

"I accept her," said Mrs. Mango, knowing how untrue the words were even as she heard them coming out of her mouth.

"You accept only parts of her," said Don Paz. "And as long as you do that, you will accept only parts of yourself."

Mrs. Mango stopped moving and stared at Don Paz. "I don't have any idea what that means."

"Or maybe it is the reverse, as long as you accept only parts of yourself, you will accept only parts of her." Don Paz nodded to himself, as if he liked that order better.

Mrs. Mango felt a chill inside. What did Don Paz know? For a moment, she panicked. Could the man read minds? Was he in her brain right now? No, there was no way. No way he could know. Could he?

"When is your birthday?" Don Paz asked.

"Huh?" Mrs. Mango was puzzled at the change of subject. "November 19. Why?"

Don Paz nodded. "Scorpio. That's what I would have guessed."

Mrs. Mango rolled her eyes. "I don't believe all that

stuff," she said, ignoring the fact that she read her horoscope every day in the newspaper.

"A water sign. Lots of deep emotion, but you don't tend to show it," said Don Paz. "Very sensitive to other people, those you care about, but quick to pull away when they upset you. I'm a water sign too—Pisces. I'll bet you are drawn to the ocean, aren't you?"

Don Paz picked his gift bags up from the counter, gave Mrs. Mango a knowing smile, and glided from the room.

Mrs. Mango dunked the tea bag hard into the water, splashing it onto the counter. "Huh! Like he knows anything about me," she huffed to herself, uncomfortable that he had gotten it so right. She did long for the ocean but hadn't seen it in years. A longing ignored for so long it seemed not even to be hers.

Back in the family room, Don Paz handed a gift bag to Rita. She pulled out a tissue-wrapped object from the bag and untied the ribbon around it. The paper fell away to reveal a pink stone set on a glass base.

"Uh, thank you. It's pretty," said Rita.

"It's rose quartz," said Don Paz, as Mrs. Mango came back in the room with her tea. "To go with her name, Rose, of course. It is a stone of unconditional love, it opens the heart chakra to all types of love." Don Paz glanced at Mrs. Mango. "It opens the heart to love, to connection, to *forgiveness*. A perfect way to start out life, opening the heart." He held his hands cupped together in front of his chest and then opened them outward as if sending love into the room.

"Thank you," said Rita. "How *love*-ly." She giggled at her pun.

Mrs. Mango made a mental note to put that thing on a high shelf. What kind of toy was that? Who gives a baby a stone? And what if it did have some kind of weird properties? What if it was hypnotizing little Emma Rose right now?

Don Paz reached down and pulled up another bag and handed it to Mr. Mango. "I got you one too! It lowers stress and tension on the heart."

"What? Hey," said Mr. Mango, flummoxed. On the one hand, he felt compelled to thank someone who had bought him a gift. On the other hand, this was a bunch of phooey. "Well, now, Don, that's very thoughtful," was the best Mr. Mango could come up with.

"Don *Paz,*" Rita said before Don Paz could correct Mr. Mango.

"Yes, yes, thank you, Don *Paz*," said Mr. Mango. As soon as Don turned his eyes back towards the baby, Mr. Mango rolled his eyes. Mrs. Mango wanted to do the same but noticed Rita's shoulders rising in a way she hadn't seen since Emma Rose had arrived.

Mrs. Mango hustled over and took the stone from Mr. Mango. "Beautiful. We have the perfect spot for it," she said, not making eye contact with Mr. Mango. For once, she could tell they were in agreement. The perfect spot would be the garbage can.

Mr. Mango stood up. "Well, I'm going to hit the road. Poker's probably tearing the house apart."

Mrs. Mango patted his arm. "Drive safely. Call us when you get home."

Don Paz smiled, feeling like the heart chakras were already opening.

CHAPTER 26
A New Normal

Mr. Mango slid out from under the truck in his driveway and wiped his face. Dang if he could figure out what that noise was—and he had figured out a lot of car noises in his life. He pulled himself up to sitting and stared out at the street. Although it was technically still winter, the air was unseasonably warm, and he had taken advantage of it to check out the bang-putt sound his truck had started to make. The unexpected warmth of the day had brought people out of their houses, and there was activity up and down the street. Dogs were being walked, gutters cleared, the last Christmas decorations taken down. It had been over three weeks since the baby arrived, and Mrs. Mango was showing no signs of giving up taking care of Emma Rose. With Mrs. Mango gone and his driving job on hold while he recovered from his 'cardiac event,' his life had taken on a new rhythm.

Rise at six—that was the same. Linger over coffee and the paper—that was new. No nattering voice in his ear to chase him out of the kitchen. Shower, clean up any stray dishes, and if it was an Artie work day, head down to the garage. If it was not an Artie day, then decide on a home project for the day. By afternoon, the couch called, and after a good nap, the dinner decision always just seemed to make itself. With Christine gone, it was even quieter. She hadn't actually moved everything out, just most of her clothes, but it still added to the silence of the house, knowing no one was going to walk through the door.

Nothing wrong with cereal for dinner, in fact he kind of enjoyed it. None of the drama of a full-cooked meal and Elsie's nagging to eat something healthy. He was torn, on the one hand enjoying the peace of making all his own decisions, on the other hand saddened that Mrs. Mango could so easily abandon her home, because she was showing no signs of coming back. It was like she had just stepped out of one life and into another.

"Earth to Joe," came a voice, startling him out of a trance he didn't realize he was in. He jumped and noticed Flora standing on the sidewalk in front of him. Velma power walked up beside her and stopped as well.

"Hi there, Joe," said Velma. "How's that new baby doing?"

Velma and Flora gave each other knowing looks.

"Doing fine, just fine," said Mr. Mango, easing himself up to standing. He pulled his phone out of his back pocket, realizing as he did so that it had been stabbing into his butt the whole time he had been working on the car. "Got some new pictures! Look at this."

Velma and Flora shuffled over. Flora sighed, "Okay, Joe, we'll look, but don't turn into one of *those* grandparents."

"What do you mean?"

"My grandchild is the cutest, smartest, most amazing thing ever, and everyone wants to look at a thousand pictures of her," sang Flora. "*That* kind of grandparent."

"Hmph," grumped Mr. Mango. "Never mind." He started to stuff the phone back in his pocket.

"Oh, don't be a Scrooge," said Velma. "Let's see. I want to see her!"

Mr. Mango pulled the phone back out and handed it to Velma, glowing with pride.

"Adorable. Just adorable. And Elsie looks so happy!"

Mr. Mango grimaced. "She's like a pig in mud."

"I wouldn't say that in front of her," said Velma. "Women don't much care for being compared to pigs."

"How long she staying up there?" asked Flora, rubbing her index finger along her eyebrow.

"Who knows?" said Mr. Mango. "Rita had to go back to work, at least for a while until she can get a real leave set up. They don't have anyone to watch the baby yet, so . . ." He gave a palms-up move.

Flora nodded and rubbed along her other eyebrow.

Velma looked at Flora. "Those still hurting?"

"A little sore, but dang, they look good, don't they?"

Mr. Mango knew he'd regret asking but couldn't help himself. "What're you talking about?"

"Got my eyebrows tattooed on," said Flora. "At my age, not much hair left in the places where it ought to be."

Velma nodded. "Not to mention our eyesight ain't so good, so there's no guarantee when you use the pencil you get it drawn on right."

Flora laughed. "I put my glasses on one day and noticed I had drawn one eyebrow an inch above the other one. Decided right then and there where my next check was going."

Mr. Mango leaned in and stared at Flora's eyebrows. "I never heard of such a thing," he said, but he had to admit, they looked realistic. Then again, he had never paid much attention to women's eyebrows.

"Going to tattoo the hair back on other places too," laughed Flora.

Mr. Mango didn't want to ask what that meant.

Velma turned to Flora. "You didn't tell me that! You mean . . .?"

"Yep! Going get me a landing strip."

Velma stared, considering. "I guess you're old school. 'Cause we kind of got natural Brazilians going, you know? People pay a lot of money to look that clean."

Mr. Mango felt sick. "I better get back to my car," he said, dropping down onto his slider. "You girls have a good walk," and with that, he slid back under the car.

He didn't even take tools with him. Just lay there under the car, waiting until he heard them shuffle away. And then he waited a good five minutes longer, to be sure, before he slid back out and ran back into the house.

Landing strips! Brazilians! The image of an old lady and a landing strip was just too much. They were going to ruin the fun of looking at naked pictures forever.

Mrs. Mango sat in the locked bathroom of the guest house on Sunday at 6:15 a.m. Not even a new baby or a change of venue could stop her Sunday ritual. She knew she didn't have to lock herself in the bathroom since she had the guest house all to herself, but it just didn't feel right to sit out in the open. She looked around her, savoring the clean look of an updated bathroom. The dark gray slate floor contrasted beautifully with the white tile of the shower and the white marble of the vanity top. The walls were painted a gray so light it was almost white. The whole thing was clean and fresh-looking. She sighed with pleasure and started writing.

Dear Raul,

Oh, my dear Raul! I have a happiness I haven't felt in many, many years. Being a grandmother is everything people say and more. There is a peace in my soul, at least in one corner of it, when I'm holding that baby. I know God meant for this child to be in this family. I knew it the moment I held her. She is as much my grandchild as any child biologically born into my family. I would run into a fire for that child. I would do anything for her. Anything. I do wish you could have lived long enough to feel this pure joy. It is even beyond what it feels like to be a parent. That, of course, is joyful too but comes with such responsibility, such fear. This is just love, day in and day out.
I think I'm going to mix things up a bit today. Instead of thinking about one of our memories together, I'm going to imagine you as a grandfather.

Mrs. Mango opened her eyes ten minutes later, face wet with tears. Maybe that wasn't such a great idea. It was beautiful, imagining Raul as a grandfather, but it had unleashed a wave of guilt. Emma Rose had a grandfather already, and Mrs. Mango couldn't forget that maybe she had hurt that grandfather. Maybe he had some sense of her divided allegiance. Maybe she had caused that heart attack, and now she wasn't even helping to take care of him. A picture of Mr. Mango sitting in his armchair in an empty house filled her brain. A brief moment of an odd feeling, what was that? Mrs. Mango couldn't put a name to it, but anyone else would have recognized it as compassion. The guilt grew—shouldn't she be there making sure he was eating properly and not overdoing the physical work yet? But how could she abandon Raul? Who else was there left to keep his memory alive? Not his parents. Not even his brother who had died in Vietnam as well. How much guilt could one heart take?

She shook her head hard, trying to shake out those thoughts. *No*, she thought. *I will not focus on that now. Now is for Emma Rose.*

Mrs. Mango scrunched her eyes together in the effort to banish the guilt thoughts. Then, she looked down at the letter in her lap. She didn't have a place to lock it. She had already figured out there was no good place in the guest house for these letters, so she walked to the kitchen, got a pack of matches from the cabinet, put the letter in the sink, and burned it. The bitter smoke stung Mrs. Mango's eyes in a perversely satisfying way, and she leaned in to inhale it. She thought of the cache of letters she had built up over the years, stuffed away in boxes behind the Christmas decorations, and wondered at the bonfire they would make if she burned them all at once.

Mrs. Mango gave a hard shake to her head; why was she thinking of burning those letters? They were her history with Raul, the only life she had with Raul. What a ridiculous thought.

A ridiculous thought that kept floating back into her brain the rest of the day.

CHAPTER 27
Marriage Interrupted

It was a Wednesday night, and Emma Rose was bathed, diapered, fed, and sleeping, at least for the moment, but hopefully for longer. Danny joined Rita on the den couch, handing her a glass of red wine. Unlike the living room, the den was where the real living happened, where TV was watched and newspapers left partly read and throw blankets actually used, not just folded artistically over a chair. Still, like the rest of the house, it showed Rita's flair for decorating, the neutrals of the rest of the house complemented in this room with sea colors, a pale turquoise ottoman for propping feet, and patterned throw pillows with a woven pattern of turquoise, sand, and navy. A star-shaped mirror with a pale gold gilt frame hung over the fireplace on the wall opposite the large flat-screen TV that was the only part of the room Danny had picked.

"Ahh," he sighed, sliding himself toward her until their legs were touching and then arranging one of the throw pillows in the hollow of his back.

"Cheers," she said, lightly tapping her glass to his.

"How was work?" Danny asked, picking up the remote and flicking around to different channels.

"Oh, I don't want to talk about that. Fine, just don't need to rehash."

Rita leaned over to the side table and tilted the baby video monitor towards them.

"What do you want to watch?" Danny asked.

"I don't care. Something light, though," Rita said.

"Night night!" sang Mrs. Mango, sticking her head into the den from the kitchen. "Off to my magical cottage."

"Are you sure? It's only 7:00," said Rita. "Come watch TV with us."

"No, no, I'm tired. Going to climb in bed and watch

The Bachelor," said Mrs. Mango. "Don't tell me what happened, I have it recorded."

After they heard the back door snick shut, Rita turned to Danny. "Your mom is being so helpful. I can't believe how well this is working out."

Danny nodded. "She's in heaven. She's wanted grandchildren forever, and now we are the favorites for giving her one."

"And she seems to be trying really hard to give us our space," added Rita, privately amazed at Mrs. Mango's sensitivity.

Danny nodded and pointed the remote at the TV. "How about an oldie goldie? Notting Hill, I know you like that one."

"Sure, that's fine. But, really, I don't know how we'd be doing this without your mother. I just can't imagine leaving Emma with a stranger." Rita shifted a stack of magazines on the ottoman to give her room to prop her feet.

"People do it all the time, besides, it wouldn't be a stranger. It would be someone we interview and check up on and get to know. The world is mostly good people, you know."

"I know. But I feel guilty. I mean, there your dad is, alone all day and recovering from a heart attack."

"Well, Christine is around, and Mrs. Melucci seems to have nothing else to do but watch the house," Danny said. "And she has Christine's number if anything comes up while she's at work. Plus, this won't be for long."

"Don't be so sure," Rita said. "Your mom is really comfortable here. If you know what I mean."

"Huh? What do you mean?"

"I don't think she and your dad, you know, get along that great," said Rita.

"Huh," said Danny, turning up the volume on the TV. "I forgot what a good movie this is. Great characters. British actors seem real, not like movie stars trying to be real. Like, look at their teeth. Not perfect."

"In fact, I don't think they really like each other that much," continued Rita.

"Of course they do," said Danny. "The whole movie is based on how attracted they are to each other."

"Not the movie characters! Your parents. They are always sniping at each other."

"Whatever. Not my business." Danny had no interest in dissecting his parents' marriage.

"Well, it kind of is our business now, because I don't think your mom is ever going to want to leave," said Rita.

"I forgot how funny his roommate is!" said Danny, gesturing at the TV. "Reminds me of one of my housemates in college. Those guys were a mess."

Rita sighed. Danny was not going to discuss this, didn't even see that there was anything to discuss. She settled back into the cushions and focused on the TV.

Out in the cottage, Mrs. Mango hummed a happy little tune as she puttered around getting ready for bed. She loved this little guest house. It was cozy and clean and uncluttered, and it had everything she needed. It had a little kitchenette and a living room area and the softest comforter on the big pillowy bed. She could climb in that lovely bed and watch her favorite shows on the perfectly sized flat-screen sitting on the narrow antique-looking dresser across from the bed. She could soak in the Jacuzzi tub as long as she wanted. No one kept her awake with his snoring or bad breath or complaints about pillows. And through the charming French doors, thirty yards away, slept the most precious baby on earth, and she would get to spend all of tomorrow with her. Life was good. Her life in Concordia seemed like something that belonged to someone else.

So, why, as she snuggled in the very middle of the double bed, did her brain keep circling back to Mr. Mango and wondering if he was taking care of himself? Why were images of the younger Joe flickering into her brain? Remembering how broad his shoulders seemed, how solid and safe he felt. How he made her laugh. How his certainty made him seem like a confident man, not just an opinionated one. No, those kinds of thoughts did her no good. She didn't want to give up her irritation with him, and yet the physical distance from him seemed to be causing old memories to surface. Or maybe it was his brush with death.

"I can't believe mom has just abandoned dad!" Christine griped into the phone. She was sitting on a deck chair on the tiny apartment porch that she now shared with Sarah, her back against the wall and her feet propped on the railing. It was an uncharacteristically balmy evening, and even though it was dark, Christine enjoyed staring into the mature trees that hid the apartment building thirty yards away. The lights from the building's windows flickered through the trees like Christmas lights.

"What are you talking about? She's just helping Danny and Rita out," answered Michael. Thirty miles away on the other side of the bay, he too was on his porch, but he was sitting in a bubbling hot tub that looked out over an artfully arranged flagstone patio, leading to a perfect green lawn, leading to a pool, leading to more lawn before the back fence. Putting his math skills towards a tech company had paid off way better than Christine's putting her math skills to a branch bank job. Michael shifted his position, wincing as his back seized up yet again despite the warmth of the water.

"He's there alone, and who knows if he is taking care of himself. I can't believe she'd leave him alone this long." Christine took a sip of her glass of wine and glanced at her watch. She still had fifteen minutes until Sarah was due home. "He still eats all kinds of unhealthy crap, and he is supposed to be cutting that stuff out. I mean, do you think he is really going to cook healthy stuff for himself?"

"He's not completely by himself, you're there," said Michael.

"Well, uh, not really," said Christine, taking a gulp of wine in preparation.

"What do you mean?"

Deep breath. "I moved in with Sarah," said Christine, glad to be on the phone and not face to face. Not that she expected Michael to protest, but still. It was hard, getting used to being so open about this.

"Huh," said Michael.

When Michael didn't add anything more, Christine got anxious. "What's that mean?"

"Nothing, just, well, now I'm going to worry more about Dad," said Michael.

Christine felt the guilt building up again. And then the resentment—why was she the one they expected to take care of him?

"Thanks, and here I thought you might be happy for me," said Christine, her voice getting edgier than she meant it to.

"No, no, you're right," said Michael quickly. "I'm sorry. That's great for you, really. When did you move?"

"Started moving stuff over about two weeks ago. And it is so great! I don't know why I lived at home so long. And Sarah, she's just, ahhh, great," said Christine, her voice happy again. "But of course I'm worried about Dad."

"Me too," said Michael. "But you are right, it isn't really your job. It should be Mom there."

"I talked to Mom, and she's not worried at all about him. That seems a little cold, you ask me," said Christine.

"Hah!" said Michael bitterly. "I'll tell you about cold. I've got one word for you: Meredith." He grabbed the beer sitting on the stone edge of the spa and took a slug.

Christine immediately regretted her words. What was she thinking, talking about marital problems with Michael? She should be comforting him, not getting him upset. And then putting her own happiness right in his face. What was she thinking? "She'll come around," she said, wondering why she even said it. What did she know about what was going on for Meredith?

"I don't know," said Michael in a subdued voice.

"Says she tired of 'not having fun,' whatever that means. I'm no different than when we met. Seemed like I was good enough for her then."

"Well, you do work a lot," said Christine. "A *lot*."

"Sure, take her side," said Michael. "Like that's such a bad thing, working hard. She doesn't seem to mind spending the money I made working hard."

"That's not fair, she made a lot too," Christine said. Christine really liked Meredith and could understand her perspective. Michael worked hard at his office and then came home and worked hard in his home office. His idea of not working was making it out to his back yard but with a laptop or phone or tablet or all three near to hand. He didn't have hobbies, he didn't care about going out for nice dinners or to any kind of entertainment. She could see how that could get boring for a wife.

"I don't mind if she goes out, I just don't know why I have to go sit in loud restaurants and loud bars and loud concerts."

"Maybe that got old for her," said Christine. "Maybe she'd like you to go with her sometimes."

"I do! I go out. Just not often enough for her. And apparently I 'don't have any friends,' at least according to her. I've got friends."

"Do you do stuff with them?" Christine asked, thinking that she rarely heard him talk about doing anything social. He barely was social with the family.

"Sure!"

"What was the last thing you did?"

"Hmm, uh, I watched the last game of the World Series with Gary," Michael said.

"The World Series?? That was months ago!" said Christine. "And who is Gary?"

"Guy on my team at work," said Michael. "Huge Giants fan. And I had a beer with Danny a couple weeks ago."

"Danny doesn't count, he's your brother."

Christine tipped her glass up to get the last swallow

and debated getting more. Maybe just half a glass. She got
up and slipped through the sliding glass door as she talked.
"Well, what have you tried with Meredith? Did you
actually try doing something fun together?"

"Like what?" said Michael.

"Oh my God, you are pathetic. You can't come up
with anything fun?" said Christine, as she opened the
refrigerator and uncorked the Chardonnay.

"Nothing that Meredith thinks is fun," said Michael.

"Well, what does she want to do? Do that."

"She wants to travel. I don't have time for that. And
she wants to have dinner parties, and I can't stand those."

"What did you guys do when you met? What was
so interesting then?" Christine moved back out to the
porch.

"We worked together. It was great. We busted our
asses and produced an amazing product, and then she
moved into HR. She's perfect for it, but now I guess we
don't have as much in common."

Christine loved her brother, but she could feel for
Meredith. Socially, Michael was a bit of a dud. Christine
and Sarah had a big group of friends and went out at least
three times a week. Christine knew her 'successful'
brothers probably thought she was underachieving with her
job, but the fact was, she loved her life. She wasn't driven
in a professional way, and she had friends and a great
girlfriend and enough money to get by. She secretly felt
sorry for Danny and Michael, working their asses off to pay
for their big houses and trying to keep their stressed-out
wives happy. She kind of felt sorry for Joe Jr. too, since he
hadn't caught that big break in Hollywood yet, but at least
he was pursuing a dream. At least he was doing what made
him happy.

"Do you love her?" Christine asked. She heard the
key in the lock and waved at Sarah through the glass doors.

"Of course I love her!" said Michael.

"You answered too fast. Think about it a moment."

Michael leaned his head back against the cool stone

of the spa coping and stared up at the dark sky. He liked nighttime. There was something restful about the dark, a certain abatement of noise and colors and people needing things from him.

"In fact, think longer than a moment," said Christine. "I have to go, Sarah is back."

"Oh, okay," said Michael. "Hey, I'd like to get to know Sarah more. I don't feel like I got much of a chance at Christmas. Maybe you guys want to come down and, you know, hang out?"

Christine felt a rush of affection for her brother. Inept socially, but a good heart. "That would be great. Sarah would love to see your house. Maybe we'll actually take you out somewhere. Introduce you to the world. You know, Palo Alto has some great restaurants."

"So I've heard. Come anytime." Michael glanced sideways as his Gallant, sitting on a table pulled up beside the spa, pinged four times in a row with a series of texts.

"Okay. Love you," said Christine.

"Back at you," said Michael, and they both hung up before Christine realized they hadn't actually come up with any plan for their parents. Oh well.

CHAPTER 28
The Angel of Death

In the inky night, Flora fumbled for the ringing cell phone by her bed, knocking her glasses to the floor in the process.

"God-darn it," she grumbled, leaning over the side of the bed and patting around for her glasses. By the time she had them on, picked up her phone, levered herself back up onto the bed, and swiped to answer, the call had ended. Peering at the 'Missed Calls' icon, she saw that Velma had been the one calling. She stared at the clock until her eyes focused and saw that it was 1:15 in the morning. Something was wrong.

Flora hit Velma's number, her heart pounding.

"Holy cow, thank God you called back," said Velma, not even bothering with hello. "I've got a bit of a situation here."

"Are you okay?" asked Flora.

"I'm fine. I'm not the problem. It's ol' Marshall that's the problem."

Marshall was Velma's latest 'honey,' the name she used for all her romantic relationships ('boyfriend' just sounded silly at her age and 'man friend' was clumsy off the tongue).

"I'm at his place, and, well, there's no easy way to say this, he's dead," said Velma.

"Oh boy," said Flora. Not another one. Velma was going to get a reputation as the Black Widow. Maybe she already had it.

"Yep. Same thing as the others. I'm telling you, these old men just don't have the stamina. Too bad I can't get more interest from the young ones."

"Did you call 911?"

"Of course I did. And I did CPR, but nothing was coming back to life, if you know what I mean."

Flora wondered what body part Velma had performed CPR on.

"The paramedics should be here any minute, but I don't want to stay here. And, uh, I don't have any clothes."

"What're you talking about?"

"We were kind of role playing, and, well, I don't have clothes."

"How in the heck did you get there without clothes? No, wait, I'm not sure I want to know."

"We pretended he was kidnapping me. He came to my place, stripped me, threw his coat over me, and off we went. Guess the excitement was too much for him."

"Well, you better put something on before the paramedics get there! Put on his robe or something."

"Right, I'm on it. But could you come get me? And bring me something to wear?"

Flora was already out of her bed and headed for the closet to get her shoes. It was the middle of the night, so there was no reason to change out of her leopard print pajamas. Who would see her? "Of course. Which unit is he again?"

"Building H, second floor, number 210."

Flora elbowed her way through the crowd in the hallway outside of Marshall's apartment. "Excuse me, excuse me, coming through."

A large woman wearing curlers and a mean expression barred her way. "What do you think you're doing? There's an emergency in there, got to stay out of their way."

"I know, my friend is there and she called me. I've got to go help her."

The furrows in Mean-faced Curler Lady smoothed a smidge. "What's going on? They won't tell us nothin'. Your friend okay?"

Flora looked around and saw the curious expressions on the faces of a hall full of people in their nighttime wear. Some in pajamas, some in t-shirts and sweat pants, some in robes. All looking more real than their pulled-together, made-up daytime selves.

"Domestic violence?" asked a skinny little old man excitedly.

"Heart attack?" asked a young woman in a hot pink t-shirt and huge baggy sweatpants.

"Someone get beat up in a burglary?" asked a middle-aged man in an ancient striped robe. "This place had been hit three times in the last month."

"No, uh, I think it is something more along the lines of natural causes," said Flora, not sure how much she should say.

"Marshall's dead?" asked Curler Lady, mean face completely gone.

Flora raised her shoulders and half nodded.

"Oh, what a shame," said Curler Lady. "Such a kind man. Well, he was almost ninety so, I guess, you know, he had a long life. Oh, your friend must be his girlfriend! Nice lady." Several people standing near Curler Lady nodded in agreement.

Curler Lady elbowed a man beside her. "Call your sister, tell her an apartment opened up."

"It's the middle of the night," the man said. "I'll call in the morning."

"It'll be rented by morning," said Curler Lady.

Flora wondered if they would all feel so friendly if they knew Velma had worn out Marshall's heart with too much sex. Or maybe they would appreciate that. Not a bad way to go. For all Flora knew, Marshall died on the happiest day of his life. Come to think of it, maybe Velma was some kind of special death facilitator, an angel offering a man the happiest possible transition between this life and the next.

"Mm-hmm, I think we could assume he died happy," said Flora. "Hey, Christine! What're you doing here?" she added, spying Christine in the crowd.

"Hi, Mrs. Gonzalez," said Christine. "Ah, visiting a friend. What's going on?"

"Bit of a problem with one of Velma's sweeties. I came to pick her up. Poor guy picked tonight to meet the Maker."

"Oh, so sorry. I'm sure you need to get to Mrs. Costa, I won't keep you," Christine said and shuffled back to the apartment before Flora could ask her any more.

Flora gave a hard stare at Christine's back. "Don't nobody sleep around this place," she said to herself with a little laugh.

CHAPTER 29
The Peace Disturbed

Mrs. Mango pulled the door to the guest cottage shut. It wasn't quite a slam but it was close, and it made Emma Rose, in Mrs. Mango's arms, jump. She muttered to herself, annoyed at the destruction of her newfound peace.

"What are they thinking?" she fumed, pulling a glass out of the cupboard and filling it with water. "Who knows what sort of spells or herbs he's going to try to give to you, my sweet?" She shook her head to herself, looking down at Emma Rose's little face. "Probably against vaccinations too."

Don Paz was now installed in the spare room in the house 'for a little while.'

If anyone knew how open-ended 'a little while' was, it was Mrs. Mango. She'd have to watch him closely. No telling what weird ideas he had about babies. For all she knew, he was in there performing some pagan ritual that would mark the child for life. With one hand, she flipped open her pill organizer and shook out the 'Tuesday Noon' compartment.

Oh sure, he said all the right things, oohed and ahhed over Emma Rose like the rest of them, but the guy was odd. Danny and Rita had enough going on without turning into a guest house for every family member who couldn't support himself! It was supposedly temporary while the building Don Paz was setting up for his 'office' was renovated. Apparently, he was pouring every bit of money into the renovation, but who knew how long *that* could take?

Mrs. Mango knew she had no say in the matter, but that didn't stop her from plotting to get Danny alone. She'd talk some sense into him. And, meanwhile, she would never let this baby out of her sight. She hugged Emma Rose closer. A fierce protectiveness burned inside her. If need be, she wouldn't even sleep until that snake oil salesman was out of the house.

"There you are!" said Rita, peeking through the door into the guest house to find Mrs. Mango and Emma Rose. "I couldn't find you anywhere."

Rita had popped home in the middle of the day to pick up some files she had accidentally left out of her briefcase. It was no annoyance to her because she was happy to look in on her sleeping baby, but the baby was not asleep. In fact, she had started panicking when she couldn't find anyone in the house.

"Oh, hello, just getting my midday pills," said Mrs. Mango, turning around while still bobbing gently up and down to soothe Emma Rose.

"Why isn't she in bed?" asked Rita. "It's nap time," she said, looking at her watch as if to prove the point.

"Oh, we're almost there," said Mrs. Mango. "Just heading up."

"Did she not sleep well this morning?" asked Rita.

"She slept fine! She's such a good baby," said Mrs. Mango. "And she took all of her bottle and gave me the best burp. I think she's getting close to tired now."

"But she should have been down forty-five minutes ago," said Rita, trying to keep her voice friendly, but annoyed that Emma Rose was not on her schedule.

"Well, she wasn't tired," said Mrs. Mango. "But, hey, why are you home in the middle of the day? Are you sick?"

"No, just forgot some files," said Rita. Maybe it was because she was in her lawyer-brain time of day or maybe it was just Rita's style, but her mind immediately got suspicious of Mrs. Mango.

"You *are* keeping the schedule, right?" asked Rita.

"Well, yes, mostly," said Mrs. Mango. "I mean, it would be impossible to do it to the minute, but I don't imagine you expect that."

Rita thought forty-five minutes was way beyond the margin for error that was acceptable, but she struggled not to bark at her mother-in-law. "Here, can I hold her? I have to leave in a few minutes, but I might as well get a little Emma Rose time."

Mrs. Mango handed Emma Rose over. Rita cooed at her and kissed her a couple of times then looked up at Mrs. Mango who was still swallowing pills. Rita gave a cold smile and turned to leave the guest house. "I'll just put her down myself, see you inside."

Mrs. Mango stared at the door after it closed behind Rita. She was mildly aware that Rita was upset but put it down to her stressful job. Her daughter-in-law was definitely high-strung.

Up in the nursery, Rita fumed as she re-swaddled Emma Rose and gently snugged her into her sleep positioner. She should have known. It was all just too good to be true. Mrs. Mango was not keeping the schedule. No wonder Emma Rose fussed at night! She was not getting proper sleep training. Probably not doing any bit of the consistent eat, play, sleep schedule Rita had showed her.

Rita gave Emma Rose one more little pat and slipped out. In the kitchen, she found the clipboard she had set up with a whole list of Emma's schedule, broken down by time and activity. She thought she was making it easy for Mrs. Mango (and reassuring for herself) to type up the time of day each thing should happen and put a little box beside it where Mrs. Mango could check off once it was done. But looking at the day's schedule, she felt her blood pressure rocket. It was only 12:30, but the boxes were checked clear through five o'clock!

Mrs. Mango came through the door right as Rita threw down the clipboard.

"Can I make you a quick bite of something to eat before you go?" Mrs. Mango said to Rita.

"No! We need to talk!" barked Rita.

Mrs. Mango recoiled at the anger in Rita's voice. "What's wrong?"

"You already checked all the boxes!" Rita said, picking up the clipboard and waving it at Mrs. Mango. In her lawyer attire, she was extra intimidating, the slate gray suit jacket and skirt showing off Rita's slim tall figure, the soft pale pink silk shirt underneath not softening her a bit. The sleek black pumps she wore added enough to her height to put her at a full foot over Mrs. Mango. She took a deep breath, trying to calm herself and talk rationally, but she was outraged. She felt duped and manipulated.

"Oh, yes," said Mrs. Mango, her face flushing. Darned hot flashes. "But I follow it."

"It doesn't look like you do!" said Rita. "She should have been down for a nap forty-five minutes ago. Almost an hour now." Rita looked at the baby monitor. "And she's not asleep yet."

"Well, maybe she's not tired," said Mrs. Mango. "That bed is so big! She gets lonely in there, and I think she does the best falling asleep in my arms anyway."

"Oh my gosh!" exploded Rita. "Remember, I told you that we are trying to teach her how to self-soothe? She will never learn that if you hold her 'til she falls asleep! She'll never learn to fall asleep on her own!"

Mrs. Mango shook her head. She thought all of this sleep training and self-soothing and other fancy terms was baloney. She had held her own children until they fell asleep, and they grew up just fine. And how could you let a baby just lie there crying? It was inhumane. A baby needed to be comforted! She was just a baby!

"The poor thing, she's just a baby," said Mrs. Mango. She knew she was headed into dangerous territory, but she couldn't stop herself. "Babies need touch, they need to be comforted, I can't let her lie there crying and not do anything!"

"You pick her up?" Rita gasped. She had been very clear that once Emma Rose was in the crib, she needed to be allowed to get herself to sleep.

"Of course! Babies cry for a reason," said Mrs. Mango.

Rita took a deep breath and called on her court self, the one that could be calm on the outside no matter how rattled she was inside. She grabbed the bottom of her suit jacket with both hands and tugged it down, pulling herself up to her full height. It was only partially effective because this was her *baby*. "I really need for you to respect my wishes, *our* wishes, on this," she said, spacing out her words to try to slow down the anger. "I know there are all sorts of theories on raising kids, and I respect that people have different ways of doing things, but this is the way I, *we*, want to raise Emma Rose. And you need to respect that."

Mrs. Mango gave a little huff. "Well," she started. She was about to continue on with her belief that Emma Rose needed more than just a robotic schedule, but the thought of Rita finding someone else to care for Emma Rose stopped her. "Well," she said again, and with great effort, "I understand. I apologize. You are right."

The words did not ring true to either of them, but Rita didn't want to fight further. Family relationships had to be treated very carefully, especially in-law relationships. Most especially a mother-in-law relationship.

"Thank you," Rita said in a hard-won cool voice. "I need to run now. See you later."

In the car, Rita dialed Danny's office and when Danny came on the phone, Rita launched into a 'you won't believe what your mother did' diatribe that lasted clear back to her office.

As Danny listened, his chest tightened. He knew it had been too good to be true. He knew his mother would somehow interfere in a way that would drive Rita crazy. Now he was going to be trapped between his wife and his mother. Nothing good ever could come of that. Maybe he should be glad it lasted this long, but he had a feeling that there would be a lot of fireworks before it was all over. And who knew what Don Paz was going to add to the mix.

Shit.

That night, the complaining continued once Rita

and Danny were shut into their bedroom. Very few problems made it past the peace this bedroom suite usually brought Rita. All of her design talents had been focused on making their bedroom, bathroom, and sitting area into a place of serene beauty. The walls were painted a dark putty, the headboard of the king-sized bed was a tufted sand-colored linen. Various shades of white and sand were scattered through the rest of the room in the form of duvet, couch, and chairs. A distressed pine chest ran the length of the end of the bed. A couple of coral pillows and a wall of built-in shelves with books were the only splashes of color.

"Don't you agree? I read the books, she needs to be on a schedule!" said Rita, pulling her shirt off and tossing it into the hamper in the corner of her walk-in closet. While in there, she grabbed her pajamas and threw the shirt of the set over her head.

Danny was happy to go along with Rita and he mildly agreed with her, but it also didn't seem like that big of a deal if Emma Rose wasn't on a strict schedule. Not that he was going to tell Rita. This had to be a united front. "Yes, that is the way to go," he agreed, sinking down onto the couch in the little seating area across from the bed. His eyes went to the remote to the small TV Rita had permitted across from the couch, but he thought better of reaching for it.

"I mean, I can't believe your mother actually lied to me—lied to us!" Rita said, pulling her silk pajama bottoms up with an angry grab.

"Lied?"

"Well, filling in a form that you did something that you didn't actually do is a lie," said Rita. "It is fraud."

Danny wanted to roll his eyes, but Rita was staring right at him.

"I'll tell you what I'm going to do!" said Rita, hands on hips. "I figured it out this afternoon. Tomorrow, I'm buying some webcams. I'll be able to see what is going on from work."

"I can't believe you are using a nanny-cam on my

mother," said Danny, pulling one of the coral pillows into his lap, unconsciously putting a barrier between him and his angry wife. And right over the tender parts.

"Do you have a better idea? Because my other option is to fire her."

"I don't know that you can fire someone you don't pay," said Danny, trying to make it funny.

"You know what I mean. If she can't respect me, she can't take care of Emma Rose. Period."

****

Dear Raul,

Oh these young people! Every generation thinks they have invented caring for babies! Like we haven't been keeping babies alive for thousands of years now, without sleep schedule spreadsheets and Babybjorns and SleepSacks. For crying out loud. But I don't want to waste my time with you talking about Rita and Danny. I want to tell you how sweet that Emma Rose is! The smell of her, oh, how I missed that baby smell. Twenty, thirty times a day, I stick my nose right next to her head and smell that delicious smell. And then her breath, oh, the smell of a baby's breath. Still so sweet, all the time. The weight of her in my arms feels like the most natural thing in the world. Oh, and the absolute joy of a baby falling asleep in your arms, it is just the most amazing feeling.

Mrs. Mango's brain drifted around all the Emma Rose images collected so far. Her peaceful face in sleep, her adorably small little figure all swaddled in that big crib. The perfect pale skin of her cheeks, the random flinging of her arms and legs, the way her face turned instinctively into Mrs. Mango's bosom, looking to feed. And the clothes! The most adorable onesies and outfits had shown up from all of Rita and Danny's friends. Mrs. Mango sat in peace, full of joy.

With a start, Mrs. Mango came out of her reverie and looked at the clock. Goodness, her Sunday half hour was already up. How had that happened? She jumped up, went to the sink, and burned the letter, and with her brain still filled with Emma Rose, ran the water to rinse it down the drain.

CHAPTER 30
A Discovery

It was Saturday, a month after Emma Rose's arrival, and Christine was back at her parent's house rounding up a few more of her belongings. After the mad rush of moving out, when she mainly took her clothes and things she used on a daily basis, she was back for some other items, like her rarely used workout clothes and the super-sized bottles of Nexxus shampoo and conditioner she had bought at Costco. She had finally finished the last gargantuan bottles and was ready for her replacements. That stuff wasn't cheap, so it was worth a trip home for that alone. Christine had hoped to also check in on her dad, but he wasn't around. She assumed he was working at Artie's since that seemed to be his new hangout. She was relieved that every time she checked in on him, he always seemed to have something going on but decided she'd stop by Artie's garage on her way home and see how her dad was doing.

Christine grabbed a few more items of clothes from her drawers and then went looking for the shampoo. She looked in the bathroom next to her room but no shampoo. She opened the linen closet in the hall but didn't find it there either. Maybe her parents had needed it, so she headed towards their bathroom. She looked in the shower but saw only dandruff shampoo and a collection of body scrubbers that looked a couple of decades old. Eww. She looked under the sink and moved the stack of towels to see if it had gotten stuck behind the towels.

No shampoo, but an interesting-looking box that Christine had never seen. She noticed a lock hanging off the box, unclamped. It was too intriguing to ignore, so she opened the box to find a stack of papers, all carefully folded in thirds. With an awareness that she was probably invading someone's privacy, Christine opened the top letter, saw her mother's handwriting, then caught sight of her own name, and started reading.

Dear Raul,

Who was Raul?

Christine read on.

> *I'm feeling very churned up inside these days. Very unsettled. Like nothing is normal anymore. Joe got scammed (and tried to blame me!). And that Vegevape party ruined everything. Somehow I've given Christine the impression that I'm okay with her, what's the word for it, lifestyle. I think there must have been something in the supplements they put in that thing because my brain got all fuzzy and Sarah seemed nice and not at all a problem. And then in the morning, it all seemed wrong again. Or maybe I'm just losing my mind. There. I said it. I can say it to you. I think I might be going crazy. This is even worse than when the menopausal stuff started, and, believe me, that was bad. One moment I feel okay, the next I'm in tears and unable to stop.*

Christine couldn't figure it out. Who was this Raul, and why was her mother writing to him? And if she was writing to him, why wasn't the letter sent? She knew she should put the letter back and walk away, but there wasn't a chance of that happening. Not when she was learning so much about what her mother thought of her. Not that it was a surprise. She picked up the next letter, and then the next, feeling as if she was falling further down a rabbit hole with each letter that she read.

> *Oh, Raul, I miss you so much. I have just never stopped loving you or remembering your love for me. I'm so sorry for all my parents did. I hated them for so long. It has been so many years that I find it hard to summon up the*

Christine sat back against the tub behind her, letting
the letter fall into her lap. What the hell was this?
Obviously, her mother had someone from her past that she
still loved. Really loved. Enough to write to. And what had
her mother's parents done? And how did her dad figure in?

No wonder her mother never seemed that loving
towards her dad. She wasn't in love with him. She was still
in love with this 'Raul' character.

Christine looked at the box, stuffed with letters. The
answers were probably all in there, but should she look?
The full meaning of violating her mother's privacy hit her.
All of a sudden, it felt incredibly invasive. And sad. And
weird. Too many emotions for her to process at one time.

How could you feel like you knew someone, knew
them well for twenty-seven years, and then find out you
really didn't know them? Her mother was a person she
didn't even know. Her mother had a whole other side to her
that Christine never even guessed about. Her mother was a
passionate person. Her mother had really loved someone.

As Christine sat there staring at the jumble of
towels over the open box, her brain whirred around, putting
pieces together into a new picture of her mother. Her
mother's seemingly constant irritation with her dad but
chatty friendliness with everyone else, her mother's
practical, matter-of-fact way of approaching the world.
Maybe that all came from this past tragedy. And Christine
was sure it was a tragedy. She could tell from just the few
letters she had already read. Her fingers itched to read
more, and yet she was fearful of what she'd find.

"Christine? You here?" she heard her father call.

She leaned over and slammed the bathroom door shut. "In the bathroom!" she yelled back. She shoved the letters back in the box and replaced the towels over it. She wished she could clamp the lock, but that would mean she couldn't look at the letters again. She couldn't make that decision this quickly. Then she worried that her dad would find the box the way she had. What to do?

She flushed the toilet and ran water in the sink to stall. She thought about taking the box, hiding it in a laundry basket under some clothes but eventually decided she'd have to leave it. What if her mother came home looking for it before Christine could sneak it back? No, she would just have to leave it.

Christine checked one more time to make sure the towels were in place and left the bathroom.

CHAPTER 31
The Kiss of Death

Rassa sauntered up the Mangos' street, his tall skinny body jangling its bones like a Halloween skeleton banging about in a stiff breeze, his long dreadlocks bouncing with each step. The walk had only been a matter of six blocks from his buddy Delbert's apartment, where Rassa was currently inhabiting the dingy couch until he worked out something better, but he was tiring. He checked off houses looking for the Mangos', thinking as he did that he could stand to live in a nice neighborhood like this. Ah, there it was, the one with the duct-taped mailbox. The Mango kids had gone to a high school where alumni took wildly divergent career paths, many starting those paths earlier than others by foregoing their degree. Although Mr. and Mrs. Mango expected their children to go to college and pursue useful careers, no one in the family acted like they were better than those who didn't have career plans. Or college plans. Or even finishing high school plans. Mr. Mango was known to be a soft touch among the less-than-gainfully-employed, and Rassa was no fool when it came to easily obtained cash. The last time around, Mr. Mango had 'lent' Rassa twenty dollars, but today he was hoping for more. He was down to his last strike and didn't want to waste it with some little burglary. He was going to plan something big and go down in a blaze of gunfire if it came to that, but until then, he needed to find a way to buy some more weed. He owed too much to his regular dealers to even ask for an extension of credit. In fact, he was doing his best to avoid running into them at all. Rassa saw Mr. Mango's feet sticking out from under his truck and got an extra hitch in his step in pleasure.

"Hey, Mr. Mango," Rassa said when he got close. "Wass' up?"

Mr. Mango didn't answer.

"Dude, hey, Mr. Mango," said Rassa. No first names for a family you kind of respected and from whom you were hoping to get money.

Still no answer. In fact, there was no movement.

Rassa bumped Mr. Mango's foot with his foot but got no response.

"Hey! You!" Rassa yelled, leaning down. As he did so, Mrs. Melucci came hustling across the street dressed in blue polyester pants, a pink smock top, and slippers.

"I been looking out the window and wondering," she said to Rassa. "He hasn't moved in a while."

Rassa crouched down and jiggled Mr. Mango's leg. "Hey, dude."

Nothing.

Mrs. Melucci sank to her knees and started shaking Mr. Mango. Getting no answer, she screamed, "Pull him out! He might've had another attack!"

Together, they pulled Mr. Mango out from under the car. His face was pale and clammy and his eyes closed.

"Holy shit," said Rassa.

Mrs. Mango leaned down and put her ear to his nose, felt his chest. "I can't tell if he's breathing! Call an ambulance!"

Rassa pulled out his phone and dialed 911, wondering if they had some kind of flag in the computer by his number. Maybe they wouldn't even come. Maybe the police would be on their way too. Shit, he better get out of there. "Hey, yeah, um, got an old dude here and think he might have had a heart attack." He looked up at the mailbox and gave the address. "Nope, not conscious. Can't tell if he's breathing."

"Tell them he had a heart attack a couple weeks ago!" screeched Mrs. Melucci, as she alternately pushed on Mr. Mango's chest and then breathed into his mouth.

Mr. Mango's eyes fluttered open and widened in horror when he saw Mrs. Melucci's mouth on his.

When Mrs. Melucci pulled back from his mouth,

Mr. Mango spat and gasped. "What the hell?" he
whispered.

Rassa shook his head. "Dude, we thought you was
dead."

Mr. Mango closed his eyes and opened them again,
as if hoping that the scene in front of him would change.
He stared at Mrs. Melucci. "I don't feel so good," he
whispered and closed his eyes again.

At the sound of sirens, Rassa stood up and, with a
careful nonchalance, slipped away.

"Jesus Christ, Dad, you got to stop scaring us like
this," said Danny to Mr. Mango. Danny, Mrs. Mango, and
Christine were gathered around Mr. Mango's hospital bed.
Thankfully, the second bed in the semiprivate room was
unoccupied because Mangos filled the room, both in space
and volume. Mrs. Mango was standing with her arms
crossed, glaring at Mr. Mango. Like it was his fault he had
another 'cardiac event.'

Mr. Mango lifted and dropped his shoulders in
resignation. "You want me to apologize?" he said. "Not
like I was trying to."

"I know, I know, I didn't mean to sound like that,"
said Danny. "It just, well, I just . . . " he couldn't finish. He
sat down on the empty bed, staring at his dad.

"My goodness, but you put the fear of God into
Danny," said Mrs. Mango. "I thought I would be the one
called home to heaven first because he broke the speed
limit the whole way down here."

Mrs. Mango's stomach felt like she had swallowed
a sack of snakes, guilt and fear wrestling with anger. She
let anger win, unable to let her mind go to the fearful place
or, even worse, the guilt. "Well, was it a heart attack or
not?" demanded Mrs. Mango.

"Sometimes they can't be sure," Mr. Mango said,
looking at Danny for confirmation. Danny nodded. "Could
be a heart attack or 'acute coronary syndrome,'" added Mr.

Mango. "Gets treated like a heart attack, so, goddamn it, the driving restriction clock starts all over again."

Danny looked puzzled.

"You know, driving my truck. Have to wait three months after the 'event' to go back to work."

"Maybe those driving days are done for," said Mrs. Mango.

"Wait and see," jumped in Danny, seeing the frustration on his dad's face.

Christine was standing there, feeling sick with guilt that she had moved out on her dad at the worst possible time. This was all her fault. It was no help to remind herself she would have been at work anyway, whether she lived at home or not. Discovered by a flipping druggie! As if reading her thoughts, Danny said, "And tell me again, who was it that found you?"

"Friend of Delbert's—you remember Delbert, was in your class, ended up in and out of jail. Rasta or Raffa or something. Guy with the dreadlocks. I assume he was coming to ask me for money." Mr. Mango remembered the rest, and his face contorted, "And Mary Melucci. I guess it's a good thing she spies on us so much." No way he was telling any of them that she had performed CPR on him. Maybe he could find a way to forget that himself. There had been a few bad moments there when he thought he might have died and landed in hell.

Danny shook his head. "Who knew it would be lucky to know Delbert and Rassa? I mean, if he hadn't been coming around, you might . . ."

Mr. Mango waved a hand. "Just not my time," he said. "Something would have saved me."

"Well, you can't be alone during the day anymore," said Danny. "Not enough that Christine is there at night."

Christine and her dad exchanged guilty looks. A tear slipped out of Christine's eye, and her dad reached over and squeezed her hand.

Mrs. Mango swiveled her head to stare at Danny. "I can't go home! There's nobody to take care of Emma

Rose!"

Mr. Mango closed his eyes. If a second 'cardiac event' wasn't enough, nothing would be. His wife was showing absolutely no compassion for him. He was getting towards the end of his patience with Mrs. Mango. Mr. Mango wasn't quick to change much of anything in his brain and had lived for years seeing his wife the way she had been when he first met her. For so long, he didn't see the wrinkles or the grumpiness, he saw the beauty and the passion of the young Elsie. But that image, he realized, was shifting. Too many years of nagging and apparent disinterest had dislodged the rose-colored glasses.

"You'll just come stay with us!" said Danny. "We've got the room. I can keep an eye on you, and Mom can take care of Emma Rose until we find a nanny. Plenty of room in the guest house." Danny gave a big smile, happy with his solution. "Not taking no for an answer this time."

Christine breathed a big sigh of relief. She had thought they might ask her to move home, and the timing would have been all wrong given how things were going with Sarah. Then, she noticed the look on her mother's face. Like a child who just had her bag of Halloween candy stolen.

"What about Poker? And the cat?" asked Mrs. Mango. "Christine can't come home in the middle of the day every day."

Christine panicked. She wasn't there at all! And no way they could take the dog to the apartment. Maybe the cat, but definitely not the dog.

Christine sighed. "I'll make sure the animals are taken care of." She had no idea how that would happen, but she'd have to make it happen.

Danny frowned. "Mom, I'm sure we'll work it out. Dad can't stay home alone, at least not for a while. *Animals are not the issue here.*" Even as he said it, he knew Rita would never let the dog come too. He could only push his wife so far.

Mr. Mango closed his eyes. Maybe if he pretended to go to sleep, they would all go away. His eyes flew open when he heard Danny say, "Michael!"

Sure enough, his second son was standing in front of him. "Dad. Jesus, Dad," said Michael, twisting at the jacket he was carrying. Michael moved forward, leaned down, and gave his dad a half hug. "Dad," he said again, like he couldn't find any other words. Michael's hand went to his back, a sight wince passing over his face. Everyone but Danny figured the wince was at his dad's 'coronary event.' Danny knew Michael was struggling with debilitating back pain, but neither of them wanted their mother to know.

Mr. Mango gave a little wave. "Ah, don't get all choked up. I'm fine. Not my time. And when it is, well, hell, then it is. When God calls you home for dinner, you don't have much of a choice."

"How do you feel? Are you in pain?" said Michael.

"Just kind of tired," said Mr. Mango. "Which is a blessing because I'm sure Obama is going to have them throw me out of here soon. Costs too much to keep a person in the hospital. Mediocrity for all, that's his slogan."

Mr. Mango's kids smiled at each other in relief. Yep, same old Dad.

The next day, Mr. Mango was dozing in his hospital bed when he heard a sound in the room. His eyes opened and darted to the second bed—no, still empty. He looked towards the door, and he thought he might be in a dream.

"Joey!" he croaked, his voice unused for several hours.

Joe Jr. was standing in front of him, smiling and crying. "Dad," he said, walking slowly toward the bed. Joe Jr. was the tallest of the Mangos, at six one, and also, incontestably, the best-looking. Mrs. Mango loved looking at him, conveniently forgetting that he looked exactly like his father had looked when she met him. Blue eyes, thick dark hair, a charming smile. Mr. Mango always told people he was the best-looking waiter in Los Angeles. When people mentioned that they looked alike Mr. Mango waved his hand and disagreed but he secretly agreed.

"What're you doing here?" said Mr. Mango, holding out his arms for Joe to give him a hug.

"Are you kidding? Do you think I wouldn't come?" said Joe, leaning in and giving his dad a gentle squeeze. "I mean, you could have just asked me to come see you, you didn't have to have a heart attack to get me here." Joe pulled back and looked at his dad.

Mr. Mango shrugged. "Hey, if that's what it takes. Hope you didn't spend too much getting here."

"Nah, don't worry, we were due for a little road trip."

"Jenny is here too?"

"She's in the hall. Wasn't sure how much company you wanted," said Joe, wiping at the corner of his eye. His voice was cheery, but his face didn't completely hide his pain at seeing his dad in a hospital bed.

"Bring her in," said Mr. Mango. "Why the hell not? I promise not to bend over in this scrap they call a hospital gown. No one needs to see old man crack."

Joe got Jenny, and after she kissed Mr. Mango and they all told each other how good they looked, Joe sat on the foot of his dad's bed and Jenny sat in a chair beside it. Jenny was a delicate-looking woman, with pretty features that were always just a smidge over the edge of looking tired. Like if she had a good rest, she'd be a knockout. Thin auburn hair framed her face in a layer cut that set off her fine nose and cheekbones. When she smiled her eyes were bright and warm. Mr. Mango had liked her from the first moment Joe brought her home, and nothing had changed his opinion in the twelve years since, especially given the way she supported Joe's dreams all these years.

"Dad, what the hell is going on with you?" said Joe. He was the only one who ever got away with talking to his dad like that, maybe because he added a warm teasing tone to the words.

"Who knows? My heart's acting up, I guess," said Mr. Mango.

"How do you feel now?" asked Jenny.

"I'm fine," Mr. Mango waved his hand, dismissing his surroundings. "I mean, I'm sleeping a lot, but I do that at home anyway."

"When do you get to go home?" asked Joe.

"That's the million dollar question, along with the two million dollar question of what home I actually go to."

Joe raised his eyebrows in question.

"Apparently, I shouldn't be by myself, and you know your mother is up there with Danny's new baby, and Christine . . ." Mr. Mango wasn't sure he should share Christine's news. How much did Joe and Jenny know?

"Christine . . . what about Christine?" said Joe.

"She's, uh, you know, she's got her own life, she's not around as much as I guess the doctors want someone around me." Mr. Mango wasn't going to be the one to tell Christine's business. "So, it looks like I'm going to Danny's house. Michael offered to have me at his house, but he's never home, and I don't want to sit around his big mausoleum with some hired lackey staring at me."

"That makes sense," said Joe. "We're sticking around for a little while, so I can take you up to Danny's if you want. And we can see the baby!"

Jenny smiled. "I can't wait! The pictures are just adorable. How great for them." A quick shadow flitted across her face—or was Mr. Mango just imagining that? Did every woman who didn't have a baby want a baby?

Mr. Mango thought it was his kids' business if and when they had babies, but he had heard Mrs. Mango ask them all repeatedly over the years when she was getting grandchildren. Joe and Jenny always said they were waiting to be 'more established,' but that hadn't happened, and they were both forty. Mr. Mango stared at Jenny, wondering if she felt like she had missed her chance.

"Yeah, great for them. And your mother is over the moon. But, you know, babies are a shitload of work."

Joe laughed. "Jenny has her hands full with me. Can't imagine a baby too!"

Jenny laughed with Joe but not as hard or long.

"Hey! I heard the famous Joe was going to make an appearance," said Danny, coming into the room carrying magazines, a paperback, and an iPad.

Jenny and Joe stood up to hug Danny.

"Hey, butthead," Joe said to Danny, whacking him on the back.

"Really?" said Danny, shaking his head. "Good to see you too."

Joe's pocket buzzed, and he pulled out his cell phone. "Oh man, I need to take this," he said, punching a button and walking out into the hall as he answered.

Jenny stared at the door Joe had just gone through. "He had a great audition the other day, this might be about that."

"Yes, I'll bet it's his big break," said Danny, still stinging from the butthead comment. Danny set his armful of stuff on the table beside his dad's bed. "Here, brought you some stuff to read and an iPad to look at."

Mr. Mango shrugged. People had interesting ideas of what to bring a hospital patient. Most seemed to bring what they themselves would want.

"He's had some good jobs lately," said Jenny. "He really has. He was in two plays for the Playwright's Workshop, he sang for a couple of commercial songs, and you can look for him on an episode of Law and Order: SVU—he's a waiter."

Danny burst out laughing. "So he's a method actor!"

"Yes, he was well prepared for that one," said Jenny, this time with a real smile.

A man in scrubs came through the door. "Hello, Joe," he said, coming alongside the bed. "Need a bedpan yet?"

"Oh, Christ," grumbled Mr. Mango. "Really? They

send a man? And in front of my daughter-in-law? I'd rather crawl to the bathroom myself."

The nurse smiled good-naturedly at Danny and Jenny. "I love this guy. Reminds me of my dad."

"I'm good, Ben," said Mr. Mango. "I'll call you if I need anything. Don't hold your breath."

"I can take a hint," the nurse laughed. This was not his first cranky old man patient. "First let me check a few vitals, then I'm out of your hair."

Once Ben the nurse was gone, Mr. Mango looked at Jenny while Danny looked through the cards and flowers lined along the window sill.

"How are you doing, Jenny?" asked Mr. Mango. "They treating you well at work?"

"Just fine, thanks," said Jenny.

"You know, I got to hand it to you, you haven't gone all Hollywood on us," said Mr. Mango. "Your face still looks real. In a good way. Please promise me you won't do all that shit to your face that the LA women seem to all do. They end up looking like plastic ducks."

"No worries," said Jenny. "That whole scene is just not me. But tell me about all this heart stuff. What happened? When? How did you know?"

Mr. Mango filled her in on the series of events that had landed him in the hospital.

"Thank goodness someone found you," Jenny said, fear in her voice. "That must really have been God looking out for you."

Mr. Mango nodded. He had been thinking a lot recently about God. Nothing like a heart attack or two to make you think about religion.

CHAPTER 32
Loaded

Several days later, Danny and Mr. Mango were headed to Danny's house after a stop at the Mangos to pick up some clothes and other belongings for Mr. Mango. As he drove, Danny thought about how, once again, Joe Jr. had somehow managed to not be available to help. Claimed he had a meeting in San Francisco so would drive up with Jenny to see them later. Some people never changed. Danny stared out at hills they were winding their way through, for once not noticing how much it felt like driving through Italy. Normally, passing one hill after another covered in neat rows of grapevines filled him with gratitude. It was his drive home from work, and work problems were always soothed by the landscape, but apparently it didn't have the same effect on family issues. As the hills receded and the road bent and straightened, allowing glimpses of the same neat rows of grapevines marching through flat land, Danny wondered how his home could have filled up so quickly. A short time ago, it was just he and Rita, and they both worked a lot. Now there was a baby, his mother, a brother-in-law, and a cardiac patient. Not to mention Joe and Jenny on their way to visit too. Danny took a deep breath and told himself it would all work out. Then he remembered the nanny cams Rita installed and knew it was not going to all work out.

"Good God, I'm ready for an election that doesn't have a Bush or a Clinton in it!" said Mr. Mango. "They're all so goddamned crooked, they move forward by walking backwards."

Danny didn't answer. He knew there was nothing he could say that would stop his dad or make his dad happy. Two years away from the next election, and his dad was already full of fury.

"This country's going to hell. This state is going to

hell—literally! We are one tossed cigarette away from the whole state burning up. Jesus, we haven't had enough rain to quench the thirst of a fruit fly. Maybe it would have been better if I'd died from that heart attack because nothing is going to get better. We are in the shits, son, the shits. I was you, I wouldn't have been so fast to take on a baby. I mean, I'm excited to be a granddad, but what kind of world has that little girl been born into? We never met a war we didn't want to be involved in, we are opening our borders to just about anyone who wants to come suck on the American teat, and our state is out of money and water. I mean, Jesus. A man could get pretty depressed thinking about all this."

Danny just nodded enough to let his dad know he was listening. No need to answer. He pulled into his driveway, puttered past the pond, and pulled up in front of the house.

Mr. Mango eased himself out of the car, and Danny walked around back, lifted the SUV door, and pulled out Mr. Mango's duffel bag. "What'd you pack in here? Gold? This thing is heavy," laughed Danny. Then he stopped and stared at his dad, having just considered the types of things his dad might bring. "You didn't bring your gun, did you?" he said.

"Yeah, yeah, I get it," said Mr. Mango, reaching back into the front seat for his jacket. "No gun."

"Did you bring the gun?"

"I told you, I get it. You don't want the gun."

"You haven't actually answered me! Did you bring it?"

"What?"

"Oh my God, just yes or no."

"Well, yes and no."

"What does that mean?"

"I brought it, but I stuck it under the seat there," he gestured towards the SUV.

"Jesus CHRIST, I don't want it in my car! I don't want it on my property. We need to get it out of here before

Rita finds out. Your ass will be on the curb if you don't."

"How am I supposed to get it out of here? I'm not even driving again yet. We can just unload it."

Danny eyes widened in disbelief. "It's *loaded?* I'll get it. And I'll hide it. *Unloaded.*"

The two of them walked through the front door and into the kitchen. Mrs. Mango was doing her baby sway with Emma Rose in her arms, and Don Paz was standing at the counter chopping peppers.

Mrs. Mango gave a nod at Danny and Mr. Mango, and Don Paz came around the counter wiping his hands on his pants.

"Hello, Joe," he beamed, taking both of Mr. Mango's hands in his and squeezing them. "Blessings on your healing."

"Thanks, Don," said Mr. Mango.

"Don Paz," Don Paz reminded him.

If Mr. Mango had known Don Paz was also in residence, he would have taken his chances alone at home with Poker.

"Right. Don *Paz.* I'm feeling a little tired, so I'm going to go lie down," said Mr. Mango. It was convenient but also true. Danny carried Mr. Mango's duffel bag out to the guest house with Mr. Mango trailing behind.

"I'm so glad we got this finished," said Danny, gesturing at the guest house as they stepped through the door. "Who knew we'd need it so soon?"

Mr. Mango looked around and nodded. "Very nice."

"The bad news is that the landscapers are coming Monday to work on the back yard. I apologize if it gets loud out there." Danny looked around the back yard, assessing the type of work still to be done. "They have maybe one more day on laying the rest of the stone for the walkways," he said. "And then it is all grass and plants and irrigation stuff."

Mr. Mango shrugged. "Maybe it's a good thing I'm here. I'll keep an eye on them. Make sure they don't rip you off or cut their day short."

"So, when is Emma Rose's christening?" asked Mrs. Mango as she set the table for dinner.

Rita paused in her salad tossing. "Christening? Hadn't thought about it." She looked towards Danny, who was pulling a pan of broiled salmon out of the oven. "What do you think?" She looked back at Mrs. Mango. "Oh, could you grab those placemats over on top of the sideboard? The striped ones. We don't eat directly on the wood of the table."

Mrs. Mango did an inner eye roll but went over to get the neat stack of placemats and added them to her table setting.

"Oh, we definitely have to baptize her!" Danny said. "You don't mind, do you?"

"We're not religious—I'm sort of surprised you want to," said Rita, throwing some shredded cheese over the top of the salad and dumping in the peppers Don Paz had cut up before he disappeared out of the kitchen.

"Of course, you have to!" exclaimed Mrs. Mango. "You want her soul to go to hell?"

"I didn't think I'd care, but I do," said Danny, slipping a spatula under each piece of fish and distributing them to the plates lined up on the counter. "But we don't exactly have a church."

"Are you telling me you two don't go to church?" asked Mrs. Mango. As she said it, she realized she had never heard them talk about it but had just assumed that they did. Her good Catholic boy would of course have been going to church.

Danny smiled sheepishly. "Not, uh, a lot."

Mrs. Mango slapped down the last of the silverware and put her hands on her hips, staring through the wide open glass doors between the dining room table and the kitchen. "Well you better start going now! You have a daughter to think about."

Rita rolled her eyes. "I'm not really a fan of

organized religion. I mean, I believe in God, but I think most of the religions are just about guilt and trying to control you. Maybe we should wait and let Emma Rose decide for herself when she is old enough.”

“What?” Mrs. Mango was outraged. “You can’t wait that long! You can have it at St. Andrews. It is such a lovely church.”

“It is a nice church,” agreed Danny.

Rita looked at him in surprise. “You really want to do this? You never go to church. I didn’t even know you cared.”

“I’m as surprised as you,” said Danny. “But I guess it feels different when you have a child. I really want to christen her.”

Mrs. Mango stared at Rita, waiting for her to fight Danny on this issue. She just had a feeling that Rita was not going to let Danny do something he wanted to. She never did.

Rita wrinkled her brow. “Well, I can’t really get excited about it one way or the other. I guess I don’t care, so if you want to, that’s okay.”

Mrs. Mango gave a big sigh of relief. “I can help you plan it!” she said excitedly.

Rita looked at Danny. “This is up to you,” she said. “I’ll go along with it, but I’m not doing the planning.”

“No problem,” said Danny carrying the plates to the table. “We need to figure out the godparents.”

Rita shook her head. “Whatever.” She walked to the back door and called outside for Don Paz and Mr. Mango. “Dinner!”

Mrs. Mango’s head buzzed with christening plans. Definitely St. Andrews. And she still had the gown that all four of her children had worn. And maybe Mimi and Leo could come, they hadn’t met Emma Rose yet. It was getting harder and harder to convince them to make the almost-three-hour drive up to Concordia but this should do it. Mrs. Mango was uncharacteristically quiet throughout dinner as all her wedding planning dreams rearranged themselves into a christening.

CHAPTER 33
A Revelation

Christine and Sarah walked out of the Mango's house into a misty fog a little after seven in the morning. Until she figured out what to do with Poker and Tripod Christine was staying back at home and Sarah had come with her. Christine was in her work uniform, which consisted of several pantsuits in varying colors and an array of interchangeable blouses. Sarah was ready for the challenges of fourth graders in slim khaki capris, a navy peasant blouse and tan ballet flats, her hair pulled up on her head in a neat bun. Christine was constantly amazed by the way Sarah put together fashionable outfits on a teacher's budget. It seemed to be a matter of knowing the colors that looked good on her and adding just the right accessories. Or maybe it was just that anything would have looked good on her.

"Hellooo! Hello Christine," Mrs. Melucci sang from across the street, having suspiciously timed her hobble towards the newspaper on her front walk with Christine and Sarah's appearance. It was amazing how often Mrs. Melucci just happened to be out in her front yard when interesting stuff was going on in the neighborhood, like she had a radar screen in her brain that pinged when gossip-worthy people were within range.

Christine turned her instinctive grimace into a fake smile. "Hi Mrs. Melucci," she called back picking up her pace towards her car. Maybe she could get away before the nosiest woman in the neighborhood made it across the street.

No luck, Mrs. Melucci left the newspaper lying on the walk and hustled across the street. "How's your father? How's the baby?" she asked. "What's all that stuff on your front porch?"

Sarah paused her walking, manners dictating she should stop when someone was talking to them. Christine silently willed her to keep moving. Mrs. Melucci could smell a secret from the other side of town. Up close there was no chance.

"Dad's doing okay. The baby is adorable! Mom is collecting for some women's center," said Christine edging towards the driveway and swinging her lunch box towards Mrs. Melucci to signal she was on her way to work. "Can't talk much longer, got to get to work."

Mrs. Melucci stared at Sarah then held out her hand towards Sarah. "Hi! I'm Mary Melucci," she said.

Sarah took her hand. "Nice to meet you. I'm Sarah."

Mrs. Melucci held onto Sarah's hand, waiting for more.

When nothing came, she dropped Sarah's hand. "I've seen you over here before. Friend of Christine's, huh?"

Sarah nodded. "Yep."

"I've known Christine all her life," said Mrs. Melucci. "All her life. I've been waiting for her to get married and have kids, and I know her mother has too. Any chance you could help find her a man? I'll bet you've got plenty, looking like that."

Sarah smiled. "Not sure that is up my alley. But nice to meet you, I need to head off to work." Sarah nodded at Mrs. Melucci and walked towards her car, parked up close behind Christine's car.

Christine followed, trying not to look back at Mrs. Melucci and give her any sense of Christine's anxiety. On the one hand, she was relieved that Mrs. Melucci seemed pretty clueless about her relationship with Sarah, on the other hand, she was really tired of Mrs. Melucci getting in her business. How was it any of her business if Christine got married or had kids? Then she panicked, thinking Mrs. Melucci was sure to tell her mother Sarah had stayed at their house.

"Tell Celia I said hello," Christine said over her shoulder, giving a little wave.

Mrs. Melucci stared at Christine until she had started her car and driven away. "Something's going on here. Something's going on."

On her way to work, Christine dialed Sarah, hit speaker, and stuck the phone on the seat beside her. No need to get pulled over for using a cell phone and make the day even worse.

"Omigod," Christine said when Sarah answered. "She knows something is up. I can feel it. And she'll tell my mom you slept over."

"Well," said Sarah. "So what?"

"I know, I know. I need to tell my mom anyway, but I want to do it myself, not have it come from Mrs. Melucci. And I don't think Mom would love it that you stayed over."

Sarah sighed.

"I think we better go back to the apartment tonight. Or at least you better," said Christine.

"So much for living together," said Sarah. "That didn't last long."

"This is an unusual circumstance!" said Christine. "My dad had a heart attack, and my mom's at my brother's, and, well, just let me handle it."

"Okay, handle it," said Sarah coolly. "I've got to go. I'm at school."

"Wait! I'll figure something out for the dog, and then I'll be back."

"Sure," said Sarah and she hung up.

That night, after a chilly dinner at Chipotle with Sarah, Christine sat alone in the Mango house trying to watch TV. She couldn't find anything interesting so turned it off. She felt restless but didn't know if it was the tension with Sarah or the odd feeling of being in the house without her parents there. In thinking about it, Christine realized that one or both of her parents were always in the house. Which made her think about the fact that she didn't remember the last time her parents had gone out somewhere together, even for, say, dinner. After sitting still for a few minutes in internal debate, Christine got up and headed to her parents' bathroom. She couldn't stay away from the letters any longer.

Pushing aside the guilt at invading her mother's private world, Christine read through each letter, carefully keeping them in the same order. Some parts of the letters were so recognizably her mother—references to Bundt cakes and aching knees—and other parts of the letter so unlike her mother it was as if another person had written them. And it was particularly odd to come across her own name, to see her mother's uncensored thoughts about her.

Christine is twenty-seven, and she's never been in love, at least not in any way it shows. And it always shows, doesn't it? It makes me sad for her, sad that she hasn't experienced what we had. I can remember, like it was just a moment ago, when I would see you again, and my body felt like it was one big beating heart. I can remember the look in your eyes when you saw me, like God had created something special just for you. It was like no one had ever really looked at me before, and then, you did. And it was everything. It was enough that I can still feel it, all these years later. I have lived on the memory of that love. I am feeling it right now and, once again, feel eternally grateful.

With love,
Elsie

Her mother was wrong about one thing. Christine knew exactly what her mother had felt like. She was feeling it herself. Sitting on the bathroom floor on a threadbare mildewey bath mat, tears started seeping from Christine's eyes. Her hand holding the letter fell to her lap, and she closed her eyes, leaning back against the side of the tub. The full force of her mother's lost love was suddenly too tragic for her to bear, and the slow flow of tears turned into a flood. Christine was in the most intense infatuation stage of love, and the thought of her mother in that, and then losing it, was heartbreaking.

Christine loved her mother and knew her mother loved her back, but there had always been something that held her mother at a slight distance away. Christine had assumed it was just a generational thing and that her mother wasn't an overly affectionate person. If asked, she might have even called her mother a simple person, with simple desires and complaints. For the first time in her life, she realized her mother was a complicated person, a whole and separate person, with parts of a life that had nothing to do with Christine or her brothers or even her dad. She had a flash of her mother as a young woman, saw her as a person just like herself, young and full of life and then devastated by it. Her mother was no different from her. Young and in love. With parents who didn't understand. And then she lost that love.

All her anger at her mother's intolerance washed away with the tears. Who could say that the way her mother survived was wrong?

Finally, Christine carefully repacked the box and returned it to its spot under the towels. She looked at her tear-stained face in the mirror and saw her mother, imagined her mother at her age, struggling to cope with the love of her life being killed. Christine wandered out to the kitchen and made a cup of tea which she then forgot about. She sat down on the couch in the living room and noticed the smoke stains around the sides of the fireplace and thought about how her mother had burned the hope chest. A new wave of tears flowed as she realized that hope chest had been holding her *mother's* hopes, not Christine's. Christine knew that her parents had married at the courthouse with no big ceremony or party, and she realized that her mother probably had dreams of a big wedding with Raul. Maybe all those dreams for Christine weren't really about Christine at all.

And then Christine started thinking about her father. How much did he know about Raul? Did he know her mother had a lost love that was still very much a part of her life? Was his heart literally breaking?

CHAPTER 34
Guns and Roses

Mr. Mango stared at his grapefruit. He didn't want to hurt Rita's feelings, but a grapefruit was no excuse for a breakfast. Eggs, bacon, couple slices of toast was a breakfast. Maybe pancakes and sausage. Not a clammy pink triangle of fruit. It was day two of his stay at Danny and Rita's, and not for the first time he was reconsidering the whole idea. He was seated on a stool at the bar side of the long cooking island.

"Morning, Dad," said Danny, coming into the kitchen soaked with sweat, wearing workout gear, with a towel draped around his neck. He had just ridden a virtual version of the Swiss Alps on his Peloton and was feeling the burn in every part of his legs. He filled a large glass of water and gulped half of it. "You got your directions to Sutter? You should probably leave by seven forty-five."

Mr. Mango rolled his eyes and poked at his grapefruit.

"Part of the deal. You got to go to the Cardiac Rehab," said Danny, grabbing a handful of almonds from a canister on the counter. "You should have been going all along. Where's Mom?"

Against both of his parents' wishes, Danny had convinced his mother to drive his father to Cardiac Rehab. Rita was working from home this morning while they went, and Danny had arranged his schedule to be home on Thursday morning, his dad's next class. After that, they weren't sure how they were going to make it work. The evening class was full, so unless a spot opened up, he was in the morning class.

Mrs. Mango bustled into the kitchen with Emma Rose. "Let me just get her bottle, and then I'll go get ready for your appointment," she said. "Not sure I will even get us there, but I guess I got no choice?"

"Mom, it is less than seven miles away. All back roads. You'll be fine."

"I just wish I had my car. It makes me nervous to drive yours."

"The insurance is fully paid," said Danny, trying to make a joke. "Plus, we still haven't fixed the dent from Thanksgiving, so you don't even need to worry about keeping it in perfect condition."

"Huh," said Mrs. Mango, and she hustled back out of the kitchen.

****

Mrs. Mango pulled out her knitting bag and settled herself onto a hard foam couch in the waiting room of the Wellness Center. Mr. Mango was checking himself in, and she figured she had a good hour and a half to spend working on the little sweater and matching hat she was planning for Emma Rose. Both would have the most charming little roses knitted right in, and the pale pink yarn she had found was the cutest, softest thing she had ever seen.

She hadn't clickety clacked more than three times before Mr. Mango appeared in front of her.

"They want you in there too," he said, not looking his wife in the eye, knowing she wanted to do this even less than he did.

"Whatever for?" asked Mrs. Mango, dropping her hands in frustration and poking her leg with one of the knitting needles. This was not part of the deal.

"They said a cardiac event affects the whole family, and they like to work with spouses as well as the patients."

"Well, we are not bringing in 'the whole family' and you are the one who has to start eating better, so I'm not sure why they need me," she said, stubbornly clacking away at her knitting. "Tell them you are fine on your own. You're a big boy."

Mr. Mango sighed, turned around, and held his hand over his chest as he went to deliver the news.

He returned with a chipper young woman with silky dark hair and a big smile. "Hello, Mrs. Mango!" she chirped, leaning forward to shake Mrs. Mango's hand, badge and silver necklace rattling against each other as she did. "I'm Julie! So happy to meet you!"

Mrs. Mango slid the knitting off her lap as she let Julie take her hand and nodded hello. She knew immediately she was no match for that kind of perky.

****

Forty minutes into the class, Mrs. Mango had a full-on hot flash. The arms that had stayed crossed on her chest in protest finally pulled apart. The sweat broke out of every pore at the same time, immediately drenching her. She shot a dagger look at Mr. Mango, who was slumped in his chair staring at his feet. There were twelve members of the class plus Julie, and they were all seated in a circle, most of them trying not to look directly at anyone else. The room was a large, pleasant meeting room with a light-colored laminate floor and pale green covered chairs. There were additional chairs stacked in the corner, presumably for larger group meetings. There was a table loaded with handouts describing every stage of recovery process for every possible disease, it seemed. Next to the table was a water cooler with both hot and cold water and a selection of teas in a neat box on the edge of the table. One wall was lined with windows covered in a privacy shade that was transparent enough to let in plenty of light.

It was probably just a coincidence that Mrs. Mango's hot flash came right when Perky Julie started talking about how soon patients could resume their sex lives.

Next to her, Mr. Mango was harrumphing inside his head. "Resume" was an interesting word. It suggested that something had actually been happening before the heart attack. He looked sideways at the other participants in the circle that Julie had insisted on, and while several were looking down like him, there were also a couple of participants sitting forward on their chairs, looking excited and curious at this turn in the class. He wondered what that must feel like.

"Most people find that they can resume sexual relations within about four weeks of the event," Perky Julie said. "Of course, each of you will be different and your doctor can discuss your specific situation, but the rule of thumb is that if you have worked up to a level of activity similar to walking up a couple of flights of stairs at a brisk pace, then you are in good enough shape for intercourse."

Mrs. Mango literally flinched at the word 'intercourse.' It was as if she had been stabbed with her own knitting needle. She promised herself she was never coming back. Ever. Joe had gotten her into some uncomfortable situations, but this was the worst. She couldn't even look up, afraid of meeting someone's eyes. If she had been standing there naked, she couldn't have been more mortified. What was wrong with the world? A whole group of people sitting in a circle talking about sex? It was a nightmare that felt like it would never end. All of a sudden, she couldn't breathe and couldn't take it one moment longer. She grabbed her purse and knitting bag and fled the room.

"What if you haven't had sex in years?" asked a slim man sitting three seats to the left of Mr. Mango. Mr. Mango glanced up at him, it was as if the man spoke the exact words in his own head. The man looked to be in his early seventies, with a full head of spiky gray hair and a neatly shaved mustache. He was wearing a crisp pressed button-down and creased khaki pants. Mr. Mango saw the woman next to him slide back in her seat and look up at the ceiling. Must be the wife.

"Well, Casper, right now we are just talking about your physical readiness," said Perky Julie. "The rest is a matter between you and your wife."

"Ha!" laughed Casper. "That has not been a matter between me and my wife for a long time."

"I hear you!" chimed in another man, this one directly across the circle from Mr. Mango. He was on the larger side of everything, height, weight, voice volume. "Maybe that is the problem!"

Casper laughed. "You got a point there, Stewart."

"Maybe the toxins just build up in your system with no release, you know? And that takes a toll on the old ticker there," said Stewart.

Perky Julie's face was starting to lose its perkiness. "We're getting a bit off topic here, at least for today," she said. "In fact, in later meetings, especially the individual ones, we are going to address relationship issues and how you can strengthen your marriage as part of recovering from the cardiac event. It is actually a good predictor of your future health if you have a supportive marriage." By the end of her speech, Julie's perk was back. She erroneously believed she had gotten control of the group.

"Huh!" said the woman sitting next to Stewart. "When a man is more interested in food than you, well, what do you think is going to happen?"

The couple next to Stewart's wife glanced at each other. They were the youngest in the group, and both were sophisticated-looking, him with a navy cashmere sweater over gray flannel pants, her with a long beige wool wrap over slim-fitting off-white pants, both with expensive-looking haircuts. The glance seemed to say 'we don't belong in this crowd and we don't have these kinds of problems.'

"What? You think you are better than us?" said Stewart's wife.

"Again, let's not get off topic. Plenty of time in individual sessions later to address any relationship concerns," said Julie.

"I, for one, am happy to receive this information," said the sophisticated man in a mild tone of voice. Mr. Mango had the feeling he was in charge of a lot of people and had handled rabble rousers plenty in his life. "Julie, please continue."

"Thank you, Chase," said Julie. "In terms of resuming an exercise program—"

Stewart cut her off. "Ha! Who do you usually talk to, Julie? You get a lot of heavy exercisers here in cardiac rehab? We're here because we *don't* exercise."

"Well, that may be true of some of the patients but certainly not all," said Julie. "And if you haven't been exercising, this is a good time to start. So we'll be covering the best ways to do that."

Meanwhile, Mrs. Mango had gotten herself to the SUV, and out of habit she got into the passenger side. Once in, she pulled the door shut, slid the window down for air, and fell back against the seat in relief. She was still sweaty, but at least she was out of that pressure cooker of a class. The sun was out and the day was warming up, but there was still a coolness in the air that was refreshing. What was wrong with those people? Talking about intimate stuff like that *in a circle*. Sitting there staring right at each other. Mrs. Mango leaned her head back on the smooth leather headrest, closed her eyes, and breathed slowly for a while. Eventually, her body cooled off, and her mind followed. She opened her eyes and took another breath.

Okay.

She was okay.

Knitting would soothe her mind, but as she fumbled with the knitting bag in her lap, one of the needles dropped to the floor. She leaned down to find it and as she fumbled around on the floor, her hand brushed against something hard. She grabbed it and pulled it up to see what it was.

Right as she came up with Mr. Mango's gun, the parking enforcement officer puttered towards her car in his fancy three-wheeled enclosed cart. Seeing the gun in her own hand, Mrs. Mango's eyes widened and she yelped, thus assuring that the officer would notice her and the gun.

The parking officer was Stan 'the Man' Lukowski,

a 24-year-old overweight college dropout living in his mother's made-over garage. He had just taken this job a week ago when his mother threatened to throw him out of the house if he didn't get some sort of work. He had found he liked wearing a uniform and had been toying with the idea of turning it into a real profession and applying to the police force. Of course, if he did that, he would have to stop going to work high. Stan the Man turned the cart towards Mrs. Mango and leaped out, forgetting to put the cart in park first. "Put down your weapon!" he yelled in his deepest, most authoritative voice. It came out a bit squeaky, as he had no real practice disarming criminals or even sort-of-past-middle-age ladies.

Mrs. Mango froze, hand in front of her face, with the gun dangling from it. When the unmanned parking enforcement cart smashed into the side of Danny's SUV, she unfroze and dropped the gun into her lap, where it landed in the middle of Emma Rose's half-completed sweater.

Stan the Man ran at the car, not sure whether to go for the gun or his smashed cart. He decided to go for the gun and stopped several feet in front of the passenger door. "Step away from the vehicle!" he yelled.

Mrs. Mango was staring at the gun nestled in the soft pink yarn in her lap. She couldn't bring herself to touch it again.

"I said, get out of the car! Keep your hands where I can see you," yelled Stan the Man again. A couple walking by stopped to stare. A teenager came running, followed by two friends, "Check it out! That parking cart ran into that SUV!"

The gathering crowd took a couple of steps backwards when they heard Stan the Man repeat "Put down the gun!" It was an unnecessary statement as the gun was already down, but he only had a couple of sentences in his repertoire for this situation, so he switched back and forth between them.

The teenager had his cell phone focused on the

scene, recording it. A line of cars was hung up near Mrs. Mango and Stan the Man as the lane was now blocked by the parking cart sticking out from Danny's car. A horn sounded, more people crowded around. Another horn sounded. The parking cart engine whined as it pushed itself against Danny's SUV.

"Get out of the car!" Stan the Man said again.

Mrs. Mango's brain finally processed what he was asking her to do, and she reached for the handle of the door, only to find the door wouldn't open because the parking enforcement cart, mostly pushing against the back door, was also partway against her door, and it was pinned shut.

"I can't get out!" Mrs. Mango cried.

"I said, get out!" yelled Stan the Man. This was all moving too fast for his reefer-soaked brain.

"I can't! Your cart hit me!" wailed Mrs. Mango.

"Get out the other side," said Stan the Man.

Mrs. Mango didn't want to touch the gun again. She knew nothing about guns and was furious with Mr. Mango for bringing this one along. Because she knew it had to be his. The old fool.

"Can you get the gun?" Mrs. Mango asked. "I'll get out the other side if you just get the gun."

Stan the Man was standing barely two feet from her, so it seemed like a reasonable request.

Stan the Man's brain tried to think quickly. Was it a trap? Was she trying to lure him closer so she could shoot him in the face?

Mrs. Mango put her hands up, touching the ceiling of the car. "Look, I'll keep my hands up, I just don't want to touch that thing. It's in my lap."

Stan the Man took a cautious step towards her.

"I'll get the gun!" yelled the cell phone-recording teenager, who was hovering behind Stan the Man.

Stan spun around. "Get out of here!" he yelled at the teenager. "This is a hostile situation!"

Stan the Man turned back towards Mrs. Mango,

who still had her hands in the air.

"I'm going to move towards you very slowly, okay?" Stan the Man said.

"Well, don't take forever," said Mrs. Mango. "I can't hold these old arms up all day."

Stan the Man crept towards the window, reached in, and grabbed the gun. His grab also netted him the half-knitted sweater, so when his arm came back out of the window, the sweater had settled around the gun like it had been made for it. The crowd laughed, probably half in relief. Stan turned in surprise, not realizing so many people were behind him, and as he turned, the gun slipped out of the sweater, landed on the ground, and discharged. As the bullet zinged through the parking cart and into the rear panel of Danny's car, the crowd screamed and most of them dove onto the ground.

Mrs. Mango shrieked, "You don't have to shoot me! I'll get out!" as she scrambled over the center console, crawled over the driver's seat, flung open the door, and fell onto the pavement on the other side of the car.

Mr. Mango, grateful the class had finally ended, was walking towards his car when he noticed a crowd and several police cars. He came around the corner of the line of parked cars into the lane where their car was parked and almost had another heart attack at the scene in front of him.

A parking enforcement cart had crashed into Danny's SUV, and there were cops gathered around it. Mrs. Mango was sitting on the ground while someone wiped at blood on her knee. Had she been attacked by the parking cart? What in Sam Hell was going on here?

He made his way up to the SUV. "Elsie, you okay? What is going on here?" he said.

Six cops turned to look at him. "Are you the husband?" asked one.

"Yes, what happened?"

The cop held Mr. Mango's gun up. "Is this yours, Sir?"

"Yes! What the hell is going on?"

"Your gun was discharged here. Luckily, no one was hurt, but you should know better than to carry a loaded gun without the safety on."

"I always have the safety on!" He turned more towards Mrs. Mango. "What were you doing with my gun?"

"I didn't know it was there! I dropped my knitting needle. And then," she gestured at the parking cart and the still-stunned Stan the Man. "And then all this happened."

Mrs. Mango's explanation, once they were detangled from the parking cart and cleared by the police and on their way back to Danny's, made no sense to Mr. Mango. He might have stayed forever in the dark, but it turned out that the teenager had the footage up on YouTube by the time they arrived home. By the time Danny got home, it had over 10,000 views and had made the evening news, so they all got to see what happened. Mrs. Mango was the most outraged by the angle the teenager had on her butt as she scrambled out of the car. She might never speak to her husband again. Danny and Rita were speechless. Don Paz nodded knowingly, as if he had predicted the whole thing.

CHAPTER 35
Cows and Crickets

"So, what, you believe in a bunch of gods?" asked Mr. Mango as Don Paz dropped into the seat beside him, sweating but not breathing hard after a run. Mr. Mango was sitting on Danny's back terrace, enjoying his coffee in the quiet of early morning, before the workers arrived. The terrace and pathways for the back yard were complete and the fire pit looked like it needed maybe one more day of work. The lawn had been torn up and graded, and Mr. Mango was guessing that the next phase would be installing the irrigation system and then the grass and plantings. Mr. Mango had been awake since five and out on the dark terrace by six. There was a peace in sitting in the dark, watching the day break as it always did whether anyone noticed or not. The sun went down and the sun came up, and nothing changed that. Mr. Mango tried to add up how many days the sun had come up since he'd been born. A lot. As the sky lightened over the trees, Mr. Mango had found himself thinking about God, a more frequent occurrence since his 'cardiac events.'

"Well, actually, I consider myself a panentheist," said Don Paz, swiping his forehead with the sleeve against his bicep, then uncapping a water bottle, "which is the belief that god exists in everything and yet is still a larger-than-us thing." Don Paz spread his arms wide in front of him, sloshing some water out of the bottle.

"Huh?" said Mr. Mango.

"Well, let me back up. There are different theories of God, and the Christian belief is called 'monotheism,' meaning there is one God and he is supreme. Then you have your 'polytheism' religions where there is a belief in more than one god. Like Hinduism."

Mr. Mango was following so far. He thought the

idea of more than one god was silly, but he was aware that people in distant countries might believe that.

"Then you have 'pantheism' which is a belief that God is in everything. The word literally means 'all is God.' Every rock and tree, every person and lizard. Even Einstein wrote about that concept." Don Paz gestured around the backyard. "For a pantheist, this is all God. Every single thing is sacred."

Mr. Mango felt uncomfortable with that one. God in the trees? The bugs?

"Then there is panENtheism, which is what I believe. It goes a bit further in that we believe that, yes, God is in everything but that there is also a larger force than us, which is God. God is in everything, but God is also a supreme force. And I believe this force, whether you call it God or not, is guiding us. If we just listen."

"So you think God is trying to tell me something with this heart business?" said Mr. Mango, a skeptical tone in his voice.

"That is a very interesting question," said Don Paz. "What do you think? Do you think God has something She wants you to know?"

"Whoa, there, cowboy," said Mr. Mango. "God is a 'He' not a 'She.'"

Don Paz tilted his head back and forth in a 'maybe' kind of motion. "That's kind of a separate issue, but I think God is bigger than gender, that God incorporates both male and female energy. And since so many people refer to God as 'he,' I'm trying to even it out a little and call God 'she,' but, really, I think of God as the 'All-That-Is.'"

This was too much for Mr. Mango. "Well, if God is 'All-That-Is,' then it isn't even a useful name. If you are referring to everything, then there is no other stuff."

Don Paz beamed. "Exactly. But we've gotten away from whether God is trying to get your attention with this heart trouble. Do you think there is something God wants you to know?"

Mr. Mango shrugged. "Hell if I know."

"Interesting choice of words," said Don Paz.

Mr. Mango rolled his eyes and took a sip of his cold coffee. "Aw jeez, you over-interpret everything."

"That may very well be true," Don Paz conceded. "But I believe everything has meaning, and nothing happens by chance. I don't think any of this life on this earth is random."

"So you think I had a heart attack for a reason?"

"Yes. But I have no idea what that reason is. Only you could know," said Don Paz.

"Well, I'm damned if I know," said Mr. Mango.

"There you go again," laughed Don Paz. "Interesting choice of words. Do you feel damned?"

"Goddamn right I do!" said Mr. Mango. "I had a heart attack and then another something or other, and now I can't work. So, yes, I do feel damned. And I don't see any reason why it happened to me." Then he thought about the secret internet porn he had visited on occasion, and a hot flush came over him. No. No way God was punishing him for that. If He was, it was a pretty harsh punishment for something that wasn't hurting anybody. Surely God did not mean for him to live with no sexual satisfaction.

"The heart is the center of our being," said Don Paz, setting down his water bottle and cupping his hands over his heart. "I think when someone has a problem with his heart, that something has really disturbed him at a deep level, a soul level."

"Nothing different in my life," said Mr. Mango. "So that kind of debunks that theory. Nothing 'disturbed my soul.'"

"Well, sometimes it is a long-time hurt that eventually is too much to bear," said Don Paz. "Or feeling isolated, that can do it. Our hearts literally sync to the people around us—it's called cardiac coherence—and if you are feeling disconnected . . . well, imagine what that would do to a heart."

Mr. Mango waved his hand in dismissal. "You are reading *way* too much into this. There is no reason except old age for my heart attack. And as far as I can tell, the world is random. Otherwise, why do kids get cancer? Why are some people born in poverty and some into mansions? It's just luck."

Don Paz could tell he had pushed his ideas too far with Mr. Mango. He stood up, pressed his hands together in front of him in prayer position, and said, "I apologize. It really isn't my business, it is your journey altogether." He looked at his watch and grabbed his water bottle. "I need to return some emails. See you later."

"God in the trees," snorted Mr. Mango after Don Paz was gone. "What a bunch of baloney." And yet. Some part of Mr. Mango longed for the comfort of knowing there really was a God, some evidence that He existed and was watching out for him.

****

"I feel just awful for them!" said Rita, scraping up the last bite of her egg white and spinach scramble. She was in full professional mode, black suit jacket over a slim black skirt and white silk blouse, sitting straight-backed at the kitchen island on a bar stool. Next to her, Danny poured himself a second bowl of granola, taking care not to splash milk onto his work uniform, which usually consisted of slim-legged pants and a starched button-down, open at the neck. Today, the pants were gray, the shirt a blue and white check. The shoes were always Adidas. When a man is on his feet all day, it helps to have comfortable shoes.

Danny grimaced. "I know. It just gets worse every day."

Mrs. Mango walked in to the kitchen carrying Emma Rose as Danny spoke.

"What's going on? What is getting worse?"

"No one you know," said Danny through a mouthful of cereal.

"Don't speak with your mouth full," said Mrs. Mango automatically. "Is there a problem?"

"Some friends of ours, the Dawsons, are just having horrible luck," explained Rita. "They had to move out of their house—some kind of mold issue—and then Charlie lost his job. They had been living at Jeanine's mother's house, but now all of Jeanine's siblings are mad because they were supposed to have sold the house after her mother died. I mean, really, their own family forcing them to move out!"

Mrs. Mango's face lit up. Nothing more fascinating than a tragedy that happened to people you don't know. "No! That is awful."

"They can't move back to their own home because they can't afford to have the mold removed," said Danny.

"And their middle son Robbie has really bad breathing issues. That mold would kill him," added Rita. She gave a little shiver of her shoulders as if the news was just too much.

"Speaking of bad luck," said Mrs. Mango. "I keep forgetting to tell you, you need to put some kind of barrier around that pond out front. What if Emma Rose falls in? It is a hazard until she learns how to swim."

Rita looked at Danny in a panic. "Oh my God, she's right! We need to drain it. Or put a fence around it."

Danny gave his mom the stink eye. "We've got time. She can't even roll over yet! We'll get someone out here to assess safety stuff, don't worry."

"I saw that look, young man," said Mrs. Mango to Danny. "No need to be rude. Just trying to protect the angel."

Mrs. Mango gave Emma Rose a little jiggle and sat down at the kitchen table across from Don Paz, who was typing away on a laptop.

Rita stood up, looking at her watch. "I need to be off. Let me just kiss my little angel first. And, Danny, call someone right away! We have no idea how to babyproof a house."

Mrs. Mango handed Emma Rose to Rita. "Leave the dishes, I'll get them," she said.

"Oh, thank you so much," said Rita. "And don't forget Emma Rose's schedule."

Mrs. Mango nodded, "Of course." Mrs. Mango was aware Rita had installed webcams but didn't fully understand the purpose of them. She had a vague sense that they were security cameras, turned on at night in case of an intruder.

Danny and Rita babytalked at Emma Rose, handed her back to Mrs. Mango, and left at the same time.

Don Paz looked up from his computer, and Mrs. Mango seized on the chance to talk. "I just don't understand why something like that has to happen to people. That poor family."

Don Paz nodded at Mrs. Mango. "Yes, it is sad, but maybe that is the journey they are meant to be on."

"Huh?" Mrs. Mango stared at Don Paz in confusion.

"Maybe they have attracted that drama into their lives," said Don Paz. "Maybe they are working something out."

"I don't really follow you," said Mrs. Mango, jiggling Emma Rose and then slipping a bottle into her mouth.

"I have come to believe that we are all born many times. And I believe we agree ahead of time who our family will be and the types of things that happen to us. We are attracted to the life we are born into and we use it to work out stuff. That bad luck didn't happen by accident."

"I can't imagine that the Dawsons chose to have all this happen!" Mrs. Mango said. "You are blaming them?"

"No, not blaming them. But they are on their own journey, and, who knows, maybe there is something in this they had to learn."

"That is just BS, excuse my French," said Mrs. Mango. "What is there to learn in a death trap of a home? In your family throwing you out of a house? In a son with breathing issues?"

"Maybe they were too trusting. Maybe there is

something they need to learn, like how to live simply. I don't know. I just believe it is no mistake that you have the children you have, the life you have. We all agreed to that ahead of time."

Mrs. Mango stared at Don Paz as if he had sprouted horns. "I can't imagine I agreed to everything that's happened to me!" she said, thinking mostly of Mr. Mango, and then Raul. And then her mind slid to Christine and the whole not-attracted-to-men issue, and she shook her head violently. "Nope, don't buy it. Next thing you'll be telling me is that I'm coming back in another life as a cow or a cricket or something."

Don Paz smiled and leaned back away from his computer, arms stretched, and then folded over his head. "I know this is not a traditional Western way of thinking. And I also know I could be completely wrong. But it feels right in my heart." He paused, then added, eyes twinkling, "Interesting that you picked those two animals. Of course, the cow is considered sacred in Hinduism in India. And in China, the cricket has been a symbol of wisdom and prosperity for thousands of years."

"Huh," said Mrs. Mango. "Doesn't say anything about crickets in my Bible."

Don Paz dropped his arms back to the table and punched a few keys. "Well, actually, the Bible does mention crickets, but only that they are okay to eat. 'Of them you may eat: the locust of any kind, the bald locust of any kind, the cricket of any kind, and the grasshopper of any kind.' Leviticus 11:12."

Mrs. Mango stared at Don Paz, unable to hide her surprise.

"I have studied many religions," said Don Paz. "And Christianity was my native language, so to speak." He gave a soft laugh. "I don't think you have to worry, though, I don't actually believe our souls ever incarnate as animals. Just people."

Mrs. Mango pulled the bottle away from Emma Rose, then shifted the baby up onto her shoulder. "Hello, little lovey! Aren't you the sleepy one." As she patted Emma Rose on the back to get her to burp, she turned her eyes back towards Don Paz. "So, you think this little one somehow set it up to come here?"

Don Paz nodded. "Absolutely. She was meant for this family. She chose her parents and her parents chose her. Not that they would be conscious of that."

This whole conversation was feeling silly to Mrs. Mango. Babies choosing parents? Ridiculous.

"You feel very connected to her, don't you?" asked Don Paz. "I can see that you share a deep bond with her."

Mrs. Mango couldn't deny that. From the first moment she held Emma Rose, she felt an attachment so deep the baby could have come from her own body. "That's just, you know, what a baby makes you feel," said Mrs. Mango.

"Maybe," said Don Paz, a slight smile on his face.

The smile was the final straw. What an imbecile, sitting there all smug like he knew the answers to the universe. Mrs. Mango stood up, "I think Emmy is ready for a diaper change." In her head, she reflected that the poop wasn't all in the diaper, some of it was coming out of Don Paz's mouth.

As she made her way to the door, Don Paz said, "You haven't felt that deep of a bond in a long time. And you've missed it."

Mrs. Mango stopped and turned around. "What's that?"

Don Paz stared at her, all trace of smile gone. "There is a sadness in your aura. A long-time sadness. Something—actually, I'm guessing someone—you cared deeply about is gone. But the sadness remains."

Mrs. Mango turned back around, unable to look Don Paz in the eye. "Nonsense," she said, bustling out the door. She made it clear to Emma Rose's room before the tears burst out.

CHAPTER 36
Mini-earthquakes

Don Paz finished pouring Rita a glass of wine and turned towards Mrs. Mango, asking her if she'd like one. It was Saturday evening, and the fading glow of the sunset seemed to have cast a feeling of calm on everyone. Mrs. Mango and Rita were sitting outside in the area Mrs. Mango referred to as 'the outdoor living room'—an area of the terrace with a plushy couch and matching wide chairs that looked like they were made of wicker but were made of some kind of rain-resistant material. The furniture set had thick off-white cushions and surrounded a table with a glass-filled fire pit in the middle of it. Planters filled with high sea grasses on either side of the couch softened the straight lines of the furniture and tied in to the pale green throw cushions lining the couch. Mrs. Mango silently reminded herself to warn Danny about the fire pit dangers later. Once Emma Rose started cruising around, he better make sure there was no fire going in that pit. Michael had finally made it up to see his new niece and was sitting with them, drinking a beer. Danny was giving Joe Jr. and Jenny, who had arrived with Michael, a tour of the backyard. Mrs. Mango and Rita were passing Emma Rose back and forth between them.

"Maybe a little bit with dinner," said Mrs. Mango, clutching Emma Rose. "When this little one is settled in to her sleeper." Mrs. Mango looked at her watch. "She's due for her bottle in ten minutes anyway." Mrs. Mango was making every effort to prove to Rita that she was on board with the schedule. At least, while Rita was around.

"Can I come help you with anything?" asked Rita, pushing herself forward on the deep couch as if to get up. Don Paz had offered to make dinner for the family, and Rita was feeling anxious just sitting and not helping.

"No, no, I've got it," said Don Paz. He gestured

towards the platter he had just set on the edge of the fire table. "Eat up, and in about twenty minutes, the pork loin should be done."

Mrs. Mango peered at the platter. "What is it?"

"Some fresh bread and an herb butter spread. And then some olives, and a couple of roasted peppers, a little soppressata—my version of an antipasti platter," answered Don Paz. "I'll be back out in a minute."

As the patio door closed behind him, Mrs. Mango said, "Well, how about that? A man who can cook."

Perched upright on a garden stool on the other side of the fire table, Michael grinned at his mother. "I can cook."

"Heating up takeout is not cooking," said Mrs. Mango, popping a roasted pepper in her mouth.

"Who would have guessed?" said Rita, eyeing the door Don Paz had just gone through. "Growing up, he was just your typical guy, you know, liked pizza, left his dirty socks everywhere, played video games. Now he's, I don't know . . ." She couldn't finish.

"People aren't always who you think they are," said Mrs. Mango, meaning it in a general way but then thinking of Christine. Who would have ever known about her? "Ooh, sweet, sweet girl, who are you going to be?" cooed Mrs. Mango to Emma Rose. How easy to love a baby before she grew up and turned into her own person and disappointed you.

"I mean, I'm really proud of him," added Rita. "He is so—how do I put it? At ease with himself. And kind," said Rita. "I know it probably seems goofy to you, renaming himself and the shaman stuff and all, but he really believes it, and he is much nicer to be around than he used to be."

"Seems like a chill dude to me," said Michael, helping himself to a piece of the bread and stacking one of everything else on it before easing himself back onto the stool.

"So, what's going on with Meredith?" said Mrs.

Mango, looking at Michael with an intense stare.

"Wow, I'm impressed, Mom," said Michael, looking at his watch. "You managed to wait a whole half hour before asking. You're off your game."

"Well? That's no answer," said Mrs. Mango. "Are you guys even talking?"

"It's complicated," mumbled Michael, stuffing soppressata in his mouth.

"Don't talk with your mouth full," Mrs. Mango said. "Of course it's complicated. *Life* is complicated. But you still didn't answer. Are you talking or not? Have you seen her? Are you just taking a break or are you divorcing?"

Michael rolled his eyes and looked at Rita for help. Rita shrugged. She had her own issues with Mrs. Mango and had no interest in joining Michael's.

Danny, Joe Jr., and Jenny came up the three steps from the lower part of the back yard. Danny headed into the house as Joe Jr. and Jenny slid onto one of the chairs, wide enough to fit them both. Joe was dressed in dark jeans and a black t-shirt with a gray V-neck sweater on top. His hair was arranged into curves that looked unarranged, and his extra-white teeth shined in the dusk. He looked like someone who was someone. Jenny was also in jeans, a white nubby sweater and knock-off Uggs. Neither tended to wear fancy clothes, but they always somehow looked stylish.

Mrs. Mango stared at Joe Jr., struck once again at how much he looked like Joe Sr. had looked at that age. She shut her eyes briefly to calm the complicated mix of feelings that thought produced.

"Wow, that backyard's going to be killer," said Joe Jr. He poked at Jenny, "You married the wrong brother. Either one of them, and you could be living in style." He gestured to Michael and then Danny's retreating back.

Rita looked down and shook her head faintly.

"What's going on with Meredith?" Mrs. Mango demanded again, this time looking at Joe Jr. "Did you see her when you were at Michael's?"

"Sounds like a good time to butt-owsky," said Joe Jr., laughing and walking around to the other side of the fire table to grab a slice of soppressata.

"I'm just worried about you, is all," said Mrs. Mango, moving side to side to rock Emma Rose.

"I'm fine," said Michael. "It's been nice to have Joe and Jenny at the house. I mean, I'm fine alone too. I'm not the first person to get separated, Mom."

"Separated! So you are officially separated?"

"Well, she's not living at home, so what else would you call it?" Michael took a long drink of his beer and stood up. "Need a refill. Anyone else?" He looked around and walked away before anyone could answer.

"Excuse me for caring," said Mrs. Mango.

"Can I hold Emma Rose?" asked Jenny.

"Of course," said Rita. "Um, could you go wash your hands first?"

Jenny jumped up. "Of course! Should have thought of that myself."

Danny caught Joe Jr.'s eye roll. "Everyone does that now, you know," Danny said. "Just makes sense not to pass on germs."

On Jenny's return, Mrs. Mango settled her back into the extra-wide chair with two cushions behind her to hold her steady and carefully handed Emma Rose to her. Jenny relaxed against the cushions and started whispering to Emma Rose. "You are just the cutest, aren't you, little angel?" Emma Rose made a sound halfway between a coo and a cry, and Jenny's body went into a slight sway and she started humming. Emma Rose stared up at her and quieted. Jenny glanced at Joe Jr. with bright eyes.

Mr. Mango, having come onto the terrace from the guest house, caught the look between Jenny and Joe Jr. Yep, Jenny wanted a baby too.

Mrs. Mango was attacking the appetizer tray. She spread some of the herb butter on a piece of bread. "Oh my goodness, this is delicious!" she said, gobbling the rest of the piece in her hand. "Joe! Come eat this! It is so good."

As she looked up Mr. Mango came to stand by Joe Jr. and Mrs. Mango's attention was caught, the younger version of Joe right there beside the older version. Mr. Mango had softened over the years but for a moment Mrs. Mango was suspended in time, looking at her husband and seeing the young, handsome Joe, still right there. Fresh out of the shower with wet hair and a big smile, he was somehow not really that old looking after all. He was still handsome, something she had not really seen for a long time, instead always so focused on the little things that annoyed her.

Huh, she thought to herself. Must be something about the angle of the dropping sun, something about having her boys all around her that made her feel overly nostalgic. Mrs. Mango gave a little shake to her head. Enough with this nonsense. She turned to Jenny, having just remembered about the christening. "Oh! Are you two going to be around for a couple more weeks? The christening is in two weeks at St. Andrews!"

Jenny and Joe looked at each other and gave a private smile.

"Looks like we might be," said Joe.

As Mr. Mango pulled a chair over to the fire table, Danny came back out of the house with a non-alcoholic beer and gave it to his dad. "Here you go, Dad."

Mr. Mango stared at the can. "What is this?"

"Well, you probably shouldn't have any alcohol just yet, so I got you this."

"Are you kidding me? It's down to this?" he grumped, but he opened the can and took a sip. He grimaced but then his face lit up as he sat down and smoothed his hand through his wet hair. "Danny, I got to tell you, that is one fine shower," said Mr. Mango, leaning back in the chair. "I'm taking two showers a day!"

Danny smiled. "I know. When we redid the bathrooms, I wanted to put in a showerhead with a lot of water pressure."

"I mean, a man feels *clean* with that kind of pressure," said Mr. Mango. "How did you work that out? No way that showerhead is legal." He looked at Michael. "Do you have one of those? It is outstanding. You gotta get one."

Danny chuckled. "You got that right! I looked into it when we were fixing the bathrooms, and there is actually a law that showerheads in California can't produce a water flow over 2.5 gallons a minute. That's why everyone has such weak showers."

Mr. Mango banged his fist on the table. "Goddamn bureaucrats. Got no place in my shower. Is there nothing private anymore? I mean, for crying out loud, regulating the water you can have in your shower? Jesus Christ, next thing they'll have cameras in there. Probably do already."

Rita looked down, hiding her guilt at putting cameras everywhere in the house to watch Mrs. Mango. At least, there was nothing in the bathrooms.

Danny smiled. "Yep, but I got around it. Found a black market showerhead and paid off the plumber to put it in."

"Black market?" Rita said, looking up. "I haven't heard about this."

"Well, Silk Road," said Danny.

"Oh my God," said Rita.

"Don't worry, I paid in bitcoin. They can't trace me."

Rita closed her eyes and sighed. "Don't be so sure."

"What's bitcoin?" asked Jenny.

"A form of currency you can use online," said Danny. "On the deep web. Untraceable," he said in a louder voice, nodding at Rita.

Mr. Mango was beaming. He lifted his can towards Danny. "Son, I don't think I was this proud of you when you graduated medical school! Finally, you are showing some sense."

Mrs. Mango was making her way around the antipasti plate. "Oh, Joe, try the butter. And the meat-thingy there!”

“Soppressata,” said Rita. “But should he?” She looked to Danny for help.

“Probably better to keep it healthy, Dad,” Danny said. “Probably best to stay away from the salty, fatty meat. Maybe just the peppers.”

“Jeezus,” said Mr. Mango. “Fake beer and limp vegetables. Life just gets better and better.”

“Well, then, it is a good thing you are enjoying the shower so much!” laughed Danny.

“Yeah, that is my one pleasure in life. A shower,” said Mr. Mango, but he laughed along with Danny. “Getting old is a bitch.”

“Joe! Watch your language. We have a little one here,” said Mrs. Mango.

Mr. Mango rolled his eyes. “She’s a baby! She can’t even control her hands yet.”

They all looked at Emma Rose, who had started whimpering. Jenny stood up and gently bounced as she walked around trying to soothe her.

Mrs. Mango looked at her watch. “Oh my, let me go get her bottle. She’s hungry!”

Don Paz came out to the patio. “Dinner is ready,” he said. “I had it set up inside, but it is so nice out tonight we could move it out here.” He looked past the couch area to the long teak table and chairs. “If we added a couple of chairs, there’d be room.”

Rita jumped up and gestured to Danny. “Great idea, we’ll help you bring everything out.”

“My goodness, this is delicious,” said Mrs. Mango as they all tucked in to the dinner. “What is it all?”

“Loin of pork with fennel and other roasted vegetables, arugula salad with goat cheese, and a rice-quinoa mix,” said Don Paz, standing at the head of the table pouring more wine. The sun had set behind him, but the sky still glowed with a warm yellow, and although the air was starting to chill, the tall skinny pyramid-shaped heaters positioned on either side of the table kept the temperature comfortable. The candles flickered in the hurricane lamps, and the mood was lighter than it had been for a while, at least in Danny's mind.

"Is this a recipe?" asked Danny. "So tasty!"

"Ina Garten," said Don Paz. "You know, the Barefoot Contessa?"

Mr. Mango shook his head. Don Paz was not anything like his definition of a man, but he had to admit the food was delicious.

"How is your building coming along?" Danny asked as Don Paz sat down and continued eating. "Don Paz is putting together a whole new kind of medical group, sort of," Danny explained to Michael, Joe Jr., and Jenny.

"On the whole, good," said Don Paz. "There's always something that gets more complicated than you expected, but it is basically on schedule."

Danny had very little understanding of what Don Paz was planning and hadn't had much interest either, but it was Saturday night and he was on a rare third glass of wine and felt expansive. "What is the whole thing going to be like?"

"My vision is to bring together like-minded practitioners of a holistic approach to health and wellness," said Don Paz, who then laughed. "That sounded like a brochure, didn't it?"

Danny smiled and avoided looking at Michael, knowing if they caught eyes, Michael would start laughing at Don Paz.

Joe Jr. was nodding in agreement with Don Paz. "Very LA-sounding."

"What I mean is that it will be a kind of one-stop shopping for body and mind. I've got a holistic physician, acupuncture and qigong, nutrition, and of course mental health and spiritual matters. I'm the spiritual matters guy on the team."

Danny nodded in support but found it hard to overcome his traditional medical training to believe in Don

Paz's plan. Michael coughed, and Danny assumed it was to cover a snort but still couldn't look at his brother.

"I've had acupuncture," said Joe Jr. "Very relaxing."

"Relaxing?" said Mr. Mango. "I can't imagine having pins jammed into you could in any way be relaxing." He looked closely at his son. "Are you on drugs?"

Joe Jr. laughed. "No. But I do like acupuncture. And yoga."

"Yoga!" Mr. Mango snorted. "You've got to be kidding me. Next thing, you'll be telling me you carry a purse."

Jenny smiled and looked down at Emma Rose, shifting the bottle she was holding to her mouth. Jenny had refused to put her down for dinner, saying she'd hold her until the others were done eating and then eat herself. Mr. Mango noticed her smile. "Oh jeez, please don't tell me he carries a purse."

Jenny shook her head. "No, no purse. But he does have a lovely teal yoga mat carrier."

Rita burst out laughing and shared a smile with Jenny. As people who had married into the Mango family, they shared a certain bond. Minor jokes like that helped to release a little tension, like mini-earthquakes along a fault line.

"I knew it would happen eventually, living in LA turns everyone into a fruit."

"Well, I am a Mango," Joe Jr. laughed.

Mr. Mango stared up at the sky. "Like I haven't heard that one before."

"Holy shit, you do yoga?" Michael asked Joe Jr.

"It's really helped my back," said Joe Jr.

"What's wrong with your back?" Mrs. Mango demanded, mother antennae shooting up. "I didn't know you had problems with your back."

"Nothing any more. It was just the normal stuff, gets tight, sore, you know," said Joe Jr. "But acupuncture and yoga have cured it."

Michael sat up and looked intently at Joe Jr. Anything that might cure back pain had his interest. He hadn't mentioned it around his mother, but nothing he was doing was helping his back pain. He could barely sleep anymore.

"Christ, that's what you're using the money I send you for?" said Mr. Mango.

"You're a doctor, don't you think the body and mind are inextricably connected?" Don Paz asked Danny, trying to get the conversation back on track.

"Well, of course," said Danny, "but not everything, right? Isn't a broken arm just a broken arm?"

"Ah, but what led to the broken arm?" asked Don Paz.

"I don't know, maybe a fall?" said Danny. "I'm not sure there is a deeper meaning in everything."

"Well, let me ask you this, do you notice any psychological causes of skin problems in your patients?" Don Paz asked. "Do you notice that people who are more anxious have more, I don't know, acne or other skin conditions?"

"Well, of course," said Danny. "I definitely see stress exacerbating a lot of conditions."

"There is even a field for that now," said Don Paz. "Psychodermatology."

Danny knew about that and felt uncomfortable that he hadn't researched it as much yet as he should. He nodded but didn't add anything.

"How are people going to pay you?" demanded Mr. Mango. "Doesn't sound like anything insurance will cover."

"Well, actually, a lot of it is covered by insurance," said Don Paz.

"Obamacare?!" Mr. Mango said. "Covering that? Are you kidding me? Jesus Christ."

Danny could tell his dad was about to say something offensive to Don Paz. He knew exactly where his dad's mind was going. "Meditation has been shown to be quite effective, as has acupuncture, Dad," Danny jumped in. He didn't believe a lot of it himself but wanted to keep the peace with Rita's brother. "I know there is some research on this stuff."

"Hmph! No one sticking me full of needles," said Mr. Mango.

"Do you use voodoo dolls?" asked Mrs. Mango.

Danny flushed with embarrassment. "Mom! I'm sure he doesn't. That is . . . you know . . ." He couldn't even finish.

Don Paz smiled. "It's not far off. We look very closely at people's beliefs about themselves and their health. And the whole concept of voodoo dolls is based on belief. In fact, some think our 'regular,'" Don Paz made air quotes, "health care system is no different than voodoo. We hypnotize people into believing in diseases like breast cancer or shingles, and then we sacrifice breasts and other organs to save them. We put public awareness ads on TV and then are surprised when people contract the illnesses. All we did was give them the suggestion and reinforce it over and over with fear."

Danny studiously avoided looking at Michael.

Don Paz could tell he had lost everyone at the table. "Well, these are some unusual concepts, aren't they? Not for everyone." He smiled. "More pork loin, anyone?"

As Don Paz went back to the kitchen for the pork loin, Rita said, "Jenny, what's new in the LA law world?" The fact that Rita was a lawyer and Jenny a para-legal gave them a common ground to retreat to when the Mangos got crazy.

Jenny stopped the pacing she was doing with Emma Rose and stood across the table facing Rita. "Same old, same old. LA can be a heartless place, and working for *lawyers* in a heartless place . . . Well." She didn't finish, unwilling to lump Rita in with all the rest of the lawyers in the world. She couldn't say that every day, she spent her hour-long drive home listing everything she was grateful for in an attempt to counteract the cold, cutthroat, unapologetic acts that pervaded her work hours. Or how she longed for a different life but loved her husband and was trying to support his dreams and couldn't find a better-paying job.

Rita laughed. "Oh, I know it. I don't know how you've lasted there so long!"

Jenny smiled, happy that she hadn't offended Rita. It was only too easy to do. "Well, it's been nice to have a regular paycheck, you know?"

Mr. Mango snorted. "Time you taught my son that lesson."

"Dad, please don't start," said Joe Jr.

"Actually, Pops, Joe's done well this year," said Jenny. "Had some good parts. Got a couple of commercials. It's just the kind of work that doesn't give a steady paycheck."

"And I might have some big news here for you soon," said Joe Jr. "I don't want to jinx it, so I'm not saying anything more."

Mr. Mango waved his empty non-alcoholic beer can at his son. "We've heard that before."

"More pork loin?" Don Paz hovered behind Mr. Mango.

"Well?" Mr. Mango looked at Danny. "I'd like more, but you better ask the food police over there."

Danny shook his head. "I'm not going to do that, Dad. I don't want to be the food police. Eat it, don't eat it."

"So you don't care about your father?" demanded Mrs. Mango. "You're the doctor! Tell him what to eat or not eat."

After dinner, Mrs. Mango harangued Michael into helping to clear the table.

On his third trip to the table, Mrs. Mango stopped him and put her arms around him.

"I miss you, Mikey," Mrs. Mango said. "Isn't that

baby just the sweetest thing?"

Michael hugged his mother back and then pulled away. "She is. I'm so happy for them."

Mrs. Mango stared intently at her son. She grabbed his face and turned it towards her. "You look like you are in pain. Literal pain. Are you okay?"

Michael shrugged. "I'm fine. Plus, I'm really enjoying Poker. I never realized how much I missed having a dog."

"*You* have Poker?" said Mrs. Mango in surprise. "Why? You work way more than Christine."

Michael froze. It hadn't occurred to him that his mother didn't know Christine had moved in with Sarah. Duh, of course if he'd given it a moment's thought, he would have realized it. He busied himself with stacking plates and then silverware on top. "Oh, I was feeling kind of lonely so said I'd take Poker for a while."

"That dog can't be left alone that much at your house!" said Mrs. Mango, arms on hips staring at Michael.

"He's not. First of all, Joe and Jenny are there, and, second, I've been taking him to work. Everyone loves him," said Michael, nonchalantly heading back to the kitchen, away from his mother.

Mrs. Mango stared at her son's retreating back. Her mother's instinct was quivering, but she didn't know why. Maybe she should set Don Paz on it, he'd read everyone's minds and tell her what was going on.

CHAPTER 37

Pass the Shaman

"What are you doing?" Danny said to his mother who was sitting at the kitchen table surrounded by rolls of toilet paper. The kitchen was mostly shadows, the only light a faint glow from the single overhead light Mrs. Mango had dimmer switched to its lowest setting. Mrs. Mango was in her fuzzy blue chenille bathrobe, and her hair was set in old-fashioned bristling rollers. Danny could count on one hand the number of times he had seen his mother in curlers and a robe. He was aware that this was her nighttime routine, but once morning hit, his mother was usually dressed and about her business.

It was two o'clock in the morning, and Danny had stumbled downstairs to get Emma Rose's bottle. He swayed back and forth to stop Emma Rose from crying in his arms. "It's okay, peanut, your bottle is coming right up," he crooned.

"I'm redistributing," said Mrs. Mango.

"What is redistributing, and why are you doing it in the middle of the night?" asked Danny.

"I couldn't sleep. Sleeping with your father is like sleeping in the engine of a jet. I'll bet you can hear his snoring from your room. So I came in here." Mrs. Mango picked up a thick new roll of toilet paper. "I'm fixing your toilet paper."

"What's wrong with our toilet paper?"

"You buy the triple layer extra large rolls and they don't fit on the spindles. So, I'm fixing them."

"We just set it by the toilet until it is small enough to put on the spindle," said Danny. "No big deal."

"Oh no, that is too messy. Then it rolls around and who wants to wipe with paper that's been dragged on the ground?" Mrs. Mango held up an empty cardboard toilet paper tube. "I just save these empty ones, roll some of the new roll onto them, and presto, everything fits!"

"I'm not using re-rolled toilet paper," said Danny. He was tired and crabby that he had lost the rock-paper-scissors contest on who would get up to get the bottle.

"Fine. I'll put the re-rolled stuff in the guest house. And I'll put some in Don Paz's bathroom. I'm sure he wouldn't mind," said Mrs. Mango. "Unless, of course, he uses hemp or something." She stood up and held out her arms for the baby. "Here, I'll hold her while you make a bottle."

An hour later, toilet paper redistribution complete, Mrs. Mango slipped outside and crept towards the guest house, clutching an armful of the rolls. The light of an almost-full moon lit up the backyard enough for her to find her way along the bumpy flagstone walkway. Halfway to the guest house, she heard a moaning sound and jumped sideways, screeching and tripping over a stack of pallets, leftover from bringing in all the flagstones. "Oh my goodness!" Mrs. Mango yelped as she fell to the side, landing on a bucket that clattered away from her, spilling the pile of toilet paper rolls she had been carrying.

"Sorry," came a voice from the shadows. "It's just me, Don Paz. Are you okay?" A dark figure appeared near her.

Mrs. Mango patted around her, found the side of the pallet stack, and pulled herself to her knees. "Holy cow. Oh my goodness. You scared the bejeezus out of me!"

"I'm so sorry I scared you. I was just meditating. The energies of the heavens are very strong tonight." Don Paz reached out a hand to help Mrs. Mango, but she didn't take it.

"Oh my goodness," Mrs. Mango repeated as she slowly got to her feet. Her head was down, looking around for the toilet paper rolls, as her arms pulled her robe more tightly around her. "I didn't expect anyone to be out here,

and, then, well, I just thought . . . I don't know." She
thought a wild animal was about to attack her, but she
wasn't going to admit to that. She bent down and started
collecting the toilet paper rolls.

As she stood up, with her head coming up near Don
Paz, she realized he was naked and she was staring directly
into his private parts. "Oh my!" she yelled and twisted
away, falling over the same pallet and scattering the toilet
paper yet again.

"I'm sorry if I startled you," said Don Paz, stepping
towards her to help her up again. "I'm communing."

"Stay away!" Mrs. Mango screeched as she
scrambled on her hands and knees towards the guest house,
toilet paper abandoned. She found a way to stand up and
ran off into the dark, whimpering.

"I'm sorry!" Don Paz called after Mrs. Mango.

Danny's cell phone rang at 6:00 a.m., just after he
hit the snooze button for the sixth time. "Fine, I'm up," he
grumbled, giving up on sleep and fumbling for the phone.
Normally, he would have been up, either treadmilling or
riding his Pelaton exercise bike in their workout room by
5:30, but it had taken him almost two hours to get Emma
Rose back to sleep.

"Hello? What? Huh? Why are you calling me,
Mom?" he said.

"You've got to get that man out of the house!" Mrs.
Mango said. "He's a pervert! Do not let him near Emma
Rose."

"What's wrong? And why are you calling me
instead of just coming in the house?"

"I don't want to see him, ever again," said Mrs.
Mango. "I had to tell you before he was around. He was
walking around your backyard last night, *naked*."

"Who was walking around naked? Dad?" Danny
was still groggy.

"Don Paz!" said Mrs. Mango. "That man is a
menace!"

"He was naked?"

"Yes! Said he was 'communing,' whatever that is."

Rita poked her head out of the bathroom with a questioning look. Danny covered the mouthpiece of the phone and said, "Your brother was walking around the backyard naked last night. Scared the crap out of my mother."

Rita giggled, then covered her mouth, causing one side of the towel she was wrapped in to drop. "I'm sorry, that's not funny, is it?"

Danny put the phone back to his face. "Mom, I'll come out there and talk to you. We'll work this out."

"Work it out? The only thing to do is get that guy out of here! He's a sex offender!"

"He's not a sex offender, he's just, uh, odd. But hang on. Let me get dressed, and I'll come talk to you." Danny hung up and looked at Rita.

"What the hell?"

Rita shrugged as she patted herself dry and pulled on underwear and a bra. "Well, it kind of fits his whole earthy-tree-hugger-one-with-the-universe thing, I guess."

"Can you imagine my mother running into him naked?" said Danny, staring at his wife thinking nakedness was not a bad thing at all. "Holy shit."

They both started laughing.

"This isn't going to end well," said Danny, pulling himself out of bed. "She is really upset. My mom is really uptight about this stuff, I mean, I don't even ever see her in a robe. She is always fully dressed and probably doesn't even change in front of my dad. Can you imagine her running into a naked man in the middle of the night?"

"What is wrong with him?" said Mrs. Mango.

Danny was sitting on the couch in the guest house, trying to calm his mother. "Rita will talk to him, don't worry. He will have to promise no nakedness, or he can't stay."

"That's not good enough!" said Mrs. Mango. "I

can't look him in the eye! I can't stay here if he is here!"

Danny looked at his watch. "I've got to get to work. I promise we'll fix it."

"I'm not coming in that house if he is there."

Danny sighed. "Fine. I'll make sure he leaves, and I'll call you and tell you he is gone. But that is just for today. Tonight, we'll sort it all out."

"Ha! No sorting out. Him or me," said Mrs. Mango, dabbing at her knees. The scabs from falling out of the car at the hospital had ripped off when she tripped over the pallet the second time.

CHAPTER 38
Poker Comes to Visit

Mr. Mango was sitting on the terrace, enjoying the newspaper on a quiet Saturday morning, when a cold nose poked him in the crotch. "What the hell?" he said, dropping his paper. "Poker! Well, I'll be damned."

Michael came around the side of the house.

"Hey, Mikey, I didn't know you were coming!" said Mr. Mango, rubbing his hands over Poker, enjoying the feel and smell of a dog again.

Michael slid gingerly into a chair. "Had some time, thought I'd take Poker for a ride."

Mr. Mango paused his petting of Poker and stared at his son. "'Had some time'? You *never* have time. You okay?"

Michael smiled to reassure his dad. "Yep, just, you know, am feeling like I never see you guys and, well, here I am. Thought I'd check on Emma Rose, you, you know."

Mr. Mango rolled his eyes. "I'm not going die, you know. I mean, not soon. I hope you didn't haul your ass up here just for me."

Michael shook his head. "Try to do a nice thing . . ."

It occurred to Mr. Mango that his son might be lonely. But then again, Joe Jr. and Jenny were at his house. Maybe he was trying to get away from them?

"It's so beautiful up here, thought I'd bring Poker, maybe go for a walk, go into town, and, I don't know, just felt like driving, I guess." Michael shivered. "It's still kind of cool, huh?"

Mr. Mango shrugged. He liked these cool mornings and was dressed for it with an extra sweater and jacket on. It was just so peaceful out here, looking at the ancient trees and the peaceful coming of the light, the way every morning it looked a little different. Today, there had been a haze caused by a faint mist that had diffused the sun and softened the green of the trees in a way that made him wish he knew how to paint, to capture those colors. And when it was chilly, no one tried to sit out here with him. Rita had unearthed an insulated cooler for the coffee, so he sat there going through maybe three cups worth, satisfied to see the steam off the coffee as he took his time with the newspaper. He didn't know that she had slipped decaf into the coffee. Probably wouldn't have mattered much if he had known.

The terrace door opened, and Don Paz came out. "Hello, Michael, Joe," he said, dipping his head in greeting. "I'm headed into the bakery, anyone want anything?"

"Anything?" said Mr. Mango. "I'll take everything."

Michael pushed his hands onto the seat of the chair to get himself up. "I'll ride along," he said.

Mr. Mango looked back and forth between Don Paz and Michael. Something was up. And Michael seemed awfully tense.

"You okay, Mikey?" he demanded.

"Sure, just a little stiff from the drive. Okay if I leave Poker here?" Michael fumbled in his pocket and came out with a tennis ball. "Here, toss it to him once in a while if you are up to it."

"Sure," said Mr. Mango, staring at Don Paz and Michael as they walked away together. He chucked the tennis ball as hard as he could towards the back fence and thought that Mrs. Mango would lose her mind completely if another one of the kids was gay.

As he had that thought, he saw Mrs. Mango making her way up the path from the guest house.

"Was that Michael?" she demanded when she reached the terrace, pulling her tan sweater around her against the cold and looking down at her bare legs wondering why she had picked a house dress over pants today. She had finished knitting her sweater right before

Christmas and was still enjoying the soft stretch and coziness of it.

Mr. Mango nodded yes.

"What's he doing here? And where's he going with *that man*?" Mrs. Mango couldn't even bring herself to say Don Paz's name. "And why hasn't Danny thrown him out yet?"

"Kind of delicate, don't you think? Him being Rita's brother and all. Danny's got to keep the peace," said Mr. Mango.

Mrs. Mango stuck her hands on her hips. "He's got to go! We can't have a pervert like that around."

Mr. Mango noticed Mrs. Mango's use of the word 'we.' As if this was her house and she made the decisions.

"He's an odd duck, that's for sure," said Mr. Mango. "But I don't think he's a pervert. Maybe a man likes to walk around in his birthday suit on occasion."

Mrs. Mango stared at Mr. Mango in horror. "You don't agree with what he did?"

Mr. Mango shrugged. "I used to skinny dip as a kid—kinda liked it."

Mrs. Mango had no interest in talking about nakedness anymore and started towards the house in a huff.

Mr. Mango chuckled to himself. He thought Don Paz was a first-class wingnut but got a kick out of getting a rise out of Mrs. Mango.

Having finally extricated the ball from under an upturned wheelbarrow, Poker came running from the back of the yard and headed straight for Mrs. Mango. Before Mr. Mango could yell out a warning, Poker leaped at her backside in excitement. After all, this was the source of his food for so many years. Mrs. Mango fell forward with a yelp, and Poker jumped on her back.

Mr. Mango recognized the position Poker had taken and leaped out of his seat, yelling at the dog. "Poker! Poker! Stop that!" Poker was one bounce away from starting to hump, and Mr. Mango knew Mrs. Mango would never get over a dog coming at her that way. She didn't even like her husband coming at her that way. All of Poker's dog years would be used up if that happened.

Mrs. Mango was on her knees trying to push herself up, but Poker kept jumping around her, barking.

Mr. Mango yelled "Poker!" again as he grabbed at Poker's collar.

The door to the kitchen opened, and Danny came out in a t-shirt and tight biking shorts. "What the hell is going on?" he said into the barking and yelling.

Mr. Mango got hold of Poker's collar after only two humping motions and prayed Mrs. Mango hadn't noticed the form of the dog's movement. "Jesus Christ, Poker," he said, yanking him back toward the chair where he'd been sitting.

"You all right, Mom?" Danny said, helping his mother to her feet and making eye contact with his dad. Mr. Mango shook his head in a 'don't tell her' move.

"Holy cow, that dog came out of nowhere," said Mrs. Mango, smoothing at her dress and then her hair. She turned towards the chair where Mr. Mango again sat, holding Poker. "What's he doing here?"

"Michael brought him," said Mr. Mango.

"Michael is here?" asked Danny, wondering what had happened to the house that used to be so quiet and peaceful.

"Went into town with Don," said Mr. Mango.

"Huh?" Danny thought he better go back and get his coffee and start over, none of this was making sense.

Mrs. Mango rolled her eyes and stomped into the house, looking over her shoulder as she walked. "Danny, put on some clothes! Those pants are obscene."

Mr. Mango pulled the tennis ball from Poker's mouth and chucked it again towards the back fence. "I don't know, he brought the dog up and decided to go into town. Hey, I'm going to go crazy just sitting around—you have any projects for me? Anything that needs to be fixed?"

Danny sighed. "Let me get some coffee, then I'll

think about it.”

In the kitchen, as Danny poured himself a cup of coffee and his mother cleaned out the dishwasher, Rita came in holding Emma Rose. “Say ‘Good morning, Grandma!’” Rita said in a high sweet voice. “Say ‘Good morning, Daddy!’” she added.

Danny poured a second cup of coffee and put it on the island in front of Rita. “Morning, my girls,” he said.

Rita bounced Emma Rose towards Danny, as if the baby were giving him a kiss. Then, she looked out the back window. “What is that dog doing here?!” she demanded, all sweetness gone.

“Oh, Michael drove up and brought Poker,” said Danny, tensing at Rita’s tone but trying to sound casual.

“That dog CANNOT come in the house,” Rita said in a severe voice.

“No problem, he won’t,” said Danny. He looked at the clock on the microwave—holy cow, it wasn’t even 8:00 yet, how could the day already be this tense and busy? All he had tried to do was grab a cup of coffee after his workout so he could run back upstairs and shower.

“What if he attacks the baby?” said Rita, hugging Emma Rose tighter at the thought.

“He’d never do that!” said Mrs. Mango.

Danny looked at his mother, hair still in disarray from Poker jumping on her, and wisely didn’t comment. “Well, we’ll just keep him away. He stays outside.”

“Go tell your dad. Right now,” demanded Rita.

Danny sighed. “Fine,” he said and went out to tell his dad.

Mr. Mango shook his head. “Jesus Christ, the dog won’t hurt anyone.”

“Dad, he just tried to hump Mom! Just keep him outside, that’s all—okay?”

“Sure, whatever,” said Mr. Mango. “It’s not like he’d even get anywhere close to the baby. She’s always in some sort of contraption. I never saw so many gizmos for holding a baby. You either got her buckled to your chest or tied up in some swing or strapped into some kind of bed. It's not like you lie her around on the floor."

Danny closed his eyes and wished he were at work. It was a Saturday morning, for crying out loud. He should be relaxing with the newspaper, nothing more on the schedule than a little yard work and maybe a nap later, but instead he was surrounded by family chaos. The workout high, so hard fought for, was already gone.

CHAPTER 39

Grannies and Trannies

Christine had her hands high over her head, fists moving back and forth in time to the pounding beat of the music. The bar was so crowded that it was almost the only place to hold her arms. She bumped into Sarah repeatedly, sometimes on purpose, other times not. They were both laughing and drenched in sweat. It was only to be expected on a Saturday night at Starfish, the latest bar/band spot/bistro in Walnut Creek. With Diamond Dave on his DJ throne, the crowd was filled with everyone from San Francisco trannies to Rossmoor grannies.

When Elton John transitioned seamlessly to Pitbull, Sarah finally gasped, "I've got to stop! I need a drink."

Christine nodded and let Sarah pull her along towards the bar. It almost didn't seem possible to move through a crowd this thick, but somehow the effect of Sarah's smile seemed to clear a path. Christine's pink flowy top was no longer flowy, instead sticking to her sweaty skin, and her feet were throbbing in the heels Sarah had talked her into, saying it made her jean-clad legs look longer. Sarah had pulled her hair up into a high pony tail to get it off her sweaty neck, and as she fought her way through the crowd, she pulled her simple black sleeveless dress away from her body to try to get some air flowing. Neither could stop smiling. Diamond Dave was their favorite night out.

They jostled their way to the six-deep bar. "We'll never get close," Christine shouted into Sarah's ear.

Sarah nodded and scanned right and left to see if there was a way to get closer. Nope. They would just have to wait their turn.

Bit by bit, as people got served and were swallowed back into the churning darkness, Sarah and Christine moved closer. Finally, only the filled bar stools were in front of them. As Christine leaned over to try to get the bartender's attention, she bumped into the woman on the stool in front of her. "So sorry," she said.

Flora turned around. "Hey, Christine! What's the dilly-oh?" Flora said, sticking her pale gnarled hand up for a high five.

"Oh hi, Mrs. Gonzalez!" said Christine, high fiving Flora. She realized she shouldn't have been surprised, Diamond Dave attracted everyone. She looked to Flora's right and sure enough, there was Velma. "And hi, Mrs. Costa!"

Flora was wearing a white scoop necked sweater with a big turquoise chunky necklace resting on her bony chest, and Velma had on a tight black sleeveless shirt with a plunging neckline showing off lots of flesh, some of it in the right places. Christine was almost glad she couldn't see what they were wearing on their bottom halves.

"You girls need a drink?" Velma asked, looking at Christine and Sarah.

"Yes! That would be great," said Christine. "We haven't even gotten close."

"Hey! Luis!" yelled Velma at the tall, broad-shouldered bartender smoothly darting to and fro. Velma turned back to Christine. "What're you drinking?"

"Stella for Sarah, a sidecar for me," said Christine. "Thanks!"

"A sidecar," said Flora. "Haven't heard of that drink in years. Velma, I think that should be our next drink."

Velma nodded. "Good idea. I'll tell Hunky Luis to make us all one. Excepting . . . " she looked at Sarah with a question.

"Sarah," said Christine. "This is Sarah, my . . ." Christine paused. She had already had two drinks and was feeling the effects of them, but the connection of Velma and Flora to her parents was too strong to just say it.

Sarah gave Christine an amused look.

Flora and Velma gave each other knowing looks.

"We weren't born yesterday," said Flora, and they both laughed hard and toasted with their almost-empty glasses.

"True dat," said Velma. "You girls are both lovely. Nice to meet you, Sarah. You got a good one here."

"My gaydar is pinging!" said Flora. "Love it!"

Luis stopped in front of Velma. "Hello, love, what can I get you?" He leaned over and kissed Velma on the cheek, then picked up Flora's hand and kissed it. "These are my best girls," he said to Christine.

Christine nodded, still stunned by the fact that she just came out to Velma and Flora.

"Three sidecars and a Stella," said Velma.

"You got it," said Luis, hustling away.

"So, how's your mom?" said Flora, staring intently at Christine.

Wow. So many ways to take that. As in, how is your mom doing with the new baby in the family? How is your mom doing with your dad? How is your mom doing with your, you know, gayness?

"Well, she is loving having a grandchild, you know," said Christine, leaning in because the music seemed to have been pumped up even louder. Iggy Azalea must be heard at high decibels. "And you probably heard about my dad? He had another cardiac thingy. Probably a heart attack but not completely sure."

Velma and Flora nodded. "Heard. Sorry," said Flora, draining the last of her cocktail in anticipation of the new drink coming.

"So, they are both at Danny's house," said Christine, as she started giggling. Danny had told her about her mom running into Don Paz naked in the middle of the night. She told Velma and Flora about it.

Once they stopped laughing and wiped their eyes, Velma said, "Damn, your mom has all the luck.

Flora chimed in, "Oh, that is the best! The best! I love your mom, but she is wound a little tight! I can't imagine her seeing that!"

Christine laughed. "I know!" When Christine had heard the story about her mother seeing Don Paz naked, it reminded her of seeing the passed-out man on Daisy Street naked, and it made her wonder what was going on with her mother that she kept finding herself in situations where she saw naked men.

Sarah was laughing too but just enough to accompany Christine, not enough to be seen to be making fun of someone she hoped might end up as her mother-in-law.

"So," said Velma, poking her finger at Sarah. "How is old Elsie treating you?"

Sarah smiled. "Uh, okay."

"I'm going to be honest here," said Velma. "I've had a couple of drinks and I'm as old as dirt, so no use beating around the bush."

Flora fistbumped Velma. "You got that right."

"You girls got to do what you want, you hear that?" Velma continued. "None of this hiding yourself bullshit. You find someone you love, it don't matter what other people think. That's none of your business. Your business is treating each other well, right?"

Sarah and Christine looked at each other and then back at Velma and nodded.

"Your job is to grab life by the balls and hang on," Velma said. "Whoops, guess that don't apply to you. But you get my point."

Luis dropped the drinks in front of Velma and Flora. "My treat," he said and sped away.

"I love that guy," said Flora, looking longingly at him. "I'd've hit that in the day."

Velma giggled. "In your dreams. When you were *twenty,* you couldn't have even got him."

"A girl can dream," said Flora.

Velma handed out the drinks and held hers up for a toast. "To sex!" she crowed, and they all bumped glasses and sipped.

Velma's face got serious, and she grabbed

Christine's hand. "I know your mom, and I know she's probably having a hard time with, you know, this—" she waved a hand around Sarah and Christine "—you know. If you've even told her. But don't worry, she'll come around. Just give her a grandchild."

CHAPTER 40
The Starter Marriage

"Elsie! What are you doing here?" Mrs. Mango looked up from her spot on the Cardiac Rehab waiting room couch where she was happily knitting away, having been permanently excused from attending the class. It turned out that Perky Julie was no match for Grumpy Elsie. Velma was standing in front of her, staring down. Mrs. Mango was so used to seeing Velma in her workout gear that she forgot how nicely Velma cleaned up. Instead of lycra running tights, she was wearing a pale green pantsuit with a finely woven white shirt underneath. Instead of an iPod with earbuds, she had a long gold chain with a pocketwatch on the end hanging around her neck. Her face was carefully made up, and her hair was arranged in soft waves, no headband to be seen. Only the bright pink lipstick was the same.

"Waiting for Joe, he's got his cardiac rehab class," said Mrs. Mango. "You look nice! What are you doing here?"

"Here to visit Ralph, my first husband," said Velma, flipping the pocket watch around on its chain to look at the time. "He's getting over a bit of heart surgery. He said, come at 11:00, and I'm early, so I guess I'll give him a few minutes. Probably wants to get presentable." She laughed and plopped herself down beside Mrs. Mango. "Like you can look that good in a hospital gown!"

"I thought both of your husbands died?" said Mrs. Mango, confused.

"Husbands two and three died," Velma said. "Ralph was my first husband. My starter marriage."

"Starter marriage? What's that?" Mrs. Mango asked.

"It's when you marry your first crush, thinking you know what love is," Velma said, shrugging out of her suit jacket. "And then pretty quickly, you find out you had no idea what marriage is and that maybe you should have broken up and gone on to date a bunch more people before settling down. Maybe shouldn't have gotten married right out of high school."

"Hmm," said Mrs. Mango, staring unseeing across to the reception desk as her brain scrambled to make sense of the idea.

"Ralph and I thought we were so in love," reminisced Velma, settling back on the couch, smoothing her jacket across her lap and staring up with a smile. "Met in high school. We went to schools on opposite sides of town, the biggest rivals. But when I met Ralph, immediate fireworks. We had to sneak around!" Velma's eyes were bright. "Not from our parents—from our friends! No one was allowed to have anything to do with East Side at that time. Like they were Germans or something."

Mrs. Mango was still circling around the idea of a starter marriage and, for once, was silent. Her knitting sat unknitted in her lap.

"We thought we had found our soul mates, and maybe, if we'd've met later, it would have worked." Velma thought for a moment. "No, it wouldn't have. It ended up we were really different in some important ways. Just couldn't make those work."

Mrs. Mango felt an uncomfortable reverberation in her brain. "How long were you married?"

"Not even a year, and then we both knew we had jumped in way too young and, ultimately, with the wrong person." Velma sighed. "Not sure I'd change it, though. We had some good times, Ralph and I. Which is why I'm here to see him now. Still have a soft spot in my heart for him."

"Any chance you are, you know, hoping to reconnect?" asked Mrs. Mango.

Velma shook her head. "No, that ship has sailed. I mean, I guess technically it is possible—his wife passed a couple of years ago—but, I don't know, I just feel a lot of fondness for him. That's all." Velma cackled. "Bet that's hard for you to believe, huh? I know I have a reputation for never turning down a man."

Mrs. Mango smiled weakly. That was true, not that she would have said it out loud.

Velma pulled a tube of lipstick out of her purse and applied another thick coat of bright pink. "Jimmy, my second husband, he's the one I really think of as my first *husband*. Ralph was my first crush, which at the time I confused with love. Real marriage is someone you can love through the hard times, through the sick baby and the lost job and the breast lump scare. And Jimmy, that's what he was. Really steady, like a rock. When you are young, you don't see how that can be attractive, that steadiness, but I think if you are lucky, you find that kind of love in a marriage." Velma shook her head and recapped the lipstick, sticking it back in her purse. "Youth! You think you know what love is, but you really don't. How could you know? Nothing to compare it to."

"I wish I could have met Jimmy," said Mrs. Mango. "He sounds like a good man."

"He was," said Velma. "We had twenty great years. Never blessed by kids, but he was a good man. Not that you might have noticed. He was the quiet type. Not showy in the least. Well, not outside of the bedroom!"

Mrs. Mango ignored the last part. She was looking at Velma in a new light. She had known Velma for maybe fifteen, twenty years and had never known this stuff about her. It occurred to her that she had always thought of Velma as a bit of a caricature, a sex-starved old woman, but clearly Velma was more complicated than that. Which shouldn't be surprising, it seemed that maybe everyone was.

"And then Jack?" asked Mrs. Mango. "I remember meeting him, I think it was not long before he, uh, passed too."

Velma nodded. "Jack was another good one. It's true that the good die young, he was only 65. I had thirteen good years with him. Different than Jimmy in some ways but alike in the important ways. Which is that he didn't run from the tough stuff. And I never felt worried that he would. Some men, you just don't know. You like them a lot, they like you, but then the going gets rough and they just can't deal with it. Saw that happen with Flora's first husband."

Mrs. Mango nodded. She had heard the stories about Flora's first husband.

Velma looked at her pocket watch again. "Well, better head on up. Ralph always was a stickler for punctuality." She laughed as she stood up, slipping back into the pantsuit jacket. "One of our many incompatibilities."

"Enjoy seeing Ralph," said Mrs. Mango.

"Tell Joe to take care of himself," said Velma, and then she sashayed away.

Mrs. Mango stared after her, admiring her for maybe the first time. Velma had found a way to stay full of life even after losing two loved husbands. Not the way Mrs. Mango would have done it, but she had to respect it.

As Velma reached the double doors leading into the rest of the hospital, an older gentleman, poker-straight back and aided by a cane, gave her a little bow and opened the door for her.

Mrs. Mango could hear Velma's flirty giggle as she thanked him, and as the two of them went through the doors, the last bit she heard was Velma asking him his name. Mrs. Mango smiled. That Velma was something else.

As she resumed clickety-clacking her knitting needles, Mrs. Mango's mind swirled with Velma's story. She couldn't help comparing her relationship with Raul to Velma and Ralph. Was it the same kind of thing? Her immediate thought was, no, of course not. Raul had really been her soul mate, if she could use that phrase without thinking of Don Paz. They were different. Of course they were. In the corner of her mind floated the idea that they

never got to test that out. That maybe Raul would have
been a 'starter marriage' too.

It was all too disturbing, the way Mrs. Mango kept
running into the idea that people were complicated.

CHAPTER 41
A Hard Karma

Rita gave a quick glance at the clock on the wall of her office. Forty-five minutes until she was due in court. She clicked the mouse in her right hand, typed in her password, and brought up the streaming video of the nanny cams at home, all eight of them. Checked her watch— Emma Rose should be in her crib sleeping. She scanned through the screens and found Emma Rose exactly where she was supposed to be. And doing what she was supposed to be doing. A quick check of the kitchen found Mrs. Mango washing baby bottles and setting them in the drying rack.

Whew. Monday morning, and all as it should be. Rita turned back to the papers in front of her, pushed her reading glasses more firmly against her nose, and got back to work.

Three hours later, Rita came back into her office, dropped a stack of files on her desk, slid into her chair, and logged in again to her security cameras. She found Emma Rose in Mrs. Mango's arms in the kitchen. Mrs. Mango was sitting at the kitchen table across from Mr. Mango. Rita turned the sound up.

"Well, just look at this little beauty," cooed Mrs. Mango. "Such a doll. You're going to drive the boys crazy."

Mr. Mango slurped at his soup and made a face.

"What?" said Mrs. Mango, catching his look.

"Nothing," said Mr. Mango.

"Well, she is a beauty! Look at those eyes. And cheeks!"

"Mm-hmm," he said, picking up the newspaper beside his bowl.

"She's a princess. And she's going to be treated like

one, aren't you, my little lovey?" Mrs. Mango said, nuzzling Emma Rose.

"There's all kinds of princesses," said Mr. Mango.

"I don't understand what you are getting at," said Mrs. Mango.

Mr. Mango set the paper down and stared at his wife. "Well, there's the Rita kind of princess, and there's the Christine kind of princess."

Mrs. Mango stood up and started swaying back and forth to soothe Emma Rose, even though Emma Rose seemed quite content staring around the room and at Mrs. Mango.

"You know, the kind of princess who marries a prince, and the kind that marries another princess," added Mr. Mango.

Rita snorted with laughter and leaned in to get a better look at Mrs. Mango's reaction.

"Why do you have to talk about that?" said Mrs. Mango, bouncing gently as she walked around the table and over towards the kitchen island.

Mr. Mango smiled to himself. He wasn't above having a little fun at his wife's expense. "Who knows what kind of princess Emma Rose is?"

"Stop that!" demanded Mrs. Mango.

"Nothing wrong with it," said Mr. Mango.

Mrs. Mango stopped her swaying and bouncing and stared straight at Mr. Mango. "You're telling me it doesn't bother you? Not even a little bit?"

"Correct-a-mundo," said Mr. Mango. "I feel like I stared death in the eye and, guess what? Life is too short to care about stuff like that. Christine seems happy, which is more than I can say for Michael or Joey, for that matter."

"Hmph," said Mrs. Mango.

"And, actually, I'm not even sure how happy Danny is," continued Mr. Mango.

Rita stiffened. What did he mean by that?

"Of course he's unhappy," said Mrs. Mango. "He seems so stressed these days. And there are a lot of rules around here, you notice that?"

Mr. Mango shrugged. "Rita really likes things her own way. That's not really news." He didn't say out loud that this was his view of all women.

Rita's eyes widened and her hands clenched. Part of her knew she should turn off the video, but she couldn't bring herself to do it.

Mrs. Mango nodded violently. "Yes, but now there is a baby she is making rules about. An *insane* number of rules." She gestured at the clipboard with the schedule. "Look at that! You can't control a baby's life down to the minute! It's crazy."

Rita's heart was beating faster, and her face was getting hot.

"Hmm," mused Mr. Mango. "I wonder if it is hard on Danny." Mr. Mango actually thought Mrs. Mango had more rules than Rita, but it was easier to talk about Danny than himself.

Rita was burning with indignation listening to them. She wanted to drive home and throw them out of her house. Here she was letting them stay at her house, and they were talking about her behind her back! Acting like she was ruining their son's life or something. How dare they?

"Of course it's hard on Danny!" said Mrs. Mango. "'Don't eat at the table without a place mat,' 'don't wear your shoes in the house'—the list is so long! Danny works those long hours, and then she expects him to help all night at home. With the dishes and the cooking and the laundry and even getting up in the middle of the night with Emma Rose!"

"Well, Rita works too," said Mr. Mango. "So . . ."

"It's not the same," said Mrs. Mango. "He is working his fingers to the bone! He should be able to relax a little when he gets home. I've done my best to get along with Rita, but I'm going to just say it, she's so *cold*. I always thought a baby would soften her, but she's still pretty hard to connect to."

Rita felt like her head was going to explode. She

never should have installed the cameras. Her hand reached for the phone to call Danny, but then she stopped herself. How could she tell him she was spying on his parents? And what if they were right? What if he was unhappy?

"It's just that I worry about him. Especially now that we know there is heart disease in the family. What if he has a heart attack?" Mrs. Mango shifted Emma Rose to her other arm. "Hello, sweetie, would you like a little bottle? Almost that time."

She walked over to Mr. Mango. "Here, hold her while I make the bottle."

Mr. Mango tucked Emma Rose into the crook of his left arm. "Hello, little one," he said. "It's nice to hold a baby again, isn't it?"

"So, you don't care that your daughter is going to hell?" said Mrs. Mango as she measured out formula. She was able to switch topics without missing a beat.

"Ah, come on, that's old stuff," said Mr. Mango. "Even the Pope is saying to be accepting of gays."

"No, he didn't," said Mrs. Mango.

"Well, just as good as."

Rita clicked off the streaming video link and sat back in her chair. Anger and shame swirled in equal amounts through her bloodstream. She had always thought Danny's parents liked her, and now all she could feel was betrayed. Too many rules. Hah. She'd show them rules! Rules of good behavior, like not talking behind the back of someone giving you a place to live. And rules about access to your only grandchild. As in, if you don't respect me, you don't get time with Emma Rose. Simple as that. They'd see how 'cold' she could be.

She couldn't go to Danny with this. He would probably say that she got what she deserved, eavesdropping on someone. And he would deny being unhappy, no matter whether it was true or not. But she had to call someone.

Rita dialed Don Paz. *Maybe it is true that blood is thicker than water,* she thought.

After trying Don Paz four times and getting no answer to a text either, Rita glanced at her schedule for the rest of the day and decided she could take off early. Nothing she couldn't finish later at home. She stuffed all the papers she'd need in her briefcase, turned off her computer, and set off for Don Paz's office work site.

Rita parked her Audi in front of the partially remodeled building, wondering idly where all the construction trucks were, most of her visits had found her turning down side streets to find parking. Don Paz's building was on a tree-lined side street, three blocks over from Main Street. It was on the edge of a residential neighborhood with neat rows of well-maintained bungalows mixed with Spanish-style stucco homes. Sun filtered through the trees arching over the street, and each house had its own version of a lush landscape despite the drought, some with thick bushes, others with spilling flowers, every one with the curb appeal of a house for sale. Last time she had been by the site, she had to park a block and a half away because of all the trucks for the construction crew, but today she easily found a spot behind Don Paz's old Saab. She stepped out and stared at the two-story building with its red tile roof, graceful arching doorways, and a mature magnolia tree to the left of the entrance. The stucco was cracked and patched and waiting to be repainted. The windows hadn't been refinished yet either, but Rita could tell the building was going to be charming when all the work was finished. She squeaked the tall carved wood door open and peered in.
"Hello? Anyone here?" She walked through the entryway, which was littered with stacks of wood, paint tarps, and various other construction accoutrements. She peered into the first room and found Don Paz, sitting against the wall, knees up, staring into his folded hands.
"Hey, what's going on?" Rita asked.
Don Paz slowly turned to look at Rita. Stared at her

for a long minute. "Well. There's been a setback," he said slowly.

"Yes?" said Rita, anxious to get to her own problems.

"More than a setback, actually," he said. He took a deep breath in and let it out in a long exhale. "So, Marla—you know, my business partner—she's the massage therapist. Well, her husband cleaned out their bank accounts, all their investments, and took off."

"So that means . . ." said Rita.

"It means we have no money. I already spent all mine on the building down payment. She was paying the mortgage on the building. And for the renovations. The hard part for her is that it was not even *their* money, it was *hers*. He took off with her inheritance from her mother."

"Oh no," said Rita, her own problems momentarily forgotten.

"Oh yes," said Don Paz. "And, of course, my name is on the loans. Loans we have no way to pay off."

Rita sank down beside Don Paz. "Oh my God, I'm so sorry. Are you sure the money is gone?"

"Well, it is nowhere anyone can find. She's a great massage therapist but apparently not so on top of financial stuff. She thinks she even signed it away, not knowing what she was signing."

"Can you find the husband? Have you talked to the police?"

Don Paz rolled his eyes. "Don't you think we've already gone down those paths? Please don't jump into problem-solving mode just yet, okay?"

"Sorry, sorry, that is just me, I know," said Rita. "That's my reaction when something goes wrong."

Don Paz gave a weak smile. "So true. Our little spitfire. Changing the world since you were ten years old."

Rita opened her mouth to speak and then closed it again, realizing she was just about to offer more advice.

Don Paz took in a deep breath and blew it out slowly. "For some reason, my deep breathing is not bringing my normal level of calm," he said, with another weak smile. He took another deep breath and blew it out again, even more slowly this time.

Rita tried to match him, slowing down her breathing in time to Don Paz's. For a minute, the only sound in the room was air being inhaled and expelled.

"Why are you here?" asked Don Paz.

"Oh, nothing as big as your problems," said Rita.

"It must be something," said Don Paz. "Come on, give."

"It's just, well, I installed webcams at home so I could look at Emma Rose during the day," Rita started.

"You mean, spy on Elsie," said Don Paz.

"What? I can't want to see my baby during the day?" said Rita, and then she laughed. "Okay, in part to see if Elsie is caring for her properly."

"And you saw something you didn't want to see," said Don Paz.

"She and Pops were talking, and both said they think I have too many rules! And that Danny is unhappy and stressed!" Rita exploded, glad to let it out. "I can't believe them! We give them a place to live, and this is how they thank me."

Don Paz nodded slowly. "Yes, that could hurt."

"Could? *Could* hurt? Of course it hurts. How could it *not* hurt?"

Don Paz reached over to Rita and rubbed her shoulder. "It is your perception of what they say that hurts, not what they are actually saying."

Rita pulled away from his hand. "I don't understand what you are saying. Of course it is my perception, but they *said* it. They said I have too many rules and am making my husband unhappy!"

"Do you think that is true?" asked Don Paz.

"No! Of course not," said Rita. "Danny and I make the rules together. My God, you've got to have rules! The world wouldn't work if there weren't agreed-upon rules and ways to behave towards each other. It would be Lord of the Flies without rules.”

“What about the unhappy husband part?” asked Don Paz in a gentle voice.

“Of course he gets stressed—we all do—but that’s not me causing it,” said Rita, her voice high and shrill. She peered closely at Don Paz, “Unless you see something else. Tell me! Do *you* think I am making Danny unhappy?”

“That is not for me to say.”

“What?! Why not? What’s your opinion?” said Rita, almost at a yell.

“Are you happy? Does Danny seem happy to you? Those are the questions to ask yourself. It really isn’t my business,” said Don Paz. “But it is interesting that Elsie and Joe’s conversation hit such a nerve for you. Maybe you are little afraid they are right?”

Rita closed her eyes and shook her head. “I should have known better than to come to you for help.”

Don Paz shrugged. “You asked my opinion. That is all I have to offer you. It really doesn’t matter what they think, they aren’t the ones living in your relationship—you are. And they aren’t the ones who can make you happy. You are.”

“Huh,” snorted Rita. “Talk about an unhappy couple. If you ask me, those two do not like each other. Anyone could see that Elsie came to stay with us to get away from Pops, and now he’s right back under her skin. And I have to live with their nattering away at each other.”

“Well, we all attract what we need to learn from,” said Don Paz. “Maybe there is some reason you attracted them to your house.”

Rita shook her head. “I don’t know where you get this stuff from. I had nothing to do with ‘attracting’ them to my house! I didn’t ask for this! I didn’t create it.” She stopped shaking her head and stared at Don Paz. “But if that’s true, that we attract what we need to learn from, then you have a hell of a lesson hitting you right now, don’t you?” She gestured around the half-renovated room.

Don Paz closed his eyes and took several long

breaths. In a whisper of a voice, he finally said, "You are absolutely right."

They sat in silence for a couple of minutes. Don Paz opened his eyes and looked around the room. "There *is* a big lesson here for me. I guess my job now is to figure out what it is."

"Don't you think sometimes there is just bad luck?" said Rita in a soft voice. "Maybe just plain bad luck, not fate or a lesson or anything."

Don Paz stared at the wall across from him and straightened his bent legs out. "No. I really don't believe in luck. You are right, somehow I helped create this situation. As Pema Chodron said, 'Nothing ever goes away until it teaches us what we need to know.'" He nodded to himself. "Yes, there is something here for me to learn."

Rita shook her head in disagreement. "I don't see what there is to learn in some asshole taking off with your money."

"You know, I thought I was leaving the whole financial world when I left business school, but clearly you can't ignore money matters. I think I need to make peace with money and the financial part of running a business. I wanted to provide services without really having to fully embrace the money part."

Don Paz pulled himself up to standing and offered Rita a hand to help her up. He pulled her into a hug. "It is all going to work out, for both of us. It may take time. But it will. And we will be the stronger from it."

They pulled away from the hug, and Rita smiled affectionately at Don Paz. "You're kooky, you know that?" she said. "I almost believe you."

Don Paz walked Rita to the door. "I'll see you later at the house. I'm going to have to refigure everything, including my living arrangements. I'm not freeloading off you forever. It was just supposed to be for a month or so."

Rita gave him a hug. "See you then." As she walked through the hallway, she stopped, looked backwards, and said, "And watch what you say at home, I may just be listening in." She gave a short laugh and stepped through the front door.

As Rita walked towards her car, she decided she was going to refigure everything too. She was taking back control of her house. She wasn't sure what that meant exactly, but she wasn't leaving Emma Rose alone so much with Elsie. She wasn't going to let Elsie run *her* house. She pulled her cell phone out of her bag and called her administrative assistant.

"Yes, hi Cheryl. Listen, I need you to reschedule the rest of the week for me. Yep, push everything you can back. I'm going to work from home. I'll come in only if it is something you really can't change. Thank you." Rita beeped her car open and threw the purse and phone onto the passenger seat. She slid in, closed the door, and smiled her toughest court smile. The icy one that said 'I'm about to put your ass in a sling.' "There's a new sheriff in town," she said to the windshield.

CHAPTER 42
The Hill to Die On

Rita found Mrs. Mango in the family room, folding laundry while she watched Emma Rose in her corner bassinet. There were neat stacks of clothes covering the couch and the armchairs, all shades of white and pink represented. In front of Mrs. Mango, a stack of darker colors was growing, and from her seat on the ottoman, she shook out what looked like a scrap of black lace as Rita came through the doorway.

"Oh no!" said Rita, darting to Mrs. Mango and grabbing her HankyPanky thong out of Mrs. Mango's hands. "I'll do these!"

Mrs. Mango frowned. "I don't mind, just trying to help out."

Rita was already angry with Mrs. Mango, and finding her with Rita's own underwear in her hands didn't help. Did the woman not have any boundaries? What if those had been period panties? A flush of embarrassment mixed with anger as she looked into the half-full basket beside Mrs. Mango and saw more fine washables and then noticed the pile of underwear and bras in front of her. Mrs. Mango must have gone in her closet to find those! She grabbed the basket and moved it out of Mrs. Mango's way. "I'll finish these."

Mrs. Mango slid back further on the ottoman and stared at Rita in bewilderment. "Whatever you want. Not like I never saw a pair of underwear."

"They're private!" said Rita, emotion at the surface. "I'd just rather you didn't. No need to do our laundry."

"I was just trying to help," said Mrs. Mango, hurt in her voice. What was wrong with Rita? Here she was doing something nice for her! Helping her out. Trying to take something off her plate. That woman was strung way too tight in Mrs. Mango's opinion. "Anything else I should stay away from?" Mrs. Mango said sarcastically.

"Well, now that you mention it, yes," said Rita. She took a couple of deep breaths to try to compose herself. "I know that you have been trying to help," she started.

Mrs. Mango cut her off. "'Trying? You say 'trying' as if I'm not really helping. Like I'm making some poor effort at it!"

Emma Rose started to cry in the bassinet, and Mrs. Mango leaped up and hustled over to her. "There, there, little one," she cooed, jiggling the bassinet. Emma Rose quieted, and Mrs. Mango looked at Rita in triumph. "Must have been *luck*, me getting her to quiet."

Rita took another deep breath. "It's just, well, I don't feel like you are completely respecting my wishes here."

Mrs. Mango put her hands on her hips. "What do you mean? I'm following the schedule. I'm not picking Emma Rose up when I'm not supposed to. How was I to know you didn't want me to do your laundry?"

"It's not about the laundry!" said Rita. "I mean, it is, a little bit. It's more that I just don't feel like you believe in what I'm trying to do with Emma Rose, and you don't respect how I want to run the house."

"I respect what you want," protested Mrs. Mango. "I'm following *all* your rules."

"Yes! That's the part that I don't like!" said Rita. "You think I have too many rules! That's what feels disrespectful."

"What do you mean?" asked Mrs. Mango. "I never said that."

"Ah, but you did!" exclaimed Rita, thrilled to catch Mrs. Mango in a lie. "I think your exact words were 'an insane number of rules.'"

Mrs. Mango stared at Rita, her mind whirling. Then her eyes narrowed, and she gasped. "You've been *spying* on me!" Mrs. Mango gestured towards the nanny cam on the mantel. "*That's* what those cameras are for! Not for security. For *spying*!"

Mrs. Mango's face got red, and her breath short. "I have never been treated so badly in my life!" she spat and stomped out of the room. She turned around and stuck her head back through the family room door. "Maybe the person you should be spying on is that pervert of a brother of yours!" she barked before leaving. "Treated like some sort of *criminal,*" she muttered, pounding through the kitchen.

Mrs. Mango banged into the guest house. "Joe! Joe! Where are you?" she yelled.

Mr. Mango had drifted off to sleep on the bed, the puffy comforter wrapped around him. With the slam of the door and Mrs. Mango's yelling, he jumped and for a moment thought his heart had stopped yet again.

"What?" he said breathlessly, hand on his chest. "What's wrong?"

"Get your stuff!" Mrs. Mango said, hauling her suitcase out of the closet. "We're leaving."

"What in the world is going on?" repeated Mr. Mango, his brain not fully awake yet. He rubbed his eyes and looked out the window. Still daylight but it was an overcast day, leaving him lost as to what time it might be.

"Rita has been *spying* on us! Listening in on those stupid cameras. Watching us! Invading our privacy!" said Mrs. Mango as she stuffed clothes haphazardly into the suitcase. "I have never been treated so disrespectfully! Here we put our lives on hold to come and help with that baby, and she acts like this! Like we are no better than some shoplifter."

"How do you know she's been watching?" asked Mr. Mango.

"She quoted something I said!" said Mrs. Mango, stopping her packing for a moment to turn and face Mr. Mango. "Something I said in privacy to you! She's been watching you too, you better know it."

Mr. Mango shrugged. He didn't feel like he had much to hide.

"Get up! We are leaving just as soon as I get packed."

"Now, Elsie, maybe hang on just a moment," said Mr. Mango, sitting up and easing his legs over the side of the bed. "We were kind of saying not nice things about her. Let's be careful, we don't want to cause a whole thing in the family."

"SHE caused the thing!" huffed Mrs. Mango, moving to the bathroom where she haphazardly tossed her creams and pills back into their ziplock bags.

"Maybe we should wait and talk to Danny?" ventured Mr. Mango.

"No!" yelled Mrs. Mango from the bathroom. "We are leaving. I'm leaving, and you are coming with me."

"Well," started Mr. Mango.

Mrs. Mango stuck her head out of the bathroom and glared at him. "You aren't going to take *her* side are you?" she said, face blotchy with anger, hair in disarray.

Mr. Mango shook his head and looked down. Just one more time in his life where he would have to put his own opinions away and go along with Elsie. Unless this was the hill he was going to pick to die on. That thought brought him a little too close to his actual potential for dying, and he breathed out, looked up, and said, "Of course not. Let me get my stuff together."

Mr. Mango sat white-knuckled in the passenger seat while Mrs. Mango zoomed down Danny's driveway towards the road. Her anger at Rita was so intense she was about to actually drive on a freeway for the first time in decades, and, then, if they even survived the freeway, the whole Christine situation was waiting for them at the other end of the trip. As Mrs. Mango slingshotted out of Danny's driveway, Mr. Mango slid his phone out and texted Christine to let her know they were on their way home. Maybe if Christine was waiting at home, the whole moving out issue wouldn't have to be addressed just yet. Then he leaned back in the passenger seat and closed his eyes, but that didn't last long. Mrs. Mango's frenzied driving on the side roads had turned into timid and shaky driving on the freeway. She drove so slowly it took them twice the time it should have and raised Mr. Mango's blood pressure to dangerous levels. He offered to drive several times, but she shut him down.

"I'm not dying because you have another 'event' while we are driving!" she said the third time he offered, fingers gripping the steering wheel in a death grip, head bare inches from the window shield. "Oh, for crying out loud!" she yelled at her window. "Look at that crazy lady! She almost rear-ended me and then flew around me like she's at Daytona or something."

Mr. Mango wanted to say that's what happens when you drive forty-five miles an hour on a freeway but knew it would do nothing to improve the situation. Sometimes a man just has to accept that the day has been shot to shit.

"What's wrong with people!?" Mrs. Mango grouched. "I think someone just flipped me off. And honked at me!"

"Where're you going?" said Mr. Mango, looking backwards. "You missed the exit."

"Holy cow! I don't know! I never paid attention before," Mrs. Mango got frantic and looked from rearview mirror to side mirror and back to rearview mirror. "What do I do?"

"Keep your eyes on the road, for one thing!" said Mr. Mango. "Just take the next one, no big deal. I'll tell you where to turn."

"Darn that Rita!" fumed Mrs. Mango. "She ruined everything! It's her fault I have to drive, and I'll never forgive her!" Not only was the driving agitating Mrs. Mango, but her heart was breaking over not seeing Emma Rose. If there was any reason to regret what had happened, it was leaving the baby. But, no, there was no possibility of staying in a house where someone was that awful to you. Rita basically kicked her out, that's what she did. Rita was ripping her apart from her grandchild.

Then Mrs. Mango remembered the christening, scheduled for the upcoming weekend. If she had to go kidnap Emma Rose, she was going to be christened. Somehow, that was going to have to happen.

"That baby is getting christened!" Mrs. Mango said fiercely.

"What?" asked Mr. Mango, not privy to Mrs. Mango's thought process.

"This weekend, that is still going to happen. I don't care how we do it—that baby is getting baptized!"

"Well, I don't know that that is a good idea right now," said Mr. Mango. "Can always do it later."

"Later? Wait on saving my only grandchild's soul? What are you, some kind of devil worshipper?" Mrs. Mango said, drifting the car from the left lane to the right, flinching at the horns that marked the disapproval of her driving skills.

Mr. Mango shrugged and didn't answer. He was busy saying his prayers, not sure he had that many lives left.

****

Sarah dropped her carryall full of ungraded papers onto the armchair and set her purse beside it. Mondays were always hard, given the stupor of her students on Monday mornings, she wondered if anyone in the class had ever heard of a bedtime. She'd get to the papers later. She went to the little kitchen for a snack and noticed Christine's phone, still plugged in its charger. No wonder Christine hadn't answered her texts—she had forgotten her phone. Sarah gave a little smile thinking of how endearing Christine's memory lapses were. She grabbed a bag of chips and swatted Tripod affectionately off the counter, checked his water dish, then headed towards the bedroom to shed her school clothes.

****

Mr. And Mrs. Mango pulled into their driveway by 6:30. Mrs. Mango stared at the dark and lonely-looking house and felt like it was from a different lifetime. It looked small and foreign and abandoned. It felt like she didn't even belong there anymore. A great loneliness welled up in her, a feeling that she didn't belong anywhere anymore. Not welcome at Danny and Rita's and rejected by her own home.

"See what happens when I'm not around?" she said, climbing out of the car. "Plants are dead, no lights left on, place looks like it's been abandoned."

Mr. Mango cringed. Obviously, Christine hadn't been coming around to take care of things. And why wasn't she back? There should be lights on, at the very least. He surreptitiously checked his phone, no return text from her. He had a feeling the day was about to get even shittier.

Mrs. Mango could barely reach the front door, edging her way through five foot high piles of donated personal products. The neighbors must be loving that. She reached the door, fumbled her key in the lock, and finally creaked it open. The dead silence and stale smell of a lifeless house greeted her. Mrs. Mango didn't need to see the dust settled on every surface to know that no one was living here anymore.

Mrs. Mango turned on the living room lamps and then headed to the kitchen, turning on lights everywhere she could. At least, she could brighten things a bit.

Mr. Mango reluctantly came in behind Mrs. Mango, bringing their bags and dropping them in the living room near the door. No sign of Christine. He took a couple of deep breaths to prepare himself for the shit storm that was about to hit.

Mrs. Mango came back into the living room. "Where is Christine? Where is Tripod? Why has no one brought the donations inside? What's going on?"

Mr. Mango stared at her, willing himself to just say it.

Mrs. Mango bustled back out and down the hall to the bedrooms.

He waited, wondering why Christine had not come home to take care of this herself.

He heard a door shut, and then a toilet flush, and then a door open.

He waited.

Finally, Mrs. Mango came back into the living room, hands on hips. "Where is all of Christine's stuff? Her room is almost empty."

"She moved in with Sarah," said Mr. Mango. There! He had done it! The words floated in the dead air, almost visibly hanging between them.

Mrs. Mango stared at her husband as if he had just spoken in Taiwanese. "What did you say?"

"You heard me."

Mrs. Mango staggered backwards, feeling behind her for a chair. She sank into an armchair and mindlessly ran her hands through her hair, leaving it standing on end. She leaned backwards and closed her eyes.

The room was silent, and Mr. Mango didn't know what to do, it was like time stopped and he was afraid if he moved, something would shatter. Yelling, crying, stomping around, these were reactions he would recognize. Just sitting in silence like this was scaring him. He wondered if this is what he looked like when his heart attacked itself.

****

Christine came into the apartment and called a hello to Sarah. She slipped out of her shoes at the door, dumped her jacket and purse on the couch, and headed towards the kitchen as she reached up inside her shirt and unhooked her bra. Ahhh, one of the best feelings in the world. She spied her phone and grabbed it. "Here it is!"

Sarah came into the kitchen behind her and gave her a hug. "Forgot the phone again, huh?"

"Yep, such a hassle and just didn't get time to come

home for it. And then I had to go to that stupid work 'mixer' after work, and I was hoping you'd remember since I couldn't call you," said Christine, scrolling through her texts. "Oh my God!"

"What?" said Sarah, leaning back against the counter.

"Oh my God, oh my God, oh my God," repeated Christine. "Crap! I missed a text from my dad—he and my mom are driving home! Oh no," she looked at the clock. "Probably already are home."

Christine and Sarah stared at each other. "Oh no. My mom must know by now," said Christine. "She must. My stuff is almost all gone from my room. Shit."

"Well, we knew it was coming at some point," said Sarah.

Christine closed her eyes and opened them again. "There's knowing, and then there's *knowing*. I don't think I really let myself *know*."

****

Mrs. Mango opened her eyes and stared a hole through her husband. "You knew about this?"

Mr. Mango shrugged.

"How long?" she asked in a quiet voice that was infinitely scarier than a yell.

Mr. Mango shrugged again. "Does it matter?"

"I guess it only matters if a person wants to trust the people around them," Mrs. Mango said. "I guess if you don't mind lying to me, maybe it doesn't matter."

Mrs. Mango stood up and walked slowly to her bedroom and into the bathroom, where she carefully locked the door and sat down on the closed toilet. She was too numb to cry. What was wrong with her family? Could she even think the word 'family' to describe them? Family doesn't spy on you. Family doesn't move out without telling you. Family doesn't keep secrets like that. Her dog and cat were gone, and even her house felt like it was rejecting her. She thought she had built some semblance of a life without Raul, but all of a sudden it was clear to Mrs. Mango that it wasn't a life. It was a construction of lies. Danny's love was a lie. Christine's love was a lie. Joe's love was a lie. Michael and Joe Jr. rarely came to see her. And now she had cut herself off from Emma Rose, the one true thing in her life. She had nothing.

****

"She called my brother a pervert!" fumed Rita to Danny. They were sitting across from each other at their kitchen table, Rita with Emma Rose in her arms taking a bottle. Danny was slumped in his chair and two glasses into the bottle of wine Rita had opened, breaking his rule against alcohol on weeknights. Having a headache at work tomorrow was the least of his worries.

"She didn't mean it," said Danny. "She was just hurt. And angry."

"Well, I'm hurt and angry too!" said Rita. "I've tried so hard with her!"

"Tell me again, what exactly started all this?" asked Danny. He still wasn't clear on it.

"I found her folding my underwear!" said Rita.

"And . . .?" said Danny.

"A woman's underwear is really private," said Rita. "She should know that! Do you think she'd be happy with *me* looking at *her* underwear?"

Danny didn't really see the big deal but wasn't about to say so. He had known this day would come. No way his mother and Rita could co-exist too long in one house.

"How do I put this delicately?" said Rita, sliding the bottle from Emma Rose's mouth and shifting her onto her shoulder for a burp. "My underwear isn't all in its, uh, newest condition. Who wants someone else to see that?"

"Maybe you should buy some new underwear then," said Danny. "We can afford it." He gave a little smile.

"Stay focused! This is not about the underwear!" exclaimed Rita.

Danny was puzzled. "I thought it *was* about the underwear."

Rita rolled her eyes and blew out her breath in frustration. "I didn't ask you to solve the problem of my old underwear! I'm talking about your mother invading my privacy!"

"Okay, okay," said Danny. "Not about the old underwear. But still, help me understand this. How did you guys fight so much she ended up leaving?" said Danny. He had arrived home to find his mother and father gone and Rita pacing in anger.

"It became a conversation about following rules, and how she hasn't—and she got all upset and then started accusing me of spying on her and invading her privacy!" said Rita, glossing over the details of how she actually *had* been spying on Mrs. Mango. "And that's when she called Don Paz a pervert! I know he is an unusual guy, but he is not a pervert!"

"Yes, I'm definitely not a pervert," said Don Paz, laughing as he entered the kitchen.

"Oh my God," yelped Rita, jumping enough that Emma Rose slid off the bottle and started crying. "Where did you come from?"

"Sorry, didn't mean to interrupt. Who thinks I'm a pervert?" he asked, standing at the island looking toward the two of them at the table.

Rita shook her head and patted Emma Rose as she set down the bottle and lifted Emma Rose to her shoulder for a burp. "No one important. Elsie. You know, from when she ran into you in the middle of the night in the backyard."

"Ah yes, when I was communing. In my birthday suit," he smiled, seemingly not upset. "Not the most normal thing to do."

Danny hadn't moved from his slumped position.

"Everything all right?" asked Don Paz, knowing it was not but not wanting to let Danny know that Rita had already confided in him.

Danny shrugged. "Apparently, my Mom and Dad left. In a huff."

Don Paz looked at Rita, more informed about the situation than Danny knew. He raised his eyebrows at her.

"Elsie and I got into it today, about her not respecting the way we want to do things. She got upset and left," said Rita.

"Hmm," said Don Paz.

"Luckily, I was able to take most of the rest of the week off," said Rita, also glossing over the fact that she had taken that time off *before* the fight with Mrs. Mango. "So I get time with this little darling here." Just as she said it, Emma Rose stopped crying, gave a robust burp, and spat milk down Rita's back.

Rita slid Emma Rose down from her shoulder into a cradle in front of her. "Hello, little sweetpea," she cooed. Then her voice shifted to anger. "I know the partners are not happy with me, but this is my *baby.*"

Danny stared at his wife, amazed at how easily she could switch between outrage at his mother and sweet baby talk to his daughter and then back to stress about her job It was like several people were living in her head, taking turns using her mouth.

Rita looked up at her brother. "Oh, I'm the worst, always focusing on myself. How are *you* coping?"

"Coping with what?" asked Danny, wondering how he was always several steps behind the news in his own house.

Don Paz started to fill Danny in on his problems, and Danny interrupted. "Grab a glass, sounds like you need a drink even more than we do."

After Don Paz's problems had been discussed, a second bottle of wine opened, and some leftover pasta heated in the microwave for a minimalist dinner, Danny dared to bring the conversation back to his parents.

"Should I call them? Make sure they got home okay?" said Danny.

"Hmph!" huffed Rita. "That's up to you. I'm done with your mother. And your father." She was afraid to mention the eavesdropping and how he had criticized her as well. "Your father always takes her side. So I guess I'm not talking to him either."

Danny stood up and walked to the living room with his cell phone. It occurred to him that his mother would not be calmed down yet, so he texted his dad.

Hey, Dad, sorry about today. Rita can be kind of emotional. Just wanted to see if you and Mom got home okay. Call you tomorrow. Danny thought about his dad's heart problems and added *love you.*

Then Danny remembered the christening scheduled for the upcoming weekend and shuddered. No way his mother was letting up on that one. No way his wife was going to agree to be in his mother's presence. The soul of a baby lost in the tension between two strong-willed women.

Before Danny could walk back to the kitchen, his dad's reply came.

We're home. Not sure I would say ok, though. Your mother found out that Christine moved in with Sarah and locked herself in the bathroom. You think Rita is emotional? She's got nothing on your mother.

****

It was not a Sunday, but sitting on the closed toilet with the door locked made Mrs. Mango think of her Raul letter ritual. That was the only good thing in her life now. Memories.

Mrs. Mango pulled the letter box out of the cupboard and fished out the blank notebook and a pen. Maybe she would make her writing ritual a daily event. Maybe that was all she had.

Dear Raul,

Mrs. Mango stared at the paper. For the first time ever she couldn't come up with what to say. Normally she would either tell him about her current life or revisit a memory from their time together but she found herself unable to do either. She searched through her mind for a good memory to focus on. Yes, the night at the beach. She could see a picture of them in the back of the truck but was unable to summon up the feelings. It was like watching someone else's life, or like watching a movie with the sound off. No sound, no emotion. Mrs. Mango switched memories, to walking in San Francisco hand in hand with Raul. Same thing—no emotion, no connection to the images. She desperately searched for a memory with feelings, anything. No image with Raul in it could touch her. Oddly enough, her mother appeared, the last time Mrs. Mango had seen her.

The memory of that fight broke through the numbness with a flood of pain. The mean words she had hurled at her mother came back so clearly it was as if someone had spoken them out loud in the tiny bathroom and they were still echoing. Her mother's crumpled face, her mother's begging words, her mother's tears and apologies. Mrs. Mango saw the scene as if she were inserted into her mother's body, felt her mother's pain at losing a daughter, felt the stab of looking at her daughter's rigid anger. Mrs. Mango had never let herself see that scene from her mother's point of view, and as it all flowed through her, she was swamped with a deep regret. Sorry that she had been so unforgiving of her parents. Sorry for all the years that she had missed out with her mother. Sorry that she had never told her mother she was sorry. The tears that had seemed gone for good came hot and strong.

Mrs. Mango didn't know how long she had cried, maybe an hour? Maybe a night? But finally, the tears slowed. She lifted the pen.

I've been wrong about everything.

Maybe even you.

Mrs. Mango's hand dropped to her lap. She was at a loss for what to do next. She felt numb and full of pain at the same time. She felt brand new and as old as time. She felt like she was teetering on the thin tip of a mountain, wondering which way to fall, which direction to point the rest of her life.

CHAPTER 43
I've Always Known

By ten o'clock, Mrs. Mango still hadn't come out of the bathroom. Mr. Mango knocked at the door, only to hear a muffled "Go away." He shrugged and returned to staring at the TV. At midnight, he started awake, the glare of the screen the only light in the family room, his neck stiff from an awkward angle to his sleep. He dragged himself up, flicked the TV off, and made his way to their bedroom, where he found the bathroom door still closed. He knocked again, this time getting no reply.

"Elsie!" he yelled. "Open up."

No answer. He pounded on the door. "Elsie, you okay?" he said.

Still no answer. His mind went to a dark place. Surely, she wouldn't . . . wouldn't hurt herself, would she?"

Mr. Mango shuffled around on his dresser but couldn't find what he wanted. He hustled to the kitchen, pulled open several junk drawers, and finally found a paper clip. As he hurried back to the bedroom, he untwisted the paper clip into a long piece of wire and jammed it into the cheap lock on the bathroom door. It had been years since he had to jimmy open a lock, maybe since the kids were little, but it still worked, and the door opened.

Mrs. Mango was sitting on the floor, back propped against the tub, eyes closed, papers scattered around her.

"Elsie!" said Mr. Mango in fear. Why wasn't she opening her eyes? His eyes darted to the medicine cabinet—it was closed—and then the sink, but no pill bottles around.

Mr. Mango took the three quick steps over to his wife and knelt beside her. "Elsie!" he said again, giving her a gentle shake.

"Wah?" Mrs. Mango mumbled, opening her eyes.

"What?" she said a little more clearly, trying to sit forward but cramped.

"Are you okay?" Mr. Mango said, putting his head closer and looking intently into her face. "Did you take anything?"

"Take anything?" Mrs. Mango mumbled, puzzled.

"Pills? Anything?" Mr. Mango said.

"No, no, just, just tired," said Mrs. Mango, pulling herself to a straighter position against the tub, the puffiness of her eyes reminding her of all the crying she had done. And then her eyes came wide open as she saw the open box of Raul's letters and the recent letters scattered around her. The ones she had re-read, trying to find some comfort.

"Oh my God!" she said, grabbing at papers around her, scrambling to shove the letters back into the box.

Mr. Mango slid backwards out of her way and stood up near the door.

"Can't a woman have any privacy?" Mrs. Mango demanded, guilt sending her voice to full anger in an instant.

Mr. Mango just stared at his wife.

"Well? You can see, I'm fine! Now give me a moment," said Mrs. Mango. Even as she spoke, tears were forming again. Frustration at being caught, fear of Mr. Mango's reaction, deep guilt at war with everything else going on in her head.

Mr. Mango didn't move, and Mrs. Mango finally looked up at him. "Well, go now," she started but then stopped at the look on his face. It wasn't anger. It wasn't surprise. It was calm—and almost kind, if that was possible.

Mr. Mango walked to the closed toilet seat and sank down onto it, putting him directly across from Mrs. Mango. He nudged the box over to the side with his foot and took her hands in his, staring down into her eyes.

"I know," he said softly. "I've always known."

Mrs. Mango stared at her husband in shock. "What? What have you known?" she whispered, afraid of the answer.

"I went to see your mother before she died," said Mr. Mango.

"What? How come you never told me?" demanded Mrs. Mango.

"You refused to ever even speak of her. And I figured it was over more than me. I'm not an idiot. I could tell I loved you more than you loved me, but I thought my love would be enough," said Mr. Mango, letting her hands go and resting his on his knees.

Mrs. Mango was in shock. "You saw my mother?"

Mr. Mango nodded. "Yep. It was about two weeks before she passed. Michael told me she was sick."

"Michael? How did HE know?" said Mrs. Mango.

"Turns out the kids were in contact with her," said Mr. Mango. "They didn't tell you because they didn't want you to feel betrayed, but they wanted to know your mother. Only saw her a couple of times because they didn't connect with her till they were grown up."

Mrs. Mango was in shock. She couldn't get her mind around the fact that her kids had met her mother. And then she panicked. What had her mother told them?

"How could they do that! Go behind my back!" she said.

"See? That's why they didn't tell you. You have to admit, it's not surprising that they would want to meet their own grandmother."

Mrs. Mango stared ahead, unseeing, in shock. Emotions fought with each other for space, anger, sadness, joy, regret. She had finally, after so many years, come to understand that her parents hadn't been bad people. They just didn't understand Raul and what he meant to her. And by the time she had realized this, they were both dead. The guilt was overwhelming—that she never apologized, that she never introduced them to their grandchildren. And now she came to find out they did meet their grandmother. And then the sadness hit again—how many years she had missed out with her mother, with her father. Pointless, her stupid pride at not being in contact. She had caused so much pain, and it couldn't be reversed.

Mrs. Mango started to sob, and she started to wonder if she was losing control.

Mr. Mango stared at her, wondering the same thing. "The kids really didn't mean to hurt you," he said, misunderstanding her tears.

Mrs. Mango waved at him through her sobbing, shaking her head no. She couldn't stand it. She put her hand on the edge of the tub and pushed herself creakily up and staggered to the bedroom, where she flung herself down on the bed, years of tears pushing themselves out of her so fast she thought her eyes might come out with them.

Mr. Mango followed her and sat on the bed beside her, laying his hand gently on her back.

Eventually, the sobs slowed down and Mrs. Mango rolled over on her back, looking up at Mr. Mango. "Such a waste of time," she choked out.

Mr. Mango nodded, understanding in his eyes. "She still loved you, you know," he said. "Never stopped."

Mrs. Mango broke into a fresh round of crying.

Mr. Mango patted her again.

Mrs. Mango put her hand on his. "I believe you," she sobbed. "Somehow, I know. I could never stop loving Christine, or Joe, or Michael, or Danny. So I know."

Mr. Mango and Mrs. Mango squeezed hands.

Clutching Mr. Mango's hand hard, Mrs. Mango wiped her eyes with her other hand. "So, you saw her? What did you talk about?"

Mr. Mango squeezed Mrs. Mango's hand again. "I told her that you had a good life, that you loved and enjoyed the kids. That you missed her and, I thought, had forgiven her."

Tears seemed to be flowing from Mrs. Mango's nose too, mixing with those coming out of her eyes. She gave up trying to wipe it all away.

"And she told me the whole story," Mr. Mango said, looking kindly at Mrs. Mango. "I already knew most of it anyway."

"What do you mean?"

"I knew that your fight with your parents wasn't really about their disappointment at your marrying me. I knew you had loved someone and lost him. I knew right from the beginning that there was a broken part of your heart. I knew it might stay that way. I thought I was willing to live with that."

Mrs. Mango closed her eyes. It felt like her whole heart was broken, not just part.

"And your mother filled me in on some of the details. I'm sorry, Elsie. I'm sorry you lost him. And—" Mr. Mango's voice got hoarse. "I'm sorry I'm not him."

Like the turn of a kaleidoscope, all the pieces of Mrs. Mango's life spun together into a completely different picture. Joe had loved her through it all. Joe had steadfastly taken care of her and their children. Joe had fixed the cars and taught the kids how to ride bikes and coached their baseball teams. Joe had helped her build a life and put up with her moodiness and her distance and never let it drive him away.

All this time, she'd been in love with a ghost, and that wasn't really love. Not returned, held unchanging, like something frozen in ice.

Of course, Joe had loved her through all these years, she could see that he did. Despite her withheld heart, he had steadily, in his own way, been there.

She saw the young Raul, the young Elsie, and all of a sudden they both seemed immature. Something real, yes, but the infatuation kind of young love. Who knows what that might have turned into eventually? Either way, it was gone, and she had pretended to herself it still lived. All the while, real love had been right there beside her all along.

Mr. Mango pulled his hand away and rested his head in his hands on his knees, staring down at the floor. He took a deep breath. "I get it. I was never enough."

Mrs. Mango felt like her heart was going to break all over again. "No! Joe! I've been a fool. A complete fool." It seemed impossible that there were any more tears, but they kept flowing. "I didn't realize it! I didn't realize it, but, I love you! I really do!" Mrs. Mango sat up and put her arm around Mr. Mango's shoulders. "I didn't see it, all these years, but I *do* love you."

Mr. Mango didn't move.

Mrs. Mango squeezed. "Oh God, please don't let it be too late!"

Mr. Mango slowly turned his head up to her. He stared into her eyes, looking for the truth inside himself as tears blurred his vision.

Time stood still.

"Please, Joe, please tell me it's not too late. I'm so sorry."

Mr. Mango stood up and gently removed Mrs. Mango's arm. "I don't know," he whispered. "I tried for so long, and then, well, I just put it away. I don't know if I can get it back." He stared at Mrs. Mango, eyes full of pain and compassion at the same time. "I have to think on this," he said and then slowly walked out of the room.

Mrs. Mango fell onto her back on the bed, staring up at the ceiling. *What have I done? What have I done?*

Unbelievably, tears continued to stream out of her eyes, down into her hair, this time in silence.

CHAPTER 44
After the Fall

In the morning, Danny was awakened by Rita standing at the foot of the bed, shaking his cell phone and yelling, "So, I'm *emotional*, huh?"

He could see her faint outline, the room still nighttime dark and lit only by a sliver of light coming from the nightlight in the bathroom.

Danny closed his eyes and wondered if he could just pull the covers over his head and disappear.

"Well?" Rita demanded. "Why would you say that? It's like you and your whole family have ganged up against me!"

Danny didn't respond.

"Oh, so now you aren't even going to answer me? Sorry, am I acting too *emotional* for you?" Rita's voice was reaching shriek level.

Without opening his eyes, Danny said, "I was just trying to let my dad know I wasn't mad at him. Everyone is emotional. It is a trait of being human."

Rita chucked the phone at Danny, and it hit him in the forehead.

"Ow! What was that for?" he said, sitting up.

"Whoops. Didn't mean for it to hit you," spat Rita. "I guess my aim isn't so good. Just a trait of being human." She whirled around and stomped out of the bedroom.

Danny rubbed his hand across his head and came up with blood. "Jesus, I'm bleeding. She actually drew blood." Holding his forehead, he got out of bed and plodded to the bathroom. He hit the lights and winced in the brightness, then stared at himself in the mirror, wondering how life could get so complicated so fast. It seemed just a few days ago that he and Rita were humming along, enjoying their jobs, each other, their home—their biggest worry picking the color of flagstones for the back terrace.

****

Mrs. Mango floated towards consciousness, first aware of a pounding headache and then eyes that seemed glued shut. Without opening her eyes, she knew that she was alone in the bed, alone in every way possible. She could sense light coming in the bedroom window and finally pried her eyes open, peering through eyelashes sticking together. The annoyingly bright light of a new day brought a paralyzing sadness, and she closed her eyes again, tempting sleep to come back.

In the living room, Mr. Mango came awake on the couch with an odd sense of peace. His mind told him he should probably feel more agitation, what with Mrs. Mango's fight with Rita, her discovery of Christine moving out, and the discovery that he knew her secret—but what he really felt was relief. The truth was finally out. In all ways. Secrets held for too many years out in the open. Mixed with the relief was an odd sense of compassion for his wife and a peace with the uncertain future. What would come would come.

Mr. Mango stretched his legs and then arms and twisted onto his side on the couch, twitching the blanket over him into place. He felt damn comfortable and maybe he'd just snooze a while longer. Instead of falling back to sleep, his mind filled with images of Mrs. Mango sobbing, telling him she loved him. The images were at a remove, as if he were watching someone across the street through his front window. Like it didn't even really include him. He wondered if he was really done with loving her or if there were still feelings in him somewhere. It was kind of hard to tell, like when your leg is asleep and you can watch yourself poke it, knowing it is your own leg but feeling nothing. Maybe his feelings for her were just asleep and would tingle back to life. Or maybe they were gone. For now, he was just tired of all the drama and secrets and agitation. This numb place was so much more peaceful. With that thought, he did drift back to sleep.

An hour later, Mr. Mango woke up to Mrs. Mango sitting in the chair staring at him. She was still wearing the same clothes as she had put on at Danny's the day before, and her eyes were puffy both above and below, like raisins pressed into marshmallows. Her back was straight in the chair, and her hands carefully folded together in her lap, like she was waiting for a job interview.

"Hmph? What? Hey," he spluttered.

"Good morning," said Mrs. Mango in a quiet voice.

Neither spoke for a good minute.

"So," said Mr. Mango, not sure if they were going to discuss real stuff or move into superficialities.

"So," said Mrs. Mango. She didn't sound like herself. All the life was gone from her voice.

They sat looking at each other like strangers who didn't know how to make conversation.

Normally, Mrs. Mango would have substituted action for feeling, would have hopped up and got coffee going, or made breakfast, or started issuing the Honey Do list for the day, but she instead just sat.

"I don't know what to say," she finally managed.

Mr. Mango sighed. "Me either, I guess."

A tear slipped out of Mrs. Mango's eye. "I'm sorry," she said, raising her hands and letting them drop back into her lap.

Mr. Mango nodded. "I know."

The quietness of the conversation felt ominous to both of them. They had never just calmly talked. There was always emotion behind Mrs. Mango's words, and reactions behind Mr. Mango's. It was like they were two train cars that had been disconnected and were rolling in separate directions.

****

"So what have you come up with?" asked Rita.

Danny had long since left for work, and she was sitting in the family room with Don Paz, finishing the folding of the laundry. The stacks Mrs. Mango had generated were still scattered around the room, and Rita was working on the load of baby blankets and sheets she had found in the dryer. She had planned on putting the laundry away before Emma Rose woke up, but the baby started crying before she had even drunk two sips of coffee. And then, somehow, it was midmorning and the kitchen was a mess and the coffee was undrunk and she was still in her pajamas.

"Well, of course, I am still seeing clients at my old office," said Don Paz. "I hadn't moved out yet. It's just that I share the space and can't get in there as much as I need to, which, of course, was a big reason for getting my own space. And I still have to refer out for acupuncture and massage and all that. I just had so hoped to get it all under one roof. I've been talking to everyone who was supposed to come and work at the center, and I was hoping we could raise some money between all of us, but it isn't anywhere close enough."

"Couldn't they all just stay independent contractors but you all work together in one place?"

"Yes, but the *place* is the issue. That is what my building was supposed to be."

"So, it is mainly an office space issue."

"Well, a bit more complicated, given that Marla and I owe on these loans, but, yes, that is the biggest limitation on going forward with the Center."

Rita nodded. "Hmm. Must think about this."

"What about you, what have you come up with?" Don Paz asked. "What are you going to do about Emma Rose?"

"I don't know," Rita said. "Hey, I have almost a whole week. Plenty of time to come up with a solution," she gave a weak smile. "I've called some people, see what turns up."

Don Paz leaned in and looked at his sister intently. "Maybe reach out to Elsie?" he said softly. "There is no doubt she loves that baby, would do anything for her."

Rita shook her head hard enough that her hair swished back and forth in front of her face. "No way. I can't have someone that disrespectful around!" Even as she said it, she looked around the room that was now cluttered with laundry and empty bottles and boxes of diapers. The kitchen was even more of a mess. Rita couldn't understand how someone like herself, organized, neat, on top of details, could have gotten so little done in a day. All she had done was take care of Emma Rose and then answer emails and calls while she was napping. Shouldn't have resulted in a house that looked like a Babies 'R Us exploded.

"I'm sure I can help out a bit," said Don Paz, rubbing a hand along his beard. "But I'm not the ultimate solution."

Rita nodded. "If you have some time next week, just for a bit, until I find someone . . ."

"Of course." Don Paz looked at his watch. "Need to run. Have clients this afternoon. I managed to get the office for extra time since my office mate only worked half a day today. But I can be back by 6:00."

Don Paz gave his sister a pat on the back and tried not to grimace at the wet milk his hand landed in on her shirt. "It's going to work out."

"Huh," Rita grunted.

As the sound of Don Paz's car faded away, Rita glanced at the baby monitor. Emma Rose was still napping, or was she? Was the sound turned off? It seemed awfully quiet. She lunged over to the monitor and hit the volume button. No, it was on. The house was just quiet.

Really quiet.

It hit Rita that this was the first time she had been home alone with Emma Rose, and a spurt of panic hit her. She tried to talk herself back down. *I've got this. It's no big deal. I'm going to focus on the peace and quiet that I finally get to feel in my own house.*

Rita stood up and started piling the stacks of

laundry into a basket. *I'm just going to put this away and then check email, and it will all be fine.* An image of Danny floated into her head, and she frowned. *Was* he unhappy? In the larger picture, who knew, but in the smaller picture of this morning, of course he'd be unhappy that she hit him in the head with his own phone. A rush of embarrassment filled Rita as she imagined him explaining to his office staff why he had a cut on his head. Would he tell the truth? Would he sell her out? The Danny she thought she knew would never tell on her. But now she wasn't so sure she knew him as well as she thought she did. Maybe he was more loyal to his family than he was to her. Maybe he'd enjoy the attention from his all female staff when he told them what a crazy person his wife was. Before she could finish that thought, the sound of Emma Rose crying came through the monitor.

Rita checked the time. Emma Rose had only gone down for her nap fifteen minutes ago. Too soon to get up. She'd just have to soothe herself back to sleep. As she carried the first load of clothes out of the room, the sound of Emma Rose's crying followed her and then got louder as she set the basket outside of Emma Rose's room.

Nope, not going in there, she'd put the clothes away when it was time to go in and get Emma Rose up.

Emma Rose was still crying when Rita got back for the next load of clothes. She found a second basket and loaded it, planning to leave it beside the first outside of Emma Rose's room. She was smart enough not to go into the room where Emma Rose could see her. The baby was still crying when she returned to the family room, but now the cries had intensified to shrieks and included gasping in the middle of them. Rita peered at the monitor and saw that Emma Rose's face was contorted and her body writhing. She had pulled herself loose from the swaddle that Rita had arranged her in.

Oh my God. What's wrong? Is this just normal crying? Is she in pain? What do I do?

Rita paced around the room and came back to the

monitor. She was sure something was wrong. She could feel it in her bones. She hurried up the stairs to Emma Rose's room and flung open the door. She moved to the bed, quickly re-swaddling Emma Rose before picking her up and pulling the squalling baby into her arms. "Shh, shh, shh," Rita whispered, doing a gentle bounce. Slowly, she eased herself towards the rocking chair in the corner and slid into it.

As Rita gently rocked back and forth in the chair, Emma Rose gave a few last half-hearted cries, then a couple of whimpers, and then fell asleep in Rita's arms.

Shit. I just soothed her to sleep, which felt like the most awesome thing in the world and which I am completely against.

****

"By the way," Rita said to Danny as he walked into the kitchen after work, as if they had been mid-discussion. "You can forget about christening Emma Rose. I went along with it because it didn't really mean much to me either way, and it seemed to matter to your family. But now, I'm done trying to please them. Call the church or whoever you call about these things, and cancel it."

Rita had just filled the sink with soapy water and dumped all the baby bottles found around the house into it. She stared defiantly over the island at Danny.

Danny knew his mom had reserved the party room at Sal's Cucina for after the ceremony. She was not going to be happy about this, and there was a part of Danny that was uncomfortable too. It seemed to be testing fate to cancel a christening.

"Uh, well, you see . . . " he started.

Rita stabbed her fists onto her hips and raised her eyebrows.

"Um, well, I kind of want Emma Rose to be christened. Not for my mom or dad—for me. And you. And *her.*"

343

"You're not even religious," said Rita.

"I think I kind of am. I mean, I know I never go to church, but I guess religion can run deep beneath the surface. It is still in there, and it would feel all wrong not to christen her."

"Fine, but we'll do it somewhere else and without family there."

Danny winced. "Well, what about godparents and all that? Family is kind of the deal with a christening."

"Do we have to have godparents?"

Danny stared at his wife. "Not have godparents? That's like saying do we have to use a car seat."

"And, speaking of that, why Michael? Why not Don Paz?"

"Technically, the godparent needs to be a practicing Catholic. It's the whole point— someone who will make sure that the child learns the faith, all that. Michael is the one who goes to church the most, aside from my mom, that is. And I think I remember you didn't want her."

"Well, maybe if Don Paz can be part of it, I'll consider it," Rita said stubbornly, plunging her hands into the soapy water and swishing bottles around with enough force to splash water out all around the sink. It was an impulsive thought, but she was tired of Danny's family running their lives.

Danny saw his opening. "Yes, let's have him be part of Emma Rose's life. For sure."

"As a godparent?" demanded Rita.

"Well, we can think of him as one, but he probably can't technically, you know, in the Catholic sense be one. But I'm sure he has a name for what he would be."

If it meant getting Rita to reconnect with his family in some way, Danny was willing to let Don Paz be a form of godparent.

Rita narrowed her eyes at Danny. "I know you don't believe in Don Paz's, uh, path, so what's with the about-face?"

"Since he's been staying here, I feel like I've gotten

to know him better," said Danny. "And he really is a decent person. And I can't argue with how peaceful he is. I do see that what he does works for him. And when it comes down to it, *family* is what is important, right?"

"So, instead of the christening, we could just have him do some sort of blessing for her," said Rita.

"Well . . ." said Danny. "I was thinking maybe do both. Church christening and then some sort of thing by Don Paz. Cover all bases, huh?" He tried a little laugh at the end.

"But what about your mother? She can't come to the church. I don't want to see her."

Danny had hoped Rita might have cooled off a bit on his mother.

"You can't even be in a church with her?" he said. "Just for a tiny amount of time?"

Rita stopped her manic washing and rinsing and stared at Danny without speaking.

"So I guess no reception either. Well, there it is." Danny's spirits dropped. He thought they were on their way to an agreement. As he stared at Rita, he let his hand drift up to rub the cut on his forehead from the cell phone. Lawyers weren't the only wily negotiators.

Rita stared in silence, brow furrowed as she thought, bottle washing forgotten. Danny was smart enough not to interrupt her thinking.

Rita suddenly smiled. "I'll go. To both the church and the reception. With your mother there. With two conditions."

Danny raised his eyebrows in question.

"Don Paz can do his own blessing for Emma Rose."

Danny nodded, "Yes."

"AND, Don Paz can live here as long as he needs to while he sorts out his money problems."

Danny couldn't believe he could get off that easily. He didn't mind Don Paz being around, and his bigger fear was that Rita would want them to give Don Paz money to bail him out of his problems. He didn't want Rita to know

it was that simple, so he didn't answer right away. "Well. .
." he said, dragging it out. "I suppose."

Rita smiled triumphantly.

Danny smiled inside himself.

"Now, what about your job, a nanny, all that?"
asked Danny.

"I'm working on it. I got a couple of names of
people and have interviews set up for Friday," said Rita.

"So you'll feel okay leaving her with, you know,
not a family member?" asked Danny, rifling around in the
refrigerator for something to eat. He already missed the
regular meals his mother had been making them, not to
mention the leftovers that were always around after those
meals.

"No, I won't feel comfortable at all. Which is why
for the first couple of weeks Don Paz will be here in the
mornings, and I will be here in afternoons. And then I'll
have the nanny cams, of course. Maybe that will work, but
who knows?"

The sound of crying came through the baby monitor
right as Rita's phone buzzed on the counter. She glanced at
the monitor, wiped her wet hands on a dishtowel, and
picked up her phone. "Shoot, I've got to go return some
emails. Can you get the baby? I'm sure she'll need a diaper
change and then a bottle."

Danny watched Rita walk away, still in her pajama
pants, a splat of dried milk down the back of her T-shirt.
Not that he would have mentioned either.

CHAPTER 45
I'm Raoul

"So. We meet again," said Timmy dramatically to Sarah as she turned away from the bar station holding two glasses of wine, handing one to Christine. Timmy smirked at Sarah and then flicked a glance at Christine. They were in the big party room at Sal's Cucina following Emma Rose's christening.

"Hey, Tim," said Christine.

"Hello," said Sarah, sliding closer to Christine and motioning Timmy to the bar. "Go ahead, they've got wine and beer."

Timmy's eyes ran up and down Sarah's body. She was dressed in a pale lavender silk dress that, while conservative in length and coverage, still showed her perfect curves.

Christine rolled her eyes. "It's like his brain never developed past junior high," Christine said to Sarah as she put her hand on Sarah's back and started to lead her away.

"Hey! I'm right here," said Timmy.

"Unfortunately," said Christine over her shoulder as they made their way away from the bar. She was done with Timmy's low-class self. For years, she had put up with Timmy's asinine comments, but she was done with that. Loyalty to family could go only so far.

Joe Jr. and Jenny fell into line behind Timmy at the bar. When he turned around, they all greeted each other.

"Hey, Joey, how's LA?" asked Timmy. "Hanging out with the celebrities?"

"Not really—plus, we are up here for a while," said Joe Jr.

Timmy nodded and winked, like they were sharing a secret. "Not getting any roles, huh?" He looked at Jenny. "You still doing that paraplegic thing?"

Jenny burst into laughter. "You mean *paralegal*?"

"Yeah, that thing," said Timmy.

"Yes, but have taken a break," said Jenny.

As Joe Jr. and Jenny watched Timmy swagger away, Joe Jr. said, "Maybe we should take that beer away from him. He can't afford to lose one more brain cell."

Velma poked Mr. Mango in the arm. "Thanks for inviting us, Joe. Haven't gone to a baptism in a year of Sundays."

Flora nodded. "Sweet baby, that's for sure. I see why you're so proud." She looked around. "What's up with Elsie? She doesn't seem like herself."

If you only knew, thought Mr. Mango. There was no short answer to that question. "Did you guys get some appetizers? A drink?" he asked instead.

"Oh, don't worry, we'll get your money's worth on those," laughed Flora. "Hey, who is the gray-haired guy over there, the one with the light blue shirt and checkered kind of tie?"

Mr. Mango peered in the direction Flora was pointing. "Oh, that's Leo, married to my sister."

"Shoot. Taken then. He's kind of good-looking, you know what I mean?" said Flora.

"How's your sister's health?" asked Velma.

"Velma! That's family!" exclaimed Flora. She shook her head at Mr. Mango. "No manners, this one. Would pick up a widower at his wife's funeral if he was good-looking."

"Hey, those guys don't stay on the market long. You can't hesitate," said Velma.

"What's with Mom?" Danny asked Michael and Joe Jr. The three were huddled around a stand-up table in a corner of the party room. "She is not herself. No meddling, no manipulating, no telling everyone what to do."

"I know," said Michael. "She is, what's the word, very subdued."

"Disconnected," said Joe Jr.

"I mean, beyond that, she seems different. Not nagging at Dad at all, did you notice that?" said Danny. "It's like when a dog that barks all the time stops barking. At first, you don't realize what is different, but then you realize the barking has stopped."

Mrs. Mango had attended the christening. She had avoided Rita, but that was no surprise. She had held Emma Rose and hugged her children hello, but it was true that she was uncharacteristically quiet. In fact, she felt like she was walking in a fog. She could make out the shapes of people and her life, but they were faint and not very colorful and seemed not real. Maybe it was all a lie.

"She must be really pissed at you guys." Joe Jr. laughed. "I'm glad not to be the problem child for once."

"You aren't the problem child!" said Michael. "*I'm* the problem child. Thinks I've somehow chased Meredith away."

"I thought *I* was the problem child," said Danny, laughing. "I'm the one with the wife she's so pissed at."

"Yeah, give, what really happened?" asked Michael.

"Long story short, Rita didn't think Mom was taking care of Emma Rose the way she wanted her to, so she set up some webcams . . ." started Danny.

Joe Jr. snorted. "And that's all she wrote."

"Man, webcams. I mean, how could *that* go wrong?" laughed Michael.

Danny was laughing too but said, "Yeah, it's funny when we talk about it, but it wasn't funny at the time. Rita watched Mom and Dad criticize her and just lost her shit."

"Yes, wives love that," said Michael. "Being criticized by their mother-in-law."

Michael held up his beer bottle as a toast. "Looks like Christine has sole possession of number one problem child."

Mrs. Mango walked up to the appetizer table and

stared at the plates of antipasto and cheeses and found nothing that interested her. She half-heartedly picked up a slice of salami rolled around a piece of cheese.

Joe Jr. strode to the middle of the room and clinked a knife against his beer bottle. "Excuse me!" he said loudly. "May I have your attention!"

The third time he clinked and said "Excuse me" the babble in the room quieted.

"I have an announcement, it is very exciting," Joe Jr. said. Jenny moved to his side and squeezed his hand.

The crowd was in a circle around him now, all staring.

"Jenny is knocked up," said Timmy. Everyone looked at him with familiar disgust, Jenny in particular.

Joe Jr. ignored Timmy. "I'm Raoul!" he crowed.

The crowd stared at him, waiting for an explanation. Before he could elaborate, there was a loud crash and then a thud as Mrs. Mango fell into the appetizer table and then slid to the floor.

Gasps and 'oh my Gods' broke the silence. Christine, eyes wide, went running for her mother. She got to her at the same time as Mr. Mango, and they looked at each other, recognition in both of their eyes. Each of them thinking they were the only person who knew the effect that name would have on Mrs. Mango. Mrs. Mango was flat on her back, arms splayed to the sides, covered in salami and cheese and artichoke hearts.

"Elsie!" Mr. Mango yelled. "Elsie, are you okay? Can you hear me?" He listened to her breath and felt her heartbeat.

"Mom, Mom," said Christine on her other side, brushing bread and salami pieces off of her. "Mom, are you okay?"

Mrs. Mango's eyes fluttered open. "What happened?" she mumbled.

Christine was afraid to tell her.

"You fainted," Mr. Mango said. "Did you hit your head? Are you injured?"

Mrs. Mango struggled to push herself up onto her elbows. "What? I don't know. I don't think so. Oh!" The memory came back. "Oh, Oh," was all she could say.

Joe Jr. had pushed his way through the crowd. "Move back everyone! Give her room," he said. "Mom? What happened?"

"I don't know. What did you say? What was your announcement?" Mrs. Mango asked, hoping she heard him wrong. Hoping it was all a bad dream.

"I said I'm Raoul! In *Phantom of the Opera*! I got the part, and we are staying in San Francisco!" he said. "Well, I started to say that and then you hit the ground."

Mrs. Mango closed her eyes and lowered herself back onto the floor. She rubbed the shoulder that had hit the appetizer table and mumbled, "My goodness."

Someone shoved a glass of water into Mr. Mango's hand. "Give her water!"

The crowd started firing off suggestions. "Give her air." "Push on her chest." "Turn her on her side." "Call 911!" "Give her smelling salts—does anyone have smelling salts?" "Who the hell carries smelling salts anymore?"

Timmy slid around Joe Jr. and tossed half a glass of water on Mrs. Mango's face.

Mrs. Mango spluttered and opened her eyes to glare at Timmy.

"Go away," hissed Christine, also glaring at Timmy.

Mr. Mango waved everyone back. "Jesus, Timmy, back off. And don't anyone call 911, for crissakes. She's okay, she just needs a moment. Just got a little lightheaded is all."

Sarah had appeared and grabbed Timmy's arm. "Come on, let's move back."

Timmy leered. "Okey dokey! Take me where you want me."

Christine stood up and shooed everyone back. "She's fine, just give her room."

Gradually, people wandered away and started talking again.

"Joe! That is so fantastic you got the part," said Mimi, giving Joe Jr. a hug.

"Thank you. I didn't want to tell anyone in case it didn't happen, but I'm completely stoked. I've wanted to do a play forever, and this one is just the best. I haven't gotten to sing in so long—I can't wait! It's going to be hella hard rehearsal, though, the current Raoul is supposed to be done in two weeks, and his understudy broke his leg and can't do it."

As people huddled around Joe getting the details of his new role, Mr. Mango and Christine helped Mrs. Mango sit up. Someone had found Danny on his way back from the bathroom and brought him over to Mrs. Mango.

Danny felt the back of her head and asked her some questions to assess her orientation. "What happened? So you just got dizzy and fainted?" he asked.

Mrs. Mango nodded slowly. "I think maybe I'm just, uh, dehydrated," she said. "That's all. Just tired and dehydrated."

Mr. Mango handed her the glass of water still in his hand. "Yes, I'm sure that's it."

"Well, I don't love it that she just up and fainted," said Danny. "When was your last checkup? Maybe you need to get some tests, check your heart, etc."

Mrs. Mango sipped the water and shook her head. "Nope. I'm fine." She took a last sip and handed the glass back to Mr. Mango. "Help me up. I'm fine!"

"So you guys are staying around for a while, huh?" Rita asked Jenny, slurping her wine and jiggling Emma Rose who was cradled in her other arm. The buffet dinner had been served, some toasts made, and now people were milling around finishing drinks and sampling the desserts. Rita and Jenny were standing next to the dessert table, nibbling on biscotti and chocolate-covered strawberries.

Jenny nodded. "I'm so happy! I think I've been looking for an excuse to leave that job for a long, long time. I have some feelers out in the city but haven't found anything yet. I go back and forth between nervous and excited."

"Hmm, I can look around for you, see if anyone I know needs a paralegal," said Rita, setting her wine glass down and shifting Emma Rose onto her shoulder. "Ooh, you are such a love," she cooed at Emma Rose. "Just an angel at the christening, weren't you?"

"Can I hold her?" asked Jenny.

"Of course," said Rita, passing the baby to Jenny.

Jenny stuck her nose to Emma Rose's head and inhaled. "Oh, I just love how she smells! Baby hair must be the best smell in the world. And look at this gown, just incredible."

Rita's eyes narrowed at Jenny. "I just had an idea. A fantastic idea."

Jenny swayed with Emma Rose. "Uh huh?"

"You and Joe should move into our guest house, and you can take care of Emma Rose! I'll pay you. And be a sort of sometime legal assistant for me!"

Jenny stopped swaying, her eyes lighting up. "Don't kid me on that. Please don't be kidding."

"I'm not! We need a nanny, and you guys need a place to live and a job for you. This is *perfect*."

Jenny gave a little scream that was loud enough to make Emma Rose jump. "Joe! Come here!"

CHAPTER 46
Cleansing

Don Paz walked slowly around his office, gently waving an abalone shell that held a sage smudge, leaving a trail of wispy smoke through the rooms. He had been waiting until the renovations were done to do this ritual but realized the building, and he, needed it now. He let all the worries, all the superficial thoughts, drift out of his brain, and he focused on the moment, on the feeling of each room. The longer his brain settled into a meditation, the more clearly he could feel the fear that clung to the rooms. He had not fully respected the leftover energy still in this building from its years of use as an insurance agency. Yes, he could feel it, the accumulation of years of fears, the thousands of people insured against fear, the way they had paid their money to deposit their fear in this building. The insurance industry making so many billions of dollars a year by assuring people that they could fix what went wrong. Don Paz knew it didn't work that way. Money couldn't buy you safety or health or longevity. It almost felt like he was walking through a huge file case, slipping past client after client who exchanged money for the mistaken belief they could be protected from the future. And people thought *he* was superstitious!

Don Paz moved his arm slowly, easily, inhaling the pungent smoke, breathing deeply as he imagined the fears dissipating, the air clearing. As his meditation deepened, he felt the connection to the centuries of cleansing rituals, felt the connection to his ancestors, felt the connection to the fearful people who had passed through the former insurance agency. He sent blessings to each. He felt the relief of rediscovering his connection to the sacred and could see the rooms lightening, the darkness receding. Once the smudge had burned out, he went back through the building and opened all the windows, silently inviting the cleansing breezes to carry the worry and darkness away. Then he lit a new smudge of Oak Moss, inviting the resolution of his money problems. Don Paz took the burning smudge in its brass bowl and sat down in the front doorway and set the bowl in front of him. He looked out the open door towards the magnolia tree to the left of the walk, crossed his legs, made sure his back was straight, and closed his eyes, breathing slowly and deeply. The peace of a new beginning diffused through his body.

An hour later, a breeze picked up and blew ashes from the copper bowl onto his lap. Don Paz opened his eyes, a deep calm settled into the very molecular level of his body. All was well, and all would be well. He belonged in this place and knew the way to stay had been cleared. He also knew he needed to stay here, at least for a while, to maintain this focus on shifting his relationship with money. He closed his eyes once more and asked the universe to help guide him to a solution for keeping the building. He imagined sending out a thin golden rope of energy, like a fly fisherman casting into a stream, to catch the answer.

Don Paz's reverie was interrupted by a screech and a thunk. He opened his eyes to see a blue Buick angled at the curb, the front driver's side tire up on the curb, the back of the car sticking out into the street. Something was hanging off of the back panel, near the gas tank. Don Paz looked closer and thought he recognized the driver. He unfolded his cramped legs up to standing and walked to the car.

"Elsie?" he said, looking in the half-open driver's side window.

Mrs. Mango's head twisted towards Don Paz. Her eyes were wild and her hair even wilder. She was shaking her head back and forth like she couldn't understand how she got to this place.

Don Paz leaned in closer. "Are you okay?"

Mrs. Mango opened her mouth but nothing came out. Instead, tears trickled down her cheeks.

Mrs. Mango was shaking. "I can't drive anymore," she mumbled.

"Okay. It's okay," said Don Paz in a soothing voice.

Mrs. Mango kept shaking her head.

Don Paz eased her door open. "Why don't you come in. I'll make you a cup of tea." He purposefully moved his deep calm around Mrs. Mango, imagining it enfolding and comforting her. She nodded and let him help her out of the car. As she stood up, Don Paz noticed that her clothes were wrinkled and her shirt half untucked from her pants. Not the normal buttoned-up and starched Mrs. Mango.

Don Paz put a gentle hand on her shoulder. "Let me get you settled, and then I'll move your car a little, uh, closer."

Mrs. Mango let herself be guided through the open front door, through the hall to a back room where a microwave and hot plate were sitting on a plank lying across two sawhorses. From a jumble of furniture and boxes in the corner of the room, Don Paz pulled out a straight back chair and brought it to Mrs. Mango.

"Here, sit down," he said, still keeping his voice slow and calm, resisting a reaction to the swirls of agitation he could almost see coming off Mrs. Mango. "I'll be right back. I'm going to move the car and get some water."

As he approached the car, Don Paz could see that the thing that was hanging off the car was a gas nozzle and a section of hose. Mrs. Mango had apparently failed to remove the gas hose when she was filling up her tank. He shuddered to think what might have happened as she pulled away, ripping the hose from the pump. That kind of thing could probably cause an explosion. And then who knew how long she had driven with that thing bouncing around? It was long enough that it would have been dragging behind her. He looked in the car, saw the keys still in the ignition and got in and moved the car to be more parallel with the curb. He pocketed the keys and went back into the building.

When he returned, Don Paz stuck the filled mugs in the microwave, picked around in a box on the table, and pulled out some tea. "Mint, chamomile, or Earl Grey?" he asked.

Mrs. Mango shrugged.

"Chamomile it is," said Don Paz.

While the microwave hummed, Don Paz went back to the furniture pile and shifted things around until he could free an ornately carved stool from the mess. He slid it in front of Mrs. Mango, retrieved the tea, gave her one of the mugs, and sat down on the stool facing her.

Don Paz sat his mug on the floor and leaned towards Mrs. Mango, his elbows on his knees. He breathed deeply, matching her breathing to try to entrain it to slow down. After ten to fifteen breaths, when Mrs. Mango seemed to be breathing more slowly with him, he spoke. "So what is going on?" he said softly.

Mrs. Mango took a sip of tea and gave a little hiccup of a cry as she tried to tell him.

"Take your time," said Don Paz.

"I didn't know where to go," Mrs. Mango sobbed. "I just couldn't stay at home. And then I thought I'd go see Emma Rose but I can't bring myself to go there. And then, well, I just didn't know what to do."

Don Paz nodded and made supportive murmurs. He envisioned extending his peaceful feeling towards Mrs. Mango, imagined surrounding her with lovingkindness.

Mrs. Mango took a deep breath. "And I was driving and people kept honking at me! So rude, drivers today."

Don Paz silently reflected that they were probably trying to alert her to the gas hose hanging off her car. Time enough to address that later.

"And I remembered this street," Mrs. Mango cried. "We parked here when we went for breakfast up around the corner."

Don Paz nodded again. "Yes," he said as if she had done exactly the right thing.

Mrs. Mango started sobbing again, unable to say

more.

Don Paz reached over and held her free hand. "Elsie, would it be okay if we prayed together?"

Mrs. Mango looked at him in surprise—that seemed too conventional for Don Paz, but she nodded yes through her tears.

Don Paz closed his eyes, still holding Mrs. Mango's hand. "Dear Father, please lead us through this pain. We pray for your guidance in all matters, knowing you are the father. We trust in your love for us, knowing there is nothing you would withhold from us, nothing you will not forgive. Guide us to be our most loving, forgiving selves. Dear God, let us start the forgiveness with ourselves and then help us bring it to those around us. Father, help us to feel the grace that you offer that is always ours. In your name we pray. Amen."

"Amen," Mrs. Mango choked out. She squeezed Don Paz's hand. "Thank you," she whispered. She took another sip of tea.

"Maybe take a few deep breaths," said Don Paz, himself breathing in and out to demonstrate.

Mrs. Mango breathed in and out several times, each one slower and deeper.

"Okay," she whispered. She leaned over and set her tea mug on the floor. "I don't know where to start."

"Start with the long-ago pain. The one you have carried for all these years. I'm guessing that is where everything starts," said Don Paz.

Mrs. Mango stared into Don Paz's face, seeing nothing but kindness, and it all came out. Raul, her letters, her fight with her parents, her discovery that Joe knew about it, her epiphany that she loved Joe, her despair that it was too late.

By the end, they were sitting on yoga mats, backs propped against the wall, four cups of tea and a box of shortbread cookies finished.

Mrs. Mango would have thought she'd feel nothing but humiliation, but the experience of telling Don Paz everything felt like she had drained a sink full of dirty dishwater. She felt relieved and cleaned out and wrung-out all at the same time. A good kind of wrung-out. Her mind felt more clear than it had in months, if not years. She giggled.

"Imagine me ending up here with you," she laughed, patting at her still-wild hair. "Although that was never in my mind. I was just driving and couldn't figure out where to go and somehow ended up here. I like that magnolia tree out front. Something made me want to just sit under it."

Don Paz laughed with her. "I like that tree too."

Mrs. Mango shook her head. "Who knew?" And before Don Paz could answer, she added, "Don't say it—you knew. Of course you did. You're a tricky rascal, Don Paz."

"So, what now?" he said. "What do you think you need to do?"

"I need to make it up to Joe. I need to make him love me again."

"Yes to the first part, the second part is not up to you."

"What do you mean?"

"You can't 'make' anyone love you. You can only do what you know to do. Express yourself to him. Act in a loving manner. Be patient. My goodness, he has been patient for many, many years with you. And then see what might happen."

Mrs. Mango sat in silence, thinking about what Don Paz had said.

"Yes. I can see that now. I can't make him do anything." She laughed. "I never could make him do anything! What makes me think I could start now? But I can be different. And, yes, I see your point about being patient."

"And what about Rita?" Don Paz asked, feeling that they had enough of a relationship now to try tackling that issue too.

Mrs. Mango's smile faded. "I don't know. She really seems to hate me."

Don Paz shook his head. "I'm sure she doesn't hate you. You've known her for some years now—she is high strung, no doubt, but she is a good person. I think she is just very uncertain about how to be a mother. It came upon her so quickly, and she is not used to being unskilled at things. And definitely not used to being uncertain. So, in reaction, she set up a bunch of rules so she can feel guided in some way. That's what I think. But then again, I'm not a parent so I could be completely wrong."

"Hmm," said Mrs. Mango, letting his words roll around in her head.

"She has always been very, uh, organized," said Don Paz. "Structure and rules are soothing to her. Can feel like a control thing to others."

"Huh," said Mrs. Mango.

"It is not personal," Don Paz added, then laughed. "Honestly, *nothing* is personal. Nothing anyone else does is ever *really* about us. It is always about them."

"Hmph" snorted Mrs. Mango. "Hard to believe that. She was yelling *at me*. She was criticizing *me*."

"Yes, but think about it. She was upset because she thinks being a good mother means following a set of rules. At least, in part. So if you weren't following the rules either, that meant she was a bad mother for not making sure the baby was 'properly' cared for—or that her rules were wrong, which again would make her a bad mother."

Mrs. Mango tried to digest that. "I raised four kids. I would think she might think I know something about taking care of babies."

"Exactly," said Don Paz. "Might have made her feel defensive about her ways. Or might just be that following rules feels comfortable. In any case, I think we all should give new mothers some latitude to be a little crazy."

"So, what am I supposed to do?" asked Mrs. Mango. "Let's just say that is all true. Now what?"

"Now you just get to be a grandmother. Now that

Jenny is going to help take care of Emma Rose, you can just be the doting grandmother.”

“No, I mean, should I apologize to Rita?”

“Are you sorry?”

Mrs. Mango thought about it. “Yes, I guess I am in a way. Sorry that I didn’t understand her anxiousness. I guess I could have been a little more understanding.”

“Well, you could tell her that. Maybe without using the word ‘anxiousness.’ Maybe saying something like, ‘I know it is stressful to be a new mom, and I’m sorry I wasn’t more understanding. Something like that.”

Mrs. Mango looked sideways at Don Paz. He returned the look, and they both smiled. “Sounds like a plan,” said Don Paz. “And the perfect time is the Blessing Ceremony. You *are* coming?”

“Oh, I guess so.” Mrs. Mango leaned forward. “Holy cow, I don’t think I’m going to be able to get up! I’m too old to be sitting this long on the ground. Everything’s gone to sleep.”

Don Paz rose in a fluid motion and offered Mrs. Mango a hand. “Next thing, we’ll have you doing yoga.”

Don Paz walked Mrs. Mango back to her car and as they approached, he said, “So, I noticed you might have forgotten to unhook the gas hose when you filled up.”

Mrs. Mango’s hands flew to her mouth. “Oh my God,” she gasped. “What have I done?”

“Where did you get gas? How long did you drive like that?” Don Paz asked.

Mrs. Mango shut her eyes and shook her head. “I have definitely lost it. Lost it. Lost my everloving mind.” She opened her eyes and looked at Don Paz.

He gave a little smile. “One could only hope.”

“You are hoping I lose my mind?”

“Hoping you lose the old way of seeing, so, in a way, yes,” said Don Paz. “Obviously, you don’t have to worry, God is looking out for you. He brought you all this way with that hose attached, and nothing bad happened.

Mrs. Mango shook her head, smiling. "I'd like to think that is true."

"Then do," said Don Paz. "It might just be that simple."

CHAPTER 47
Beginner's Brain

After Don Paz removed the gas hose for her, Mrs. Mango drove home. Her body felt different, lighter. Her mind felt different too, more clear. It didn't even bother her when other cars went zooming by her, honking. It occurred to her that carrying a secret for so many years had weighed her down to the earth. She felt a hundred pounds lighter now that the secret was out. All those years, it was a guilty mass in the center of her body, not that she had understood exactly how heavy it had been until that mass was gone. The energy previously devoted to keeping her secret shut away was now flooding through her, enlivening the part of herself that never got to live in the light, making her want to dance and skip. A bubbling silliness rose in her, a childlike playfulness. What had Don Paz called that? 'Beginner's Mind.' She felt as new as Emma Rose.

As she thought about Emma Rose, it became completely clear that she had to make up with Rita. And apologize to both Rita and Danny for judging them. All she wanted was to play with Emma Rose and love her family. She couldn't wait to get home and tell Joe.

With that, a cloud slid over the sunny feeling. Oh, Joe. Poor Joe. How long she had shut him out! How long she had ignored his steady, quiet love. Her mind filled with the image of him as a young man, standing in front of her asking her to dance. His whole face lit up with a smile, his blue eyes full of charm. She had always felt a guilt over marrying him, assuming that it was a superficial choice since he was so handsome and every girl liked him, but she realized now that he had held something more for her right from the start. In her grief over Raul a part of her had still been able to recognize the kindness in him. She had felt safe with him, instinctively knowing he would be careful with her heart. Mrs. Mango felt like a school girl, a crush filling her body. Oh how desperately she wanted his attention now! Mindful of Don Paz's words, she knew she'd have to go slow and be patient but it was going to be hard. She thought about how casually she had treated his love, how she had just always assumed it would be there waiting for her. And now it might be gone forever. And with that thought, her mind jumped to Christine. She could not risk losing her too. No matter what it took inside her, she needed to make sure Christine knew she loved her. She couldn't risk losing her too.

Before she knew it, Mrs. Mango was pulling back into her driveway, pleased to see Mr. Mango's truck parked there.

Mrs. Mango found Mr. Mango snoozing on the couch. She tiptoed past him, happy to have a chance to be good to him by letting him sleep. In the past, she would have almost gone out of her way to make noise to wake him. Like that bit in the Bible about scales falling off of eyes, Mrs. Mango saw how she had been a grump to him for many, many years. The man was a saint to still be around.

In the kitchen, she set to baking a chocolate cake with Seven-Minute Frosting, one of his favorites and a cake she hadn't made in years. As she sorted through the cupboard to pull out the mixer, she came across the box of "Boost Your Juice" Vegevape herbs. She had forgotten about those and set them up on the counter so she could ask Christine if she wanted them along with the Vegevape itself. She never seemed to get around to using it.

She was three ingredients into the mixing of the cake when she realized she had planned to give Christine the Vegevape blender and herbs without even thinking about the fact that she was gay. Huh. She hadn't been able to think of Christine in that way since she came out. Literally every thought of Christine had led to heartbreak and worry until today. She could feel a loosening in how she felt about Christine—had a thought that maybe the most important thing wasn't who she loved, but that she loved.

Confession really *was* good for the soul.

By the time Mr. Mango had woken and wandered into the kitchen, Mrs. Mango was just finishing icing the cake.

"What's that?" he said, peering at the cake.

"Yep! It's what you think. Chocolate cake with Seven-Minute Frosting," said Mrs. Mango triumphantly.

"Are we going somewhere?" asked Mr. Mango. "'Cause I'm kind of beat."

"No. It's for you. I figure I have a lot to make up to you, and I'm starting with this cake," said Mrs. Mango.

Mr. Mango waved a hand at Mrs. Mango. "I don't know that you can do that kind of thing. Change years' worth of, I don't know, stuff."

"Can I make you a cup of coffee to go with the cake? I can cut you a slice right now, it's still warm," said Mrs. Mango. One negative comment from Mr. Mango was not going to put her off. Don Paz had prepared her for this. Just keep doing what she knew to do and ignore his protests. It can take a long time for an old dog to notice you are doing new tricks.

Mrs. Mango put on a pot of coffee and cut them both slices of cake.

Mr. Mango sat down at the kitchen table and looked at the clock as Mrs. Mango slid the piece of cake in front of him. "It's almost dinner. You don't care if I eat this now?"

Mrs. Mango smiled. "Maybe this should be dinner. Maybe I need to loosen up!"

Mr. Mango stared at his wife, not trusting this bubbly woman. This was the girl he fell in love with, the one he tried to believe was there for so many years without evidence. And now, here she was again. Mr. Mango was having trouble trusting his perceptions, his ability to see his wife for who she was. He thought about the young Elsie, how she had been a wild mix of things, and sometimes joyful and bubbly had been one of the things. He thought about how when he first met her, she had seemed like a couple of different people all rolled into one. That had been intriguing, it felt like life would always stay interesting with someone like that. Now, he realized that had been a young woman still in grief. Sometimes the real girl, the joyful one, had come through, and at other times, what seemed like a sophisticated, in-control woman came out. Maybe the sophisticated woman had really been a girl trying to harden herself against pain.

"Huh," was all Mr. Mango could manage.

Mr. Mango dug into his cake and took a huge bite. "Goddammit, I forgot how good this is," he said, holding his fork up like a salute.

"It *is* good, isn't it?" said Mrs. Mango. "I know we need to eat healthy and all, but maybe we should have a cheat day once a week. A lot of those really fit people do that. The Rock does that, eats like a couple of pizzas at once."

Mr. Mango nodded. "I am in full support of that idea."

"Well, you just tell me what you want me to make, and I'll do it," said Mrs. Mango.

Mr. Mango frowned. "You don't have to do this," he said.

"Do what?"

"Try to, I don't know, make up for stuff. It feels kind of awkward."

Mrs. Mango scraped the last of the frosting left on her plate onto her fork and licked it clean. "Don't think of it as making up for stuff, then. Think of it as me being me. Being a nice person. I *do* have that in me, you know."

Mr. Mango laughed uncomfortably. "I know. I think at times I've known that more than you have. Then again, I'm not sure I'd want Suzy Sunshine blowing bubbles up my ass all day."

It was one thing to feel compassion for his wife, it was a whole different thing to try to restart a heart.

Mrs. Mango giggled. "You're funny. It's okay. I don't expect you to believe I can really be different until you have more evidence."

Mr. Mango shrugged.

"So the Blessing Ceremony is coming up, and I want to go," said Mrs. Mango. "Are you coming?"

"You want to go to that craziness?" said Mr. Mango.

"Yes. I want to apologize to Danny and Rita, and I want to hold that baby. How bad could it be? She's been baptized—she's protected. And I'll bet Don Paz makes it really interesting."

For the first time, Mr. Mango started to believe it might be possible for Mrs. Mango to find the person he knew she could be, the one he had seen in the beginning. Apologize to Rita? He would have bet his left nut that would never happen.

"Well, sure, then," said Mr. Mango, realizing this could be very entertaining.

CHAPTER 48
The Way to a Man's Heart

Mrs. Mango eased the Buick into her driveway, still smiling from the drop-off she had just completed. Such a good feeling to provide all those women's products to the shelter. Those ladies who worked there always seemed so cheerful and so appreciative every time she made a delivery. The fact that she had not fully latched the trunk and had scattered several hundred panty liners down Daisy Drive before she noticed was not going to ruin her good mood. There had still been plenty left when she pulled over and closed the trunk more firmly. The wind would take care of the rest.

As she climbed out of the car in the driveway Mrs. Mango reflected that Mr. Mango would stop grumbling about his porch being constantly stacked with unmentionables, at least for a while. Then she glanced towards the front door and saw another big bag sitting beside a box, and her smile faded. Holy cow, but her friends were active in their donations!

The first onslaught of donations had been from all the women who had hit menopause and still had products in their bathrooms, but now it seemed they were going out and buying more just to donate. Maybe out of gratitude not to need that stuff anymore.

Mrs. Mango popped her trunk and moved the latest set of donations to her trunk, pushing down extra hard to hear the trunk latch completely. At least, she could keep the porch clean for an evening, right?

****

An hour later, Mrs. Mango hummed a little song as she opened the oven door and reached for the tray in it. She jerked back and blinked a couple of times as the wave of heat hit her in the face. When would she ever learn to wait a beat after opening the oven door? No wonder her hair was always frizzing up. She carefully set the cookie sheet on the cool stove and peered at the crinkles of green covering it. Didn't look like something a person would eat, but she was willing to give it a try. She picked up the edge of one of the crinkles, held it in front of her, blew on it, and then nibbled on a corner.

"Hmm," she said to herself, reaching for the salt and flinging it around over the cookie sheet. She liked the bit of flourish she gave her wrist when she salted, like she was a chef on TV.

After the tray cooled a bit, Mrs. Mango used a spatula to scrape the thin, dark green pieces onto a plate. Then she sprinkled some shredded Parmesan over the plate and took it into the family room where Mr. Mango was on his hands and knees by the desk, which was pulled out from the wall.

"Damn rat's nest of cords back here!" he grumbled. "Time they were in some sort of order. Lamp isn't working, and I went to unplug it and couldn't find the end. Now everything's unplugged.

"Here you go, made a snack for you," said Mrs. Mango, setting the plate on the desk.

"What the hell is that?" said Mr. Mango, coming up off his hands and staring at the plate.

"Kale chips. Supposed to be good for you. You know, as a replacement for potato chips."

Mr. Mango stared at his wife, unable to fathom a world in which it would occur to her to make kale chips. Unable to fathom who could possibly even think of making kale into a chip.

"All the celebrities eat them. Taste one, they aren't bad."

Mr. Mango shook his head as if to say no but reached for a chip. It crumbled in his hand so he scooped his fingers under about five chips and stuck them in his mouth.

Mrs. Mango waited.

"Hmm," he said, reaching for some more. "Not bad. Don't get any ideas, though. I'm not doing any kind of cleanse or whatever somesuch those millionaires with too much time on their hands do."

Mrs. Mango smiled. "Don't worry, I'm not turning into Gwyneth Paltrow on you."

Mr. Mango scooped another handful of chips and shoved them in his mouth. "I don't even know who that is."

"You know her, she's been in a ton of movies. And has a 'lifestyle' website." Mrs. Mango made air quotes around 'lifestyle.'

"Huh," grunted Mr. Mango, bending back over the mess of cords behind the desk, his butt sticking out. "I got a life. Don't think I've ever needed the style part."

"I'm just thinking, when Danny or Christine bug us about eating healthier, now we can say we eat kale chips," said Mrs. Mango.

"I wouldn't mind getting Christine off my back," agreed Mr. Mango. "Like she's so healthy in her food! I have a little heart hiccup, and now everybody cares what I eat."

"Exactly," nodded Mrs. Mango. Like her whole intention was to just get people off her husband's back. "So, final verdict on the kale chips?"

"Uh, not bad," mumbled Mr. Mango. "You can leave the plate."

Mrs. Mango left the plate and returned to the kitchen where she helped herself to some of the chips left on the cookie sheet. If a person closed her eyes, they really were kind of tasty.

She pulled a cookbook from under the dishcloth where she had hidden it and glanced towards the family room to make sure her husband was still occupied. No need for him to see her new cookbook. She opened "The Cardiac Recovery Meal Plan" and looked for a chicken recipe.

Maybe the way to a man's heart really was through his stomach. Or maybe the way to *save* a man's heart was through his stomach. By hook or crook, by sneaky healthy food or sneaky exercise (did he really think she needed to go to both ends of the mall three times?), she was going to get him healthy. She was tired of losing things just as she discovered how much she loved them.

CHAPTER 49
Mango Mimosas

"Here, hold Emma Rose while I get her sweater. I must have left it upstairs," Rita said, handing Emma Rose to Danny and darting out of the kitchen. It was ten o'clock on Sunday morning, one week after the baptism, and they were standing in the kitchen, waiting for the arrival of the Blessing Ceremony guests. The caterer and his assistant were moving in and out of the kitchen, but it was empty right now. Danny shifted Emma Rose into his left arm and opened the refrigerator. He pulled out one of the pitchers of Mango Mimosas intended for the brunch after the ceremony, deciding not to wait. He was finding it increasingly hard to be around his family, not to mention his wife, without some sort of help. He dumped a generous amount into a coffee travel cup, took several big gulps, and screwed on the top of the cup.

"Okay, sweet pea," he said to Emma Rose as he heard the front door open. "Here we go." He took another quick sip. "Oh my God, that's good." The caterer had come up with the idea to make a mango juice mimosa in honor of their last name. "How have we never made these before?" he asked Emma Rose. She responded with a powerful burst of gas from her bottom.

Danny's parents came into the kitchen at the same time as Rita arrived with Emma Rose's sweater. She slid Emma Rose's arms into the soft pink sweater that Mrs. Mango had knitted and gave Mrs. Mango a quick smile.

"Oh, look at that angel," gushed Mrs. Mango, dropping her shopping bag full of food and rushing to kiss Emma Rose. "I just knew that pink would be perfect for her." Mrs. Mango beamed at Rita.

"It is beautiful. And so soft," said Rita, her voice a

bit strained but clearly trying to be gracious. "I hope her skin isn't sensitive to the yarn, though."

Danny took another sip of his 'coffee.'

"Rita, I apologize for not respecting your wishes in taking care of Emma Rose," said Mrs. Mango, clearly a rehearsed speech but sincere, stroking the soft yarn of Emma Rose's sweater. "I know the old ways aren't always the best ways. And I know Jenny is going to care for her now, but if you ever need me, I promise I'll follow everything you ask."

Rita smiled. "Thank you. I'm sorry too, that I was so . . . uptight." As she spoke, she gently moved Emma Rose from Danny to Mrs. Mango's arms.

Mrs. Mango gave a big happy sigh and started swaying with Emma Rose.

Mr. Mango surreptitiously moved the food bag under the table, thinking he'd sneak it back outside. No need to ruin the thawing between Rita and his wife by offending Rita with extra food. He glanced around the kitchen and saw platters and bowls and all sorts of food already set out. Yes, definitely needed to get rid of the stuff Mrs. Mango had insisted on bringing. No need to bring Entenmann's when there was a three-layer fondant cake displayed on a silver cake stand.

Just as he had that thought, a short, slim man dressed in all black bustled into the kitchen carrying a large, Saran-wrapped tray. "Okay, my dear, I have it all in hand!" he gushed to Rita. "I have everything cold laid out, and the hot stuff will be done just when you finish the ceremony."

Rita hugged the man. "Jules, you are the best. Thank you. I feel so good knowing you are here."

Rita motioned to Danny and Mr. and Mrs. Mango. "Let's get out of the caterer's way. There is coffee set up outside if you want some before the ceremony starts."

On the way out, Mr. Mango snagged the shopping bag full of Mrs. Mango's food and slipped back to the car, stowing it in the trunk.

By eleven, the group was gathered on the newly finished patio extension where Don Paz had set up the Blessing Ceremony. He told the group they would start by standing in a circle on the grass and then move to encircle the fire pit, where a fire was already snapping in the soft breeze.

Rita had Emma Rose back in her arms, dressed in a white cotton onesie with a white mini-tutu fluffed out around her waist. Over the onesie she wore the pink sweater knitted by Mrs. Mango.

Don Paz walked to Rita. "May I?" he asked, motioning to Emma Rose.

Rita handed her over. "Of course."

Don Paz motioned the group into a circle on the grass. He held Emma Rose against his chest, his hands under her bottom, her body upright, facing the group. "The name 'Emma' means whole, or universal, and one of the meanings of 'Rose' is 'heart.' So the choice of the name Emma Rose was really inspired, even if it wasn't intentional." Don Paz smiled at Danny and Rita. "Although I do believe you were led to that name, whether you knew so or not. Emma Rose is 'whole heart,' meaning she is intact, not missing anything, not damaged."

Don Paz moved his body to face Mrs. Mango on his left, and slowly shifted to face each person in the circle: Mr. Mango, Joe Jr., Jenny, Christine, Sarah, Rita, and finally Danny on his right.

"Growing into adulthood can mean feeling like you have lost parts of yourself, but in fact, each of you are whole and can feel your whole heart too. This little girl is whole, and we are all the same.

Don Paz paused, letting a silence linger. "Now I'd like you all to hold hands and feel the power of an unbroken circle of love for Emma Rose." As he spoke, he moved forward so that Mrs. Mango, on his left, could join hands with Danny, on his right.

Sarah grabbed Christine's hand and gave an extra

squeeze. This was a small version of the family group, and they both felt it was right that Sarah was here.

Don Paz turned to face Mrs. Mango. "Elsie, I'm sure you looked at each one of your children this way when they were born. Looked at Joe Jr. and knew he was whole and without sin. Looked at Danny and knew the same. Looked at Michael and knew the same. Looked at Christine and knew she was whole and without sin. They all still are. And your mother looked at you and knew that you were whole and perfect. Rita, our mother, rest her soul, looked at you and at me the same way. And God, however you think of Him or Her, God still sees us all that way. So while we celebrate this baby, this whole heart, let us also celebrate *our own* whole hearts."

Don Paz turned and looked around the circle. "While you continue to hold hands, please let your mind focus on your own heart."

The group glanced at each other and then stared either off into the distance or down at the ground. Mr. Mango made a face but tried to think about his heart. His heart did not feel whole to him, but he kept that to himself.

Don Paz continued. "Feel it, feel that beat that has sustained you for so many years. Realize that is the Divine, right there inside you. Giving you evidence of the Divine in every beat. And let us ask the Divine to let our love for Emma Rose allow us to guide her as she grows up. Let our love keep her safe even while we encourage her to live fully, wholeheartedly. And may our love stay unconditional, even as we teach her how to behave, even as we teach her right and wrong, let us teach her that there is nothing she can do to lose our love. Just as there is nothing you can do to lose God's love."

As Don Paz spoke, Mrs. Mango let go of Mr. Mango's hand and made her way to Christine and Sarah. Still staring into the center of the circle she slipped her right hand into Christine's hand and her left into Sarah's hand. Mrs. Mango forced her brain to focus on how much she loved Christine, not how uncomfortable it felt to hold

Sarah's hand. She told herself she could probably get used to anything. She just needed to give it time.

Christine and Sarah snuck a look at each other and smiled. A tear formed at the edge of Christine's eye, but she didn't want to let go of holding hands so she let it trickle down her cheek.

Don Paz had stopped speaking when Mrs. Mango reached Christine and Sarah. He let the group notice Mrs. Mango's act and waited until glances had been exchanged, smiles had formed. He nodded at Mrs. Mango, and she nodded back at him.

"I have spoken with Danny and Rita about their wishes for Emma Rose," Don Paz continued. "Rita wants to make sure Emma Rose grows up strong and confident and not bound by gender stereotypes. At the same time, she wishes for her to feel comfortable with all her femininity." Don Paz shifted Emma Rose to his left arm and from a stone table in the center of the circle, he picked up a bouquet of white roses, bound with a blue ribbon. He held it in the air above his head. "We summon the Goddess energy to flow through Emma Rose for all her days. Let these flowers represent softness and beauty."

He set the bouquet back on the table and then picked up a piece of stone, similar to the stone of the fire pit but smaller. He held it aloft. "Let the God energy flow through Emma Rose as effortlessly as the Goddess energy. This stone represents strength and a foundation that does not crumble."

Don Paz set the stone beside the flowers and picked up a pitcher of water. "Let Emma Rose be ever fluid and adaptable," he said as he poured a few drops of water onto her head.

Don Paz set the pitcher down and picked up a compass. Showing the compass to the group, he said, "Emma Rose, may you always allow the Divine to guide you. May we all be guided in our own journey to support you."

As he set the compass down, Emma Rose began to whimper. He shifted her into a cradled position and gave a little sway to soothe her. He walked around the circle, looking at each person as he spoke. "I am deeply honored to be an earthly god to this soul, this beautiful little girl, but I am not enough. My offerings to her would best be balanced by the holy feminine, and so I am choosing my earthly goddess counterpart." Don Paz was back to his original position near Mr. Mango and Danny. He smiled and looked around the circle. He stared towards Christine, gripping her mother's hand, eyes wet.

Danny and Rita glanced at each other in surprise. There had been no discussion of adding another "earthly god." Danny felt himself tense and then noticed Rita's beaming face. He relaxed, realizing she was happy with this turn. Christine would be a great person to add to the gods and godparents helping to guide Emma Rose. Emma Rose would never lack for adult guidance, that was for sure.

Don Paz walked towards Christine and then handed Emma Rose to Mrs. Mango. "Elsie, will you join me in spiritually guiding this baby? Are you willing to be the earthly goddess in her life?

There was an intake of breath from the circle. No one had seen that coming.

"What could be better than a grandma, a devoted, loving grandma, the wise woman of the tribe, one who has accumulated wisdom to pass along, one *not in charge of all the little things*, but one who can oversee the big things?" said Don Paz.

Don Paz paused, looking around the circle. Then he laughed, breaking the seriousness of the moment. "And by oversee, I don't mean micromanage."

Rita snorted with laughter and then broke hold with Sarah to cover her mouth. Danny squeezed Rita's hand, hoping his touch would help him assess whether she was going to accept his mother as a 'spiritual guide' for Emma Rose. Danny had to hand it to Don Paz, this ceremony was brilliant. It got everyone emotional, it made them all feel loved and accepted, and then the stroke of genius to invite Mrs. Mango back into Emma Rose's life.

Mrs. Mango snuggled Emma Rose in her arms. "Of course I will."

There was a loud eruption from Emma Rose's bottom. Everyone in the circle froze, afraid that Mrs. Mango would take it as a dark sign.

"Whoops, someone has had a movement," laughed Mrs. Mango, and everyone relaxed and laughed with her. A dark stain appeared up Emma Rose's back.

"Those things can be explosive!" exclaimed Danny, and he ran to a chair on the patio where there was a baby blanket. He brought it back and wrapped it around Emma Rose and handed her back to his mother. "There. Fine for now," he said.

"Are you ready to do what is best for Emma Rose? In every way?" Don Paz asked Mrs. Mango, easily able to stay focused.

"Of course," said Mrs. Mango. Christine put her arm around her mother.

Don Paz stepped backwards and looked behind him. He wheeled around and walked to Rita, grabbing her hand and pulling her closer to Mrs. Mango. "And Rita, are you ready to do what is best for Emma Rose?"

"Of course," said Rita.

"Let us all move to the fire pit to consecrate this union of protection." Don Paz led the group over to the fire pit and motioned for them to reconstruct their circle around it.

"There it is," muttered Mr. Mango, thinking of the only definition of 'consecrate' that he knew. He had had a feeling all along Don Paz would get weird, but this was incredibly perverted. He tensed, ready to stop the orgy he thought was coming. *You just try it, buddy,* he thought. *I'll be on you like white on rice.*

Don Paz positioned Rita on the other side of Mrs. Mango from Christine. Mr. Mango stood with his arms folded, laser eye stare at Don Paz. "Look at this!" said Don Paz. "Emma Rose has so much love around her. A mother, a grandmother, an aunt"—here he nodded at Sarah—"and so many more. The three of you represent the feminine energy that she will need to develop through her life. And her father and uncles and I will all be the masculine energy that balances so exquisitely when paired with powerful feminine energy."

Don Paz faced the fire. "Fire represents purity, righteousness, and truth. May these things be ever present in Emma Rose's life." He turned back to face Mrs. Mango holding Emma Rose. "Now let us all walk in a circle around this fire to show Emma Rose we hold her in the center of our love and our willingness to help her lead her wholehearted, truthful life."

The group obediently walked in a circle. Danny was shocked to feel himself welling up with emotion, and just as it threatened to spill out into tears, he noticed his dad rolling his eyes as he plodded in the circle, arms still folded tightly against his chest. Danny smiled to himself. Some things about his dad would never change. Thank the goddess.

After Don Paz said his final blessings and Emma Rose had been handed back to Rita, who hurried up to the nursery to change her diaper and outfit, Christine grabbed Sarah's hand and turned to her mother. "Thank you," she started and then got choked up and couldn't speak.

Mrs. Mango squeezed her lips together and nodded. Then she awkwardly put her arms up and around both Sarah and Christine, hugged them, and stepped back. "I'm new to this. I'm probably going to step in it once in a while, but I'm going to do my best."

Sarah grinned. "You're doing great."

"Well, I'm a goddess now, so maybe I've got a chance," said Mrs. Mango with a wry smile. Then she thought of the years lost with her own mother and the way she might have lost Joe forever, and her smile disappeared.

"I just, I just, I can't, I don't want to miss your life," she said to Christine, reaching a hand up and patting Christine's cheek. "I was stupid with my own mother, and whatever it takes, I don't want that kind of thing to happen with us."

"I'm buying Don Paz's building," said Michael. After the Blessing Ceremony, the group had scattered around the terrace, eating and drinking and laughing. Michael was sitting at the table with his dad, drinking a mango mimosa.

"What the hell?" said Mr. Mango, waving his own mimosa at Michael. He figured the mango juice cut the alcohol down to almost nothing and it would be okay to have one. Plus, it was named after him, for crying out loud.

"I'm buying his building and renting it back to him," said Michael. "He cured my back pain. In, like, a week."

Mr. Mango waved his hand in the air. "Come on. Your back gets better so you're going give that quack all your money?"

Michael laughed. "First of all, it's not *all* my money. I got plenty. It's actually a good investment for me. Plus, I had one of my VC buddies look at his business plan. It is sound. He was impressed. I mean, the guy was at *Stanford Business School,* for crying out loud."

"What's the Viet Cong got to do with any of this?" said Mr. Mango, mystified.

"Huh?" said Michael. "Who said anything about the Viet Cong?"

"VC," said Mr. Mango. "Viet Cong. Viet Charlie, you know."

Michael laughed. "Venture Capital, that's what VC stands for. The guys who invest in start-ups and such."

Mr. Mango shook his head. "Jesus, a bit of back pain relief, and you hand the guy your balls."

"Hey, I didn't complain about it, didn't want to

worry you, but my back was *really* bad. Like, close-to-surgery bad. And it is completely cured. It was so obvious I couldn't see it, but I had to address my issues with Meredith. And I did. And boom, back pain gone. I'm a believer."

Mr. Mango stared across the lawn at Don Paz who was walking around the edge of the back fence with Danny as Danny gestured at parts of the landscaping that had just been finished. "Does that guy have some sort of hypnotic powers? How is he influencing everyone like this?"

"We *are* all so stuck in Western ways of looking at the world," said Michael. "There are so many other ways to think about life and health and, I don't know, God."

"Oh good Christ, he's sucked you in too," said Mr. Mango. "You drank the Kool-aid."

"Just trying to keep an open mind," said Michael. "And the proof is in the pudding. My back is completely better."

"Well, whatever," said Mr. Mango. "It's your money."

Danny and Don Paz made their way back to the terrace. Danny picked up a pitcher of mimosas that Jules had just put on the table and refilled both of their glasses.

"Well, it is all working out, isn't it?" said Danny, beaming. "Rita and Mom are good again, Christine and Mom are good again, Michael is buying Don Paz's building, Joe and Jenny have moved into the guest house and are helping with Emma Rose. Life is good!" The amount of champagne in his bloodstream allowed Danny to ignore the thought that all was not good with his dad's health. He held up his glass. "Cheers!"

Danny clinked glasses with Don Paz and then his dad.

"Mango mimosas, what an idea!" said Don Paz. "Delicious."

"Cheers," said Mr. Mango reluctantly, in a gruff voice. Too much happiness always seemed to him to just be an invitation to fate to come and disappoint you again. And what did the kid really know about life anyway? *Wait till you're married for forty-some years and then talk to me about happiness,* he thought. Young people these days felt so entitled to a life of happiness and love and, boy, were most of them going to be disappointed. You had to find a way to just get through. That was what life was about. Get through with a few comforts, enjoy your sports, enjoy your coworkers, wait for the time you get some grandkids to play with. Maybe it would be enough. Maybe it wouldn't.

CHAPTER 50

Boost Your Juice

Mr. Mango drove home from the Blessing Ceremony and Mrs. Mango was relieved to have him back in the driver role. Not because she was afraid to drive on the highway—she was feeling more and more comfortable with that—but because it felt like a return to the natural order of things. Plus, she had sipped on the mimosas for the better part of the afternoon.

Mrs. Mango gave a contented sigh. "I don't know what I expected, but that was just lovely. And the food! Did you try the tea sandwiches? One was better than the next! And the idea of Mango mimosas, well, it was just perfect." Since she wasn't much of a drinker, Mrs. Mango was feeling the effect of all those mimosas. And was feeling the uplift of being called a goddess. And the relief of not being at war with Rita anymore.

Wait a minute, wasn't she mad at Rita? Well, probably still a bit. But she wanted that baby in her arms as often as she could get her, and it was worth eating a little crow. Or a lot of crow.

Mr. Mango snorted. "Bunch of hooey, you ask me." He snuck a sideways glance at Mrs. Mango and realized maybe he could be a little less gruff. "But, yeah, nice I guess. And, yeah, that was a good spread. Maybe having a baby around has loosened up Rita's food rules."

"I didn't even know I'd like watercress sandwiches! But they were so good."

"And you get to be a 'goddess' for Emma Rose. That's a good thing, huh?" Mr. Mango said, trying to get into the spirit of pleasant conversation. It felt awkward, but maybe it would be a good idea to encourage Mrs. Mango's amiable mood.

"That Don Paz, he's kind of a clever one," said Mrs. Mango. She might never tell Mr. Mango about her visit with Don Paz, but then again, maybe she would. She laughed at herself in her own head, realizing how immediately her impulse was to hide something. She'd have to work on changing that instinct because keeping secrets was not something she wanted to do anymore.

"I thought he was a 'pervert,'" said Mr. Mango, chuckling at the use of Mrs. Mango's word for Don Paz.

Mrs. Mango shrugged and looked out her side window. The smooth undulations of the Wine Country hills matched the smooth undulations in her brain. "He's definitely out there, but he is also pretty wise. He, uh, he helped me calm down. Helped me realize some things."

The buzzy head made her bolder than she might normally have been. "I ended up talking to him the other day. I was kind of a mess and—you know when I went out for a drive?"

"Uh huh?" said Mr. Mango.

"Well, I ended up at his office and we talked for a long time. And, I don't know. I just felt more peaceful."

Mr. Mango nodded, his eyes still on the road in front of him. Smooth undulations take focus when you are the driver. "Peaceful is a good thing."

"He helped me see that I have been unfair to you. For a long time." Mrs. Mango looked out her window again, unable to look at Mr. Mango while she spoke. "And that I cannot expect you to just, I don't know, get over that right away. So, take your time."

There was silence for a minute or so.

"I was misguided. For *so* long," said Mrs. Mango quietly. "And I can't expect you to just get with the program since I have had this big realization."

"It's okay," said Mr. Mango, ill at ease and not sure what to say.

"It's not okay. I mean, what I've done all these years is not okay. You've been nothing but—" Mrs. Mango got choked up and couldn't speak for a moment. "You've been nothing but a good husband. A good father. A good man."

"Ah, no need to go over that again," said Mr. Mango, eyes straight ahead, shoulders stiff.

"We never talk like this," said Mrs. Mango. "About real stuff. And now I want to. And I understand *you* might not want to. But here's my side of it. No one helped me get over losing . . . Raul." She couldn't believe she just said his name. Out loud. To her husband. "And I know I should have moved on. But I didn't know how. And I didn't know a person *could* move on. And now I know people do. It seems impossible, but people do. And I know that it was you, there, all along."

"You don't need to do this," said Mr. Mango.

"But I do!" said Mrs. Mango. "And it's not just the mimosas talking. You don't have to say a word. You don't have to do anything. I just want you to know. I am still working on sorting it all out, but I know a couple of things. I know I love you. I know I love Christine and will never let anything separate us the way I let myself be separated from my mother. I have some big regrets, and the biggest is not appreciating you all these years, and the second biggest is being cut off from my parents."

Mrs. Mango finally looked sideways at her husband and gave a little laugh. "I know you so well. I know you feel like you should say something to comfort me, but you can't right now. And that's okay." She reached over and patted Mr. Mango's shoulder. "That's okay."

Mrs. Mango watched the landscape change from pastoral to the rush of a busy highway in silence the rest of the way home. Each time she had an impulse to say something, she stopped herself. *Give Joe time to think on what I've said,* she thought to herself. *Patience.*

****

"What is that contraption anyway?" Mr. Mango said, gesturing to the Vegevape 6200 Pro on the kitchen counter. Enough hours had passed for the mimosas to wear off, and Mrs. Mango was getting dinner started.

"That's the Vegevape thingy I bought. Am going to pass it along to Christine . . . and Sarah. Have just never gotten around to using it." Mrs. Mango gave a little smile to herself, proud she had included Sarah in the conversation. It was a start. As long as they didn't start kissing or some such in front of her, maybe she could handle it. She continued chopping the broccoli she was preparing for dinner.

"You put vegetables in it?" asked Mr. Mango. "'Cause at Cardiac Rehab they keep harping about eating more vegetables. Among all sorts of other shit I'm supposed to change."

"It is so powerful it *vaporizes* the vegetables and then you inhale the vapor," said Mrs. Mango. "Sounded silly to me, but the vapor was actually quite pleasant."

"And what are these?" Mr. Mango asked, picking up one of the "Boost Your Juice" boxes that had been arriving steadily in the mail.

"Supplements you add to the mix, gives you extra energy and such," answered Mrs. Mango.

"Let's give it a try," said Mr. Mango. "Maybe there's a way I might actually like broccoli. Toss it in there."

Eager for any connection with her husband, Mrs. Mango agreed immediately. They added broccoli, apple, a couple of carrots, and two scoops of the "Boost Your Juice" supplement, even though it only called for one. Then the two cups of water that allowed the powerful blade to do its work.

An hour and half later, Christine and Sarah stopped by the Mangos' to pick up Christine's bike. They were going to try biking on the weekends for exercise, and Mr. Mango had fixed up the bike Christine had left unused for years.

"Hello? Mom? Dad?" Christine called, coming into the kitchen with Sarah trailing behind her.

"What the—" Christine stopped short, Sarah

running into her from behind.

Christine's eyes and mouth hung wide open at the sight of her mother sitting on her father's lap, the two of them laughing so hard they were crying.

"Oh, hello dear," giggled Mrs. Mango. "And you too, my other dear," she said to Sarah as she came around Christine.

"Come on in! Have a puff!" said Mr. Mango, waving expansively at the Vegevape sitting on the table in front of them. "Goddamn it, but that stuff's good!"

Christine giggled and elbowed Sarah in the side. "They're vaping!"

"Can't believe someone came up with a way to make me like vegetables, but there it is," said Mr. Mango as Mrs. Mango slid off his lap.

"Let me get you girls some cake," bubbled Mrs. Mango, staggering slowly towards the far counter where the cake keep had half of the chocolate cake left.

Mr. Mango leaned in and fired up the Vegevape Pro and gave a deep inhale on the cone. "Whew! But that is good."

Christine was still processing the fact that her mother had been on her father's lap and that her father seemed fine with that. Maybe moving out had been an even better idea than she had known. Maybe they were rediscovering each other.

"We don't have any extra time," said Christine. "Just going to grab the bike and go."

Sarah looked at her with a puzzled expression. They had nowhere they had to be.

Christine gave Sarah a little push towards the garage. "See you guys!" she said over her shoulder.

Mrs. Mango slid back onto Mr. Mango's lap.

"What the hell is in that Vegevape stuff?" said Mr. Mango, laughing. "I think we are high."

"Is this what high feels like?" said Mrs. Mango. "Because I like it."

Mr. Mango gave his wife a squeeze. "Me too."

"I think I'm going to keep that Vegevape Pro," said Mrs. Mango. "Let Christine get her own if she wants one."

In the morning, Mr. Mango's eyes opened to an unfamiliar sight and it took him a beat to realize he was staring into Mrs. Mango's hair on the back of her head, about two inches from his face. And his body was aligned closely to hers, two spoons back in their rightful place in the drawer. His arm was over her side, and as he moved it, she shifted enough to wake up.

"Hmm, what?" she mumbled, turning over to face directly into Mr. Mango's eyes.

They both floated towards consciousness slowly, arriving at the same realization at about the same time.

"Oh my," whispered Mrs. Mango.

"Huh," grunted Mr. Mango, his mind sorting through the images of the previous night. Blurry, floaty, but definite memories of laughing with his wife while they enjoyed something they hadn't done in years.

Mrs. Mango looked anxiously at Mr. Mango, almost as if the relationship was new and they had just had a drunken hookup and one didn't know yet whether it was the beginning of something or just a one-night stand. Silly thought to have about your own husband.

"Well," said Mr. Mango, realizing his arm was still cast over his wife's body, wondering if she would want it there.

Mrs. Mango was afraid to move, liking having her husband that close to her. She wanted, so badly, to ask her husband what the night before meant, if it meant anything. Was it just that they were snockered or did that experience mean he was back with her? Something told her to not ruin the moment. To just let it unfold and see what happened next.

Mr. Mango decided that Mrs. Mango's frozen position meant that she was uncomfortable being that close, which would make sense. She had never really been that physical, and it was only those herbs that had freed her up last night. He carefully removed his arm and rolled out of bed.

"Damn prostate, can't go even a couple of hours without peeing," he grumbled.

Mrs. Mango stared at her husband's back as he walked to the bathroom, wishing that wasn't what had happened next

CHAPTER 51

No Spikes

Mrs. Mango strolled down the sidewalk towards her house, sweat pouring down her face and dripping from her neck into her well-covered cleavage. She realized she was going to have to buy a couple of those sports bra thingies because her regular bras were getting ruined by all this sweating. She was determined to keep up with her walking program and had invited Mr. Mango, but he passed on this morning's walk. The walk had given her plenty of time to analyze everything Joe had done and said since the Raul revelation. He had definitely made an effort to be more pleasant. And there was of course the Vegevape night two days ago. The thought of that one made her sweat even more.

Although they both had seemed to enjoy that night, it was hard to overcome the habits of that many years, so there was no discussion of it once they had gotten out of bed in the morning. Mrs. Mango was shy about saying anything, and Mr. Mango—well, who knew? Maybe it had just been a physical thing for him, maybe it didn't have that much meaning. Or maybe it was his way of saying he had found a way back to Mrs. Mango. The entire walk Mrs. Mango had examined the evidence for each side. Did it mean he loved her? Or was it just the result of inhaling too many vegetables?

There had been no more affection, but they had never been hand holders or even much for kissing. So how was a woman to know if her husband could love her again?

"Elsie!" Mrs. Melucci waved as she hurried across the street, breaking into Mrs. Mango's thoughts.

"Oh, hello Mary," said Mrs. Mango as the two of them intersected by the Mangos' mailbox and stopped.

"I haven't had a chance to catch up with you,"

scolded Mrs. Melucci, pulling her thin cotton robe around her. She must have seen Mrs. Mango coming and run out of the house. "How is that little baby? And how did the christening go? And why aren't you up there taking care of her?

Mrs. Mango realized a lot had happened since she last talked to Mary. "Emma Rose is just wonderful. And Jenny and Joe are living there now, so Jenny is taking care of her."

Mrs. Melucci's eyes widened. "Joe's up from LA?"

Mrs. Mango nodded. "Yes, going to be in *Phantom of the Opera* in San Francisco! I just love that play. I can't wait to see him."

"Well, don't that beat all! *Phantom of the Opera*."

"And Jenny, well, she's never said exactly, but I think she'd love to have had children and she just loves taking care of Emma Rose. Plus, she's helping Rita with legal stuff. It's nice for them," said Mrs. Mango, rubbing her hand across her forehead to try to mop off some of the sweat.

"The christening was lovely, and then Rita's brother, Don Paz, did a Blessing Ceremony too. Made me a goddess in her life!" Mrs. Mango puffed out her chest a bit, awkward with the word 'goddess' but loving it all the same.

"Goddess? What the heck does that mean?" asked Mrs. Melucci, frowning. "That's not some Satan cult kind of thing, is it?"

"No, no, just that I am an important female influence in her life," said Mrs. Mango. "Kind of like a Godparent, but not Catholic."

"Huh," said Mrs. Melucci, crossing her arms across her chest.

"Hey, girls," said a voice behind them. Mrs. Mango and Mrs. Melucci turned to see Velma and Flora powerwalking at them, elbows flying.

Velma and Flora slowed up and joined Mrs. Mango and Mrs. Melucci beside the duct-taped mail box. Velma gave the mailbox a little push. "That thing is holding tight! Good job, Elsie."

"Elsie was just filling me in on everything going on in her family," said Mrs. Melucci.

"*Everything*?" asked Flora, looking meaningfully at Velma and then Mrs. Mango.

Mrs. Mango laughed. "No one gets to hear *everything*. You couldn't handle the truth." She laughed, pleased at quoting *A Few Good Men,* which she and Mr. Mango had watched last night. "Or maybe you could?"

Mrs. Melucci snapped to attention, sniffing out good gossip. "Oh, *really,*" she said, eyes darting back and forth between Flora and Mrs. Mango.

Mrs. Mango smiled at Mrs. Melucci. "Yes, like, could you handle Christine having a girlfriend? Because she does. Lovely girl." Mrs. Mango sighed and looked off into the distance as if picturing the happy couple. "Ahh, just a lovely pair, those two." Out of the corner of her eye, she watched for Mrs. Melucci's reaction. For so long, she had tried to hide the family dirty laundry from Mrs. Melucci, and it just now was occurring to her to wonder why. It was actually fun to shock her. And every time she told the truth, she felt lighter and freer.

"What?" said Mrs. Melucci, mouth agape, predictably outraged. "Are you saying what I think you're saying?"

"Yes, they are *lesbians*," said Mrs. Mango, holding back a giggle as she emphasized the word 'lesbians.' Mary Melucci's face was contorted, her mouth wide open, her eyes wild with shock.

Velma and Flora were both thrilled that they had happened upon this scene. Watching Mrs. Mango shock Mrs. Melucci hadn't been on the day's agenda, but it was the most entertaining thing to happen in months. It was even better than when Harvey Mathison fell at bingo night, landing on his own dentures in his pocket and biting himself in the ass.

"Oh no! I'm so sorry!" spluttered Mrs. Melucci.

"Christine was such a nice girl! You know that means she's going to hell."

"Hey!" said Flora protectively. "Don't be dirtying Elsie's chakras! She has gotten a lot straightened out in her life, and I'm proud of her! And proud of Christine."

"You know, that was my first reaction too," said Mrs. Mango to Mrs. Melucci. "But a lot has happened that has, uh, opened up my mind. Maybe as we age, we get too rigid in our thinking, you know?" Mrs. Mango looked at Flora and Velma. "You girls, you have the right idea."

Flora nodded. "Got to keep it real!"

"Try new things. Think new things," agreed Velma. "Hey, life just *starts* at 70, that's what I say."

"No one to please anymore, that's for sure," chimed in Flora. "What do I care what anyone thinks? Old people are invisible, so no one notices anyway."

"Exactly," said Mrs. Mango. "You know what matters? Family. And you're right," she pointed at Mrs. Melucci. "Christine IS a nice girl. Was and still is. Not going to let some old-fashioned ideas separate me from my only daughter."

Mrs. Melucci was shaking her head and took a step away from the group. These ladies were crazy and what if it was contagious?

"Mary, we are too old to try to hide all our flaws. It is a huge waste of energy," said Mrs. Mango. "For instance, I know that Celia was separated from her husband. I know they are trying to make it work again. I know that little Parker has a learning disorder. Doesn't mean anything bad about your family! That's just a family—all families have issues."

Velma and Flora looked at each other, delighted with Mrs. Mango's new attitude.

"And me, I screwed up my marriage holding a torch for a long-ago love. And poor Joe, he put up with it," Mrs. Mango shook her head and wiped again at the sweat that wouldn't stop coming. "I always thought I had been faithful to him because I didn't physically cheat, but I wasn't all there for him emotionally."

Mrs. Melucci closed her eyes. "Stop!" she said, holding up a hand. "Just stop."

"Really? Stop? Because this is *exactly* the kind of thing you would love to talk about behind my back," said Mrs. Mango. "I'm sorry to say I participated in that kind of thing for so long. We knew everybody's business, but we never talked to *them* about it, never offered compassion or support. Just got some weird pleasure out of gossiping. Well, it's out now."

Velma started clapping, and Flora joined in. "Way to go, Elsie!"

Mrs. Mango gave a little bow, enjoying herself.

The three of them watched Mrs. Melucci shuffle back across the street and into her house.

"She's just not ready for it," said Velma sadly.

Mrs. Mango nodded. "I wasn't either. So I kind of feel for her." She paused and then burst out laughing. "But her face! Did you see her face when I told her about Christine?"

Flora slung an arm around Mrs. Mango's waist, unable to reach her neck. "Good job, Elsie. I mean, with Christine and all. Life's too short to be so uptight about who loves who. Sarah's a winner."

"And now, after all those boys, you get another girl in the family," said Flora, stepping back.

Mrs. Mango looked surprised. "You know, I hadn't even thought of it that way."

Velma gave Mrs. Mango an intense stare. The comment about a long-ago love had just sunk in. "That long-ago love, was that your starter marriage?"

Mrs. Mango shrugged. "Not a marriage, but a starter something. When you told me about that, it really hit a nerve. But mine, he died before I had a chance to know if it would have turned into the real thing."

"Oh, honey," said Velma, giving Mrs. Mango a hug. "You been suffering that alone all these years?"

Tears started to flow from Mrs. Mango's eyes,

Velma's kindness taking her by surprise.

Velma hugged tighter. "You poor baby. What was his name?"

"Raul," whispered Mrs. Mango.

Flora patted Mrs. Mango's shoulder. "You just go ahead and cry. Never too late to grieve properly."

Mrs. Mango nodded through her tears and reached a hand out to grasp Flora's hand. With her other hand, she reached up and wiped away the tears. "Whew, didn't know it would hit me again that hard."

"We all make mistakes," said Velma. "Lord knows I made more than my share. But we don't have to live unhappy. When we know better, we do better. I heard that somewhere once."

"Must've read it online," said Flora. "That Velma, she's addicted to her screens," Flora added to Mrs. Mango. "I think she might have a problem with sexting too," she added, giggling.

"Oh my, I don't know anything about that," said Mrs. Mango as Velma finally let her out of the hug. "Maybe bring me along slowly, okay? You girls have had more time to get used to all this."

Mrs. Mango glanced across the street and saw Mrs. Melucci peeking out from behind her curtains. Mrs. Mango gave a cheerful wave at her.

"Nice how you didn't mention Manny's drinking," said Velma. Everyone knew that Mrs. Melucci's husband Manny's 'back pain' was code for hangover.

"Well, not sure if she is even really admitting to that, so probably not my business," said Mrs. Mango. "I'm thinking I've got enough of my own business to keep me busy for a while."

"So you and Joe, how're the two of you?" asked Flora.

"Not sure, to be honest," said Mrs. Mango. She paused to think, and tears welled up in her eyes again. "My goodness, all I do is cry," she half-laughed to try to get herself under control. "I was a fool. He's been a good man, a good husband, all these years, and I never really let myself . . . love him."

"You got to tell him!" said Flora.

"I did. But, you know," Mrs. Mango got choked up, "it might be too late."

"I'll bet it's not," said Velma. "Women, now when we decide a relationship is over, *it is over,* we can't go back. It's like them spikes you drive over to get out of a parking lot - no backing up. But men, you can get them back. No spikes at the exit of their parking lots. Men will drive in and out of love till the car falls apart."

Mrs. Mango shrugged. "Well, we'll see. I know I can't expect him to get over it all right away. And he has been acting less grumpy, but that makes me just think he is being polite, like you would be to a stranger. It's almost worse because it seems kind of, I don't know, forced."

"Fake it to make it," said Flora, looking at the big sports watch on her wrist. "Come on, Velma, we better get moving again. Need at least five thousand more steps."

Mrs. Mango looked at her own watch. "Oh, I got to go too. Heading up to Danny's this afternoon."

Velma gave Mrs. Mango another hug. "You go makc that man *happy*, you know what I mean," she raised her perfectly tattooed eyebrows.

Mrs. Mango gave an awkward giggle. "Uh, okay," she said, thinking that she already did and it still didn't feel like enough.

"Danny, could you run this pack of wipes up to Emma Rose's room? Your mom is up there changing her, and I think the wipes are all gone."

"I'll take it," said Mr. Mango, looking at the band on his wrist. "They're keeping track of my activity so I guess I better actually be active." He laughed and took the wipes from Rita's hand.

As he got closer to Emma Rose's room, Mr. Mango

could hear a kiddie tune version of "The Lord of the Dance" blasting out of her door. As he came into the doorway, he saw Mrs. Mango dancing in front of Emma Rose's crib, Emma Rose's eyes transfixed on her grandmother. Mr. Mango took a step back so that his wife wouldn't see him and, peering around the side of the door, watched her skip and sway and spin for Emma Rose, singing along to the words.

"Dance, dance, wherever you may be," sang Mrs. Mango, her back to the door, swaying up to her left tiptoe and then her right, her arms gracefully following her feet.

With her back to him and if he squinted, it was as if Mr. Mango was spun back in time and looking at a young Elsie, the way he had seen her at the dance where they met. A bright, spinning, dancing young woman. He thought about how he had seen her then, thought about all that had seemed to lie in front of them.

He peeked around the side of the door at Emma Rose, so young and unformed and innocent. He thought about how Don Paz had compared them all to a baby, how easy it was to love babies before they grew up and had so many expectations on them. He looked back at Mrs. Mango, still seeing the young woman, and felt his heart soften. She really had done her best. None of them had known how to handle Vietnam or death or war, overseas or in their own homes. His brain argued with his heart. Could he really forget all those years of being held at a distance? Of being the second choice? He looked back at Emma Rose and felt like he could forgive her anything. He thought about his daughter Christine and realized he could forgive her anything. Could he feel the same way about Elsie?

"And I lead you all in the dance said he," Mrs. Mango sang, her voice a surprisingly clear and lovely tone. She started to turn around, and Mr. Mango ducked back into the hall, not wanting her to see him spying.

Mr. Mango crept back a couple of feet and then called out. "Elsie? I have wipes if you need them," he said

as he walked slowly towards the room, giving her time to
compose herself.

CHAPTER 52
The Real Phantom

The Mangos were sitting in a line in the fifth row, right center section, facing the stage where *The Phantom of the Opera* was about to begin. Thanks to that prostate business, Mr. Mango was on the aisle for his likely trips to the bathroom, and somehow Danny and then Rita had ended up next to him. To the right of Rita was Jenny, trembling with pride and excitement, then Mrs. Mango, then Christine, Sarah, and then Michael on the far right end.

It was amazing they had actually made it to the theater on time. Mrs. Mango had tried on six different outfits, unable to make up her mind. Christine and Sarah finally just picked a navy dress and made her put it on so they wouldn't be late. By the time they got to the theater, Jenny, Michael, Danny, and Rita had already had dinner at a restaurant down the street and made it to their seats.

"He's had almost no time to rehearse," said Jenny, worried and flustered. Aside from the worry, Jenny looked beautiful, hair done in a French twist, makeup accenting the angles of her face and eyes in perfect ways. She looked every inch the wife of a star.

Michael patted her hand. "He'll be fine! He's loved this show since he was a kid. Could probably have stepped into this role when he was fifteen." Michael rolled his eyes. "I've heard him sing these songs a thousand times. *I* could step into this role just from hearing him."

Jenny smiled, but her hands kept moving in her lap, playing with the program, staring at Joe's name in it as if that finally made it real.

And then the theater darkened and the orchestra started and Mrs. Mango felt like her body was one big beating heart. She couldn't quite believe her son was part of this. She remembered bringing him to see a production of the show when he was a teenager—how he had begged and finally wore her down. Nobody else in the family had wanted to come, so she and Joe Jr. had gone to a matinee, just the two of them. She remembered enjoying the musical more than she had expected to, but it had never, ever occurred to her that she might return to see her son starring in it.

Mrs. Mango scanned the elaborate set, stared up at the chandelier over the audience, and felt the music carry her into the story as she waited, seemingly forever, until Joe appeared as Raoul. Her hand went to her heart, and it was all she could do not to jump up and yell to the crowd, 'That is my son!'

Joe was so confident, so at ease on the stage. And his voice! Mrs. Mango hadn't realized how perfectly made it was for these songs. She snuck a glance at Jenny to see that she was also beaming. Mrs. Mango felt a pang of guilt that she had dismissed Joe's acting aspirations for so long. She had never really believed he would make it as an actor and was grateful he hadn't listened to her. It occurred to her that all of her children knew themselves better than she knew them. Christine was right about herself. Michael was probably right about his marriage. Danny, well, she wasn't sure about him yet, but she was starting to believe that maybe she could trust her children to know what they needed. Because Joe was made for the stage, there was no doubt.

Mrs. Mango thought back to watching the play with Joe Jr. years ago, trying to remember the basic story of a chorus girl who makes a kind of deal with the devil when the Phantom helps her to sing like an angel. And then an old acquaintance hears her and falls in love with the Phantom's creation.

Watching the story unfold, Mrs. Mango couldn't help but think about how easily love can turn to jealousy, to possessiveness, to conflict.

Just enjoy Joey. Just enjoy this story. It is not your

story, she told herself as her mind started to compare her Raul and this Raoul. Spelled differently but spoken the same. It was a challenge to just focus on the *Phantom of the Opera* story, complicated as it was by names from her own life. Raoul, of course, but then there was the coincidence of the chorus girl being named Christine. All the parts of Mrs. Mango's life that had stayed separate for so long were mixing together in a very uncomfortable way. Her brain swirled with emotion—joy and sadness as intertwined as the duets being sung in front of her.

Rita slid her hand into her purse and manipulated her phone to get to the webcams at home, wanting to check on Don Paz, home with Emma Rose. As she peered in, hoping the light from the phone wasn't showing outside of the purse, Danny elbowed her. "Put that away," he whispered. "She's fine."

The man sitting in front of Danny turned around and gave him a 'shush' look. Danny leaned forward. "Sorry," he whispered. "New mom here," he said pointing at Rita.

The man glared at Danny and turned back around towards the stage.

Mrs. Mango tried to remember how Raoul manages to find Christine after the Phantom takes her but then was drawn back into the production in front of her, as Christine began to sing "Think of Me." The song was too much, Mrs. Mango couldn't keep her own story separate from the story in front of her. It was as if Christine had opened the box under the Mangos' bathroom sink and was singing the words from one of Mrs. Mango's letters. Tears formed and started to trickle down Mrs. Mango's face as Christine sang about taking your heart back and being free. Exactly what Mrs. Mango was trying to do. Exactly what she should have done years ago. She turned her head ever so slightly to glance at Joe, wishing desperately that he was sitting right next to her. Knowing he was the owner of her heart.

Mr. Mango caught his wife's look and saw the tears, misinterpreting them as being for her lost love of Raul. He closed his eyes, unable to look at the scene in front of him, or the one to his side. *This is ridiculous,* he thought. He got up and made his way to the back of the theater, deciding he would watch from back there. He wanted to see his son in such a big moment in his life, but what kind of man could sit and watch his wife cry for someone else?

Looking at the Phantom, Mrs. Mango thought about how she turned her Raul into a phantom. The real Raul hadn't been in her life for almost fifty years, and yet she let herself believe she had kept him. The real Raul was long gone, it was a phantom of Raul that lingered, the phantom of Raul who seduced her into believing he was making her life better when in fact he was keeping her from life. Mrs. Mango felt the tears coming even harder as she realized that the danger of a phantom is that the life he offered, an imagined one, was always superior to the life she had. For years, her real life looked pale in comparison.

I've had it wrong for so long, she thought, wiping at her wet face.

In the back of the theater, Mr. Mango stared at the stage, willing himself to enjoy his son, and nothing else. Goddamn it, but that kid was good. He couldn't help but put himself in the story, though. It was just too similar to his life. This phantom trying to steal away his wife, he had lived with this scenario for so many years. He got caught up in a desperate hope that Raoul would kill the Phantom, that some sort of spell would be broken and Raoul and Christine would live happily ever after. He laughed bitterly at himself—he had never thought of himself as a fairy tale kind of guy.

Christine kept sneaking looks at her mother, increasingly worried about the effect of watching star-crossed lovers, particularly since one was named Raoul.

Sarah noticed Mrs. Mango's tears too and squeezed Christine's hand, trying to send a message of support.

Mrs. Mango let herself get caught up in the malevolence of the Phantom against the opera owners, the story within a story of an opera and the workings of an opera. And then Christine and Raoul sang "All I Ask of You," and the words dragged her back yet again to her own Raul. The words her son was up there singing were exactly how she had felt about her Raul, how he was there to guard her and guide her—and then he wasn't. It was so odd for Mrs. Mango to hear her son singing these words. And singing them to Christine, her daughter's name. All so confusing. She shouldn't have wished for that from Raul for so long. And in fact, it was *Joe* who had been guarding her all these years. The longer she watched the musical, the more it became clear that her Raul was the Phantom, and Joe was the musical's Raoul.

This was her and *Joe's* story.

Completely unaware of the drama going on with his parents, Danny watched his brother with growing amazement. He had led the teasing for so long, and here it turned out that Joe was actually incredibly talented. He hadn't realized that he worried about his older brother until this very moment when he finally seemed to have found success. Danny settled back into his chair, happy. Who cared if people around them gave them nasty looks for a little whisper here and there? Life was working out.

Michael was also unaware of the drama with their parents, but more because the story was resonating with his own relationship dramas. If he hadn't met those times with Don Paz, he probably wouldn't have seen it, but now he did. His obsession and possessiveness of Meredith had driven her away, just like the Phantom's towards Christine. Not to mention his insistence on doing things his way. He felt a freedom in the realization. Felt able to let Meredith move on to something or someone that was a better fit for her. Truly understood that love is wanting the person to be happy, even if that happiness didn't come from you. That peaceful thought, combined with the warmth of the theater, sent Michael to sleep.

Mrs. Mango remained lost in her own thoughts until another song grabbed her attention. She looked down at her program, what was this song that seemed to have flowed straight from her own brain? "Wishing You Were Somehow Here Again." At the end, when the singer spoke of trying to stop looking to the past, begging to learn to say goodbye, Mrs. Mango felt ripped open, naked. This was her.

This beautiful and brutal scene in front of her was life made into art. Other people had felt this raw, this uncertain, this desperate. And someone took those feelings and made art out of it. And her son was up there, helping to create that art. Her chest didn't feel adequate to contain all her feelings. Her heart was full with the beauty of the play and her son's part in it, but it was broken with the way it reflected her own life.

Mrs. Mango couldn't sit still one more minute. She jumped up, mumbling something about needing the restroom.

As Mrs. Mango slipped out to the aisle, she woke up Michael, who jumped, then surreptitiously wiped the drool off the side of his mouth. He wondered if Joe Jr. could actually see them in the audience, knowing he'd catch hell for falling asleep at Joe's big moment.

Christine knew this moment was probably coming, having watched her mother so carefully all evening. With a last squeeze of Sarah's hand, she followed her mother, giving Michael a little slap on the shoulder as she got up. "Stay awake!" she whispered.

In the restroom, Christine found her mother leaning against the sink, head bowed.

"Mom, are you okay?"

"Of course not! I couldn't control myself in there," said Mrs. Mango, staring in the mirror and wiping carefully at her face with a tissue. She sniffled.

"Is it just too hard, thinking of, uh, him?" said Christine. "Of your Raul."

Mrs. Mango froze, staring at her daughter. She was unable to speak.

"I know," said Christine. "I saw the letters."

Mrs. Mango looked around and saw a velvet bench against the wall. She stumbled to it and sank down onto it.

"I'm so sorry, Mom," Christine said in a soft voice, coming to sit down next to her mother.

"I didn't read them all," Christine said, thinking a bit of a white lie might not be so bad in this situation. "Just enough to realize you had someone you loved from long ago. And that he died."

Mrs. Mango stared straight ahead, as if she couldn't hear.

Christine slid her hand over and grabbed her mother's hand. "It must be hard, seeing Joe up there playing a guy named *Raoul*."

Mrs. Mango shook her head. Christine didn't understand. Mr. Mango didn't understand either. They all thought she was crying for Raul, but she was crying for her Joe.

"No, it is not that," started Mrs. Mango and then she couldn't speak for a few moments. Then, "It is that I have wasted so many years thinking of him. I mean, I didn't think of him most of the time, but I thought of him enough to ruin everything. And so I never let him go, not really."

Mrs. Mango turned and faced her daughter. "I was so caught up in the romance of it, the Romeo and Juliet of it all. And this," she swept her hand towards the theater, "this is so beautiful and emotional, but it is your *dad* I feel this all for now. It was *him* all along and I just didn't know. Raul was the phantom! Your dad is Raoul, you know, the Raoul of the play."

Mrs. Mango stood up. "I've got to find him. I've

got to explain."

But when they came out of the restroom, they could not find Mr. Mango. Not in his seat, not in the back of the theater. It did not occur to either of them to look up in the balcony, high above the stage, way in the back where Mr. Mango had landed, courtesy of paying off an usher.

Christine convinced her mother to return to her seat, watch the rest of the show, and then find Mr. Mango. "Mom, you've got to watch Joe! This is his big moment."

Mrs. Mango, back in her seat, did her best to giving herself over to watching her son.

Christine poked her mother in the side as the Phantom, having felt love for the first time when Christine kisses him, sets Christine and Raoul free.

"See, Mom," Christine whispered. "They are free. You are free."

Mrs. Mango shrugged, sure her freedom had come too late.

In the balcony, Mr. Mango struggled to believe there could be a good ending. Sure, the play had one, but that wasn't real life. Phantoms didn't just let go like that. Besides, it wasn't the Phantom's attachment that was the problem.

At the end of the play, as her son took his bow to the wild applause, Mrs. Mango stood clapping, wondering just how much emotion a person could take in one night. She felt like a guitar with strings made of pain, and joy, and pride, and regret, and sorrow, and it was as if some god was plucking each at random. It was too much. The tears were dripping down her face yet again, pride mixing with pain.

Mrs. Mango looked around, still not seeing Mr. Mango. She was sure he would not have left, would not have missed seeing Joe Jr., but couldn't figure out where he might be.

Eventually, as they waited to go backstage to see

Joe, Mr. Mango sauntered up to the group.

"How about that?!" he exclaimed to Michael and Danny, who were standing closest to where he appeared. "Wasn't he good?"

Danny and Michael both nodded.

"Amazing," said Michael.

"Like you saw it," said Christine, poking Michael. "You were asleep."

"Just for a moment," said Michael.

"I finally get it," said Danny. "I see why he wants to do this. He was *made* for this."

Jenny was glowing. "He did it! He really did it! He was perfect."

They all hugged Jenny, praising Joe, and her for supporting him so long to get to this moment.

Mrs. Mango realized Mr. Mango was not going to make eye contact with her. He was acting like she wasn't even there. Well, if that was how he wanted to play it. She tried to repeat Don Paz's words in her head, to remember how Don Paz said to be patient, to give him time. But she desperately wanted to talk to Mr. Mango, to tell him she was not crying for Raul. She just needed him to know that.

Mrs. Mango looked around at the group, none of whom knew the real Raul story besides Christine and Mr. Mango. Sarah gave her a warm smile.

Oh, Sarah must know too. Of course, Christine would have told her.

Mrs. Mango felt like such a fool.

On the way home, the conversation in the car was completely focused on the details of the production, on Joe's performance, on the beauty of the story. Mrs. Mango barely spoke, letting Christine and Sarah talk, with Mr. Mango adding a few comments here and there. It felt like they were riding with a huge elephant in the car, a huge and obvious secret that no one was mentioning. The ride seemed to take forever.

Finally, finally, they were home, and Christine and Sarah were in Christine's car driving away with a honk and a wave.

"Joe," Mrs. Mango said, following him into the kitchen.

"We don't need to talk about it," said Mr. Mango, pulling a beer out of the refrigerator.

"We do!"

"I can't keep doing this," said Mr. Mango, cracking the cap off the bottle.

"It wasn't him! I was crying for *you*!" cried Mrs. Mango, picking up a dishtowel and twisting it in her hands. "Those songs, those words, oh my God, it made me realize how stupid I've been. How I let the past ruin my life. And I realized it has always been you!"

Mr. Mango took a long drink of his beer and walked towards the family room. "Okay," he said as she followed him.

"It's not okay!" screamed Mrs. Mango. "You have to know! You *have* to. I was crying for you, and for *us*. And for how I took so long to realize it. Those words in the song, oh my God, those wasted years. I've been such a fool."

Mrs. Mango sat down on the chair facing the couch as Mr. Mango pointed the remote at the TV and flicked it on.

"Please," she begged. "Please just look at me."

Mr. Mango dragged his eyes to his wife.

"I love you. I loved the other night when we used the Vegevape and ended up in bed. I enjoyed it. That was *fun*. You are fun. You are amazing. You have been a rock—strong, steady, caring for me and the kids all these years. Caring for the community. Working hard, teaching the boys how to throw a ball, coaching their teams, Doing all my Honey Do's without complaining—well, not much—making sure Christine knew to make sure a man respected her because you respected her." Here, Mrs. Mango gave a half-laugh, "Of course that didn't have the result we wanted, but that's not your fault."

Mr. Mango shrugged. "I don't know what to say."

"You don't have to say anything, just please, *please*, listen to me when I tell you I was crying for you. That I love *you*. That I realized it wasn't Raul that I was thinking of all these years. It was some *phantom*, a *ghost*. And that attraction I felt to you when we met, I'll be honest, I thought it was mostly about your looks. And of course you were fun. But now I realize that a part of me saw the full you, the real you, and knew that you were kind, that you were good and honest and brave. That part of me knew that it was more than just a superficial attractiveness that brought us together. Without getting all, I don't know, God-squad, on you, maybe God was looking out for me bringing me you. It's like the clouds finally cleared from the sky and I can see. And I see that I love you. And always have, except that the guilt over Raul, over," Mrs. Mango stopped and held back a sob, 'over, his death, how maybe it was my fault." Mrs. Mango held her fist over her mouth to keep from sobbing. "That guilt got in the way of really seeing you," she finally choked out.

Mr. Mango gave a little nod. "Okay."

"Okay—you believe me? Okay—you will think about it? What do you mean by 'okay'?"

Mr. Mango took a deep breath and let it out slowly. "I guess I mean I'll think about what you have said. I promise." He turned back towards the TV and picked up his beer, finishing it in several long gulps. The pain in her eyes, it was just too much to look straight at.

Mrs. Mango stared at her husband until it was clear he wasn't going to talk about it any longer. She wandered back to their bedroom and took off her dress. She went into the bathroom and closed the door and sat down on the lid of the toilet. She stared at the shower wall in front of her, numb. Then she looked towards the cupboard with the letter box and knew what she needed to do. One part she could do right now, one part she'd need help with.

Mrs. Mango put on her robe and went to the computer. She had never done a search but she had heard about Google and it didn't take her very long to figure out how to find the lyrics to Phantom of the Opera, and to eventually find the song "All I Ask of You." She printed out the words to the song and wrote on the top, "Joe, this says how I feel about you better than I can. Please believe that. Love, Elsie." Then she pinned it to his pillow and went to sleep in Christine's old room. If those passionate words of love, of wanting only each other, weren't enough, she wasn't sure what would be.

CHAPTER 53
The Last Letter

Mrs. Mango waited until she heard Mr. Mango's truck pull out of the driveway. Danny had found him a new Cardiac Rehab closer to home, and he was liking this one a lot more. There was a gym set up that led him through exercises, and that seemed a better fit than the circle of emotion up at the Sutter near Danny. Mrs. Mango grabbed her phone and checked to see if Don Paz had texted. He had, and the text said he was on time.

Mrs. Mango went to the garage and actually put the door up. She needed the light and she needed a way to get to the other side, something not possible with the piles of boxes and equipment and bags and other detritus that grow like kudzu in a dark garage.

By the time Don Paz pulled into the driveway, Mrs. Mango had freed up several dusty cardboard boxes and stacked them in the driveway.

"Good morning," said Don Paz, making a prayer position with his hands and giving a little bow. A slight breeze picked up and ruffled his thin flowy shirt against his faded jeans.

"Morning," said Mrs. Mango. "Do you want some coffee for the ride?"

"That would be nice," said Don Paz. "I'll start loading these."

Mrs. Mango went in the house to get the coffee but came out with the box from under the bathroom sink. "Add this to the stuff too, I'll be right back."

"Don't forget a jacket," Don Paz called after Mrs. Mango. "It always seems windy there."

Coffees in hand, Mrs. Mango in the passenger seat, Don Paz backed into the street, and as he pulled forward, Mrs. Mango waved at Mrs. Melucci's house. "She must be

going crazy in there, wondering who you are!" she giggled.
"Slow down and give a wave."

Don Paz obligingly gave a wave and a big smile. "I
can't see anyone."

"Oh, she's there, don't you doubt it."

Don Paz pulled the car off the side of the rutted set
of tracks that passed for a road. "I think this should work,
the path is right up there," he pointed ahead of the car about
twenty feet. "If you don't like it, we'll try another spot."

They got out of the car and found the path and went
down the narrow sandy trail coming out on a stretch of
beach.

Mrs. Mango felt her chest expand, like there was
more room to breathe, like there was space for her heart to
actually do its job. Oh, the ocean—here it was spread out in
front of her, welcoming her as if it hadn't been decades
since she saw it. A lump formed in her throat. The slate
blue of the water, the gray blue of the sky, the faded sand
were all colors that felt like home. Colors that matched the
inside of her and called to her to stay.

Don Paz looked sideways at Mrs. Mango. They had
come to a stop and were standing side by side looking out
at the water. "You are a water child, that is for sure."

Mrs. Mango nodded. "I've always loved the water.
And especially the ocean." She laughed. "Maybe I was a
turtle in another life."

Don Paz gave an easy smile. "Interesting that turtle
is what first came to mind."

Mrs. Mango wrinkled her brow in thought. "I'm
just thinking of how the mama turtle comes up to the sand
to lay her eggs, and then when they hatch, the way those
little babies scrape their way back to the ocean. And how
treacherous that return can be, all exposed to birds and
other animals. But they have to get there. They were born
one place, but they belong another. They know that right
from the beginning."

Mrs. Mango closed her eyes in thought.

Don Paz remained quiet, letting her put the pieces together for herself.

Eventually, with a sigh, Mrs. Mango opened her eyes. "Don't know why I never come."

"Well, you are here now. Reclaiming that part of you. It was always there, you know. Just like the ocean."

"Buried, though!" laughed Mrs. Mango. She reached down and grabbed a handful of sand. Standing up, she inhaled deeply. "Ahh, the smell! And the colors. Just amazing. And the sound." She looked up the coast to the north and then to the south, taking in the mist that seem to soften the edges in either direction. "I forgot how loud the beach is. The waves, and the wind, and the birds." She stared at the breaking waves as if hypnotized. "The best music, these sounds."

After standing in silence for a few minutes longer, Don Paz said, "So, shall we get started?"

"Yep. Let's do this," said Mrs. Mango, and they turned around and headed back to the car.

After several trips, they had all the boxes on the beach, stacked back near an indent in the bluffs that blocked some of the worst of the wind and where there were the remains of a makeshift fire pit. Together, they gathered driftwood and arranged it in the fire pit.

Don Paz got a fire going and tossed some bundles of dried herbs on it, adding an extra smell to all the other sensations Mrs. Mango was taking in.

"In India, this would be called a yagna, which is a sacred fire. You are to offer your attachment to Raul to whatever God you worship so as to let go of that attachment. Just let go."

When Mrs. Mango nodded, Don Paz looked up towards the sky and said, "Oh Divine, please release Elsie from the pain of the past. Please help her release all that needs to go and welcome all that needs to come. Please help her keep the good from her past without sacrificing the good in the present. Bless her life in all its parts as she lets go of the old."

Don Paz looked at Mrs. Mango and gave a nod. She opened the first box and grabbed as many letters as two hands could hold, and tossed them into the fire.

"You can give thanks for those," Don Paz said.

Mrs. Mango looked at the burning letters. "Thank you," she whispered.

"And now the rest," Don Paz said.

Mrs. Mango repeated her actions, tossing in letters, whispering thanks, holding her hands over her heart at each batch burned.

The cardboard boxes were emptied, and then the fancy box with the lock was emptied.

"Now the coconut," said Don Paz, pulling a coconut out of his backpack. "Put all your negative energy into this coconut. Put all your grief and sadness and anger and resentment. Everything negative about that time in your life, put it in here."

He paused and let Mrs. Mango hold the coconut and stare intently at it, until she looked up and said, "Okay."

Don Paz handed Mrs. Mango a small hatchet. "Now smash the hell out of it. Not really in anger, but as a way to let go of what happened."

Mrs. Mango put the coconut down, kneeled near it and started hacking at it. With the first hack, the coconut squirted sideways and she dissolved into giggles. She pulled it back and aimed more carefully and whacked it. It took many hits and whacks and Mrs. Mango ended up sweaty but finally she had the coconut in pieces. "Whew!" she said and sat back down.

"Let it all go," said Don Paz in a serene voice.

"Hmm, it's going. It's gone," said Mrs. Mango, still puffing.

"Now, toss the pieces into the fire," said Don Paz.

Mrs. Mango did as he said, and they both stared into the fire for a couple of minutes. The sounds of the wind and the waves were interrupted by some loud voices and laughing. Five young men came into view, bubbling around each other like puppies, pushing, laughing, falling, as they banged into each other.

"Hey, dudes! It's a bonfire," yelled one of the boys, and they made their way towards Don Paz and Mrs. Mango.

"Greetings," said the boy as he got to the fire. "Cool fire! We were going to make one too, but the wind kept blowing it out."

"Awesome!" agreed a second boy.

"Yes, it's hard to get a fire going here sometimes," agreed Don Paz. "What are you boys up to today?"

"Just hangin'," said the first boy, swinging his backpack around to the front. "Day off! Want a beer?"

"No thanks," said Don Paz. "We've kind of got a thing going here, a ritual, if you will."

"Oh cool! What are you celebrating?"

Don Paz looked at Mrs. Mango, thinking she might be annoyed with this interruption.

Mrs. Mango smiled at the boys. "We are celebrating young love. And we are celebrating learning to let go. And we are celebrating keeping your heart open. So we are, I guess, celebrating life."

"All right!" said another one of the boys. "I can drink to that."

Mrs. Mango held out her hand. "I'll take one of those beers, thank you."

Boy Number One opened a Coors Light and handed it to Mrs. Mango. He opened one for himself and held it up to Mrs. Mango to toast. They clinked cans. "To life," said the boy.

"I have one last part to do," said Mrs. Mango, carefully wedging her can into the sand. She reached into her shirt and pulled a letter out of her bra. "The last letter," she said to Don Paz. To the boys she said, "I loved a boy once, when I was your age. And then he died in Vietnam. And I never really got over that."

Boy Number One stared at Mrs. Mango with kindness. "So sorry."

Several other boys echoed him. "That's harsh, yeah,

so sorry."

"So this is saying goodbye," said Mrs. Mango.

Mrs. Mango read the letter silently to herself, one last time.

Dear Raul,

Oh dear Raul, I'm so sorry I've held you in purgatory for so long. I imagine my need for you might have kept you from doing whatever it is you are to be doing in the next world, and if it did, I'm sorry. I'm ready to let you go. I'm ready to say goodbye.

Thank you for our time together. Our actual time together, not this obsession I've held onto for too long. Thank you for seeing the real me and helping me to be proud of that person. I lost her for a long time, but I think I feel her coming back. And I think you would be proud of that. I don't think that you would have wished for me to live such a half-hearted life all these years. In fact, I know you wouldn't.

Raul, I will never forget that you were such an important part of my life. I will always treasure our memories, but I will not live on those memories anymore. I am ready to live with what I have now, in the present. I have found a way to accept and love Christine exactly as she is, the way I always wished my mother could love me. In fact, I feel that way about all my children. I love Michael with or without his wife. I love Danny no matter how he raises Emma Rose. I love Joe as an actor and am beyond proud of him. And I am ready to give my whole heart to the now, to the man in front of me. My Joe. If he will only have me. Oh Raul, he is such a good man. And I didn't see that all these years. I am very scared because I may have hurt him for too long. His heart may be too scarred to love me back, but I'm going to give it everything. And live with whatever happens.

Live.

She kissed the letter, put it in the fancy box, and tossed the whole thing into the fire. "Goodbye, Raul," she whispered. Then she picked up the beer, drank most of it, and set it down. She stood up and pulled the chain with the key to the letter box from around her neck. She walked down to the edge of the waves, held it once against her heart, and tossed it into the ocean.

When she returned to the fire, the boys all held up their beers (as did Don Paz who had finally accepted one) and said, "To Raul!"

"To Raul," echoed Mrs. Mango.

"Boys, I've made a lot of mistakes in my life," Mrs. Mango said, standing and looking around the circle they had formed around the fire. "But I can tell you this. You can recover from the thing you think will destroy you. You just have to keep your heart open to change. Don't freeze up and try to hold onto the past."

They all nodded.

"Don Paz? I think we can leave the boys to the fire," said Mrs. Mango.

Don Paz stood up. "Thanks for the beer. Nice to meet you guys. Make sure you douse the fire before you move on."

Mrs. Mango felt a sudden fondness for these boys. They were probably close to the age Raul had been when she met him. They had their whole lives ahead of them, or so she hoped. She hugged each one and told him to have a good life, and then she and Don Paz walked back up the path.

As they got to Don Paz's car, Mrs. Mango looked with surprise at the truck now parked behind it. It was Mr.

Mango's truck, and he was sitting there, looking at her. She looked at Don Paz.

"Guilty," said Don Paz, holding up his hands and looking sheepish. "I told him where we'd be. Didn't think he should be part of the ritual, but, well, I thought it seemed right he might be here at the end. I invited him to come *if he wanted to*."

Mrs. Mango stared at Mr. Mango as Don Paz slipped into his car. "I have a feeling you'll be riding back with him," Don Paz whispered before shutting his door. "But I'm going to be up the road getting something to eat, so if it doesn't work out, call me and I'll come get you."

Don Paz shut the door, pulled the car forward, did a U-turn, and left.

Mrs. Mango smiled and walked toward the truck. As she did, Mr. Mango got out and stood by the door.

"So, you're here," she said.

Mr. Mango shrugged. "Don Paz told me you might, I don't know, need something," he said, glancing side to side as if afraid to make eye contact. "Said you were laying the past to rest. So . . . " Mr. Mango looked uncomfortable but raised his eyes to Mrs. Mango's face. He raised a shoulder again. "Thought I'd hang out here in case you needed something."

Mrs. Mango realized those words represented everything she knew about Joe. Always close by, waiting to see if anyone needed anything. Not making a big deal out of it.

Mrs. Mango stared into Mr. Mango's eyes with a smile that was lighter than he'd ever seen from her. A smile that seemed to emanate from her whole body, not just her mouth. She walked to him and put her arms around him, and he put his arms around her.

The wind blowing through the trees mixed with the muffled sound of the ocean as they hugged each other, unspeaking, as they squeezed bodies that held years of distance and misunderstandings in every cell. For the first time ever, Mrs. Mango let herself truly sink into the feeling of Mr. Mango's body. Let herself feel the pleasure of being close to *him.* Let herself feel the relief of a heart not divided. The phrase that Don Paz had used so often finally made sense.

Wholehearted.

And for Mr. Mango, it was like he was feeling the full warmth of the sun for the first time. Not the weak sun through clouds or the half-warmth through a window but the full force. Even that sun couldn't melt an iceberg in a minute, but if it was allowed to continue to shine, it might just melt it in what was left of a lifetime.

Finally, they pulled back enough to see each other's faces.

Mr. Mango cleared his throat. "My heart's been through it, you know? Kind of trampled on."

Mrs. Mango nodded, tears forming. She left her arms around him but pulled slightly backwards and looked down at the ground. She couldn't stand to look him in the eye when he said goodbye.

"But you know what I've realized?" Mr. Mango put his index finger under Mrs. Mango's chin and gently raised it so that she was looking at him. "This heart, it's still beating. It's tougher than I thought."

Mrs. Mango didn't want to let herself hope.

Mr. Mango's eyes stayed on Mrs. Mango's. "I know we started off kind of wrong, and I know it's been many years." He paused and coughed to cover rising emotion. "And I'm an old dog." He paused again and took a deep breath. "I don't know exactly how it will go, but I think we should try," he finished. "I *want* to try."

"Really?" sobbed Mrs. Mango.

Mr. Mango gave a slow nod.

"Maybe, and this might sound weird after forty-some years of being married, but maybe we should kind of pretend to start at the beginning," said Mr. Mango, dropping his hands down to rest on Mrs. Mango's waist.

Mrs. Mango looked down at his arms, holding her on either side. It felt steadying. Mrs. Mango nodded her head 'yes.' "Okay."

Mr. Mango let go, stepped back, and bowed at the waist. "Elsie Walker," he said in a formal but teasing kind of voice, "would you like to join me for a walk on the beach?"

He held his hand out, palm up.

Mrs. Mango gave a girlish giggle and put her hand into his. "I'd love to, Joe Mango."

The End.
(Or actually, The Beginning.)

Note from the Author

I've long been a beneficiary of an "Esquer grant" (aka, my husband supporting my writing) and could not be more appreciative of his generosity (literally and otherwise). No books would have been published without that opportunity. My longtime writing group, KalKrew, has relit my fire so many times.

This book started out when I noticed an older couple who seemed very disgruntled with each other and I never anticipated it would end the way it did! The magic of characters coming to life is delicious.

About the Author

I'm a California girl (transplanted from Pennsylvania via North Carolina). Well, girl might be stretching it, I'm a mom (Thing One is 22 and Thing Two is 21), a baseball coach's wife, a runner (slogger is more like it; I jog very slowly), an obsessed pickleballer, and a lapsed cook. My whole world lit up the second I deciphered *Fun with Dick and Jane*, and it has never dimmed. I am endlessly enthralled with how stories come out of someone's head into my hands then into my head. Every book feels like it is enchanted. I love the beach, Lemonheads, and baseball. I've sampled several professions including psychologist, college professor, rat lab tech, and waitress (not in that order). And these days, I am a writer, taking pieces of everything I know and love and putting them together in one place. Sometimes that place is imaginary (my novels), and sometimes that place is my twist on the real world (my blog). It is a most delicious way to live life, tinkering with words, occasionally glimpsing magic.

If you'd like to be informed when my book comes out, please let me know at my website: https://lynnrankin-esquer.com

Or via QR code:

www.ingramcontent.com/pod-product-compliance
Lightning Source LLC
Chambersburg PA
CBHW061045310726
48969CB00004B/1093